ENC
Short

ENGLISH
Short Stories

English Short Stories

Stories selected from
The Masterpiece Library of Short Stories, Volume VII, English,
issued by Allied Newspapers Ltd., in association with
The Educational Book Company Ltd, London.

This edition published in 1995 by Senate, an imprint of
Studio Editions Ltd, Princess House, 50 Eastcastle Street,
London W1N 7AP, England

ISBN 1 85958 096 3
Printed and bound in Guernsey by
The Guernsey Press Co. Ltd

Contents

"Hundred Merry Tales"
The Welshman's Confession 19
The Overmasterful Husband 21
Sir Thomas Elyot
The Wonderful History of Titus and Gisippus 22
Sir Philip Sidney
The Story of the Unkind King 34
Sixteenth Century
King Lewis and the Husbandman 41
Anonymous
The Waking Man's Dream 43
The Tale told by the Fishwife of Strand-on-the-Green 47
Daniel Defoe
The Apparition of Mrs. Veal 57
The Ghost of Dorothy Dingley 65
Joseph Addison
The Vision of Mirzah 72
Henry Fielding
The History of Leonora, or The Unfortunate Jilt 76
Samuel Taylor Coleridge
Maria Schöning 91
Charles Lamb
Dream-Children 103
Juke Judkins' Courtship 107
James Morier
Hajji Baba andthe Stolen Money 113
Mary Russell Mitford
The Election 123
Thomas Ingoldsby
The Lady Rohesia 129

CONTENTS

Captain Marryat
S.W. and by W. 3/4 W. ....136.
Mary Wollstonecraft Shelley
The Sisters of Albano 150
The False Rhyme 163
Thomas Hood
A Tale of Terror 166
Mrs Gore
Ehrenbreitstein 169
Douglas Jerrold
The Tragedy of the Till 175
Jacques Cocast, the Hunchback Philosopher 184
Benjamin Disraeli
A True Story 190
Samuel Warren
The Resurrectionist 192
Mrs. Gaskell
The Squire's Story 203
The Half-Brothers 217
W. M. Thackeray
Dennis Haggarty's Wife 227
A Gambler's Death 244
A Little Dinner in Bittlestone Street 252
The Princess's Tragedy 260
"Dimond Cut Dimond" 277
Charles Dickens
The Bagman's Story 290
The Poor Relation's Story 302
The Story of Richard Doubledick 311
Boots at the Holly-Tree 323
Dr. Manette's MS 332
To be taken with a Grain of Salt 344
No.1 Branch Line: The Signalman 354

"HUNDRED MERRY TALES" 15TH CENTURY

THE WELSHMAN'S CONFESSION

A WELSHMAN dwelling in a wild place in Wales came to his Curate in the time of Lent and was confessed; and when his confession was in manner at the end, the Curate asked him whether he had any other thing to say that grieved his conscience, which, sore abashed, answered no word a great while.

At last, by exhortation of his ghostly father, he said that there was one thing in his mind that greatly grieved his conscience, which he was ashamed to utter, for it was so grievous that he trowed God would never forgive him.

To whom the Curate answered and said that God's mercy was above all, and bade him not despair in the mercy of God, for, whatsoever it was, if he were repentant, God would forgive him.

And so, by long exhortation, at the last he showed it, and said thus:

"Sir, it happened once, that as my wife was making a cheese on a Friday I would have said whether it had been salt or fresh, and took a little of the whey in my hand and put it in my mouth, and, or I was ware, part of it went down my throat against my will, and so I brake my fast."

To whom the Curate said, "If there be none other thing, I warrant God shall forgive thee."

So when he had well comforted him with the mercy of God the Curate prayed him to answer a question and to tell him truth.

The Curate said that there were robberies and murders done nigh the place where he dwelt, and divers men found slain, and asked him whether he were consenting to any of them.

To whom he answered and said "Yes"; and said he was party to many of them, and did help to rob and to slay divers of them.

Then the Curate asked him why he did not confess him thereof.

The Welshman answered and said he took it for no sin, for it was a custom among them that when any booty came of any rich merchant riding, it was but a good neighbour's deed one to help another when one called another, and so they took that but for good fellowship and neighbourhood.

Here ye may see that some have remorse of conscience of small venial sins, and fear not to do great offences without shame of the world or dread of God: and as the common proverb is, they stumble at a straw and leap over a block.

"HUNDRED MERRY TALES"

THE OVERMASTERFUL HUSBAND

A YOUNG man late married to a wife thought it was good policy to get the mastery of her in the beginning.

Came to her, the pot seething over the fire, although the meat therein was not cooked enough, suddenly commanded her to take the pot from the fire.

Which answered and said, that the meat was not ready to eat.

And he said again, " I will have it taken off, for my pleasure."

This good woman, loth yet to offend him, set the pot beside the fire as he bade.

And anon after he commanded her to set the pot behind the door, and she said thereto again, " Ye be not wise therein."

But he precisely said, it should be so as he bade.

And she gently again did his commandment.

This man, yet not satisfied, commanded her to set the pot ahigh upon the hen-roost.

" What ! " quoth the wife again ; " I trow ye be mad."

And he fiercely then commanded her to set it there, or else, he said, she should repent.

She, somewhat afeared to move his patience, took a ladder and set it to the roost, and went herself up the ladder, and took the pot in her hand, praying her husband then to hold the ladder fast, for sliding ; which so did.

And when the husband looked up and saw the pot stand there on height he said thus, " So now standeth the pot there as I would have it."

This wife, hearing that, suddenly poured the hot pottage on his head, and said thus, " And now ben the pottage there as I would have them."

By this tale men may see that it is no wisdom for a man to attempt a meek woman's patience too far, lest it turn to his own hurt and damage.

SIR THOMAS ELYOT
1499–1546

THE WONDERFUL HISTORY OF TITUS AND GISIPPUS

THERE was in the city of Rome a noble senator, named Fulvius, who sent his son, called Titus, being a child, to the city of Athens, in Greece (which was the fountain of all manner of doctrine), there to learn good letters : and caused him to be hosted with a worshipful man of that city, called Chremes.

This Chremes happened to have also a son named Gisippus, who not only was equal to the said young Titus in years, but also in stature, proportion of body, favour, and colour of visage, countenance, and speech. The two children were so like, that without much difficulty it could not be discerned of their proper parents, which was Titus from Gisippus, or Gisippus from Titus.

These two young gentlemen, as they seemed to be one in form and personage, so shortly after acquaintance, the same nature wrought in their hearts such a mutual affection, and their wills and appetites daily more and more so confederated themselves, that it seemed none other, when their names were declared, but that they had only changed their places, issuing (as I might say) out of the one body, and entering into the other. They together, and at one time went to their learning and study, at one time to their meals and refection, they delighted both in one doctrine, and profited equally therein ; finally, they together increased in doctrine, that within a few years few within Athens might be compared unto them.

At the last died Chremes, which was not only to his son, but also to Titus cause of much sorrow and heaviness. Gisippus, by the goods of his father, was known to be a man of great substance : wherefore there were offered to him great and rich marriages. And he then being of ripe years, and of an able and goodly personage, his friends, kin, and allies exhorted him busily to take a wife, to the intent he might increase his lineage and progeny. But the young man, having his heart already wedded to his friend Titus, and his mind fixed to the study of philosophy, fearing that marriage should be the occasion to sever him both from the one and the other, refused of long time to be persuaded, until at the last, partly by the importunate calling on of his kinsmen, partly by the consent and advice of his dear friend Titus, thereto by other desired, he assented to marry such a one as should like him.

What shall need any words ? His friends found a young gentlewoman, which in equality of years, virtuous conditions, nobility of blood, beauty, and sufficient riches, they thought was for such a young man apt and convenient. And when they and her friends upon the covenants of marriage were thoroughly accorded, they counselled Gisippus to repair unto the maiden, and to behold how her person contented him : and he so doing found her in every form and condition according to his expectation and appetite, whereat he much rejoiced, and became of her amorous, insomuch as many and oftentimes leaving Titus at his study, he secretly repaired unto her.

Notwithstanding, the fervent love that he had to his friend Titus at the last surmounted his shamefacedness, wherefore he disclosed to him his secret journeys, and what delectation he took in beholding the excellent beauty of her whom he intended to marry, and how with her good manners and sweet entertainment, she had constrained him to be her lover. And on a time he, having with him his friend Titus, went to his lady, of whom he was received most joyously.

But Titus forthwith as he beheld so heavenly a personage, adorned with beauty inexplicable, in whose visage was a most amiable countenance, mixed with maidenly shamefacedness, and the rare and sober words and well couched, which issued out of her pretty mouth, Titus was thereat abashed, and had the heart through pierced with the fiery dart of blind Cupid, of the which wound the anguish was so exceeding and vehement, that neither the study of philosophy, neither the remembrance of his dear friend Gisippus, who so much loved and trusted him, could anything withdraw him from that unkind appetite, but that of force he must love inordinately that lady, whom his said friend had determined to marry. Albeit with incredible pains he kept his thoughts secret until that he and Gisippus were returned unto their lodgings.

Then the miserable Titus, withdrawing him as it were to his study, all tormented and oppressed with love, threw himself on a bed, and there rebuking his own most despiteful unkindness, which by the sudden sight of a maiden, he had conspired against his most dear friend Gisippus, against all humanity and reason, cursed his fate or constellation, and wished that he had never come to Athens. And therewith sent he out from the bottom of his heart deep and cold sighs, in such plenty, that it lacked but little that his heart was not riven in pieces.

In dolour and anguish tossed he himself by a certain space, but to no man would he discover it. But at the last, the pain became so intolerable, that would he or no, he was enforced to keep his bed, being for lack of sleep and other natural sustenance, brought in such feebleness, that his legs might not sustain his body.

Gisippus missing his dear friend Titus, was much abashed, and hearing that he lay sick in his bed, had forthwith his heart pierced with heaviness, and with all speed came to him, where he lay. And beholding the rosial colour, which was wont to be in his visage, turned into sallow, the residue pale, his ruddy lips wan, and his eyes leaden and hollow, might unneth[1] keep himself from weeping: but to the intent he would not discomfort his friend Titus, dissimulated his heaviness, and with a comfortable countenance demanded of Titus, what was the cause of his disease, blaming him of unkindness, that he so long had sustained it, without giving him knowledge, that he might for him have provided some remedy, if any might have been got, though it were with the dispensing of all his substance.

With which words the mortal sighs renewed in Titus, and the salt tears burst out of his eyen in such abundance, as it had been a land flood running down of a mountain after a storm. That beholding Gisippus, and being also resolved into tears, most heartily desired him, and (as I might say) conjured him, for the fervent and entire love that had been, and yet was between them, that he would no longer hide from him his grief, and that there was nothing to him so dear and precious (although it were his own life) that might restore Titus to health, but that he would gladly, and without grudging employ it, with which words, obtestations, and tears of Gisippus, Titus constrained, all blushing and ashamed, holding down his head, brought forth with great difficulty his words in this wise:

" My dear and most loving friend, withdraw your friendly offers, cease of your courtesy, refrain your tears and regrettings, take rather your knife, and slay me here where I lie, or otherwise take vengeance on me, most miserable and false traitor unto you, and of all other most worthy to suffer shameful death. For where as God of nature, like as He hath given to us similitude in all the parts of our body, so hath He conjoined our wills, studies, and appetites together in one, so that between men was never like concord and love, as I suppose. And now notwithstanding, only with the look of a woman, those bonds of love be dissolved, reason oppressed, friendship is excluded, there availeth no wisdom, no doctrine, no fidelity or trust: yea, your trust is the cause that I have conspired against you this treason.

" Alas! Gisippus, what envious spirit moved you to bring me to her, whom you have chosen to be your wife, where I received this poison? I say, Gisippus, where was then your wisdom, that ye

[1] *Unneth*, First English, " uneath," not easily.

remembered not the fragility of our common nature? what need ye to call me for a witness of your private delights? why would ye have me see that, which you yourself could not behold without ravishing of mind and carnal appetite? Alas, why forgot ye, that our minds and appetites were ever one? and that also what so ye liked was ever to me in like degree pleasant. What will ye more? Gisippus, I say your trust is the cause that I am entrapped. The rays or beams issuing from the eyen of her whom ye have chosen, with the remembrance of her incomparable virtues, hath thrilled throughout the midst of my heart, and in such wise burneth it, that above all things I desire to be out of this wretched and most unkind life, which is not worthy the company of so noble and loving a friend as ye be."

And therewith Titus concluded his confession, with so profound and bitter a sigh, received with tears, that it seemed that all his body should be dissolved and relented into salt drops.

But Gisippus, as he were therewith nothing astonished or discontented, with an assured countenance, and merry regard, embracing Titus, and kissing him, answered in this wise:

"Why, Titus, is this your only sickness and grief that ye so uncourteously have so long concealed, and with much more unkindness kept from me, than ye have conceived it? I acknowledge my folly wherewith ye have with good right upbraided me, that in showing to you her whom I loved, I remembered not the common estate of our nature, neither the agreeableness, or (as I might say) the unity of our two appetites. Surely that default can be by no reason excused, wherefore it is only I that have offended. For who may by right prove that ye have trespassed, that by the inevitable stroke of Cupid's dart are thus bitterly wounded? Think ye me such a fool or ignorant person, that I know not the power of Venus, where she liketh to show her importable[1] violence? Have not ye well resisted against such a goddess, that for my sake have striven with her almost to the death? What more loyalty or truth can I require of you? Am I of that virtue, that I may resist against celestial influence, preordinate by providence divine? If I so thought, what were my wits? where were my study so long time spent in noble philosophy? I confess to you, Titus, I love that maiden as much as any wise man might possible: and took in her company more delight and pleasure than of all the treasure and lands that my father left me, which ye know was right abundant.

"But now I perceive that the affection of love toward her surmounteth in you above measure, what, shall I think it of a wanton lust, or sudden appetite in you, whom I have ever known of grave and sad disposition, inclined alway to honest doctrine, flying all vain dalliance and dishonest pastime? Shall I imagine to be in

[1] *Importable*, unbearable.

you any malice or fraud, since from the tender time of our childhood, I have alway found in you, my sweet friend Titus, such a conformity with all my manners, appetites, and desires, that never was seen between us any manner of contention? May God forbid, that in the friendship of Gisippus and Titus should happen any suspicion: or that any fantasy should pierce my head whereby that honourable love between us should be the mountenance of a crumb[1] perished. Nay, nay, Titus, it is as I said, the only providence of God: she was by Him from the beginning prepared to be your lady and wife. For such fervent love entereth not into the heart of a wise man and virtuous, but by a divine disposition: whereat if I should be discontented or grudge, I should not only be unjust to you, withholding that from you which is undoubtedly yours, but also obstinate and repugnant against the determination of God, which shall never be found in Gisippus.

"Therefore, gentle friend Titus, dismay you not at the chance of love, but receive it joyously with me, that am with you nothing discontented, but marvellous glad, since it is my hap to find for you such a lady, with whom ye shall live in felicity, and receive fruit to the honour and comfort of all your lineage. Here I renounce to you clearly all my title and interest, that I now have or might have in the fair maiden. Call to your pristinate courage, wash clean your visage and eyes thus bewept, and abandon all heaviness. The day appointed for our marriage approacheth: let us consult how, without difficulty, ye may wholly attain your desires. Take heed this mine advice: ye know well that we two be so like, that being apart, and in one apparel, few men do know us. Also ye do remember that the custom is that, notwithstanding any ceremony done at the time of the espousals, the marriage, notwithstanding is not confirmed until at night that the husband putteth a ring on the finger of his wife, and unlooseth her girdle. Therefore, I myself will be present with my friends, and perform all the parts of a bridegroom. And ye shall abide in a place secret, where I shall appoint you, until it be night. And then shall ye quickly convey yourself into the maiden's chamber, and for the similitude of our personages, and of our apparel, ye shall not be espied of the women, which have none of us any acquaintance, and shortly get you to bed, and put your own ring on the maiden's finger, and undo the girdle of virginity, and do all other thing that shall be to your pleasure.

"Be now of good cheer, Titus, and comfort yourself with good reflections and solace, that this wan and pale colour, and your cheeks meagre and lean, be not the cause of your discovering. I know well, that, ye having your purpose, I shall be in obloquy and derision of all men, and so hated of all my kindred, that they shall seek

[1] *The mountenance of a crumb*, to the amount of a crumb.

occasion to expulse me out of this city, thinking me to be a notable reproach to all my family. But let God therein work, I force not [1] what pain that I abide, so that ye, my friend Titus, may be safe, and pleasantly enjoy your desires, to the increasing of your felicity."

With these words Titus began to move, as it were, out of a dream, and doubting whether he heard Gisippus speak, or else saw but a vision, lay still as a man abashed. But when he beheld the tears trickling down by the face of Gisippus, he then comforted him, and thanking him for his incomparable kindness, refused the benefit that he offered, saying that it were better that a hundred such unkind wretches as he was should perish, than so noble a man as was Gisippus should sustain reproach or damage.

But Gisippus eftesoones comforted Titus, and therewith sware and protested, that with free and glad will he would that this thing should be in form aforesaid accomplished, and therewith embraced and sweetly kissed Titus. Who perceiving the matter sure, and not feigned, as a man not sick, but only awaked out of his sleep, set himself up in his bed; the quick blood somewhat resorted unto his visage, and after a little good meats and drinks taken, he was shortly, and in a few days, restored into his old fashion and figure.

To make the tale short: the day of marriage was come. Gisippus, accompanied with his allies and friends, came to the house of the damosel, where they were honourably and joyously feasted. And between him and the maiden was a sweet entertainment, which to behold, all that were present, took much pleasure and comfort, praising the beauty, goodliness, virtue, and courtesy, which in this couple were excellent above all other that they had ever seen. What shall I say more? The covenants were read and sealed, the dower appointed, and all other bargains concluded, and the friends of either part took their leave and departed: the bride with a few women (as was the custom) brought into her chamber; then, as it was before agreed, Titus conveyed himself, after Gisippus returned to his house, or perchance to the chamber appointed for Titus, nothing sorrowful, although that he heartily loved the maiden, but with a glad heart and countenance that he had so recovered his friend from death, and so well brought him to the effect of his desire. . . . The morrow is come. Gisippus, thinking it expedient that the truth should be discovered, assembled all the nobility of the city at his own house, where also by appointment was Titus, who among them had these words that do follow:—

"My friends, Athenians, there is at this time showed among you an example, almost incredible, of the divine power of honourable love, to the perpetual renown and commendation of this noble city of Athens, whereof he ought to take excellent comfort, and therefore

[1] *I force not*, I care not.

give due thanks to God, if there remain among you any token of the ancient wisdom of your most noble progenitors. For what more praise may be given to people that benevolence, faithfulness, and constancy? without whom all countries and cities be brought unto desolation and ruin, like as by them they become prosperous and in most high felicity. What, shall I long tarry you in conjecturing mine intent and meaning? Ye all know from whence I came unto this city, that of adventure I found in the house of Chremes his son Gisippus, of mine own age, and in everything so like to me that neither his father nor any other man could discern of us the one from the other, but by our own insignment or showing: in so much as there were put about our necks laces of sundry colours to declare our personages. What mutual agreement and love have been alway between us during the eight years that we have been together, ye all be witnesses, that have been beholders and wonderers of our most sweet conversation and consent of appetites, wherein was never any discord or variance.

"And, as for my part, after the decease of my father, notwithstanding that there was descended and happened unto me great possessions, fair houses, with abundance of riches; also I being called home by the desirous and importunate letters of mine allies and friends, which be of the most noble of all the senators, offered the advancement to the highest dignities in the public weal, I will not remember the lamentations of my most natural mother, expressed in her tender letters, all besprent and blotted with abundance of tears, wherein she accuseth me of unkindness, for my long tarrying, and especially now in her most discomfort. But all this could not remove me the breadth of my nail from my dear friend, Gisippus. And but by force could not I, nor yet may be drawn from his sweet company, but if he thereto will consent. I choosing rather to live with him as his companion and fellow, yea, and as his servant rather than to be Consul of Rome. Thus my kindness hath been well acquitted (or as I might say), redoubled, delivering me from the death, yea from the most cruel and painful death of all other.

"I perceive ye wonder hereat, noble Athenians, and no marvel. For what person should be so hardy to attempt any such thing against me, being a Roman, and of the noble blood of the Romans? Or who should be thought so malicious to slay me, who (as all ye be my judges) never trespassed against any person within this city. Nay, nay, my friends, I have none of you all therein suspected. I perceive you desire and hearken to know what he was that presumed to do so cruel and great an enterprise. It was love, noble Athenians, the same love which, as your poets do remember, did wound the more part of all the gods, that ye do honour, that constrained Jupiter to transform himself in a swan, a bull, and divers other likenesses:

the same love that caused Hercules, the vanquisher and destroyer of monsters and giants, to spin on a rock, sitting among maidens in a woman's apparel: the same love that caused to assemble all the noble princes of Asia and Greece in the fields of Troy: the same love, I say, against whose assaults may be found no defence or resistance, hath suddenly and unaware stricken me unto the heart with such vehemence and might, that I had in short space died with most fervent torments had not the incomparable friendship of Gisippus holpen me. I see you would fain know who she is that I loved.

"I will no longer delay you, noble Athenians. It is Sophronia, the lady whom Gisippus had chosen to have to his wife, and whom he most entirely loved. But when his most gentle heart perceived that my love was in a much higher degree than his toward that lady, and that it proceeded neither of wantonness, neither of long conversation, nor of any other corrupt desire or fantasy, but in an instant, by the only look, and with such fervence, that immediately I was so cruciate, that I desired, and in all that I mought provoked death to take me. He by his wisdom soon perceived (as I doubt not but that ye do) that it was the very provision of God that she should be my wife and not his: whereto he giving place, and more esteeming true friendship than the love of a woman, whereunto he was induced by his friends and not by violence of Cupid constrained, as I am, hath willingly granted to me the interest that he had in the damosel. And it is I, Titus, that have verily wedded her, I have put the ring on her finger, I have undone the girdle of her shamefacedness: what will ye more? I have lain with her, and confirmed the matrimony, and made her a wife."

At these words all they that were present began to murmur, and to cast a disdainous and grievous look upon Gisippus. Then spake again Titus:

"Leave your grudgings and menacing countenance towards Gisippus; he hath done to you all honour, and no need of reproach. I tell you he hath accomplished all the parts of a friend: that love, which was most certain, hath he continued. He knew he might find in Greece another maiden, and fair and as rich as this that he had chosen, and one, perchance, that he mought love better. But such a friend as I was, having respect to our similitude, the long approved concord, also mine estate and condition, he was sure to find never none. Also the damosel suffereth no disparagement in her blood, or hindrance in her marriage, but is much rather advanced (no dispraise to my dear friend Gisippus).

"Also consider, noble Athenians, that I took her not my father living, when ye mought have suspected that as well her riches as her beauty should have thereto allured me: but soon after my father's decease, when I far exceeded her in possessions and substance, when the most notable men of Rome and Italy desired mine alliance ; ye have therefore all cause to rejoice and thank Gisippus, and not to be angry, and also to extol his wonderful kindness toward me, whereby he hath won me and all my blood, such friends to you and your city, that ye may be assured, to be by us defended against all the world : which being considered, Gisippus hath well deserved a statue or image of gold, to be set on a pillar, in the midst of your city, for an honourable monument, in the remembrance of our incomparable friendship, and of the good that thereby may come to your city.

" But if this persuasion cannot satisfy you, but that ye will imagine anything to the damage of my dear friend Gisippus after my departing, I make my vow unto God, creator of all thing, that as I shall have knowledge thereof, I shall forthwith resort hither, with the invincible power of the Romans, and revenge him in such wise against his enemies that all Greece shall speak of it to their perpetual dishonour, shame, and reproach."

And therewith Titus and Gisippus rose, but the other for fear of Titus dissembleth their malice, making semblant as they had been with all thing contented.

Soon after, Titus, being sent for by the authority of the Senate and people of Rome, prepared to depart out of Athens, and would fain have had Gisippus to have gone with him, offering to divide with him all his substance and fortune. But Gisippus, considering how necessary his counsel should be to the city of Athens, would not depart out of his country. Notwithstanding that above all earthly things he most desired the company of Titus : which above also, for the said consideration, Titus approved.

Titus with his lady is departed towards the city of Rome, where, at their coming, they were of the mother of Titus, his kinsmen, and of all the Senate and people joyously received. And there lived Titus with his lady in joy inexplicable, and had by her many fair children : and for his wisdom and learning was so highly esteemed that there was no dignity or honourable office within the city that he had not with much favour and praise achieved and occupied.

But now let us resort to Gisippus, who immediately upon the departing of Titus was so maligned at, as well by his own kinsmen as by the friends of the lady, that he, to their seeming, shamefully abandoned, leaving her to Titus, that they spared not daily to vex him with all kinds of reproach that they could devise or imagine : and first they excluded him out of their council, and prohibited him from all honest company.

And yet not being therewith satisfied, finally they adjudged him unworthy to enjoy any possessions or goods left to him by his parents whom he (as they supposed) by his indiscreet friendship had so distained. Wherefore they despoiled him of all things, and almost naked, expelled him out of the city.

Thus is Gisippus, late wealthy, and one of the most noble men of Athens, for his kind heart, banished his country for ever, and as a man dismayed, wandering hither and thither, finding no man that would succour him. At the last remembering in what pleasure his friend lived with his lady, for whom he suffered these damages, concluded to go to Rome, and declare his infortune to his said friend Titus. What shall need a long tale ? In conclusion, with much pain, cold, hunger, and thirst, he is come to the city of Rome, and diligently enquiring for the house of Titus, at the last he came to it : but beholding it so beautiful, large and princely, he was ashamed to approach nigh to it, being in so simple estate and unclad, but standeth by, that in case Titus came forth out of his house, he might present himself to him.

He being in this thought, Titus, holding his lady by the hand, issued out from his door, and taking their horses to solace themselves, beheld Gisippus, and beholding his vile apparel, regarded him not, but passed forth on their way, wherewith Gisippus was so wounded to the heart, thinking Titus had contemned his fortune, that oppressed with mortal heaviness, fell in a sownde,[1] but being recovered by some that stood by, thinking him to be sick, forthwith departed, intending not to abide any longer, but as a wild beast to wander abroad in the world. But for weariness he was constrained to enter into an old barn without the city ; where he, casting himself on the bare ground with weeping and dolorous crying, bewaileth his fortune ; but most of all accusing the ingratitude of Titus, for whom he suffered all that misery, the remembrance whereof was so intolerable that he determined no longer to live in that anguish and dolour. And therewith drew his knife, purposing to have slain himself. But ever wisdom (which he by the study of philosophy had attained) withdrew him from that desperate act. And in this contention between wisdom and will, fatigued with long journeys in watch, or as God would have it, he fell into a deep sleep. His knife (wherewith he would have slain himself) falling down by him.

In the meantime, a common and notable ruffian or thief, which had robbed and slain a man, was entered into the barn where Gisippus lay, to the intent to sojourn there all that night. And seeing Gisippus bewept, and his visage replenished with sorrow, and also the naked knife by him, perceived well that he was a man desperate, and surprised with heaviness of heart, was weary of his life : which the said ruffian taking for a good occasion to escape, took the knife of Gisippus, and putting it in the wound of him that was slain, put

[1] *Sownde*, swoon.

it all bloody in the hand of Gisippus, being fast asleep, and so departed.

Soon after, the dead man being found, the officers made diligent search for the murderer : at the last they entering into the barn, and finding Gisippus asleep, with the bloody knife in his hand, awaked him ; wherewith he entered again into his old sorrows, complaining his evil fortune. But when the officers laid unto him the death of the man, and the having of the bloody knife, thereat rejoiced, thanking God that such occasion was happened, whereby he should suffer death by the laws, and escape the violence of his own hands.

Wherefore he denied nothing that was laid to his charge, desiring the officers to make haste that he might be shortly out of his life. Whereat they marvelled. Anon, report came to the Senate that a man was slain, and that a stranger, and a Greek born, was found in such form as is before-mentioned. They forthwith commanded him to be brought unto their presence, sitting there at that time, Titus being then Consul, or in other like dignity. The miserable Gisippus was brought to the bar, with bills and staves like a felon, of whom it was demanded if he slew the man that was founden dead. He nothing denied, but in most sorrowful manner cursed his fortune, naming himself of all other most miserable.

At the last one demanding him of what country he was, he confessed to be an Athenian, and therewith he cast his sorrowful eye upon Titus with much indignation, and burst out into sighs and tears abundantly. That beholding Titus, and espying by a little sign in his visage, which he knew, that it was his dear friend Gisippus, and anon considering that he was brought into despair by some misadventure, rose out of his place where he sat, and falling on his knees before the judges, said that he had slain the man for old malice that he bare toward him, and that Gisippus, being a stranger, was guiltless, and all men mought perceive that the other was a desperate person. Wherefore to abbreviate his sorrows, he confessed the act whereof he was innocent, to the intent that he would finish his sorrows with death, wherefore Titus desired the judges to give sentence on him according to his merits. But Gisippus, perceiving his friend Titus (contrary to his expectation) to offer himself to the death for his safeguard, more importunately cried to the Senate to proceed in their judgment on him, that was the very offender.

Titus denied, and affirmed with reasons and arguments that he was the murderer, and not Gisippus. Thus they of long time, with abundance of tears, contended which of them should die for the other, whereat all the Senate and people were wonderfully abashed, not knowing what it meant. The murderer in deed happened to be in the prease [1] at that time, who, perceiving the marvellous conten-

[1] *Prease*, press, crowd.

tion of these two persons, which were both innocent, and that it proceeded of an incomparable friendship, was vehemently provoked to discover the truth. Wherefore he brake through the prease, and coming before the Senate, spake in this wise :

"Noble fathers, I am such a person, whom ye know have been a common barrator [1] and thief by a long space of years : ye know also, that Titus is of a noble blood, and is approved to be alway a man of excellent virtue and wisdom, and never was malicious. This other stranger seemeth to be a man full of simplicity, and that more is desperate for some grievous sorrow that he hath taken, as it is to you evident. I say to you, fathers, they both be innocent ; I am that person that slew him that is founden dead by the barn, and robbed him of his money. And when I found in the barn this stranger lying asleep, having by him a naked knife, I, the better to mine offence, did put the knife into the wound of the dead man, and so all bloody laid it again by this stranger. This was my mischievous desire to escape your judgment. Whereunto now I remit me wholly, rather than this noble man Titus, or this innocent stranger, should unworthily die."

Hereat all the Senate and people took comfort, and the noise of rejoicing hearts filled all the court. And when it was further examined, Gisippus was discovered ; the friendship between him and Titus was throughout the city published, extolled, and magnified. Wherefore the Senate consulted of this matter, and finally, at the instance of Titus and the people, discharged the felon. Titus recognised his negligence in forgetting Gisippus.

And Titus, being advertised of the exile of Gisippus, and the despiteful cruelty of his kindred, was therewith wonderful wroth, and having Gisippus home to his house (where he was with incredible joy received of the lady, whom some time he should have wedded) honourably apparelled him ; and there Titus offered to him to use all his goods and possessions at his own pleasure and appetite. But Gisippus desiring to be again in his proper country, Titus, by the consent of the Senate and people, assembled a great army, and went with Gisippus unto Athens, where he, having delivered to him all those which were causers of banishing and despoiling of his friend Gisippus, did on them sharp execution ; and restoring to Gisippus his lands and substance, stablished him in perpetual quietness, and so returned to Rome.

[1] *Barrator*, mischief-maker.

SIR PHILIP SIDNEY
1554–1586

THE STORY OF THE UNKIND KING

It was in the kingdome of Galacia, the season being (as in the depth of winter) very cold, and as then sodainely growne to so extreame and foule a storme, that never any winter (I thinke) brought foorth a fowler child ; so that the princes were even compelled by the haile, that the pride of the winde blew into their faces, to seeke some shrowding place within a certain hollow rocke offering it unto them, they made it their shield against the tempests furie.

And so staying there, till the violence thereof was passed, they heard the speach of a couple, who not perceiving them (being hidde within that rude canapy) helde a straunge and pitifull disputation which made them steppe out ; yet in such sort, as they might see unseene. There they perceaved an aged man, and a young, scarcely come to the age of a man, both poorely arayed, extreamely weather beaten ; the olde man blinde, the young man leading him : and yet, through all those miseries, in both these seemed to appeare a kind of noblenesse, nut sutable to that affliction.

But the first words they heard, were these of the old man.

" Well, Leonatus " (said he), " since I cannot perswade thee to leade me to that which should end my griefe, and my trouble, let me now entreat thee to leave me : feare not, my miserie cannot be greater then it is, and nothing doth become me but miserie ; feare not the danger of my blind steps, I cannot fall worse then I am. And doo not, I pray thee, doo not obstinately continue to infect thee with my wretchedness. But flie, flie from this region, onely worthy of me."

" Deare father " (answered he), " doo not take away from me the onely remnant of my happinesse : while I have power to doo you service, I am not wholly miserable."

" Ah, my sonne " (saide he, and with that he groned, as if sorrow strave to breake his herte), " how eville fits it me to have such a sonne, and how much doth thy kindness unbraide my wickednesse ? "

These dolefull speeches, and some others to like purpose (well shewing they had not been borne to the fortune they were in) moved the princes to goe out unto them, and aske the younger what they were.

"Sirs" (answered he, with a good grace, and made the more agreable by a certaine noble kinde of pitiousnes), "I see well you are straungers, that know not our miserie so well here knowne, that no man dare know, but that we must be miserable. In deede, our state is such, as though nothing is so needfull unto us as pittie, yet nothing is more daungerous unto us, then to make our selves so knowne as may stirre pittie. But your presence promiseth that cruelty shall not over-runne hate. And if it did, in truth our state is soncke below the degree of feare.

"This old man (whom I leade) was lately rightfull prince of this countrie of Paphlagonia, by the hard-harted ungratefulnes of a sonne of his, deprived, not onely of his kingdome (whereof no forraine forces were able to spoyle him) but of his sight, the riches which nature graunts to the poorest creatures. Whereby, and by other his unnaturall dealings, he hath bin driven to such griefe, as even now he would have had me to have led him to the toppe of this rocke, thence to cast himself headlong to death: and so would have made me (who received my life of him) to be the worker of his destruction. But, noble gentlemen (said he), if either of you have a father, and feele what duetifull affection is engraffed in a sonnes hart, let me intreate you to convey this afflicted prince to some place of rest and securitie. Amongst your worthie actes it shall be none of the least, that a king, of such might and fame, and so unjustly oppressed, is in any sort by you relieved."

But before they could make him answere, his father began to speake:

"Ah, my sonne" (said he), "how evill an historian are you, that leave out the chiefe knotte of all the discourse: my wickednes, my wickednes. And if thou doest it to spare my eares (the onely sense nowe left me proper for knowledge) assure thy selfe thou dost mistake me. And I take witnesse of that sunne which you see (with that he cast up his blinde eyes, as if he would hunt for light), and wish my selfe in worse case then I do wish my selfe, which is as evill as may be, if I speake untruely; that nothing is so welcome to my thoughts as the publishing of my shame. Therefore, know you, gentlemen (to whom from my harte I wish that it may not prove ominous foretoken of misfortune to have mettle with such a miser as I am), that whatsoever my sonne (O God, that trueth binds me to reproach him with the name of my sonne) hath said, is true.

"But, besides those truthes, this is also true: that, having had in lawful mariage, of a mother fitte to beare royall children, this sonne (suche one as partly you see, and better shall knowe by my shorte declaration), and so enjoyed the expectations in the world of him, till he was growen to justifie their expectations (so as I needed envie no father for the chiefe comfort of mortalitie, to leave an other ones-selfe after me), I was caried by a bastarde sonne of mine (if, at least, I be bounde to beleeve the words of that base woman my concubine, his mother) first to mislike, then to hate, lastly to destroy, to doo my best to destroy, this sonne (I thinke you thinke) undeserving destruction. What waies he used to bring me to it, if I should tell you, I should tediously trouble you with as much poysonous hypocrisie, desperate fraud, smoothe malice, hidden ambition, and smiling envie, as in any living person could be harbored. But I list it not, no remembrance of naughtines delights me, but mine own: and, methinks, the accusing his traines might in some manner excuse my fault, which certainly I loth to doo. But the conclusion is, that I gave order to some servants of mine, whom I thought as apte for such charities as my selfe, to leade him out into a forrest, and there to kill him.

" But those theeves (better natured to my sonne then my selfe) spared his life, letting him goe, to learn to live poorely: which he did, giving himselfe to be a private soldier, in a countrie hereby. But as he was redy to be greatly advanced for some noble peeces of service which he did, he hearde newes of me: who (dronke in my affection to that unlawfull and unnaturall sonne of mine) suffered my selfe so to be governed by him, that all favors and punishments passed by him, all offices, and places of importance, distributed to his favourites; so that ere I was aware, I had left my selfe nothing but the name of a king: which he shortly wearie of too, with many indignities (if any thing may be called an indignity which was laid upon me), threw me out of my seat, and put out my eies; and then (proud in his tyrannie) let me goe, neither imprisoning, nor killing me: but rather delighting to make me feele my miserie; miserie, indeed, if ever there were any; full of wretchednes, fuller of disgrace, and fullest of guiltines.

" And as he came to the crowne by so unjust meanes, as unjustlie he kept it, by force of stranger souldiers in cittadels, the nestes of tyranny, and murderers of libertie; disarming all his own countrimen, that no man durst shew himself a welwiller of mine: to say the trueth (I think) few of them being so (considering my cruell follie to my good sonne, and foolish kindnes to my unkinde bastard): but if there were any who fell to pitie of so great a fall, and had yet any sparkes of unstained duety lefte in them towardes me, yet durst they not shewe it, scarcely with giving me alms at their doores; which yet was the onelie sustenaunce of my distressed life, no bodie daring to shewe so much charitie as to lende me a handle to guide my darke steppes : till this sonne of mine (God knowes, woorthie of a more vertuous, and more fortunate father) forgetting my abhominable wrongs, not recking danger, and neglecting the present good way he was in doing himselfe good, came hether to doo this kind office you see him performe towards me, to my unspeakable griefe ; not onelie because his kindnes is a glasse even to my blind eyes, of my naughtines, but that above all griefes, it greeves me he should desperatly adventure the losse of his well-deserving life for mine, that yet owe more to fortune for my deserts, as if he would cary mudde in a chest of christall. For well I know, he that now raigneth, how much soever (and with good reason) he despiseth me, of all men despised ; yet he will not let slippe any advantage to make away with him, whose just title (ennobled by courage and goodnes) may one day shake the seat of a never secure tyrannie. And for this cause I craved of him to leade me to the toppe of this rocke, indeede I must confesse, with meaning to free him from so serpentine a companion as I am. But he finding what I purposed, onelie therein since he was borne, shewed himselfe disobedient unto me.

" And now, gentlemen, you have the true storie, which I pray you publish to the world, that my mischievous proceedings may be the glorie of his filiall pietie the onelie reward now left for so great a merite. And if it may be, let me obtaine that of you, which my sonne denies me ; for never was there more pitie in saving any, then in ending me ; both because therein my agonies shall ende, and so shall you preserve this excellent young man, who els wilfully followes his owne ruine."

The matter, in itself lamentable, lamentably expressed by the old prince (which needed not take to himselfe the gestures of pitie, since his face could not put of the markes thereof) greatly moved the two princes to compassion, which could not stay in such harts as theirs without seeking remedie. But by and by the occasion was presented : for Plexirtus (so was the bastard called) came thether with fortie horse, onelie of purpose to murder this brother ; of whose comming he had soone advertisement, and thought no eyes of sufficient credite in such a matter, but his owne ; and therefore came himselfe to be actor, and spectator.

And as soone as he came, not regarding the weake (as he thought) garde of but two men, commaunded some of his followers to set their handes to his, in the killing of Leonatus. But the young prince (though not otherwise armed but with a sworde), how falsely soever he was dealt with by others, would not betray himselfe : but bravely drawing it out, made the death of the first that assayled him, warne his fellowes to come more warily after him. But then Pyrocles and Musidorus were quickly become parties (so just a defence deserving as much as old friendship), and so did behave them among that companie (more injurious then valiant) that many of them lost their lives for their wicked maister.

Yet perhaps had the number of them at last prevailed, if the King of Pontus (lately by them made so) had not come unlooked for to their succour. Who (having had a dreame which had fixt his imagination vehemently upon some great daunger, presently to follow those two princes whom he most deerely loved) was come in all hast, following as well as he could their tracke with a hundreth horses in that countrie, which he thought (considering who then raigned) a fit place inough to make the stage of any tragedie.

But then the match had ben so ill made for Plexirtus, that his ill-led life, and worse-gotten honour, should have tumbled together to destruction : had there not come in Tydeus and Telenor, with fortie or fiftie in their suit, to the defence of Plexirtus. These two were brothers, of the noblest house of that country, brought up from their infancie with Plexirtus : men of such prowesse as not to know feare in themselves, and yet to teach it others that should deale with them : for they had often made their lives triumph over most terrible daungers ; never dismayed, and ever fortunate ; and truely no more settled in their valure, then disposed to goodnesse and justice, if either they had lighted on a better friend, or could have learned to make friendship a child, and not the father vertue.

But, bringing up (rather then choise) having first knit their minds unto him (indeed, craftie inough, eyther to hide his faults, or never to shewe them, but when they might pay home) they willingly held out the course, rather to satisfie him, then all the world ; and rather to be good friendes then good men : so, as though they did not like the evill he did, yet they liked him that did the evill, and, though not councellors of the offence, yet protectors of the offender.

Now, they having heard of this sodaine going out, with so small a company, in a country full of evil-wishing minds toward him (though they knew not the cause), followed him ; till they found him in such case as they were to venture their lives, or else he to loose his : which they did with such force of minde and bodie, that truly I may justly say, Pyrocles and Musidorus had never till then found any that could make them so well repeate their hardest lesson in the feates of armes. And briefly so they did, that, if they overcame not, yet were they not overcome, but caried away that ungratefull maister of theirs to a place of securitie ; howsoever the princes laboured to the contrary.

But this matter being thus far begun, it became not the constancie of the princes so to leave it ; but in all hast making forces both in Pontus and Phrygia, they had in fewe dayes lefte him but only that one strong place where he was.

For feare having bene the onelie knot that had fastened his people unto him, that once untied by a greater force, they all scattered from him, like so many birdes, whose cage had bene broken.

In which season the blind king (having in the chief citie of his realme set the crowne upon his sonne Leonatus' head) with many teares (both of joy and sorrow) setting forth to the people his owne fault and his sonnes vertue, after he had kist him, and forst his sonne to accept honour of him (as of his newe-become subject) even in a moment died, as it should seeme: his hart broken with unkindnes and affliction, stretched so farre beyond his limits with this excesse of comfort, as it was able no longer to keep safe his vitall spirits.

But the new king (having no lesse lovingly performed all duties to him dead, then alive) pursued on the siege of his unnatural brother, inasmuch for the revenge of his father, as for the establishing of his owne quiet. In which siege, truly I cannot but acknowledge the prowesse of those two brothers, then whom the princes never found in all their travell two men of greater habilitie to performe, nor of habler skill for conduct.

But Plexirtus, finding that, if nothing else, famin would at last bring him to destruction, thought better by humblenes to creepe, where by pride he could not march. For certainly so had nature formed him, and the exercise of craft conformed him to all turnings of sleights, that, though no man had lesse goodnes in his soule then he, no man could find better the places whence arguments might grow of goodnesse to another: though no man felt lesse pitie, no man could tel better how to stir pitie: no man more impudent to deny, where proofes were not manifest; no man more ready to confesse with a repenting manner of aggravating his owne evill, where denial would but make the fault fowler.

Now, he tooke this way, that, having gotten a pasport for one (that pretended he would put Plexirtus alive into his hands) to speak with the king his brother, he himselfe (though much against the minds of the valiant brothers, who rather wished to die in brave defence) with a rope about his neck, barefooted, came to offer himselfe to the discretion of Leonatus.

Where what submission he used, how cunningly in making greater the fault he made the faultines the lesse, how artificially he could set out the torments of his own conscience, with the burdensome comber he had found of his ambitious desires; how finely seeming to desire nothing but death, as ashamed to live, he begd life in the refusing it, I am not cunning inough to be able to expresse: but so fell out of it, that though, at first sight, Leonatus saw him with no other eie then as the murderer of his father; and anger already began to paint revenge in many colours, ere long he had not only gotten pitie, but pardon; and if not an excuse of the fault past, yet an opinion of a future amendment: while the poor villaines (chiefe ministers of his wickednes, now betraied by the author thereof) were delivered to many cruell sorts of death; he so handling it, that it rather seemed he had rather come into the defence of an unremediable mischiefe already committed, then that they had done it at first by his consent.

In such sort the princes left these reconciled brothers (Plexirtus in all his behavious carying him in far lower degree of service than the ever-noble nature of Leonatus would suffer him), and taking likewise their leaves of their good friend the King of Pontus (who returned to enjoy their benefite, both of his wife and kingdome), they privately went thence, having onelie with them the two valiant brothers, who would needs accompanie them through divers places; they foure dooing actes more daungerous, though lesse famous, because they were but privat chivalries: till hearing of the faire and vertuous Queen Erona of Lycia, besieged by the puissant King of Armenia, they bent themselves to her succour, both because the weaker (and weaker as being a ladie), and partly, because they heard the King of Armenia had in his company three of the most famous men living for matters of armes, that were knowe to be in the worlde.

Whereof one was the Prince Plangus (whose name was sweetened by your breath, peerlesse ladie, when the last daie it pleased you to mention him unto me), the other two were two great princes (though holding of him), Barzanes and Euardes, men of giant-like both hugenes and force: in which two especially the trust the King had of victory was reposed. And of them, those two brothers of Tydeus and Telenor (sufficient judges in warlike matters) spake so high commendations, that the two young princes had even a youthfull longing to have some triall of their vertue. And, therefore, as soone as they were entred into Lycia, they joyned themselves with them that faithfully served the poore Queene, at that time besieged: and, ere long, animated in such sort of their almost over-throwne harts, that they went by force to relieve the towne, though they were deprived of a great part of their strength by the parting of the two brothers, who were sent for in all hast to returne to their old friend and maister, Plexirtus: who (willingly hoodwinking themselves from seeing his faultes, and binding themselves to beleeve what he said) often abused the vertue of courage to defend his fowle vice of injustice. But now they were sent for to advaunce a conquest he was about; while Pyrocles and Musidorus pursued the deliverie of the Queene Erona.

"MERY TALES, WITTIE QUESTIONS AND QUICK ANSWERES" 16TH CENTURY

KING LEWIS AND THE HUSBANDMAN

WHAT time King Lewis of France the XI. of that name, because of the trouble that was in the realm kept himself in Burgoyne, he chanced, by occasion of hunting, to become acquainted with one Conon, a homely husbandman and a plain-meaning fellow, in which manner of men the high princes greatly delight them.

To this man's house the king oft resorted from hunting, and with great pleasure he would eat radish roots with him.

Within a while after, when Lewis was restored home and had the governance of France in his hand, this husbandman was counselled by his wife to take a goodly sort of radish roots and to go and give them to the king, and put him in mind of the good cheer that he had made him at his house. Conon would not assent thereto.

"What, foolish woman!" quoth he; "the great princes remember not such small pleasures."

But for all that she would not rest till Conon took out a great sight of the fairest roots and took his journey toward the Court. But as he went by the way he ate up all the radishes save one of the greatest.

Conon peaked into the Court, and stood where the king should pass by; by and by the king knew him and called him to him. Conon stepped to the king and presented his root with a glad cheer.

And the king took it more gladly, and bade one that was nearest to him to lay it up among those jewels that he loved best; and then commanded Conon to dine with him.

When dinner was done, he thanked Conon: and when the king saw that he would depart home, he commanded to give him a thousand crowns of gold for his radish root.

When this was known in the king's house, one of the Court gave the king a proper minion horse. The king perceiving that he did it because of the liberality showed unto Conon, with very glad cheer he took the gift, and counselled with his lords how and with what gift he might recompense the horse that was so goodly and fair.

This meanwhile the pickthank had a marvellous great hope, and, thought in his mind thus: If he so well recompensed the radish root that was given of a rustical man, how much more largely will he recompense such an horse, that is given of me that am of the Court?

When every man had said his mind as though the king had counselled about a great weighty matter, and that they had long fed the pickthank with vain hope, at last the king said:

"I remember now what we shall give him"; and so he called one of his lords, and bade him in his ear go fetch him that that he found in his chamber (and told him the place where) featly folded up in silk.

Anon he came and brought the radish root, and even as it was folded up the king gave it with his own hand to the courtier, saying:

"We suppose your horse is well recompensed with this jewel, for it hath cost us a thousand crowns."

The courtier went his way never so glad, and when he had unfolded it, he found none other treasure but the radish root almost withered.

ANONYMOUS
1570

THE WAKING MAN'S DREAM

In the time that Phillip Duke of Burgundy (who by the gentlenesse and curteousnesse of his carriage purchaste the name of good) guided the reines of the country of Flanders, this prince, who was of an humour pleasing, and full of judicious goodnesse, rather then silly simplicity, used pastimes which for their singularity are commonly called the pleasures of Princes: after this manner he no lesse shewed the quaintnesse of his wit then his prudence.

Being in Bruxelles with all his court, and having at his table discoursed amply enough of the vanities and greatnesse of this world, he let each one say his pleasure on this subject, whereon was alleadged grave sentences and rare examples: walking towards the evening in the towne, his head full of divers thoughts, he found a Tradesman lying in a corner sleeping very soundly, the fumes of Bacchus having surcharged his braine. I describe this man's drunkenesse in as good manner as I can to the credit of the party. This vice is so common in both the superior and inferiour Germany, that divers, making glory and vaunting of their dexterity in this art, encrease their praise thereby, and hold it for a brave act. The good Duke, to give his followers an example of the vanity of all the magnificence with which he was invironed, devised a meanes farre lesse dangerous than that which Dionysius the Tyrant used towards Democles, and which in pleasantnesse beares a marvellous utility. He caused his men to carry away this sleeper, with whom, as with a blocke, they might doe what they would, without awaking him; he caused them to carry him into one of the sumptuosest parts of his Pallace, into a chamber most state-like furnished, and makes them lay him on a rich bed. They presently strip him of his bad cloathes, and put him on a very fine and cleane shirt, instead of his own, which was foule and filthy. They let him sleepe in that place at his ease, and whilest he settles his drinke the Duke prepares the pleasantest pastime that can be imagined.

In the morning, this drunkard being awake drawes the curtaines of this brave rich bed, sees himselfe in a chamber adorned like a Paradice, he considers the rich furniture with an amazement such as you may imagine: he beleeves not his eyes, but layes his fingers on them, and feeling them open, yet perswades himselfe they are shut by sleep, and that all he sees is but a pure dreame.

As soone as he was knowne to be awake, in comes the officers of the Dukes house, who were instructed by the Duke what they should do. There were pages bravely apparelled, Gentlemen of the chamber, Gentleman waiters, and the High Chamberlaine, who, all in faire order and without laughing, bring cloathing for this new guest: they honour him with the same reverences as if he were a Soveraigne Prince; they serve him bare headed, and aske him what suite he will please to weare that day.

This fellow, affrighted at the first, beleeving these things to be inchantment or dreames, reclaimed by these submissions, tooke heart, and grew bold, and setting a good face on the matter, chused amongst all the apparell that they presented unto him that which he liked best, and which he thought to be fittest for him: he is accommodated like a King, and served with such ceremonies, as he had never seene before, and yet beheld them without saying anything, and with an assured countenance. This done, the greatest Nobleman in the Dukes Court enters the chamber with the same reverence and honour to him as if he had been their Soveraigne Prince (Phillip with Princely delight beholds this play from a private place); divers of purpose petitioning him for pardons, which he grants with such a continuance and gravity, as if he had had a Crowne on his head all his life time.

Being risen late, and dinner time approaching, they asked him if he were pleased to have his tables covered. He likes that very well. The table is furnished, where he is set alone, and under a rich Canopie; he eates with the same ceremony which was observed at the Dukes meales; he made good cheere, and chawed with all his teeth, but only drank with more moderation then he could have wisht, but the Majesty which he represented made him refraine. All taken away, he was entertained with new and pleasant things; they led him to walk about the great Chambers, Galleries, and Gardens of the Pallace (for all this merriment was played within the gates, they being shut only for recreation to the Duke and the principall of his Court): they shewed him all the richest and most pleasantest things therein, and talked to him thereof as if they had all beene his, which he heard with an attention and contentment beyond measure, not saying one word of his base condition, or declaring that they tooke him for another. They made him passe the afternoone in all kinds of sports; musicke, dancing, and a

Comedy, spent some part of the time. They talked to him of some State matters, whereunto he answered according to his skill, and like a right Twelftetide King.

Super time approaching, they aske this new created Prince if he would please to have the Lords and Ladies of his Court to sup and feast with him; whereat he seemed something unwilling, as if he would not abase his dignity unto such familiarity; neverthelesse, counterfeiting humanity and affability, he made signes that he condiscended thereunto: he then, towards night, was led with sound of Trumpets and Hoboyes into a faire hall, where long tables were set, which were presently covered with divers sorts of dainty meates, the Torches shined in every corner, and made a day in the midst of a night: the Gentlemen and Gentlewomen were set in fine order, and the Prince at the upper end in a higher seat. The service was magnificent; the musicke of voyces and instruments fed the eare, whilest mouthes found their food in the dishes. Never was the imaginary Duke at such a feast: carousses begin after the manner of the Country; the Prince is assaulted on all sides, as the Owle is assaulted by all the Birds, when he begins to soare. Not to seeme uncivill, he would doe the like to his good and faithfull subjects. They serve him with very strong wine, good Hipocras, which he swallowed downe in great draughts, and frequently redoubled; so that, charged with so many extraordinaryes, he yeelded to deaths cousin german, sleep, which closed his eyes, stopt his eares, and made him loose the use of his reason and all his other sences.

Then the right Duke, who had put himselfe among the throng of his Officers to have the pleasure of this mummery, commanded that this sleeping man should be stript out of his brave cloathes, and cloathed againe in his old ragges, and so sleeping carried and layd in the same place where he was taken up the night before. This was presently done and there did he snort all the night long, not taking any hurt either from the hardnesse of the stones or the night ayre, so well was his stomacke filled with good preservatives. Being awakened in the morning by some passenger, or it may bee by some that the good Duke Phillip had thereto appointed, "Ha!" said he, "my friends, what have you done? You have rob'd mee of a Kingdome, and have taken mee out of the sweetest and happiest dreame that ever man could have fallen into."

Then, very well remembring all the particulars of what had passed the day before, he related unto them, from point to point, all that had happened unto him, still thinking it assuredly to bee a dreame. Being returned home to his house, he entertaines his wife, neighbours, and friends, with this his dreame, as he thought: the truth whereof being at last published by the mouthes of those Courtiers who had been present at this pleasant recreation, the good man could not beleeve it, thinking that for sport they had framed this history upon his dreame ; but when Duke Phillip, who would have the full contentment of this pleasant tricke, had shewed him the bed wherein he lay, the cloathes which he had worne, the persons who had served him, the Hall wherein he had eaten, the gardens and galleries wherein he had walked, hardly could he be induced to beleeve what he saw, imagining that all this was meere inchantment and illusion.

The Duke used some liberality towards him for to helpe him in the poverty of his family ; and, taking an occasion thereon to make an Oration unto his Courtiers concerning the vanity of this worlds honours, he told them that all that ambitious persons seeke with so much industry is but smoake, and a meere dreame, and that they are strucken with that pleasant folly of the Athenian, who imagined that all the riches that arrived by shipping in the haven of Athens to be his, and that all the Marchants were but his factors : his friends getting him cured by a skilfull Physitian of the debility of his brain, in lieu of giving them thanks for this good office, he reviled them, saying that, whereas he was rich in conceit, they had by this cure made him poore and miserable in effect.

Harpaste, a foole that Senecaes wife kept, and whose pleasant imagination this grave Phylosopher doth largely relate, being growne blind, could not perswade herselfe that she was so, but continually complained that the house wherein she dwelt was dark, that they would not open the windowes, and that they hindred her from setting light, to make her beleeve she could see nothing : hereupon this great Stoick made this fine consideration, that every vitious man is like unto this foole, who, although he be blind in his passion, yet thinks not himself to be so, casting all his defect on false surmises, whereby he seeks not only to have his sinne worthy of excuse and pardon, but even of praise : the same say the covetous, ambitious, and voluptuous persons, in defence of their imperfections ; but in fine (as the Psalmist saith) all that must passe awaye, and the images thereof come to nothing, as the dreame of him that awaketh from sleepe.

If a bucket of water be as truly water, as all the sea, the difference only remaining in the quantity, not in the quality, why shall we not say, that our poore Brabander was a Soveraigne Prince for the space of fowre and twenty houres, being that he received all the honours and commodities thereof : how many Kings and Popes have not lasted longer, but have dyed on the very day of their Elections or Coronations ? As for those other pompes, which have lasted longer, what are they else but longer dreames ? This vanity of worldly things is a great sting to a well composed soule, to helpe it forward towards the heavenly kingdome.

ANONYMOUS
1620

THE TALE TOLD BY THE FISHWIFE OF STRAND-ON-THE-GREEN

In the troublesome raigne of King Henry the sixt, there dwelt in Waltam (not farre from London) a gentleman, which had to wife a creature most beautifull: so that in her time there were few found that matched her (none at all that excelled her), so excellent were the gifts that nature had bestowed on her. In body was she not onely so rare, and unparalleled, but also in her gifts of minde: so that this creature, it seemed, that Grace and Nature strove who should excell each other in their gifts toward her.

The gentleman her husband thought himselfe so happy in his choise, that he beleeved, in choosing her, he tooke hold of that blessing which heaven proffereth every man once in his life. Long did not this opinion hold for currant, for in his height of love he began so to hate her, that he sought her death: the cause I will tell you.

Having businesse one day to London, he took his leave very kindly of his wife, and accompanied with one man, he rode to London: being toward night, he tooke up his inne, and, to be briefe, he went to supper amongst other gentlemen. Amongst other talke at table, one tooke occasion to speake of women, and what excellent creatures they were, so long as they continued loyall to man. To whom answered one, saying:

"This is truth, Sir: so is the Divell so long as he doth no harme, which is neaver: his goodnes and women's loyaltie will come both in one yeere, but it is so farre off, that none in this age shall live to see it."

This gentleman loving his wife dearely (and knowing her to be free from this uncivill gentleman's generall taxation of women) in her behalfe, saide:

"Sir, you are too bitter against the sexe of women, and doe ill (for some one's sake that hath proved false to you) to taxe the generalitie of women-kinde with lightnesse ; and but I would not be counted uncivill amongst these gentlemen, I would give you the reply that approved untruth deserveth, you know my meaning, Sir : construe my words as you please : excuse me, gentlemen, if I be uncivill : I answere in the behalfe of one who is as free from disloyaltie as the sunne from darknes, or the fire from the cold."

" Pray, Sir," said the other, " since wee are opposite in opinions, let us rather talke like lawyers, that wee may be quickly friends again, then like souldiers which end their wordes with blowes. Perhaps this woman that you answer for is chaste, but yet against her will : for many women are honest 'cause they have not the means and opportunitie to bee dishonest (so is a thiefe true in prison 'cause he hath nothing to steale) : had I but opportunitie, and knew this same saint you so adore, I would pawne my life and whole estate, in a short while to bring you some manifest token of her disloyaltie. Sir, you are yong in the knowledge of women's slights, your want of experience makes you too credulous ; therefore be not abused."

This speech of his made the gentleman more out of patience then before, so that with much adoe he held himselfe from offering violence ; but his anger beeing a little over, he said :

"Sir, I doe verily beleeve that this vaine speech of yours proceedeth rather from a loose and ill manner'd minde, then of any experience you have had of women's loosenes : and since you thinke your selfe so cunning in that (divellish art) of corrupting women's chastitie, I will lay downe heere a hundred pounds, against which you shall lay fifty pounds, and before these gentlemen I promise you, if that within a month's space you bring me anie token of this gentlewoman's disloyaltie (for whose sake I have spoken in the behalfe of all women) I doe freely give you leave to enjoy the same ; conditionally you not performing it, I may enjoy your money. If that it be a match, speake, and I will acquaint you where she dwelleth : and besides, I vow, as I am a gentleman, not to give her notice of any such intent that is toward her."

" Sir," quoth the man, " your proffer is faire, and I accept the same " : so the money was delivered into the oast of the house his hands, and the sitters by were witnesses : so drinking together like friends, they went every man in his chamber.

The next day this man having knowledge of the place, rid thither, leaving the gentleman at the inne, who being assured of his wives chastitie, made no other account but to winne the wager, but it fell out otherwise : for the other vowed either by force, policie, or free will to get some jewell or other toy from her, which was enough to perswade the gentleman that he was a cuckold and win the wager he had laid. This villaine (for he deserved no better stile) lay at Waltam a whole day, before he came to the sight of her: at last he espyed her in the fields, to whom he went and kissed her (a thing no modest woman can deny): after his salutation, he said:

"Gentlewoman, I pray pardon me if I have beene too bold: I was intreated by your husband which is at London (I riding this way) to come and see you: by me he hath sent his commends to you, with a kinde intreat that you would not be discontented for his long absence, it being serious businesse that keepes him from your sight."

The gentlewoman very modestly bade him welcome, thanking him for his kindnes, withall telling him that her husband might command her patience as long as he pleased. Then intreated shee him to walke homeward, where shee gave him such entertainment as was fit for a gentleman, and her husband's friend.

In the time of his abiding at her house, he oft would have singled her in private talke, but she perceiving the same (knowing it to bee a thing not fitting a modest woman) would never come in his sight but at meales, and then were there so many at boord, that it was no time to talke of love-matters; therefore he saw he must accomplish his desire some other way, which he did in this maner:—

He having layne two nights at her house, and perceiving her to bee free from lustfull desires, the third night he fained himselfe to be something ill, and so went to bed timelier then he was wont. When he was alone in his chamber, he began to think with himselfe that it was now time to do that which he determined; for if he tarried any longer, they might have cause to think that he came for some ill intent, and waited opportunity to execute the same: therefore he resolved to doe something that night, that might winne him the wager, or utterly bring him in despaire of the same.

With this resolution he went to her chamber, which was but a paire of staires from his, and finding the doore open, he went in, placing himselfe under the bed: Long had he not lyne there, but in came the gentlewoman with her maiden; who having been at prayers with her household, was going to bed. She preparing herselfe to bedward, laid her head-tyre and those jewels she wore on a little table thereby: at length he perceived her to put off a littel crucifix of gold, which dayly she wore next to her heart, this jewell he thought fittest for his turne, and therefore observed where she did lay the same. At length the gentlewoman having untyred her selfe, went to bed: her maid then bolting of the doore, took the candle, and went to bed in a withdrawing roome onely separated with arras. This villaine lay still under the bed, listening if he could heare her draw her breath long: then thought he all sure, and like a cunning villaine rose without noise, going straight to the table, where, finding of the crucifix, he lightly went to the doore, which he cunningly unbolted ; all this performed he with so little noise, that neither the mistris nor the maid heard him.

Having gotten into his chamber, he wished for day, that he might carry this jewell to her husband as signe of his wives disloyaltie ; but seeing his wishes but in vaine, he laid him downe to sleepe : happy had she beene had his bed proved his grave.

In the morning, so soone as the folkes were stirring, he rose and went to the horse-keeper, praying him to helpe him to his horse, telling him that he had took his leave of his mistris the last night. Mounting his horse, away rid he to London, leaving the gentlewoman in bed ; who, when she rose, attiring her selfe hastily ('cause some one tarried to speake with her) missed not her crucifix : so passed she the time away, as shee was wont other dayes to doe, no whit troubled in mind, though much sorrow was toward her ; onely she seemed a little discontented that her ghest went away so unmannerly, she using him so kindely.

So leaving her, I will speake of him, who the next morning was betimes at London ; and comming to the inne, he asked for the gentleman, who then was in bed, but he quickly rose and came downe to him, who seeing him return'd so suddenly he thought he came to have leave to release himselfe of his wager ; but this chanced otherwise : for having saluted him, he said in this manner :

" Sir, did not I tell you that you were too yong in experience of woman's subtilties, and that no woman was longer good then she had cause, or time to doe ill ? this you beleeved not, and thought it a thing so unlikely, that you gave me a hundred pounds for the knowledge of it. In brief know your wife is a woman, and therefore a wanton, a changeling : to confirme that I speake, see heere (shewing him the crucifix), know you this ? if this be not sufficient proofe, I wil fetch you more."

At the sight of this, his blood left his face, running to comfort his faint heart, which was ready to breake at the sight of this crucifix, which he knew she alwayes wore next to her heart, and therefore he must (as he thought) goe something neere, which stole so private a jewell. But remembering himselfe, he cheeres his spirits, seeing that was sufficient proofe and he had wonne the wager, which he commanded should be given to him.

Thus was the poore gentleman abused, who went into his chamber, and beeing weary of this world (seeing where he had put onely his trust, he was deceived) he was minded to fall upon his sword, and so end all his miseries at once : but his better genius perswaded him contrary, and not so (by laying violent hands on himselfe) to leape into the Divel's mouth.

Thus being in many mindes, but resolving no one thing, at last he concluded to punish her with death, which had deceived his trust, and himselfe utterly to forsake his house and lands, and follow the fortunes of King Henry.

To this intent he called his man, to whom he said:

"George, thou knowest I have ever held thee deare, making more account of thee then thy other fellowes, and thou hast often told me that thou diddest owe thy life to me, which at any time thou wouldest bee ready to render up to doe me good."

"True, Sir (answered his man), I said no more then, then I will now at any time, whensoever you please, performe."

"I beleeve thee, George (replyed he): but there is no such need: I onely would have thee doe a thing for me, in which is no great danger, yet the profit which thou shalt have thereby shall amount to my wealth: for the love that thou bearest to me, and for thy own good, will thou do this?"

"Sir (answered George), more for your love, then any reward, I will doe it (and yet money makes many men valiant); pray tell me what it is?"

"George (said his master), this it is, thou must goe home, praying thy mistris to meete me halfe the way to London; but having her by the way, in some private place kill her: I meane as I speake; kill her, I say, this is my command, which thou hast promised to performe, which if thou performest not, I vow to kill thee the next time thou commest in my sight. Now for thy reward it shall be this: Take my ring, and when thou hast done my command, by vertue of it, doe thou assume my place till my returne, at which time thou shalt know what my reward is, till then govern my whole estate: and for thy mistris absence, and mine own, make what excuse thou please: so be gone."

"Well, Sir (said George), since it is your will, tho unwilling I am to doe it, yet I will performe it."

So went he his way towards Waltam, and his master presently rid to the court, where he abode with King Henry, who a little before was inlarged by the Earle of Warwicke, and placed in the throne againe.

George beeing come to Waltam, did his dutie to his mistris, who wondred to see him, and not her husband, for whom she demanded of George: he answered her, that he was at Enfield, and did request her to meet him there.

To which shee willingly agreed, and presently rode with him toward Enfield.

At length they being come into a by-way, George began to speake with her in this manner:

"Mistris, I pray you tel me what that wife deserves, who through some lewd behaviour of hers, hath made her husband to neglect his estate, and meanes of life, seeking by all meanes to dye, that he might be free from the shame which her wickednesse hath purchased him ?"

"Why, George (quoth shee), hath thou met with some such creature ? Be it whomsoever might I be her judge, I should thinke her worthy of death: how thinkest thou ?"

"Faith, mistris (said he), I thinke so too, and am so fully perswaded that her offence deserveth that punishment, that I purpose to bee executioner to such a one my selfe. Mistris, you are this woman: you have so offended my master (you know best how your selfe) that he hath left his house, vowing never to see the same till you be dead, and I am the man appointed by him to kill you; therefore, those words which you meane to utter, speake them presently, for I cannot stay."

Poor gentlewoman, at the report of these unkinde words (ill-deserved at her hands) she looked as one dead, and uttering aboundance of teares, she at last spake these words:

"And can it bee, that my kindnes and loving obedience hath merited no other reward at his hands then death ? It cannot be; I know thou onely tryest me, how patiently I would endure such an unjust command. I'le tell thee heere, thus with body prostrate on the earth, and hands lift up to heaven, I would pray for his preservation, those should be my worst words: for death's fearfull visage shewes pleasant to that soule that is innocent."

"Why, then, prepare your selfe (said George), for by heaven I doe not jest."

With that shee prayed him stay, saying:

"And is it so ? then, what should I desire to live, having lost his favour (and without offence) whom I so dearly loved, and in whose sight my happiness did consist ? come, let me die. Yet, George, let mee have so much favour at thy hands, as to commend me in these few words to him: Tell him my death I willingly embrace, for I have owed him my life (yet no otherwise but by a wives obedience) ever since I call'd him husband; but that I am guilty of the least fault toward him, I utterly deny, and doe (at this houre of my death) desire that heaven would powre down vengeance upon me, if ever I offended him in thought. Intreat him that he would not speake ought that were ill on mee, when I am dead, for in good troth I have deserved none. Pray heaven blesse him. I am prepared now; strike, prethee, home, and kill me and my griefes at once."

George, seeing this, could not withhold himselfe from shedding teares, and with pitie he let fall his sword, saying:

"Mistris, that I have used you so roughly, pray pardon me, for I was commanded so by my master, who hath vowed, if I let you live, to kill me. But I being perswaded that you are innocent, I will rather undergoe the danger of his wrath, then to staine my hands with the bloud of your cleere and spotlesse brest: Yet let mee intreat you (so much) that you would not come in his sight (lest in his rage he turne your butcher), but live in some disguise till time have opened the cause of his mistrust, and shewed you guiltlesse, which (I hope) will not be long."

To this she willingly granted (being loth to die causelesse), and thanked him for his kindnes: so parted they both, having teares in their eyes. George went home, where he shewed his master's ring for the government of the house till his master and mistris returne, which he said lived a while at London, 'cause the time was so troublesome, and that was a place where they were more secure then in the countrey. This his fellowes beleeved, and were obedient to his will, amongst whom he used himselfe so kindely, that he had all their loves.

This poore gentlewoman (mistris of the house) in short time got man's apparell for her disguise; so wandred she up and downe the countrey, for she could get no service, because the time was so dangerous that no man knew whom he might trust; onely she maintained her selfe with the price of those jewels which she had, all which she sold. At the last, being quite out of money, and having nothing left (which she could well spare) to make money of, she resolved rather to starve, then so much to debase herself to become a beggar: with this resolution she went to a solitary place beside Yorke, where shee lived the space of two dayes on hearbs, and such things as shee could there finde.

In this time it chanced that King Edward (beeing come out of France, and lying thereabout with the small forces hee had) came that way with some two or three noblemen, with an intent to discover if any ambushes were laid to him at an advantage. He seeing there this gentlewoman, whom he supposed to be a boy, asked her what she was, and what she made there in that private place? To whom shee very wisely and modestly withall answered, that she was a poore boy, whose bringing up had bin better then her outward parts then shewed, but at that time she was both friendlesse, and comfortlesse, by reason of the late warre.

He being moved to see one so well featur'd (as she was) to want, entertained her for one of his pages, to whom she shewed her selfe so dutifull and loving, that (in short time) shee had his love above all her fellows. Still followed she the fortunes of King Edward, hoping at last (as not long after it did fall out) to be reconciled to her husband.

After the battell at Barnet (where King Edward got the best), she going up and downe amongst the slaine men (to know whether her husband, which was on King Henries side, were dead or escaped) happened to see the other, who had been her ghest, lying there for dead: she remembring him, and thinking him to be one whom her husband loved, went to him, and finding him not dead, she caused one to helpe her with him to a house there-by: where opening of his brest to dresse his wounds, she espied her crucifix; at sight of which her heart was joyfull (hoping by this to find him that was the originall of her disgrace), for she remembring her selfe, found that she had lost that crucifix ever since that morning he departed from her house so suddenly.

But saying nothing of it at that time, she caused him to be carefully looked unto, and brought up to London after her, whither she went with the king, carrying the crucifix with her.

On a time when he was a little recovered, shee went to him, giving him the crucifix which shee had taken from about his necke: to whom he said:

"Good, gentle youth, keep the same; for now in my misery of sicknes, when the sight of that picture should be most comfortable, it is to me most uncomfortable, and breedeth such horrour in my conscience (when I think how wrongfully I got the same), that so long as I see it, I shall never be in rest."

Now knew she that he was the man that caused the separation twixt her husband and her selfe; yet said shee nothing, using him as respectively as shee had before; only shee caused the man, in whose house he lay, to remember the words he had spoken concerning the crucifix.

Not long after, she being alone, attending on the king, beseeched his grace to doe her justice on a villain that had been the cause of all the misery she had suffered. He loving her (above all his other pages) most dearely, said:

"Edmund (for so had she named herself), thou shalt have what right thou wilt on thy enemy; cause him to be sent for, and I will be thy judge myself."

She being glad of this (with the king's authority) sent for her husband, whom she heard was one of the prisoners that was taken at the battell of Barnet, she appointing the other, now recovered, to be at the court at the same time.

They being both come (but not one seeing of the other), the king sent for the wounded man into the presence; before whom the page asked him how he came by the crucifix? He, fearing that his villany would come forth, denyed the words he had said before his oast, affirming he bought it. With that shee called in the oast of the house where he lay, bidding him boldly speake what he had heard this man say concerning the crucifix.

The oast then told the king, that in the presence of this page he heard him intreat that the crucifix might be taken from his sight, for it did wound his conscience to thinke how wrongfully he had gotten the same. These words did the page averre ; yet he utterly denyed the same, affirming that he bought it, and that if he did speake such words in his sicknesse, they proceeded from the lightnesse of his braine, and were untruthes.

Shee, seeing this villain's impudency, sent for her husband in, to whom she shewed the crucifix, saying :

" Sir, doe you know, doe you know this ? "

" Yes," answered hee, " but would God I ne're had knowne the owner of it ! It was my wives, a woman vertuous, till this divell (speaking to the other) did corrupt her purity, who brought me this crucifix as a token of her inconstancie."

With that the king said :

" Sirra, now you are found to be a knave ; did you not even now affirm that you bought it ? " To whom he answered (with fearful countenance) :

" And it like your grace, I said so, to preserve this gentleman's honour, and his wives, which by my telling of the truth would have been much indamag'd ; for indeed she being a secret friend of mine, gave me this, as a testimony of her love."

The gentlewoman, not being able longer to cover herself in that disguise, said :

" And it like your majesty, give mee leave to speake, and you shall see me make this villaine confesse, how he hath abused that good gentleman."

The king having given her leave, she said :

" First, sir, you confessed before your oast, and myself, that you had wrongfully got this jewell ; then, before his majestie you affirmed you bought it, so denying your former words ; now you have denyed that which you so boldly affirmed before, and have said it was this gentleman's wives gift. (With his majesties leave) I say thou art a villaine, and this is likewise false : (with that she discovered herself to be a woman, saying), Hadst thou (villaine) ever any strumpet's favour at my hands ? Did I (for any sinfull pleasure I received from thee) bestow this on thee ? Speake, and if thou have any goodnes left in thee, speake the truth."

With that, he, being daunted at her sudden sight, fell on his knees before the king, beseeching his grace to be mercifull unto him, for he had wronged that gentlewoman : therewith told he the king of the match betweene the gentleman and himselfe, and how he stole the crucifix from her, and by that meanes perswaded her husband that she was a wanton.

The king wondred how he durst (knowing God to bee just) commit so great villany, but more admired he to see his page to turn a gentlewoman : but ceasing to admire, he said :

" Sir (speaking to her husband), you did the part of an unwise man to lay so foolish a wager, for which offence the remembrance of your folly is punishment inough ; but seeing it concernes me not, your wife shall be your judge."

With that mistris Dorrill (thanking his majestie) went to her husband, saying:

" All my anger to you I lay downe with this kisse."

He, wondring all this while to see this strange and unlooked-for change, wept for joy, desiring her to tell him how shee was preserved, wherein shee satisfied him at full.

The king was likewise glad that he had preserved this gentlewoman from wilfull famine, and gave judgment on the other in this manner: That he should restore the money treble which he had wrongfully got from him ; and so was to have a yeeres imprisonment.

So this gentleman and his wife went (with the king's leave) lovingly home, where they were kindly welcomed by George, to whom for recompense he gave the money which he received. So lived they ever after in great content.

DANIEL DEFOE
1659–1731

THE APPARITION OF MRS. VEAL

THIS thing is so rare in all its circumstances, and on so good authority, that my reading and conversation has not given me anything like it. It is fit to gratify the most ingenious and serious inquirer.

Mrs. Bargrave is the person to whom Mrs. Veal appeared after her death ; she is my intimate friend, and I can avouch for her reputation for these last fifteen or sixteen years, on my own knowledge ; and I can confirm the good character she had from her youth to the time of my acquaintance ; though since this relation she is calumniated by some people that are friends to the brother of Mrs. Veal who appeared, who think the relation of this appearance to be a reflection, and endeavour what they can to blast Mrs. Bargrave's reputation and to laugh the story out of countenance. But by the circumstances thereof, and the cheerful disposition of Mrs. Bargrave, notwithstanding the unheard-of ill-usage of a very wicked husband, there is not the least sign of dejection in her face ; nor did I ever hear her let fall a desponding or murmuring expression ; nay, not when actually under her husband's barbarity, which I have been witness to, and several other persons of undoubted reputation.

Now you must know Mrs. Veal was a maiden gentlewoman of about thirty years of age, and for some years last past had been troubled with fits, which were perceived coming on her by her going off from her discourse very abruptly to some impertinence. She was maintained by an only brother, and kept his house in Dover. She was a very pious woman, and her brother a very sober man, to all appearance ; but now he does all he can to null or quash the story. Mrs. Veal was intimately acquainted with Mrs. Bargrave from her childhood. Mrs. Veal's circumstances were then mean ; her father did not take care of his children as he ought, so that they were exposed to hardships ; and Mrs. Bargrave in those days had as unkind a father, though she wanted neither for food nor clothing, while Mrs. Veal wanted for both; so that it was in the power of Mrs. Bargrave to be very much her friend in several instances, which mightily endeared Mrs. Veal; insomuch that she would often say: "Mrs. Bargrave, you are not only the best, but the only friend I have in the world; and no circumstance in life shall ever dissolve my friendship." They would often condole each other's adverse fortune, and read together Drelincourt upon Death, and other good books; and so, like two Christian friends, they comforted each other under their sorrow.

Some time after, Mr. Veal's friends got him a place in the Custom House at Dover, which occasioned Mrs. Veal, by little and little, to fall off from her intimacy with Mrs. Bargrave, though there was never any such thing as a quarrel; but an indifferency came on by degrees, till at last Mrs. Bargrave had not seen her in two years and a half; though above a twelvemonth of the time Mrs. Bargrave had been absent from Dover, and this last half-year had been in Canterbury about two months of the time, dwelling in a house of her own.

In this house, on the 8th of September last, viz. 1705, she was sitting alone, in the forenoon, thinking over her unfortunate life, and arguing herself into a due resignation to Providence, though her condition seemed hard. "And," said she, "I have been provided for hitherto, and doubt not but I shall be still; and am well satisfied that my afflictions shall end when it is most fit for me"; and then took up her sewing-work, which she had no sooner done but she hears a knocking at the door. She went to see who it was there, and this proved to be Mrs. Veal, her old friend, who was in a riding-habit: at that moment of time the clock struck twelve at noon.

"Madam," says Mrs. Bargrave, "I am surprised to see you, you have been so long a stranger"; but told her she was glad to see her, and offered to salute her, which Mrs. Veal complied with, till their lips almost touched; and then Mrs. Veal drew her hand across her own eyes and said: "I am not very well," and so waived it. She told Mrs Bargrave she was going a journey, and had a great mind to see her first.

"But," says Mrs. Bargrave, "how came you to take a journey alone? I am amazed at it, because you have so fond a brother."

"Oh," says Mrs. Veal, "I gave my brother the slip, and came away, because I had so great a desire to see you before I took my journey." So Mrs. Bargrave went in with her into another room within the first, and Mrs. Veal set her down in an elbow-chair, in which Mrs. Bargrave was sitting when she heard Mrs. Veal knock. Then says Mrs. Veal:

"My dear friend, I am come to renew our old friendship again, and beg your pardon for my breach of it; and if you can forgive me, you are one of the best of women."

"Oh," says Mrs. Bargrave, "don't mention such a ting; I have not had an uneasy thought about it; I can easily forgive it."

"What did you think of me?" said Mrs. Veal.

Says Mrs. Bargrave: "I thought you were like the rest of the world, and that prosperity had made you forget yourself and me."

Then Mrs. Veal reminded Mrs. Bargrave of the many friendly offices she did her in former days, and much of the conversation they had with each other in the time of their adversity; what books they read, and what comfort in particular they received from Drelincourt's *Book of Death*, which was the best, she said, on that subject ever wrote. She also mentioned Dr. Sherlock, and two Dutch books which were translated, wrote upon death, and several others; but Drelincourt, she said, had the clearest notions of death and of the future state of any who handled that subject.

Then she asked Mrs. Bargrave whether she had Drelincourt. She said: "Yes." Says Mrs. Veal: "Fetch it." And so Mrs. Bargrave goes upstairs and brings it down. Says Mrs. Veal:

"Dear Mrs. Bargrave, if the eyes of our faith were as open as the eyes of our body, we should see numbers of angels about us for our guard. The notions we have of heaven now are nothing like what it is, as Drelincourt says. Therefore be comforted under your afflictions, and believe that the Almighty has a particular regard to you, and that your afflictions are marks of God's favour; and when they have done the business they are sent for, they shall be removed from you. And believe me, my dear friend, believe what I say to you, one minute of future happiness will infinitely reward you for all your sufferings; for I can never believe [and claps her hand upon her knee with great earnestness, which indeed ran through most of her discourse] that ever God will suffer you to spend all your days in this afflicted state; but be assured that your afflictions shall leave you, or you them in a short time." She spake in that pathetical and heavenly manner, that Mrs. Bargrave wept several times, she was so deeply affected with it.

Then Mrs. Veal mentioned Dr. Horneck's *Ascetick*, at the end of which he gives an account of the lives of the primitive Christians. Their pattern she recommended to our imitation, and said their conversation was not like this of our age; "for now," says she, "there is nothing but frothy, vain discourse, which is far different from theirs. Theirs was to edification, and to build one another up in faith; so that they were not as we are, nor are we as they were; but," said she, "we might do as they did. There was a hearty friendship among them; but where is it now to be found?"

Says Mrs. Bargrave: "'Tis hard indeed to find a true friend in these days."

Says Mrs. Veal: "Mr. Norris has a fine copy of verses, called *Friendship in Perfection*, which I wonderfully admire. Have you seen the book?" says Mrs. Veal.

"No," says Mrs. Bargrave, "but I have the verses of my own writing out."

"Have you?" says Mrs. Veal; "fetch them then." Which she did from above-stairs, and offered them to Mrs. Veal to read, who refused, and waived the thing, saying, holding down her head would make it ache; and then desired Mrs. Bargrave to read them to her, which she did.

As they were admiring *Friendship* Mrs. Veal said: "Dear Mrs. Bargrave I shall love you forever." In the verses there is twice used the word Elysian. "Ah!" says Mrs. Veal, "these poets have such names for heaven!" She would often draw her hand across her own eyes and say: "Mrs. Bargrave, don't you think I am mightily impaired by my fits?"

"No," says Mrs. Bargrave, "I think you look as well as ever I knew you."

After all this discourse, which the apparition put in words much finer than Mrs. Bargrave said she could pretend to, and was much more than she can remember (for it cannot be thought that an hour and three-quarters' conversation could all be retained, though the main of it she thinks she does), she said to Mrs. Bargrave she would have her write a letter to her brother, and tell him she would have him give rings to such and such, and that there was a purse of gold in her cabinet, and that she would have two broad pieces given to her cousin Watson.

Talking at this rate, Mrs. Bargrave thought that a fit was coming upon her, and so placed herself in a chair just before her knees, to keep her from falling to the ground, if her fit should occasion it (for the elbow-chair, she thought, would keep her from falling on either side); and to divert Mrs. Veal, as she thought, she took hold of her gown-sleeve several times and commended it. Mrs. Veal told her it was a scoured silk, and newly made up. But for all this, Mrs. Veal persisted in her request, and told Mrs. Bargrave she must not deny her; and she would have her tell her brother all their conversation when she had an opportunity.

"Dear Mrs. Veal," said Mrs. Bargrave, "this seems so impertinent that I cannot tell how to comply with it; and what a mortifying story will our conversation be to a young gentleman!"

"Well," says Mrs. Veal, "I must not be denied."

"Why," says Mrs. Bargrave, "'tis much better, methinks, to do it yourself."

"No," says Mrs. Veal, "though it seems impertinent to you now, you will see more reason for it hereafter."

Mrs. Bargrave then, to satisfy her importunity, was going to fetch a pen and ink; but Mrs. Veal said: " Let it alone now, and do it when I am gone; but you must be sure to do it "; which was one of the last things she enjoined her at parting; and so she promised her.

Then Mrs. Veal asked for Mrs. Bargrave's daughter. She said she was not at home: " but if you have a mind to see her," says Mrs. Bargrave, " I'll send for her."

" Do," says Mrs. Veal. On which she left her, and went to a neighbour's to send for her; and by the time Mrs. Bargrave was returning, Mrs. Veal was got without the door in the street, in the face of the beast-market, on a Saturday (which is market-day), and stood ready to part as soon as Mrs. Bargrave came to her.

She asked her why she was in such haste. She said she must be going, though perhaps she might not go her journey until Monday; and told Mrs. Bargrave she hoped she should see her again at her cousin Watson's before she went whither she was a-going. Then she said she would take her leave of her, and walked from Mrs. Bargrave in her view, till a turning interrupted the sight of her, which was three-quarters after one in the afternoon.

Mrs. Veal died the 7th of September, at twelve o'clock at noon, of her fits, and had not above four hours' senses before death, in which time she received the sacrament.

The next day after Mrs. Veal's appearance, being Sunday, Mrs. Bargrave was mightily indisposed with a cold and a sore throat, that she could not go out that day; but on Monday morning she sends a person to Captain Watson's to know if Mrs. Veal were there. They wondered at Mrs. Bargrave's inquiry, and sent her word that she was not there, nor was expected.

At this answer, Mrs. Bargrave told the maid she had certainly mistook the name, or made some blunder. And though she was ill, she put on her hood, and went herself to Captain Watson's, though she knew none of the family, to see if Mrs. Veal was there or not. They said they wondered at her asking, for that she had not been in town; they were sure, if she had, she would have been there. Says Mrs. Bargrave: " I am sure she was with me on Saturday almost two hours." They said it was impossible; for they must have seen her, if she had.

In comes Captain Watson while they are in dispute, and said that Mrs. Veal was certainly dead, and her escutcheons were making. This strangely surprised Mrs. Bargrave, who went to the person immediately who had the care of them, and found it true.

Then she related the whole story to Captain Watson's family, and what gown she had on, and how striped, and that Mrs. Veal told her it was scoured. Then Mrs. Watson cried out: " You have seen her indeed, for none knew but Mrs. Veal and myself that the gown was scoured." And Mrs. Watson owned that she described the gown exactly; "for," said she, "I helped her to make it up." This Mrs. Watson blazed all about the town, and avouched the demonstration of the truth of Mrs. Bargrave's seeing Mrs. Veal's apparition; and Captain Watson carried two gentlemen immediately to Mrs. Bargrave's house to hear the relation from her own mouth.

And then it spread so fast that gentlemen and persons of quality, the judicious and sceptical part of the world, flocked in upon her, which at last became such a task that she was forced to go out of the way; for they were in general extremely satisfied of the truth of the thing, and plainly saw that Mrs. Bargrave was no hypochondriac, for she always appears with such a cheerful air and pleasing mien, that she has gained the favour and esteem of all the gentry, and 'tis thought a great favour if they can but get the relation from her own mouth.

I should have told you before that Mrs. Veal told Mrs. Bargrave that her sister and brother-in-law were just come down from London to see her.

Says Mrs. Bargrave: "How came you to order matters so strangely?"

"It could not be helped," says Mrs. Veal. And her sister and brother did come to see her, and entered the town of Dover just as Mrs. Veal was expiring.

Mrs. Bargrave asked her whether she would drink some tea. Says Mrs. Veal: "I do not care if I do; but I'll warrant this mad fellow [meaning Mrs. Bargrave's husband] has broke all your trinkets."

"But," says Mrs. Bargrave, "I'll get something to drink in for all that." But Mr. Veal waived it, and said: "It is no matter; let it alone"; and so it passed.

All the time I sat with Mrs. Bargrave, which was some hours, she recollected fresh sayings of Mrs. Veal. And one material thing more she told Mrs. Bargrave—that old Mr. Breton allowed Mrs. Veal ten pounds a year, which was a secret, and unknown to Mrs. Bargrave till Mrs. Veal told it her.

Mrs. Bargrave never varies in her story, which puzzles those who doubt the truth, or are unwilling to believe it. A servant in a neighbour's yard adjoining to Mrs. Bargrave's house heard her talking to somebody an hour of the time Mrs. Veal was with her.

Mrs. Bargrave went out to her next neighbour's the very moment she parted with Mrs. Veal, and told what ravishing conversation she had with an old friend, and told the whole of it. Drelincourt's *Book of Death* is, since this happened, bought up strangely. And it is to be observed that, notwithstanding all this trouble and fatigue Mrs. Bargrave has undergone upon this account, she never took the value of a farthing, nor suffered her daughter to take anything of anybody, and therefore can have no interest in telling the story.

But Mr. Veal does what he can to stifle the matter, and said he would see Mrs. Bargrave ; but yet it is certain matter of fact that he has been at Captain Watson's since the death of his sister, and yet never went near Mrs. Bargrave ; and some of her friends report her to be a great liar, and that she knew of Mr. Breton's ten pounds a year. But the person who pretends to say so has the reputation of a notorious liar among persons whom I know to be of undoubted repute.

Now, Mr. Veal is more a gentleman than to say she lies, but says a bad husband has crazed her ; but she needs only to present herself, and it will effectually confute that pretence. Mr. Veal says he asked his sister on her deathbed whether she had a mind to dispose of anything, and she said : "No." Now, the things which Mrs. Veal's apparition would have disposed of were so trifling, and nothing of justice aimed at in their disposal, that the design of it appears to me to be only in order to make Mrs. Bargrave so to demonstrate the truth of her appearance, as to satisfy the world of the reality thereof as to what she had seen and heard, and to secure her reputation among the reasonable and understanding part of mankind.

And then again, Mr. Veal owns that there was a purse of gold ; but it was not found in her cabinet, but in a comb-box. This looks improbable ; for that Mrs. Watson owned that Mrs. Veal was so very careful of the key of her cabinet, that she would trust nobody with it ; and if so, no doubt she would not trust her gold out of it. And Mrs. Veal's often drawing her hand over her eyes, and asking Mrs. Bargrave whether her fits had not impaired her, looks to me as if she did it on purpose to remind Mrs. Bargrave of her fits, to prepare her not to think it strange that she should put her upon writing to her brother to dispose of rings and gold, which looked so much like a dying person's request ; and it took accordingly with Mrs. Bargrave, as the effects of her fits coming upon her ; and was one of the many instances of her wonderful love to her, and care of her, that she should not be affrighted ; which indeed appears in her whole management, particularly in her coming to her in the day-time, waiving the salutation, and when she was alone ; and then the manner of her parting, to prevent a second attempt to salute her.

Now, why Mr. Veal should think this relation a reflection (as 'tis plain he does by his endeavouring to stifle it) I can't imagine, because the generality believe her to be a good spirit, her discourse was so heavenly. Her two great errands were to comfort Mrs. Bargrave in her affliction, and to ask her forgiveness for her breach of friendship, and with a pious discourse to encourage her. So that, after all, to suppose that Mrs. Bargrave could hatch such an invention as this from Friday noon till Saturday noon (supposing that she knew of Mrs. Veal's death the very first moment), without jumbling circumstances, and without any interest too, she must be more witty, fortunate, and wicked too, than any indifferent person, I dare say, will allow.

I asked Mrs. Bargrave several times if she was sure she felt the gown. She answered modestly: "If my senses be to be relied on, I am sure of it." I asked her if she heard a sound when she clapped her hand upon her knee. She said she did not remember she did; and she said: "She appeared to be as much a substance as I did, who talked with her; and I may," said she, "be as soon persuaded that your apparition is talking to me now as that I did not really see her; for I was under no manner of fear; I received her as a friend, and parted with her as such. I would not," says she, "give one farthing to make any one believe it; I have no interest in it. Nothing but trouble is entailed upon me for a long time, for aught I know; and had it not come to light by accident, it would never have been made public."

But now she says she will make her own private use of it, and keep herself out of the way as much as she can; and so she has done since. She says she had a gentleman who came thirty miles to her to hear the relation, and that she had told it to a room full of people at a time. Several particular gentlemen have had the story from Mrs. Bargrave's own mouth.

This thing has very much affected me, and I am as well satisfied as I am of the best grounded matter of fact. And why we should dispute matter of fact because we cannot solve things of which we have no certain or demonstrative notions, seems strange to me. Mrs. Bargrave's authority and sincerity alone would have been undoubted in any other case.

DANIEL DEFOE

THE GHOST OF DOROTHY DINGLEY

In the beginning of this year, a disease happened in this town of Launceston, and some of my scholars died of it. Among others who fell under the malignity then triumphing, was John Elliot, the eldest son of Edward Elliot of Treherse, Esq., a stripling of about sixteen years of age, but of more than common parts and ingenuity. At his own particular request, I preached at the funeral, which happened on the 20th day of June 1665. In my discourse (*ut mos reique locique postulabat*), I spoke some words in commendation of the young gentleman; such as might endear his memory to those that knew him, and, withal, tended to preserve his example to the fry which went to school with him, and were to continue there after him. An ancient gentleman, who was then in the church, was much affected with the discourse, and was often heard to repeat, the same evening, an expression I then used out of Virgil:—

Et puer ipse fuit cantari dignus.

The reason why this grave gentleman was so concerned at the character, was a reflection he made upon a son of his own, who being about the same age, and, but a few months before, not unworthy of the like character I gave of the young Mr. Elliot, was now, by a strange accident, quite lost as to his parent's hopes and all expectation of any further comfort by him.

The funeral rites being over, I was no sooner come out of the church, but I found myself most courteously accosted by this old gentleman; and with an unusual importunity almost forced against my humour to see his house that night; nor could I have rescued myself from his kindness, had not Mr. Elliot interposed and pleaded title to me for the whole of the day, which, as he said, he would resign to no man.

Hereupon I got loose for that time, but was constrained to leave a promise behind me to wait upon him at his own house the Monday following. This then seemed to satisfy, but before Monday came I had a new message to request me that, if it were possible, I would be there on the Sunday. The second attempt I resisted, by answering that it was against my convenience, and the duty which mine own people expected from me.

Yet was not the gentleman at rest, for he sent me another letter on the Sunday, by no means to fail on the Monday, and so to order my business as to spend with him two or three days at least. I was indeed startled at so much eagerness, and so many dunnings for a visit, without any business ; and began to suspect that there must needs be some design in the bottom of all this excess of courtesy. For I had no familiarity, scarce common acquaintance with the gentleman or his family ; nor could I imagine whence should arise such a flush of friendship on the sudden.

On the Monday I went, and paid my promised devoir, and met with entertainment as free and plentiful as the invitation was importunate. There also I found a neighbouring minister who pretended to call in accidentally, but by the sequel I suppose it otherwise. After dinner this brother of the coat undertook to show me the gardens, where, as we were walking, he gave me the first discovery of what was mainly intended in all this treat and compliment.

First he began to tell the infortunity of the family in general, and then gave an instance in the youngest son. He related what a hopeful, sprightly lad he lately was, and how melancholic and sottish he was now grown. Then did he with much passion lament, that his ill-humour should so incredibly subdue his reason ; for, says he, the poor boy believes himself to be haunted with ghosts, and is confident that he meets with an evil spirit in a certain field about half a mile from this place, as often as he goes that way to school.

In the midst of our twaddle, the old gentleman and his lady (as observing their cue exactly) came up to us. Upon their approach, and pointing me to the arbour, the parson renews the relation to me ; and they (the parents of the youth) confirmed what he said, and added many minute circumstances, in a long narrative of the whole. In fine, they all three desired my thoughts and advice in the affair.

I was not able to collect thoughts enough on the sudden to frame a judgment upon what they had said, only I answered, that the thing which the youth reported to them was strange, yet not incredible, and that I knew not then what to think or say of it ; but if the lad would be free to me in talk, and trust me with his counsels, I had hopes to give them a better account of my opinion the next day.

I had no sooner spoken so much, but I perceived myself in the springe their courtship had laid for me ; for the old lady was not able to hide her impatience, but her son must be called immediately.

This I was forced to comply with and consent to, so that drawing off from the company to an orchard near by, she went herself and brought him to me, and left him with me.

It was the main drift of all these three to persuade me that either the boy was lazy, and glad of any excuse to keep from the school, or that he was in love with some wench and ashamed to confess it; or that he had a fetch upon his father to get money and new clothes, that he might range to London after a brother he had there; and therefore they begged of me to discover the root of the matter, and accordingly to dissuade, advise, or reprove him, but chiefly, by all means, to undeceive him as to the fancy of ghosts and spirits.

I soon entered into a close conference with the youth, and at first was very cautious not to displease him, but by smooth words to ingratitate myself and get within him, for I doubted he would be too distrustful or too reserved. But we had scarcely passed the first situation, and begun to speak to the business, before I found that there needed no policy to screw myself into his breast; for he most openly and with all obliging candour did aver, that he loved his book, and desired nothing more than to be bred a scholar; that he had not the least respect for any of womankind, as his mother gave out; and that the only request he would make to his parents was, that they would but believe his constant assertions concerning the woman he was disturbed with, in the field called the Higher-Broom Quartils. He told me with all naked freedom, and a flood of tears, that his friends were unkind and unjust to him, neither to believe nor pity him; and that if any man (making a bow to me) would but go with him to the place, he might be convinced that the thing was real, etc.

By this time he found me apt to compassionate his condition, and to be attentive to his relation of it, and therefore he went on in this way:—

"This woman which appears to me," saith he, "lived a neighbour here to my father, and died about eight years since; her name, Dorothy Dingley, of such a stature, such age, and such complexion. She never speaks to me, but passeth by hastily, and always leaves the footpath to me, and she commonly meets me twice or three times in the breadth of the field.

"It was about two months before I took any notice of it, and though the shape of the face was in my memory, yet I did not recall the name of the person, but without more thoughtfulness, I did suppose it was some woman who lived thereabout, and had frequent occasion that way. Nor did I imagine anything to the contrary before she began to meet me constantly, morning and evening, and always in the same field, and sometimes twice or thrice in the breadth of it.

"The first time I took notice of her was about a year since, and when I first began to suspect and believe it to be a ghost, I had courage enough not to be afraid, but kept it to myself a good while, and only wondered very much about it. I did often speak to it, but never had a word in answer. Then I changed my way, and went to school the Under Horse Road, and then she always met me in the narrow lane, between the Quarry Park and the Nursery, which was worse.

"At length I began to be terrified at it, and prayed continually that God would either free me from it or let me know the meaning of it. Night and day, sleeping and waking, the shape was ever running in my mind, and I often did repeat these places of Scripture (with that he takes a small Bible out of his pocket), Job vii. 14: 'Thou scarest me with dreams, and terrifiest me through visions.' And Deuteronomy xxviii. 67: 'In the morning, thou shalt say, Would God it were even; and at even thou shalt say, Would God it were morning; for the fear of thine heart, wherewith thou shalt fear, and for the sight of thine eyes, which thou shalt see.'"

I was very much pleased with the lad's ingenuity in the application of these pertinent Scriptures to his condition, and desired him to proceed.

"When," says he, "by degrees, I grew very pensive, inasmuch that it was taken notice of by all our family; whereupon, being urged to it, I told my brother William of it, and he privately acquainted my father and mother, and they kept it to themselves for some time.

"The success of this discovery was only this; they did sometimes laugh at me, sometimes chide me, but still commanded me to keep to my school, and put such fopperies out of my head. I did accordingly go to school often, but always met the woman in the way."

This, and much more to the same purpose, yea, as much as held a dialogue of near two hours, was our conference in the orchard, which ended with my proffer to him, that, without making any privy to our intents, I would next morning walk with him to the place, about six o'clock. He was even transported with joy at the mention of it, and replied, "But will you, sure, sir? Will you, sure, sir? Thank God! Now I hope I shall be relieved."

From this conclusion we retired into the house.

The gentleman, his wife, and Mr. Sam were impatient to know the event, insomuch that they came out of the parlour into the hall to meet us; and seeing the lad look cheerfully, the first compliment from the old man was, "Come, Mr. Ruddle, you have talked with him; I hope now he will have more wit. An idle boy! an idle boy!"

At these words, the lad ran up the stairs to his own chamber, without replying, and I soon stopped the curiosity of the three expectants by telling them I had promised silence, and was resolved to be as good as my word ; but when things were riper they might know all. At present, I desired them to rest in my faithful promise, that I would do my utmost in their service, and for the good of their son. With this they were silenced ; I cannot say satisfied.

The next morning before five o'clock, the lad was in my chamber, and very brisk. I arose and went with him. The field he led me to I guessed to be twenty acres, in an open country, and about three furlongs from any house. We went into the field, and had not gone about a third part, before the spectrum, in the shape of a woman, with all the circumstances he had described her to me in the orchard the day before (as much as the suddenness of its appearance and evanition would permit me to discover), met us and passed by. I was a little surprised at it, and though I had taken up a firm resolution to speak to it, yet I had not the power, nor indeed durst I look back ; yet I took care not to show any fear to my pupil and guide, and therefore only telling him that I was satisfied in the truth of his complaint, we walked to the end of the field and returned, nor did the ghost meet us that time above once. I perceived in the young man a kind of boldness, mixed with astonishment : the first caused by my presence, and the proof he had given of his own relation, and the other by the sight of his persecutor.

In short, we went home : I somewhat puzzled, he much animated. At our return, the gentlewoman, whose inquisitiveness had missed us, watched to speak with me. I gave her a convenience, and told her that my opinion was that her son's complaint was not to be slighted, nor altogether discredited ; yet, that my judgment in his case was not settled. I gave her caution, moreover, that the thing might not take wind, lest the whole country should ring with what we had yet no assurance of.

In this juncture of time I had business which would admit no delay ; wherefore I went for Launceston that evening, but promised to see them again next week. Yet I was prevented by an occasion which pleaded a sufficient excuse, for my wife was that week brought home from a neighbour's house very ill. However, my mind was upon the adventure. I studied the case, and about three weeks after went again, resolving, by the help of God, to see the utmost.

The next morning, being the 27th day of July 1665, I went to the haunted field by myself, and walked the breadth of the field without any encounter. I returned and took the other walk, and then the spectrum appeared to me, much about the same place where I saw it before, when the young gentleman was with me. In my thoughts, it moved swifter than the time before, and about ten feet distance from me on my right hand, insomuch that I had not time to speak, as I had determined with myself beforehand.

The evening of this day, the parents, the son, and myself being in the chamber where I lay, I propounded to them our going all together to the place next morning, and after some asseveration that there was no danger in it, we all resolved upon it. The morning being come, lest we should alarm the family of servants, they went under the pretence of seeing a field of wheat, and I took my horse and fetched a compass another way, and so met at the stile we had appointed.

Thence we all four walked leisurely into the Quartils, and had passed above half the field before the ghost made appearance. It then came over the stile just before us, and moved with that swiftness that by the time we had gone six or seven steps it passed by. I immediately turned head and ran after it, with the young man by my side; we saw it pass over the stile by which we entered, but no farther. I stepped upon the hedge at one place, he at another, but could discern nothing; whereas, I dare aver, that the swiftest horse in England could not have conveyed himself out of sight in that short space of time. Two things I observed in this day's appearance. 1. That a spaniel dog, who followed the company unregarded, did bark and run away as the spectrum passed by; whence it is easy to conclude that it was not our fear or fancy which made the apparition. 2. That the motion of the spectrum was not gradation, or by steps, and moving of the feet, but a kind of gliding, as children upon the ice, or a boat down a swift river, which punctually answers the description the ancients gave of their *Lemures*, which was Κατὰ ῥύμτω ἀέριον καὶ ὁρμὴν ἄπζαποδισον (Heliodorus).

But to proceed. This ocular evidence clearly convinced, but, withal, strangely frightened the old gentleman and his wife, who knew this Dorothy Dingley in her lifetime, were at her burial, and now plainly saw her features in this present apparition. I encouraged them as well as I could, but after this they went no more. However, I was resolved to proceed, and use such lawful means as God hath discovered, and learned men have successfully practised in these irregular cases.

The next morning being Thursday, I went out very early by myself, and walked for about an hour's space in meditation and prayer in the field next adjoining to the Quartils. Soon after five I stepped over the stile into the disturbed field, and had not gone above thirty or forty paces before the ghost appeared at the farther stile. I spoke to it with a loud voice, in some such sentences as the way of these dealings directed me, whereupon it approached, but slowly, and when I came near, it moved not. I spake again, and it answered, in a voice neither very audible nor intelligible. I was not in the least terrified, and therefore persisted until it spake again, and gave me satisfaction. But the work could not be finished at this time; wherefore the same evening, an hour after sunset, it met me again near the same place, and after a few words on each side, it quietly vanished, and neither doth appear since, nor ever will more to any man's disturbance. The discourse in the morning lasted about a quarter of an hour.

These things are true, and I know them to be so, with as much certainty as eyes and ears can give me; and until I can be persuaded that my senses do deceive me about their proper object, and by that persuasion deprive myself of the strongest inducement to believe the Christian religion, I must and will assert that these things in this paper are true.

As for the manner of my proceeding, I find no reason to be ashamed of it, for I can justify it to men of good principles, discretion, and recondite learning, though in this case I choose to content myself in the assurance of the thing, rather than be at the unprofitable trouble to persuade others to believe it; for I know full well with what difficulty relations of so uncommon a nature and practice obtain relief. He that tells such a story may expect to be dealt withal as a traveller in Poland by the robbers, viz., first murdered and then searched,—first condemned for a liar, or superstitious, and then, when it is too late, have his reasons and proofs examined. This incredulity may be attributed—

1. To the infinite abuses of the people, and impositions upon their faith by the cunning monks and friars, etc., in the days of darkness and popery; for they made apparitions as often as they pleased, and got both money and credit by quieting the *terriculamenta vulgi*, which their own artifice had raised.

2. To the prevailing of Somatism and the Hobbean principle in these times, which is a revival of the doctrine of the Sadducees; and as it denies the nature, so it cannot consist with the apparition of spirits; of which, see *Leviathan*, p. 1, c. 12.

3. To the ignorance of men in our age, in this peculiar and mysterious part of philosophy and of religion, namely, the communication between spirits and men. Not one scholar in ten thousand (though otherwise of excellent learning) knows anything of it or the way how to manage it. This ignorance breeds fear and abhorrence of that which otherwise might be of incomparable benefit to mankind.

But I being a clergyman and young, and a stranger in these parts, do apprehend silence and secrecy to be my best security.

In rebus abstrusissimis abundans cautela non nocet.

JOSEPH ADDISON
1672–1719

THE VISION OF MIRZAH

WHEN I was at Grand Cairo, I picked up several oriental manuscripts, which I have still by me. Among others I met with one entitled *The Visions of Mirzah*, which I have read over with great pleasure. I intend to give it to the public when I have no other entertainment for them, and shall begin with the first vision, which I have translated word for word as follows:

" On the fifth day of the moon, which, according to the custom of my forefathers, I always kept holy, after having washed myself, and offered up my morning devotions, I ascended the high hills of Bagdat, in order to pass the rest of the day in meditation and prayer. As I was here airing myself on the tops of the mountains, I fell into a profound contemplation on the vanity of human life; and passing from one thought to another, 'Surely,' said I, 'man is but a shadow, and life a dream.' Whilst I was thus musing, I cast my eyes towards the summit of a rock that was not far from me, where I discovered one in the habit of a shepherd, with a little musical instrument in his hand. As I looked upon him, he applied it to his lips, and began to play upon it. The sound of it was exceeding sweet, and wrought into a variety of tunes that were inexpressibly melodious, and altogether different from anything I had ever heard: they put me in mind of those heavenly airs that are played to the departed souls of good men upon their first arrival in Paradise, to wear out the impressions of the last agonies, and qualify them for the pleasures of that happy place. My heart melted away in secret raptures.

" I had been often told that the rock before me was the haunt of a genius, and that several had been entertained with music who had passed by it, but never heard that the musician had before made himself visible. When he had raised my thoughts by those transporting airs which he played, to taste the pleasures of his conversation, as I looked upon him like one astonished, he beckoned to me, and by the waving of his hand directed me to approach the place where he sat. I drew near with that reverence that is due to a superior nature ; and as my heart was entirely subdued by the captivating strains I had heard, I fell down at his feet and wept. The genius smiled upon me with a look of compassion and affability that familiarised him to my imagination, and at once dispelled all the fears and apprehensions with which I approached him. He lifted me from the ground, and taking me by the hand, 'Mirzah,' said he, 'I have heard thee in thy soliloquies ; follow me.'

"He then led me to the highest pinnacle of the rock, and placing me on the top of it, 'Cast thy eyes eastward,' said he, 'and tell me what thou seest.' 'I see,' said I, 'a huge valley, and a prodigious tide of water rolling through it.' 'The valley that thou seest,' said he, 'is the vale of misery, and the tide of water that thou seest is part of the great tide of eternity.' 'What is the reason,' said I, 'that the tide I see rises out of a thick mist at one end, and again loses itself in a thick mist at the other ?' 'What thou seest,' said he, 'is that portion of eternity which is called time, measured out by the sun, and reaching from the beginning of the world to its consummation. Examine now,' said he, 'this sea that is thus bounded with darkness at both ends, and tell me what thou discoverest in it.' 'I see a bridge,' said I, 'standing in the midst of the tide.' 'That bridge thou seest,' said he, 'is human life : consider it attentively.' Upon a more leisurely survey of it, I found that it consisted of threescore and ten entire arches, with several broken arches, which, added to those that were entire, made up the number about an hundred. As I was counting the arches, the genius told me that this bridge consisted at first of a thousand arches ; but that a great flood swept away the rest, and left the bridge in the ruinous condition I now beheld it. 'But tell me further,' said he, 'what thou discoverest on it.' 'I see multitudes of people passing over it,' said I, 'and a black cloud hanging on each end of it.' As I looked more attentively, I saw several of the passengers dropping through the bridge, into the great tide that flowed underneath it ; and upon further examination, perceived there were innumerable trap-doors that lay concealed in the bridge, which the passengers no sooner trod upon, but they fell through into the tide, and immediately disappeared. These hidden pitfalls were set very thick at the entrance of the bridge, so that throngs of people no sooner broke through the cloud, but many of them fell into them. They grew thinner towards the middle, but multiplied and lay closer together towards the end of the arches that were entire.

"There were indeed some persons, but their number was very small, that continued a kind of hobbling march on the broken arches, but fell through one after another, being quite tired and spent with so long a walk.

"I passed some time in the contemplation of this wonderful

structure, and the great variety of objects which it presented. My heart was filled with a deep melancholy to see several drooping unexpectedly in the midst of mirth and jollity, and catching at everything that stood by them to save themselves. Some were looking up towards the heavens in a thoughtful posture, and in the midst of a speculation stumbled and fell out of sight. Multitudes were very busy in the pursuit of bubbles that glittered in their eyes and danced before them, but often, when they thought themselves within the reach of them, their footing failed, and down they sank. In this confusion of objects, I observed some with scimitars in their hands, and others with pill-boxes, who ran to and fro upon the bridge, thrusting several persons on trap-doors which did not seem to lie in their way, and which they might have escaped had they not been thus forced upon them.

"The genius, seeing me indulge myself in this melancholy prospect, told me I had dwelt long enough upon it; 'Take thine eyes off the bridge,' said he, 'and tell me if thou yet seest anything thou dost not comprehend.' Upon looking up, 'What mean,' said I, 'those great flights of birds that are perpetually hovering about the bridge, and settling upon it from time to time? I see vultures, harpies, ravens, cormorants, and among many other feathered creatures several little winged boys, that perch in great numbers upon the middle arches.' 'These,' said the genius, 'are envy, avarice, superstition, despair, love, with the like cares and passions that infest human life.'

"I here fetched a deep sigh; 'Alas,' said I, 'man was made in vain! how is he given away to misery and mortality! tortured in life, and swallowed up in death!' The genius, being moved with compassion towards me, bid me quit so uncomfortable a prospect. 'Look no more,' said he, 'on man in the first stage of his existence, in his setting out for eternity; but cast thine eye on that thick mist into which the tide bears the several generations of mortals that fall into it.' I directed my sight as I was ordered, and (whether or no the good genius strengthened it with a supernatural force, or dissipated part of the mist that was before too thick for the eye to penetrate) I saw the valley opening at the further end, and spreading forth into an immense ocean, that had a huge rock of adamant running through the midst of it, and dividing it into two equal parts. The clouds still rested on one half of it, insomuch that I could discover nothing in it: but the other appeared to me a vast ocean planted with innumerable islands, that were covered with fruits and flowers, and interwoven with a thousand little shining seas that ran among them. I could see persons dressed in glorious habits, with garlands upon their heads, passing among the trees, lying down by the sides of the fountains, or resting on beds of flowers; and could hear a confused harmony of singing birds, falling waters, human voices, and musical instruments. Gladness grew in me upon the discovery of so delightful a scene. I wished for the wings of an eagle, that I might fly away to those happy seats ; but the genius told me there was no passage to them, except through the gates of death that I saw opening every moment upon the bridge. 'The islands,' said he, 'that lie so fresh and green before thee, and with which the whole face of the ocean appears spotted as far as thou canst see, are more in number than the sands on the sea-shore ; there are myriads of islands behind those which thou here discoverest, reaching farther than thine eye or even thine imagination can extend itself. These are the mansions of good men after death, who, according to the degree and kinds of virtue in which they excelled, are distributed among these several islands, which abound with pleasures of different kinds and degrees, suitable to the relishes and perfections of those who are settled in them ; every island is a paradise accommodated to its respective inhabitants. Are not these, O Mirzah, habitations worth contending for ? Does life appear miserable, that gives thee opportunities of earning such a reward ? is death to be feared, that will convey thee to so happy an existence ? Think not man was made in vain, who has such an eternity reserved for him.' I gazed with inexpressible pleasure on these happy islands. At length, said I, 'Show me now, I beseech thee, the secrets that lie hidden under those dark clouds which cover the ocean on the other side of the rock of adamant.' The genius making me no answer, I turned about to address him a second time, but I found that he had left me. I then turned again to the vision which I had been so long contemplating ; but instead of the rolling tide, the arched bridge, and the happy islands, I saw nothing but the long hollow valley of Bagdat, with oxen, sheep, and camels grazing upon the sides of it."

HENRY FIELDING
1707–1754

THE HISTORY OF LEONORA, OR THE UNFORTUNATE JILT

LEONORA was the daughter of a gentleman of fortune : she was tall and well-shaped, with a sprightliness in her countenance, which often attracts beyond more regular features, joined with an insipid air : nor is this kind of beauty less apt to deceive than allure, the good humour which it indicates being often mistaken for good nature, and the vivacity for true understanding.

Leonora, who was now at the age of eighteen, lived with an aunt of hers, in a town in the north of England. She was an extreme lover of gaiety, and very rarely missed a ball or any other public assembly, where she had frequent opportunities of satisfying a greedy appetite of vanity, with the preference which was given her by the men to almost every other woman present.

Among many young fellows who were particular in their gallantries towards her, Horatio soon distinguished himself in her eyes beyond all his competitors : she danced with more than ordinary gaiety when he happened to be her partner ; neither the fairness of the evening, nor the music of the nightingale, could lengthen her walk like his company. She affected no longer to understand the civilities of others, whilst she inclined so attentive an ear to every compliment of Horatio, that she often smiled even when it was too delicate for her comprehension.

Horatio was a young gentleman of a good family, bred to the law, and had been some few years called to the degree of a barrister. His face and person were such as the generality allowed handsome, but he had a dignity in his air very rarely to be seen. His temper was of the saturnine complexion and without the least taint of moroseness. He had wit and humour, with an inclination to satire, which he indulged rather too much.

This gentleman, who had contracted the most violent passion for Leonora, was the last person who perceived the probability of its success. The whole town had made the match for him before he himself had drawn a confidence from her actions sufficient to mention his passion to her; for it was his opinion, and perhaps he was there in the right, that it is highly impolitic to talk seriously of love to a woman before you have made such progress in her affections that she herself expects and desires to hear it.

But whatever diffidence the fears of a lover may create, which are apt to magnify every favour conferred on a rival, and to see the little advances towards themselves through the other end of the perspective, it was impossible that Horatio's passion should so blind his discernment as to prevent his conceiving hopes from the behaviour of Leonora, whose fondness for him was now as visible to an indifferent person in their company as his for her.

It was in the midst of a gay conversation in the walks one evening, when Horatio whispered Leonora that he was desirous to take a turn or two with her in private; for that he had something to communicate to her of great consequence.

"Are you sure it is of consequence?" said she, smiling.

"I hope," answered he, "you will think so too, since the whole future happiness of my life must depend on the event."

Leonora, who very much suspected what was coming, would have deferred it till another time; but Horatio, who had more than half conquered the difficulty of speaking by the first motion, was so very importunate that she at last yielded, and, leaving the rest of the company, they turned aside into an unfrequented walk.

They had retired far out of sight of the company, both maintaining a strict silence. At last, Horatio made a full stop, and taking Leonora, who stood pale and trembling, gently by the hand, he fetched a deep sigh, and then, looking on her eyes with all the tenderness imaginable, he cried out, in a faltering accent:

"O Leonora! is it necessary for me to declare to you on what the future happiness of my life must be founded? Must I say there is something belonging to you which is a bar to my happiness, and which, unless you will part with, I must be miserable!"

"What can that be?" replied Leonora.

"No wonder," said he, "you are surprised that I should make an objection to anything which is yours: yet sure you may guess, since it is the only one which the riches of the world, if they were mine, should purchase of me. Oh, it is that which you must part with to bestow all the rest! Can Leonora, or rather, will she, doubt longer? Let me, then, whisper it in her ears.—It is your name, madam. It is by parting with that, by your condescension to be for ever mine, which must at once prevent me from being the most miserable, and will render me the happiest of mankind."

Leonora, covered with blushes, and with as angry a look as she could possibly put on, told him, that had she suspected what his declaration would have been, he should not have decoyed her from her company; that he had so surprised and frighted her, that she begged him to convey her back as quick as possible; which he, trembling very near as much as herself, did.

Many weeks had not passed after this interview before Horatio and Leonora were what they call on a good footing together. All ceremonies, except the last, were now over; the writings were now drawn, and everything was in the utmost forwardness, preparative to the putting Horatio in possession of all his wishes. I will, if you please, repeat you a letter from each of them, and which will give you no small idea of their passion on both sides.

" *Horatio to Leonora.*

" How vain, most adorable creature, is the pursuit of pleasure in the absence of an object to which the mind is entirely devoted, unless it has some relation to that object! I was last night condemned to the society of men of wit and learning, which, however agreeable it might have formerly been to me, now only gave me a suspicion that they imputed my absence in conversation to the true cause. For which reason, when your engagements forbid me the ecstatic happiness of seeing you, I am always desirous to be alone; since my sentiments for Leonora are so delicate that I cannot bear the apprehension of another's prying into those delightful endearments with which the warm imagination of a lover will sometimes indulge him, and which I suspect my eyes then betray.

" To fear this discovery of our thoughts may, perhaps, appear too ridiculous a nicety to minds not susceptible of all the tenderness of this delicate passion; and surely we shall suspect there are few such when we consider that it requires every human virtue to exert itself in its full extent; since the beloved, whose happiness it ultimately respects, may give us charming opportunities of being brave in her defence, generous to her wants, compassionate to her afflictions, grateful to her kindness; and, in the same manner, of exercising every other virtue, which he, who would not do to any degree, and that with the utmost rapture, can never deserve the name of a lover. It is therefore with a view to the delicate modesty of your mind that I cultivate it so purely in my own; and it is that which will sufficiently suggest to you the uneasiness I bear from those liberties which men, to whom the world allow politeness, will sometimes give themselves on these occasions.

" Can I tell you with what eagerness I expect the arrival of that blessed day when I shall experience the falsehood of a common assertion that the greatest human happiness consists in hope?—a doctrine which no person had ever stronger reason to believe than myself at present, since none ever tasted such bliss as fires my bosom with the thoughts of spending my future days with such a companion, and that every action of my life will have the glorious satisfaction of conducing to your happiness."

" *Leonora to Horatio.*

" The refinement of your mind has been so evidently proved by every word and action, ever since I had the first pleasure of knowing you, that I thought it impossible my good opinion of Horatio could have been heightened to any additional proof of merit. This very thought was my amusement when I received your last letter, which, when I opened, I confess I was surprised to find the delicate sentiments expressed there so far exceeded what I thought could come even from you (although I know all the generous principles human nature is capable of are centred in your breast) that words cannot paint what I feel on the reflection that my happiness shall be the ultimate end of all your actions.

" O Horatio! what a life must that be where the meanest domestic cares are sweetened by the pleasing consideration that the man on earth who best deserves, and to whom you are most inclined to give your affections, is to reap either profit or pleasure from all you do! In such a case toils must be turned into diversions, and nothing but the unavoidable inconveniences of life can make us remember that we are mortal.

" If the solitary turn of your thoughts and the desire of keeping them undiscovered make even the conversation of men of wit and learning tedious to you, what anxious hours must I spend, who am condemned by custom to the conversation of women, whose natural curiosity leads them to pry into all my thoughts, and whose envy can never suffer Horatio's heart to be possessed by anyone, without forcing them into malicious designs against the person who is so happy as to possess it? But, indeed, if ever envy can possibly have any excuse, or even alleviation, it is in this case, where the good is so great that it must be equally natural to all to wish for it for themselves; nor am I ashamed to own it: and to your merit, Horatio, I am obliged, that prevents my being in that most uneasy of all the situations I can figure in my imagination, of being led by inclination to love the person whom my own judgment forces me to condemn."

Matters were in so great forwardness between this fond couple that the day was fixed for their marriage, and was now within a fortnight, when the sessions chanced to be held for that county in a town about twenty miles' distance from that which is the scene of our story. It seems it is usual for the young gentlemen of the bar to repair to these sessions, not so much for the sake of profit, as to show their parts, and learn the law of the justices of peace; for which purpose one of the wisest and gravest of all the justices is appointed speaker, or chairman as they modestly call it, and he reads them a lecture, and instructs them in the true knowledge of the law.

Hither repaired Horatio, who, as he hoped by his profession to advance his fortune, which was not at present very large, for the sake of his dear Leonora, resolved to spare no pains, nor lose any opportunity of improving or advancing himself in it.

The same afternoon in which he left the town, as Leonora stood at her window, a coach and six passed by, which she declared to be the completest, genteelest, prettiest equipage she ever saw; adding these remarkable words: "Oh, I am in love with that equipage!" which, though her friend Florella at that time did not greatly regard, she has since remembered.

In the evening an assembly was held, which Leonora honoured with her company; but intended to pay her Horatio the compliment of refusing to dance in his absence. Oh, why have not women as good resolution to maintain their vows as they have often good inclinations in making them!

The gentleman who owned the coach and six came to the assembly. His clothes were as remarkably fine as his equipage could be. He soon attracted the eyes of the company; all the smarts, all the silk waistcoats with silver and gold edgings, were eclipsed in an instant. I have been told he had on a cut velvet coat of a cinnamon colour lined with a pink satin, embroidered all over with gold; his waistcoat, which was cloth of silver, was embroidered with gold likewise. I cannot be particular as to the rest of his dress, but it was all in the French fashion; for Bellarmine, that was his name, was just arrived from Paris.

This fine figure did not more entirely engage the eyes of every lady in the assembly than Leonora did his. He had scarce beheld her but he stood motionless and fixed as a statue, or at least would have done so if good breeding had permitted him. However, he carried it so far, before he had power to correct himself, that every person in the room easily discovered where his admiration was settled. The other ladies began to single out their former partners, all perceiving who would be Bellarmine's choice, which they however endeavoured by all possible means to prevent, many of them saying to Leonora, "O madam! I suppose we sha'n't have the pleasure of seeing you dance to-night!" and then crying out, in Bellarmine's hearing, "Oh, Leonora will not dance, I assure you: her partner is not here."

One maliciously attempted to prevent her, by sending a disagreeable fellow to ask her, that so she might be obliged either to dance with him, or sit down; but this scheme proved abortive.

Leonora saw herself admired by the fine stranger and envied by every woman present. Her little heart began to flutter within her, and her head was agitated with a convulsive motion ; she seemed as if she would speak to several of her acquaintance, but had nothing to say, for as she would not mention her present triumph, so she could not disengage her thoughts one moment from the contemplation of it. She had never tasted anything like this happiness. She had before known what it was to torment a single woman, but to be hated and secretly cursed by a whole assembly was a joy reserved for this blessed moment. As this vast profusion of ecstasy had confounded her understanding, so there was nothing so foolish as her behaviour : she played a thousand childish tricks, distorted her person into several shapes, and her face into several laughs, without any reason.

In a word, her carriage was as absurd as her desires, which were to affect an insensibility of the stranger's admiration, and at the same time a triumph, from that admiration, over every woman in the room.

In this temper of mind, Bellarmine, having inquired who she was, advanced to her, and with a low bow begged the honour of dancing with her, which she, with as low a curtsey, immediately granted. She danced with him all night, and enjoyed perhaps the highest pleasure that she was capable of feeling.

Leonora retired about six in the morning, but not to rest ; she tumbled and tossed in her bed, with very short intervals of sleep, and those entirely filled with dreams of the equipage and fine clothes she had seen, and the balls, operas and ridottos which had been the subject of their conversation.

In the afternoon Bellarmine, in the dear coach and six, came to wait on her. He was indeed charmed with her person, and was, on inquiry, as well pleased with the circumstances of her father—for he himself, notwithstanding all his finery, was not quite so rich as a Crœsus or an Attalus.

He was so pleased that he resolved to make his addresses to her directly. He did so accordingly, and that with so much warmth and briskness that he quickly baffled her weak repulses, and obliged the lady to refer him to her father, who, she knew, would quickly declare in favour of a coach and six.

Thus what Horatio had by sighs and tears, love and tenderness, been so long obtaining, the French-English Bellarmine with gaiety and gallantry possessed himself of in an instant ; in other words, what modesty had employed a full year in raising, impudence demolished in twenty-four hours.

From the opening of the assembly till the end of Bellarmine's visit Leonora had scarce one thought of Horatio ; but he now began, though an unwelcome guest, to enter into her mind. She wished she had seen the charming Bellarmine and his charming equipage before matters had gone so far.

"Yet why," says she, "should I wish to have seen him before? or what signifies it that I have seen him now? Is not Horatio my lover, almost my husband? Is he not as handsome, nay handsomer, than Bellarmine? Ay, but Bellarmine is the genteeler and the finer man; yes, that he must be allowed: yes, yes, he is that, certainly. But did not I, no longer ago than yesterday, love Horatio more than all the world? Ay, but yesterday I had not seen Bellarmine. But does not Horatio dote on me, and may he not in despair break his heart if I abandon him? Well, and has not Bellarmine a heart to break too? Yes, but I promised Horatio first; but that was poor Bellarmine's misfortune; if I had seen him first, I should certainly have preferred him. Did not the dear creature prefer me to every woman in the assembly, when every she was laying out for him? When was it in Horatio's power to give me such an instance of affection? Can he give me an equipage, or any of those things which Bellarmine will make me mistress of? How vast is the difference between being the wife of a poor counsellor, and the wife of one of Bellarmine's fortune! If I marry Horatio I shall triumph over no more than one rival, but by marrying Bellarmine I shall be the envy of all my acquaintance. What happiness! But can I suffer Horatio to die? for he has sworn he cannot survive my loss; but perhaps he may not die; if he should, can I prevent it? Must I sacrifice myself to him? Besides, Bellarmine may be as miserable for me too."

She was thus arguing with herself, when some young ladies called her to the walks, and a little relieved her anxiety for the present.

The next morning Bellarmine breakfasted with her in presence of her aunt, whom he sufficiently informed of his passion for Leonora. He was no sooner withdrawn than the old lady began to advise her niece on this occasion.

"You see, child," says she, "what fortune has thrown in your way; and I hope you will not withstand your own preferment."

Leonora, sighing, begged her not to mention any such things when she knew her engagements to Horatio.

"Engagements to a fig!" cried the aunt; "you should thank Heaven, on your knees, that you have it in your power to break them. Will any woman hesitate a moment whether she shall ride in a coach or walk on foot all the days of her life? But Bellarmine drives six, and Horatio not even a pair."

"Yes, but, madam, what will the world say?" answered Leonora; "will not they condemn me?"

"The world is always on the side of prudence," cries the aunt, "and would surely condemn you if you sacrified your interest to any motive whatever. Oh, I know the world very well; and you show your ignorance, my dear, by your objection. On my conscience, the world is wiser : I have lived longer in it than you ; and, I assure you, there is not anything worth our regard besides money ; nor did I ever know one person who married from other considerations who did not afterwards heartily repent it. Besides, if we examine the two men, can you prefer a sneaking fellow who has been bred at the university to a fine gentleman just come from his travels ? All the world must allow Bellarmine to be a fine gentleman,—positively a fine gentleman, and a handsome man."

" Perhaps, madam, I should not doubt, if I knew how to be handsomely off with the other."

" Oh, leave that to me," says the aunt ; " you know your father has not been acquainted with the affair. Indeed, for my part, I thought it might do well enough, not dreaming of such an offer ; but I'll disengage you : leave me to give the fellow an answer. I warrant you shall have no further trouble."

Leonora was at length satisfied with her aunt's reasoning ; and Bellarmine supping with her that evening, it was agreed he should the next morning go to her father and propose the match, which she consented should be consummated at his return.

The aunt retired soon after supper ; and the lovers being left together, Bellarmine began in the following manner :

" Yes, madam ; this coat, I assure you, was made at Paris, and I defy the best English tailor even to imitate it. There is not one of them can cut, madam ; they can't cut. If you observe how this skirt is turned, and this sleeve ; a clumsy English rascal can do nothing like it. Pray, how do you like my liveries ? "

Leonora answered, she thought them very pretty.

" All French," says he, " I assure you, except the great coats : I never trust anything more than a great coat to an Englishman. You know one must encourage our own people what one can, especially as before I had a place I was in the country interest : he, he, he ! But for myself, I would see the dirty island at the bottom of the sea, rather than wear a single rag of English work about me ; and I am sure, after you have made one tour to Paris, you will be of the same opinion with regard to your own clothes. You can't conceive what an addition a French dress would be to your beauty ; I positively assure you, at the first opera I saw since I came over, I mistook the English ladies for chambermaids : he, he, he ! "

With such sort of polite discourse did the gay Bellarmine entertain his beloved Leonora, when the door opened on a sudden, and Horatio entered the room. Here it is impossible to express the surprise of Leonora.

A long silence prevailed in the whole company. If the familiar entrance of Horatio struck the greatest astonishment into Bellarmine, the unexpected presence of Bellarmine no less surprised

Horatio. At length Leonora, collecting all the spirit she was mistress of, addressed herself to the latter, and pretended to wonder at the reason of so late a visit.

" I should, indeed," answered he, " have made some apology for disturbing you at this hour, had not my finding you in company assured me I do not break in upon your repose."

Bellarmine rose from his chair, traversed the room in a minuet step, and hummed an opera tune; while Horatio, advancing to Leonora, asked her, in a whisper, if that gentleman was not a relation of hers; to which she answered with a smile, or rather sneer:

" No, he is no relation yet"; adding, she could not guess the meaning of his question.

Horatio told her softly it did not arise from jealousy.

" Jealousy! I assure you, it would be very strange in a common acquaintance to give himself any of those airs."

These words a little surprised Horatio; but before he had time to answer, Bellarmine danced up to the lady, and told her, he feared he interrupted some business between her and the gentleman.

" I have no business," said she, " with the gentleman, nor any other, which need be any secret to you."

" You'll pardon me," said Horatio, " if I desire to know who this gentleman is, who is to be entrusted with all our secrets."

" You'll know soon enough," cried Leonora; " but I can't guess what secrets can ever pass between us of such mighty consequence."

" No, madam!" cries Horatio; " I'm sure you would not have me understand you in earnest."

" 'Tis indifferent to me," says she, " how you understand me; but I think so unseasonable a visit is difficult to be understood at all, at least when people find one engaged; though one's servants do not deny one, one may expect a well-bred person should soon take the hint."

" Madam," said Horatio, " I did not imagine any engagement with a stranger, as it seems this gentleman is, would have made my visit impertinent, or that any such ceremonies were to be preserved between persons in our situation."

" Sure you are in a dream," says she, " or would persuade me that I am in one. I know no pretensions a common acquaintance can have to lay aside the ceremonies of good breeding."

" Sure," says he, " I am in a dream; for it is impossible I should be really esteemed a common acquaintance by Leonora, after what has passed between us."

" Passed between us! Do you intend to affront me before this gentleman?"

" D—n me, affront the lady?" says Bellarmine, cocking his hat, and strutting up to Horatio; " does any man dare affront this lady before me, d—n me ? "

" Harkee, sir," says Horatio, " I would advise you to lay aside that fierce air ; for I am mightily deceived if this lady has not a violent desire to get your worship a good drubbing."

" Sir," said Bellarmine, " I have the honour to be her protector ; and d—n me, if I understand your meaning."

" Sir," answered Horatio, " she is rather your protectress ; but give yourself no more airs, for you see I am prepared for you " (shaking his whip at him).

" *Oh ! serviteur très humble,*" says Bellarmine ; " *je vous entend parfaitement bien.*"

At which time, the aunt, who had heard of Horatio's visit, entered the room, and soon satisfied all his doubts. She convinced him that he was never more awake in his life, and that nothing more extraordinary had happened in his three days' absence, than a small alteration in the affections of Leonora, who now burst into tears, and wondered what reason she had given him to use her in so barbarous a manner.

Horatio desired Bellarmine to withdraw with him ; but the ladies prevented it, by laying violent hands on the latter ; upon which the former took his leave without any great ceremony, and departed, leaving the lady with his rival to consult for his safety, which Leonora feared her indiscretion might have endangered ; but the aunt comforted her with assurances, that Horatio would not venture his person against so accomplished a cavalier as Bellarmine : and that, being a lawyer, he would seek revenge in his own way, and the most they had to apprehend from him was an action.

They at length therefore agreed to permit Bellarmine to retire to his lodgings, having first settled all matters relating to the journey which he was to undertake in the morning, and their preparations for the nuptials at his return. But, alas ! as wise men have observed, the seat of valour is not the countenance ; and many a grave and plain man will, on a just provocation, betake himself to that mischievous metal, cold iron ; while men of a fiercer brow, and sometimes with that emblem of courage, a cockade, will more prudently decline it.

Leonora was awaked in the morning, from a visionary coach and six, with the dismal account that Bellarmine was run through the body by Horatio ; that he lay languishing at an inn, and the surgeon had declared the wound mortal. She immediately leaped out of the bed, danced about the room in a frantic manner, tore her hair and beat her breast in all the agonies of despair ; in which sad condition her aunt, who likewise arose at the news, found her.

The good old lady applied her utmost art to comfort her niece. She told her, while there was life there was hope ; but that if he should die, her affliction would be of no service to Bellarmine, and would only expose herself, which might probably keep her some time without any future offer; that as matters had happened, her wisest way would be to think no more of Bellarmine, but to endeavour to regain the affections of Horatio.

"Speak not to me," cried the disconsolate Leonora; "is it not owing to me that poor Bellarmine has lost his life? Have not these cursed charms" (at which words she looked steadfastly in the glass) "been the ruin of the most charming man of this age? Can I ever bear to contemplate my own face again?" (with her eyes still fixed on the glass). "Am I not the murderess of the finest gentleman? No other woman in the town could have made any impression on him."

"Never think of things past," cries the aunt; "think of regaining the affections of Horatio."

"What reason," said the niece, "have I to hope he would forgive me? No, I have lost him as well as the other, and it was your wicked advice which was the occasion of all: you seduced me, contrary to my inclinations, to abandon poor Horatio" (at which words she burst into tears); "you prevailed upon me, whether I would or no, to give up my affections for him: had it not been for you, Bellarmine never would have entered into my thoughts: had not his addresses been backed by your persuasions, they never would have made any impression on me; I should have defied all the fortune and equipage in the world: but it was you, it was you, who got the better of my youth and simplicity, and forced me to lose my dear Horatio for ever."

The aunt was almost borne down with this torrent of words; she, however, rallied all the strength she could, and, drawing her mouth up in a purse, began:

"I am not surprised, niece, at this ingratitude. Those who advise young women for their interest must always expect such a return: I am convinced my brother will thank me for breaking off your match with Horatio at any rate."

"That may not be in your power yet," answered Leonora, "though it is very ungrateful in you to desire or attempt it, after the presents you have received from him."

For indeed true it is, that many presents, and some pretty valuable ones, had passed from Horatio to the old lady; but as true it is, that Bellarmine, when he breakfasted with her and her niece, had complimented her with a brilliant from his finger, of much greater value than all she had touched of the other.

The aunt's gall was on float to reply, when a servant brought a letter into the room; which Leonora, hearing it came from Bellarmine, with great eagerness opened, and read as follows:

"MOST DIVINE CREATURE—The wound which I fear you have heard I received from my rival is not like to be so fatal as those shot into my heart, which have been fired from your eyes, tout brilliant. Those are the only cannons by which I am to fall; for my surgeon gives me hopes of being soon able to attend your ruelle; till when, unless you would do me an honour which I have scarcely the hardiesse to think of, your absence will be the greatest anguish which can be felt by, madam, avec tout le respect, in the world, your most obedient, most absolute dévoté, BELLARMINE."

As soon as Leonora perceived such hopes of Bellarmine's recovery, and that the gossip Fame had, according to custom, so enlarged his danger, she presently abandoned all further thoughts of Horatio, and was soon reconciled to her aunt, who received her again into favour with a more Christian forgiveness than we generally meet with. Indeed, it is possible she might be a little alarmed at the hints which her niece had given her concerning the presents: she might apprehend such rumours, should they get abroad, might injure a reputation, which, by frequenting church twice a day, and preserving the utmost rigour and strictness in her countenance and behaviour for many years, she had established.

Leonora's passion returned now for Bellarmine with greater force, after its small relaxation, than ever. She proposed to her aunt to make him a visit in his confinement, which the old lady, with great and commendable prudence, advised her to decline:

"For," says she, "should any accident intervene to prevent your intended match, too forward a behaviour with this lover may injure you in the eyes of others. Every woman, till she is married, ought to consider of, and provide against, the possibility of the affair's breaking off."

Leonora said she should be indifferent to whatever might happen in such a case: for she had now so absolutely placed her affections on this dear man (so she called him), that, if it was her misfortune to lose him, she should for ever abandon all thoughts of mankind. She therefore resolved to visit him, notwithstanding all the prudent advice of her aunt to the contrary, and that very afternoon executed her resolution.

Leonora, having once broken through the bounds which custom and modesty impose on her sex, soon gave an unbridled indulgence to her passion. Her visits to Bellarmine were more constant, as well as longer, than his surgeon's: in a word, she became absolutely his nurse; made his water-gruel, administered him his medicines, and, notwithstanding the prudent advice of her aunt to the contrary, almost entirely resided in her wounded lover's apartment.

The ladies of the town began to take her conduct under consideration: it was the chief topic of discourse at their tea-tables, and was severely censured by the most part, especially by Lindamira, a lady, whose discreet and starch carriage, together with a constant attendance at church three times a day, had utterly defeated many malicious attacks on her own reputation; for such was the envy that Lindamira's virtue had attracted, that, notwithstanding her own strict behaviour, and strict inquiry into the lives of others, she had not been able to escape being the mark of some arrows herself, which, however, did her no injury; a blessing, perhaps, owed by her to the clergy, who were her chief male companions, and with two or three of whom she had been barbarously and unjustly calumniated.

The extreme delicacy of Lindamira's virtue was cruelly hurt by those freedoms which Leonora allowed herself: she said it was an affront to her sex; that she did not imagine it consistent with any woman's honour to speak to the creature, or to be seen in her company; and that, for her part, she should always refuse to dance at an assembly with her, for fear of contamination by taking her by the hand.

But to return to my story: as soon as Bellarmine was recovered, which was somewhat within a month from his receiving the wound, he set out, according to agreement, for Leonora's father, in order to propose the match, and settle all matters with him, touching settlements, and the like.

A little before his arrival, the old gentleman had received an intimation of the affair by the following letter, which I can repeat verbatim, and which, they say, was written neither by Leonora nor her aunt, though it was in a woman's hand. The letter was in these words:

"SIR—I am sorry to acquaint you, that your daughter Leonora has accepted one of the basest, as well as most simple parts, with a young gentleman to whom she has engaged herself, and whom she has (pardon the word) jilted for another of inferior fortune, notwithstanding his superior figure. You may take what measures you please on this occasion: I have performed what I thought my duty; as I have, though unknown to you, a very great respect for your family."

The old gentleman did not give himself the trouble to answer this kind epistle; nor did he take any notice of it after he had read it, till he saw Bellarmine. He was, to say the truth, one of those fathers who look on children as an unhappy consequence of their youthful pleasures; which, as he would have been delighted not to have had attended them, so was he no less pleased with any opportunity to rid himself of the encumbrance. He passed, in the world's language, as an exceeding good father; being not only so rapacious as to rob and plunder all mankind to the utmost of his power, but even to deny himself the conveniences, and almost necessaries of life; which his neighbours attributed to a desire of raising immense fortunes for his children; but, in fact, it was not so: he heaped up money for its own sake only, and looked on his children as his rivals, who were to enjoy his beloved mistress when he was incapable of possessing her; and which he would have been much more charmed with the power of carrying along with him: nor had his children any other security of being his heirs than that the law would constitute them such without a will, and that he had not affection enough for any one living to take the trouble of writing one.

To this gentleman came Bellarmine on the errand I have mentioned. His person, his equipage, his family, and his estate, seemed to the father to make him an advantageous match for his daughter; he, therefore, very readily, accepted his proposals: but when Bellarmine imagined the principal affair concluded, and began to open the incidental matters of fortune, the old gentleman presently changed his countenance saying, he resolved never to marry his daughter on a Smithfield match; that whoever had love for her to take her, would, when he died, find her share of his fortune in his coffers; but he had seen such examples of undutifulness happen from the too early generosity of parents, that he had made a vow never to part with a shilling whilst he lived.

He commended the saying of Solomon, "He that spareth the rod, spoileth the child"; but added, he might have likewise asserted, that he that spares the purse saves the child. He then ran into a discourse on the extravagance of the youth of the age; whence he launched into a dissertation on horses; and came at length to commend those Bellarmine drove.

That fine gentleman, who at another season would have been well enough pleased to dwell a little on that subject, was now very eager to resume the circumstance of fortune. He said he had a very high value for the young lady, and would receive her with less than he would any other whatever; but that even his love to her made some regard to worldly matters necessary; for it would be a most distracting sight for him to see her, when he had the honour to be her husband, in less than a coach and six.

The old gentleman answered, "Four will do, four will do," and then took a turn from horses to extravagance, and from extravagance to horses, till he came round to the equipage again; whither he was no sooner arrived, than Bellarmine brought him back to the point; but all to no purpose: he made his escape from that subject in a minute; till at last the lover declared, that, in the present situation of his affairs, it was impossible for him, though he loved Leonora more than *tout le monde*, to marry her without any fortune.

To which the father answered, he was sorry then his daughter must lose so valuable a match; that if he had an inclination, at present it was not in his power to advance a shilling; that he had had great losses, and been at great expense on projects, which, though he had great expectations from them, had yet produced him nothing; that he did not know what might happen hereafter, as on the birth of a son, or such accident; but he would make no promise, nor enter into any article; for he would not break his vow for all the daughters in the world.

In short, Bellarmine, having tried every argument and persuasion which he could invent, and finding them all ineffectual, at length took his leave, but not in order to return to Leonora: he proceeded directly to his own seat, whence, after a few days' stay, he returned to Paris, to the great delight of the French and the honour of the English nation. But as soon as he arrived at his home, he presently despatched a messenger with the following epistle to Leonora:

"ADORABLE AND CHARMANTE—I am sorry to have the honour to tell you I am not the heureux person destined for your divine arms. Your papa has told me so with a politesse not often seen on this side Paris; you may, perhaps, guess his manner of refusing me. Ah, mon Dieu! you will certainly believe me, madam, incapable myself of delivering this triste message, which I intend to try the French air, to cure the consequence of. A jamais! Cœur! Ange! Au diable! If your papa obliges you to a marriage, I hope we shall see you at Paris; till when, the wind that flows from thence will be the warmest dans le monde, for it will consist almost entirely of my sighs. Adieu, ma princesse! Ah l'amour!

BELLARMINE."

I shall not attempt to describe Leonora's condition when she received this letter; it is a picture of horror, which I should have as little pleasure in drawing as you in beholding. She immediately left the place where she was the subject of conversation and ridicule, and retired to the country, where she has ever since led a disconsolate life, and deserves, perhaps, pity for her misfortunes, more than our censure for a behaviour to which the artifices of her aunt very probably contributed, and to which very young women are often rendered too liable by that blameable levity in the education of their sex.

SAMUEL TAYLOR COLERIDGE
1772–1834

MARIA SCHÖNING

Maria Eleonora Schöning was the daughter of a Nuremberg wine-drawer. She received her unhappy existence at the price of her mother's life, and at the age of seventeen she followed, as the sole mourner, the bier of her remaining parent. From her thirteenth year she had passed her life at her father's sick-bed, the gout having deprived him of the use of his limbs; and beheld the arch of heaven only when she went to fetch food or medicines. The discharge of her filial duties occupied the whole of her time and all her thoughts. She was his only nurse, and for the last two years they lived without a servant. She prepared his scanty meals, she bathed his aching limbs, and though weak and delicate from constant confinement and the poison of melancholy thoughts, she had acquired an unusual power in her arms, from the habit of lifting her old and suffering father out of and into his bed of pain.

Thus passed away her early youth in sorrow: she grew up in tears, a stranger to the amusements of youth and its more delightful schemes and imaginations. She was not, however, unhappy; she attributed indeed, no merit to herself for her virtues, but for that reason were they the more her reward.

The peace which passeth all understanding disclosed itself in all her looks and movements. It lay on her countenance, like a steady unshadowed moonlight; and her voice, which was naturally at once sweet and subtle, came from her like the fine flute-tones of a masterly performer, which still floating at some uncertain distance, seem to be created by the player rather than to proceed from the instrument. If you had listened to it in one of those brief sabbaths of the soul, when the activity and discursiveness of the thoughts are suspended, and the mind quietly eddies round, instead of flowing onward—(as at late evening in the spring I have seen a bat wheel in silent circles round and round a fruit-tree in full blossom, in the midst of which, as within a close tent of the purest white, an unseen nightingale was piping its sweetest notes)—in such a mood you might have half fancied, half felt, that her voice had a separate being of its own; that it was a living something, whose mode of existence was for the ear only: so deep was her resignation, so entirely had it become the unconscious habit of her nature, and in all she did or said, so perfectly were both her movements and her utterance without effort, and without the appearance of effort! Her dying father's last words, addressed to the clergyman who attended him, were his grateful testimony, that during his long and sore trial his good Maria had behaved to him like an angel; that the most disagreeable offices, and the least suited to her age and sex, had never drawn an unwilling look from her, and that whenever his eye had met hers he had been sure to see in it either the tear of pity or the sudden smile expressive of her affection and wish to cheer him.

"God," said he, "will reward the good girl for all her long dutifulness to me!"

He departed during the inward prayer which followed these his last words. His wish will be fulfilled in eternity; but for this world the prayer of the dying man was not heard!

Maria sat and wept by the grave which now contained her father, her friend, the only bond by which she was linked to life. But while yet the last sound of his death-bell was murmuring away in the air, she was obliged to return with two revenue officers, who demanded entrance into the house, in order to take possession of the papers of the deceased, and from them to discover whether he had always given in his income, and paid the yearly income-tax according to his oath and in proportion to his property.

After the few documents had been looked through and collated with the registers, the officers found, or pretended to find, sufficient proofs that the deceased had not paid his tax proportionably, which imposed on them the duty to put all the effects under lock and seal. They therefore desired the maiden to retire to an empty room, till the ransom office had decided on the affair. Bred up in suffering, and habituated to immediate compliance, the affrighted and weeping maiden obeyed. She hastened to the empty garret, while the revenue officers placed the lock and seal upon the other doors, and finally took away the papers to the ransom office.

Not before evening did the poor faint Maria, exhausted with weeping, rouse herself with the intention of going to her bed; but she found the door of her chamber sealed up, and that she must pass the night on the floor of the garret. The officers had had the humanity to place at the door the small portion of food that happened to be in the house.

Thus passed several days, till the officers returned with an order that Maria Eleonora Schöning should leave the house without delay, the commission court having confiscated the whole property to the city treasury. The father before he was bedridden had never possessed any considerable property ; but yet, by his industry, had been able not only to keep himself free from debt, but to lay up a small sum for the evil day. Three years of evil days, three whole years of sickness, had consumed the greatest part of this ; yet still enough remained not only to defend his daughter from immediate want, but likewise to maintain her till she could get into some service or employment, and should have recovered her spirits sufficiently to bear up against the hardships of life. With this thought her dying father comforted himself, and this hope too proved vain !

A timid girl, whose past life had been made up of sorrow and privation, she went indeed to solicit the commissioners in her own behalf ; but these were, as is mostly the case on the Continent, advocates—the most hateful class, perhaps, of human society, hardened by the frequent sight of misery, and seldom superior in moral character to English pettifoggers or Old Bailey attorneys.

She went to them, indeed, but not a word could she say for herself ! Her tears and inarticulate sounds—for these her judges had no ears or eyes. Mute and confounded, like an unfledged dove fallen out from its mother's nest, Maria betook herself to her home, and found the house door too now shut upon her. Her whole wealth consisted in the clothes she wore. She had no relations to whom she could apply, for those of her mother had disclaimed all acquaintance with her, and her father was a Nether Saxon by birth. She had no acquaintance, for all the friends of old Schöning had forsaken him in the first year of his sickness. She had no playfellow, for who was likely to have been the companion of a nurse in the room of a sick man ?

Surely, since the creation never was a human being more solitary and forsaken than this innocent poor creature, that now roamed about friendless in a populous city, to the whole of whose inhabitants her filial tenderness, her patient domestic goodness, and all her soft yet difficult virtues, might well have been the model.

> But homeless near a thousand homes she stood,
> And near a thousand tables pined, and wanted food !

The night came, and Maria knew not where to find a shelter. She tottered to the churchyard of the St. James' Church in Nuremberg, where the body of her father rested. Upon the yet grassless grave she threw herself down ; and could anguish have prevailed over youth, that night she had been in heaven.

The day came, and, like a guilty thing, this guiltless, this good being stole away from the crowd that began to pass through the churchyard, and hastening through the streets to the city gate, she hid herself behind a garden hedge just beyond it, and there wept away the second day of her desolation.

The evening closed in ; the pang of hunger made itself felt amid the dull aching of self-wearied anguish, and drove the sufferer back again into the city.

Yet what could she gain there ? She had not the courage to beg, and the very thought of stealing never occurred to her innocent mind. Scarce conscious whither she was going, or why she went, she found herself once more by her father's grave, as the last relic of evening faded away in the horizon. I have sat for some minutes with my pen resting ; I can scarce summon the courage to tell, what I scarce know whether I ought to tell. Were I composing a tale of fiction the reader might justly suspect the purity of my own heart, and most certainly would have abundant right to resent such an incident, as an outrage wantonly offered to his imagination.

As I think of the circumstance, it seems more like a distempered dream ! but alas ! what is guilt so detestable other than a dream of madness, that worst madness, the madness of the heart ? I cannot but believe that the dark and restless passions must first have drawn the mind in upon themselves, and as with the confusion of imperfect sleep, have in some strange manner taken away the sense of reality, in order to render it possible for a human being to perpetrate what it is too certain that human beings have perpetrated. The churchyards in most of the German cities, and too often, I fear, in those of our own country, are not more injurious to health than to morality. Their former venerable character is no more. The religion of the place has followed its superstitions, and their darkness and loneliness tempt worse spirits to roam in them than those whose nightly wanderings appalled the believing hearts of our brave forefathers ! It was close by the new-made grave of her father that the meek and spotless daughter became the victim to brutal violence, which weeping and watching and cold and hunger had rendered her utterly unable to resist. The monster left her in a trance of stupefaction, and into her right hand, which she had clenched convulsively, he had forced a half-dollar.

It was one of the darkest nights of autumn : in the deep and dead silence the only sounds were the slow blunt ticking of the church clock, and now and then the sinking down of bones in the nigh charnel-house. Maria, when she had in some degree recovered her senses, sat upon the grave near which—not her innocence had been sacrificed, but—that which, from the frequent admonitions and almost the dying words of her father, she had been accustomed to consider as such.

Guiltless, she felt the pangs of guilt, and still continued to grasp the coin which the monster had left in her hand, with an anguish as sore as if it had been indeed the wages of voluntary prostitution. Giddy and faint from want of food, her brain becoming feverish from sleeplessness, and in this unexampled concurrence of calamities, this complication and entanglement of misery in misery, she imagined that she heard her father's voice bidding her leave his sight.

His last blessings had been conditional, for in his last hours he had told her that the loss of her innocence would not let him rest quiet in his grave. His last blessings now sounded in her ear like curses, and she fled from the churchyard as if a demon had been chasing her; and hurrying along the streets, through which it is probable her accursed violater had walked with quiet and orderly step to his place of rest and security, she was seized by the watchmen of the night—a welcome prey, as they receive in Nuremberg half a gulden from the police chest for every woman that they find in the streets after ten o'clock at night. It was midnight, and she was taken to the next watch-house.

The sitting magistrate before whom she was carried the next morning prefaced his first question with the most opprobrious title that ever belonged to the most hardened street-walkers, and which man born of woman should not address even to these, were it but for his own sake. The frightful name awakened the poor orphan from her dream of guilt, it brought back the consciousness of her innocence, but with it the sense likewise of her wrongs and of her helplessness. The cold hand of death seemed to grasp her, she fainted dead away at his feet and was not without difficulty recovered.

The magistrate was so far softened, and only so far, as to dismiss her for the present, but with a menace of sending her to the House of Correction if she were brought before him a second time. The idea of her own innocence now became uppermost in her mind; but mingling with the thought of her utter forlornness, and the image of her angry father, and doubtless still in a state of bewilderment, she formed the resolution of drowning herself in the river Pegnitz—in order (for this was the shape which her fancy had taken) to throw herself at her father's feet, and to justify her innocence to him in the world of spirits. She hoped that her father would speak for her to the Saviour, and that she should be forgiven.

But as she was passing through the suburb she was met by a soldier's wife, who during the lifetime of her father had been occasionally employed in the house as a charwoman. This poor woman was startled at the disordered apparel and more disordered looks of her young mistress, and questioned her with such an anxious and heartfelt tenderness, as at once brought back the poor orphan to her natural feelings and the obligations of religion. As a frightened child throws itself into the arms of its mother, and hiding its head on her breast, half tells amid sobs what has happened to it, so did she throw herself on the neck of the woman who had uttered the first words of kindness to her since her father's death, and with loud weeping she related what she had endured and what she was about to have done, told her all her affliction and her misery, the wormwood and the gall! Her kind-hearted friend mingled tears with tears; pressed the poor forsaken one to her heart; comforted her with sentences out of the hymn-book; and with the most affectionate entreaties conjured her to give up her horrid purpose, for that life was short, and heaven was for ever.

Maria had been bred up in the fear of God; she now trembled at the thought of her former purpose, and followed her friend Harlin, for that was the name of her guardian angel, to her home hard by. The moment she entered the door she sank down and lay at her full length, as if only to be motionless in a place of shelter had been the fulness of delight. As when a withered leaf, that has been long whirled about by the gusts of autumn, is blown into a cave or hollow tree, it stops suddenly, and all at once looks the very image of quiet—such might this poor orphan appear to the eye of a meditative imagination.

A place of shelter she had attained, and a friend willing to comfort her in all that she could; but the noble-hearted Harlin was herself a daughter of calamity, one who from year to year must lie down in weariness and rise up to labour; for whom this world provides no other comfort but the sleep which enables them to forget it; no other physician but death, which takes them out of it! She was married to one of the city guards, who, like Maria's father, had been long sick and bedridden. Him, herself, and two little children, she had to maintain by washing and charing; and some time after Maria had been domesticated with them, Harlin told her that she herself had been once driven to a desperate thought by the cry of her hungry children, during a want of employment, and that she had been on the point of killing one of the little ones, and of then surrendering herself into the hands of justice.

In this manner, she had conceived, all would be well provided for; the surviving child would be admitted, as a matter of course, into the Orphan House, and her husband into the Hospital; while she herself would have atoned for her act by a public execution, and, together with the child that she had destroyed, would have passed into a state of bliss. All this she related to Maria, and those tragic ideas left but too deep and lasting impression on her mind. Weeks after, she herself renewed the conversation, by expressing to her benefactress her inability to conceive how it was possible for one human being to take away the life of another, especially that of an innocent little child.

" For that reason," replied Harlin, " because it was so innocent and so good, I wished to put it out of this wicked world. Thinkest thou, then, that I would have my head cut off for the sake of a wicked child ? Therefore it was little Nan that I meant to have taken with me, who, as you see, is always so sweet and patient ; little Frank has already his humours and naughty tricks, and suits better for this world."

This was the answer. Maria brooded a while over it in silence, then passionately snatched the children up in her arms, as if she would protect them against their own mother.

For one whole year the orphan lived with the soldier's wife, and by their joint labours barely kept off absolute want. As a little boy (almost a child in size though in his thirteenth year) once told me of himself, as he was guiding me up the Brocken, in the Hartz Forest, they had but " little of that, of which a great deal tells but for little."

But now came the second winter, and with it came bad times, a season of trouble for this poor and meritorious household. The wife now fell sick : too constant and too hard labour, too scanty and too innutritious food, had gradually wasted away her strength. Maria redoubled her efforts in order to provide bread, and fuel for their washing which they took in ; but the task was above her powers. Besides, she was so timid and so agitated at the sight of strangers, that sometimes, with the best good-will, she was left without employment. One by one, every article of the least value which they possessed was sold off, except the bed on which the husband lay. He died just before the approach of spring ; but about the same time the wife gave signs of convalescence.

The physician, though almost as poor as his patients, had been kind to them : silver and gold had he none, but he occasionally brought a little wine, and often assured them that nothing was wanting to her perfect recovery but better nourishment and a little wine every day. This, however, could not be regularly procured, and Harlin's spirits sank, and as her bodily pain left her she became more melancholy, silent, and self-involved. And now it was that Maria's mind was incessantly racked by the frightful apprehension, that her friend might be again meditating the accomplishment of her former purpose. She had grown as passionately fond of the two children as if she had borne them under her own heart ; but the jeopardy in which she conceived her friend's salvation to stand—this was her predominant thought. For all the hopes and fears, which under a happier lot would have been associated with the objects of the senses, were transferred, by Maria, to her notions and images of a future state.

In the beginning of March, one bitter cold evening, Maria started up and suddenly left the house. The last morsel of food had been divided between the two children for their breakfast; and for the last hour or more the little boy had been crying for hunger, while his gentle sister had been hiding her face in Maria's lap, and pressing her little body against her knees, in order by that mechanic pressure to dull the aching from emptiness. The tender-hearted and visionary maiden had watched the mother's eye, and had interpreted several of her sad and steady looks according to her preconceived apprehensions. She had conceived all at once the strange and enthusiastic thought that she would in some way or other offer her own soul for the salvation of the soul of her friend. The money, which had been left in her hand, flashed upon the eye of her mind, as a single unconnected image; and faint with hunger and shivering with cold, she sallied forth—in search of guilt!

Awful are the dispensations of the Supreme, and in His severest judgments the hand of mercy is visible. It was a night so wild with wind and rain, or rather rain and snow mixed together, that a famished wolf would have stayed in his cave, and listened to a howl more fearful than his own. Forlorn Maria! thou wert kneeling in pious simplicity at the grave of thy father, and thou becamest the prey of a monster! Innocent thou wert, and without guilt didst thou remain. Now thou goest forth of thy own accord—but God will have pity on thee! Poor bewildered innocent; in thy spotless imagination dwelt no distinct conception of the evil which thou wentest forth to brave! To save the soul of thy friend was the dream of thy feverish brain, and thou wert again apprehended as an outcast of shameless sensuality, at the moment when thy too spiritualised fancy was busied with the glorified forms of thy friend and of her little ones interceding for thee at the throne of the Redeemer!

At this moment her perturbed fancy suddenly suggested to her a new means for the accomplishment of her purpose; and she replied to the night-watch—who with a brutal laugh bade her expect on the morrow the unmanly punishment, which to the disgrace of human nature the laws of Protestant states (alas! even those of our own country) inflict on female vagrants—that she came to deliver herself up as an infanticide.

She was instantly taken before the magistrate, through as wild and pitiless a storm as ever pelted on a houseless head! through as black and tyrannous a night as ever aided the workings of a heated brain! Here she confessed that she had been delivered of an infant by the soldier's wife, Harlin, that she deprived it of life in the presence of Harlin, and according to a plan preconcerted with her, and that Harlin had buried it somewhere in the wood, but where she knew not. During this strange tale she appeared to listen, with a mixture of fear and satisfaction, to the howling of the wind; and never sure could a confession of real guilt have been accompanied by a more dreadfully appropriate music!

At the moment of her apprehension she had formed the scheme of helping her friend out of the world in a state of innocence. When the soldier's widow was confronted with the orphan, and the latter had repeated her confession to her face, Harlin answered in these words, "For God's sake, Maria! how have I deserved this of thee?" Then turning to the magistrate, said, "I know nothing of this."

This was the sole answer which she gave, and not another word could they extort from her. The instruments of torture were brought, and Harlin was warned, that if she did not confess of her own accord, the truth would be immediately forced from her. This menace convulsed Maria Schöning with affright; her intention had been to emancipate herself and her friend from a life of unmixed suffering, without the crime of suicide in either, and with no guilt at all on the part of her friend. The thought of her friend's being put to the torture had not occurred to her.

Wildly and eagerly she pressed her friend's hands, already bound in preparation for the torture—she pressed them in agony between her own, and said to her, "Anna! confess it! Anna, dear Anna! it will then be well with all of us! all, all of us! and Frank and little Nan will be put into the Orphan House!"

Maria's scheme now passed, like a flash of lightning, through the widow's mind; she acceded to it at once, kissed Maria repeatedly, and then serenely turning her face to the judge, acknowledged that she had added to the guilt by so obstinate a denial, that all her friend had said was true, save only that she had thrown the dead infant into the river, and not buried it in the wood.

They were both committed to prison, and as they both persevered in their common confession, the process was soon made out and the condemnation followed the trial: and the sentence, by which they were both to be beheaded with the sword, was ordered to be put in force on the next day but one. On the morning of the execution the delinquents were brought together, in order that they might be reconciled with each other, and join in common prayer for forgiveness of their common guilt.

But now Maria's thoughts took another turn. The idea that her benefactress, that so very good a woman, should be violently put out of life, and this with an infamy on her name which would cling for ever to the little orphans, overpowered her. Her own excessive desire to die scarcely prevented her from discovering the whole plan; and when Harlin was left alone with her, and she saw her friend's calm and affectionate look, her fortitude was dissolved; she burst into loud and passionate weeping, and throwing herself into her friend's arms, with convulsive sobs she entreated her forgiveness.

Harlin pressed the poor agonised girl to her arms; like a tender mother, she kissed and fondled her wet cheeks, and in the most solemn and emphatic tones assured her that there was nothing to forgive. On the contrary, she was her greatest benefactress, and the instrument of God's goodness to remove her at once from a miserable world and from the temptation of committing a heavy crime. In vain! Her repeated promises, that she would answer before God for them both, could not pacify the tortured conscience of Maria, till at length the presence of the clergyman and the preparations for receiving the sacrament occasioned the widow to address her thus: "See, Maria! this is the Body and Blood of Christ, which takes away all sin! Let us partake together of this holy repast with full trust in God and joyful hope of our approaching happiness."

These words of comfort, uttered with cheering tones, and accompanied with a look of inexpressible tenderness and serenity, brought back peace for a while to her troubled spirit. They communicated together, and on parting, the magnanimous woman once more embraced her young friend; then stretching her hand toward heaven, said, "Be tranquil, Maria! by to-morrow morning we are there, and all our sorrows stay here behind us."

I hasten to the scene of the execution; for I anticipate my reader's feelings in the exhaustion of my own heart. Serene and with unaltered countenance the lofty-minded Harlin heard the strokes of the death-bell, stood before the scaffold while the staff was broken over her, and at length ascended the steps, all with a steadiness and tranquillity of manner which was not more distant from fear than from defiance and bravado. Altogether different was the state of poor Maria: with shattered nerves and an agonising conscience that incessantly accused her as the murderess of her friend, she did not walk but staggered towards the scaffold and stumbled up the steps.

While Harlin, who went first, at every step turned her head round and still whispered to her, raising her eyes to heaven, "But a few minutes, Maria! and we are there!"

On the scaffold she again bade her farewell, again repeating, "Dear Maria! but one minute now, and we are together with God."

But when she knelt down and her neck was bared for the stroke, the unhappy girl lost all self-command, and with a loud and piercing shriek she bade them hold and not murder the innocent "She is, innocent! I have borne false-witness! I alone am the murderess!"

She rolled herself now at the feet of the executioner, and now at those of the clergymen, and conjured them to stop the execution: declaring that the whole story had been invented by herself; that she had never brought forth, much less destroyed, an infant; that for her friend's sake she made this discovery; that for herself she wished to die, and would die gladly, if they would take away her friend, and promise to free her soul from the dreadful agony of having murdered her friend by false-witness.

The executioner asked Harlin if there were any truth in what Maria Schöning had said.

The heroine answered with manifest reluctance: "Most assuredly she hath said the truth; I confessed myself guilty, because I wished to die and thought it best for both of us; and now that my hope is on the moment of its accomplishment, I cannot be supposed to declare myself innocent for the sake of saving my life—but any wretchedness is to be endured rather than that poor creature should be hurried out of the world in a state of despair."

The outcry of the attending populace prevailed to suspend the execution: a report was sent to the assembled magistrates, and in the meantime one of the priests reproached the widow in bitter words for her former false confession.

"What," she replied, sternly but without anger, "what would the truth have availed? Before I perceived my friend's purpose I did deny it: my assurance was pronounced an impudent lie; I was already bound for the torture, and so bound that the sinews of my hands started, and one of their worships in the large white peruke, threatened that he would have me stretched till the sun shone through me! and that then I should cry out, Yes, when it was too late."

The priest was hard-hearted or supersitious enough to continue his reproofs, to which the noble woman condescended no further answer.

The other clergyman, however, was both more rational and more humane. He succeeded in silencing his colleague, and the former half of the long hour, which the magistrate took in making speeches on the improbability of the tale instead of re-examining the culprits in person, he employed in gaining from the widow a connected account of all the circumstances, and in listening occasionally to Maria's passionate descriptions of all her friend's goodness and magnanimity. For she had gained an influx of life and spirit from the assurance in her mind, both that she had now rescued Harlin from death and was about to expiate the guilt of her purpose by her own execution.

For the latter half of the time the clergyman remained in silence, lost in thought, and momentarily expecting the return of the messenger. All that during the deep silence of this interval could be heard was one exclamation of Harlin to her unhappy friend :

"Oh ! Maria ! Maria ! couldst thou but have kept up thy courage but for another minute, we should have been now in heaven ! "

The messenger came back with an order from the magistrates to proceed with the execution ! With reanimated countenance Harlin placed her neck on the block, and her head was severed from her body amid a general shriek from the crowd. The executioner fainted after the blow, and the under-hangman was ordered to take his place.

He was not wanted. Maria was already gone : her body was found as cold as if she had been dead for some hours. The flower had been snapt in the storm, before the scythe of violence could come near it.

CHARLES LAMB
1775–1834

DREAM-CHILDREN

A REVERIE

CHILDREN love to listen to stories about their elders when *they* were children ; to stretch their imagination to the conception of a traditionary great-uncle, or grandame, whom they never saw. It was in this spirit that my little ones crept about me the other evening to hear about their great-grandmother Field, who lived in a great house in Norfolk (a hundred times bigger than that in which they and papa lived), which had been the scene—so at least it was generally believed in that part of the country—of the tragic incidents which they had lately become familiar with from the ballad of the *Children in the Wood*.

Certain it is, that the whole story of the children and their cruel uncle was to be seen fairly carved out in the wood upon the chimney-piece of the great hall—the whole story down to the Robin Redbreasts—till a foolish rich person pulled it down to set up a marble one of modern invention in its stead, with no story upon it. Here Alice put out one of her dear mother's looks, too tender to be called upbraiding.

Then I went on to say how religious and how good their great-grandmother Field was, how beloved and respected by everybody, though she was not, indeed, the mistress of this great house, but had only the charge of it (and yet in some respects she might be said to be the mistress of it too) committed to her by the owner, who preferred living in a newer and more fashionable mansion, which he had purchased somewhere in the adjoining county ; but still she lived in it in a manner as if it had been her own, and kept up the dignity of the great house in a sort while she lived, which afterwards came to decay, and was nearly pulled down, and all its old ornaments stripped and carried away to the owner's other house, where they were set up, and looked as awkward as if some one were to carry away the old tombs they had seen lately at the Abbey, and stick them up in Lady C.'s tawdry gilt drawing-room.

Here John smiled, as much as to say, "That would be foolish indeed."

And then I told how, when she came to die, her funeral was attended by a concourse of all the poor, and some of the gentry too, of the neighbourhood, for many miles round, to show their respect for her memory, because she had been such a good and religious woman—so good, indeed, that she knew all the Psalter by heart, aye, and a great part of the Testament besides.

Here little Alice spread her hands. Then I told what a tall, upright, graceful person their great-grandmother Field once was; and how in her youth she was esteemed the best dancer—here Alice's little right foot played an involuntary movement, till, upon my looking grave, it desisted—the best dancer, I was saying, in the county, till a cruel disease, called a cancer, came, and bowed her down with pain; but it could never bend her good spirits, or make them stoop; but they were still upright, because she was so good and religious.

Then I told how she was used to sleep by herself in a lone chamber of the great lone house; and how she believed that an apparition of two infants was to be seen at midnight gliding up and down the great staircase near where she slept; but she said, "Those innocents would do her no harm"; and how frightened I used to be, though in those days I had my maid to sleep with me, because I was never half so good or religious as she, and yet I never saw the infants.

Here John expanded all his eyebrows, and tried to look courageous. Then I told how good she was to all her grandchildren, having us to the great house in the holidays, where I in particular used to spend many hours by myself in gazing upon the old busts of the twelve Caesars, that had been emperors of Rome, till the old marble heads would seem to live again, or I to be turned into marble with them; how I never could be tired with roaming about that huge mansion, with its vast empty rooms, with their worn-out hangings, fluttering tapestry, and carved oaken panels, with the gilding almost rubbed out—sometimes in the spacious old-fashioned gardens, which I had almost to myself, unless when now and then a solitary gardening man would cross me—and how the nectarines and peaches hung upon the walls without my ever offering to pluck them, because they were forbidden fruit, unless now and then,—and because I had more pleasure in strolling about among the old melancholy-looking yew-trees, or the firs, and picking up the red berries, and the fir-apples, which were good for nothing but to look at—or in lying about upon the fresh grass, with all the fine garden smells around me—or basking in the orangery, till I could almost fancy myself ripening too along with the oranges and the limes, in that grateful warmth—or in watching the dace that darted to and fro in the fish-pond, at the bottom of the garden, with here and there a great sulky pike hanging midway down the water in silent state, as if it mocked at their impertinent friskings,—I had more pleasure in these busy-idle diversions than in all the sweet flavours of peaches, nectarines, oranges, and such-like common baits of children.

Here John slily deposited back upon the plate a bunch of grapes, which, not unobserved by Alice, he had meditated dividing with her, and both seemed willing to relinquish them for the present as irrelevant. Then, in somewhat a more heightened tone, I told how, though their great-grandmother Field loved all her grandchildren, yet, in an especial manner, she might be said to love their uncle, John L——, because he was so handsome and spirited a youth, and a king to the rest of us; and, instead of moping about in solitary corners like some of us, he would mount the most mettlesome horse he could get, when but an imp no bigger than themselves, and make it carry him half over the county in a morning, and join the hunters when there were any out—and yet he loved the old great house and gardens too, but had too much spirit to be always pent up within their boundaries—and how their uncle grew up to man's estate as brave as he was handsome, to the admiration of everybody, but of their great-grandmother Field most especially; and how he used to carry me upon his back when I was a lame-footed boy—for he was a good bit older than me—many a mile when I could not walk for pain;—and how, in after-life, he became lame-footed too, and I did not always (I fear) make allowances enough for him when he was impatient, and in pain, nor remember sufficiently how considerate he had been to me when I was lame-footed; and how, when he died, though he had not been dead an hour it seemed as if he had died a great while ago, such a distance there is betwixt life and death; and how I bore his death, as I thought, pretty well at first, but afterwards it haunted and haunted me; and though I did not cry or take it to heart as some do, and as I think he would have done if I had died, yet I missed him all day long, and I knew not till then how much I had loved him.

I missed his kindness, and I missed his crossness, and wished him to be alive again, to be quarrelling with him (for we quarrelled sometimes), rather than not have him again, and was as uneasy without him as he, their poor uncle, must have been when the doctor took off his limb.

Here the children fell a-crying, and asked if their little mourning which they had on was not for Uncle John, and they looked up, and prayed me not to go on about their uncle, but to tell them some stories about their pretty dead mother.

Then I told how, for seven long years, in hope sometimes, sometimes in despair, yet persisting ever, I courted the fair Alice W—n;

and, as much as children could understand, I explained to them what coyness, and difficulty, and denial meant in maidens, when suddenly turning to Alice, the soul of the first Alice looked out at her eyes, with such a reality of representment that I became in doubt which of them stood there before me, or whose that bright hair was ; and while I stood gazing, both the children gradually grew fainter to my view, receding, and still receding, till nothing at last but two mournful features were seen in the uttermost distance, which, without speech, strangely impressed upon me the effects of speech :

" We are not of Alice, nor of thee, nor are we children at all. The children of Alice call Bartrum father. We are nothing ; less than nothing, and dreams. We are only what might have been, and must wait upon the tedious shores of Lethe millions of ages before we have existence and a name "——and immediately awaking, I found myself quietly seated in my bachelor arm-chair, where I had fallen asleep with the faithful Bridget unchanged by my side.

CHARLES LAMB

JUKE JUDKINS' COURTSHIP

I AM the only son of a considerable brazier in Birmingham, who, dying in 1803, left me successor to the business, with no other encumbrance than a sort of rent-charge, which I am enjoined to pay out of it, of ninety-three pounds sterling *per annum*, to his widow, my mother: and which the improving state of the concern, I bless God, has hitherto enabled me to discharge with punctuality. (I say, I am enjoined to pay the said sum, but not strictly obligated: that is to say, as the will is worded, I believe the law would relieve me from the payment of it; but the wishes of a dying parent should in some sort have the effect of law.) So that, though the annual profits of my business, on an average of the last three or four years, would appear to an indifferent observer, who should inspect my shop-books, to amount to the sum of one thousand three hundred and three pounds, odd shilling, the real proceeds in that time have fallen short of that sum to the amount of the aforesaid payment of ninety-three pounds sterling annually.

I was always my father's favourite. He took a delight to the very last in recounting the little sagacious tricks and innocent artifices of my childhood. One manifestation thereof I never heard him repeat without tears of joy trickling down his cheeks. It seems, that when I quitted the parental roof (Aug. 27, 1788), being then six years and not quite a month old, to proceed to the Free School at Warwick, where my father was a sort of trustee, my mother—as mothers are usually provident on these occasions—had stuffed the pockets of the coach, which was to convey me and six more children of my own growth that were going to be entered along with me at the same seminary, with a prodigious quantity of gingerbread, which I remembered my father said was more than was needed: and so indeed it was; for, if I had been to eat it all myself, it would have got stale and mouldy before it had been half spent. The consideration whereof set me upon my contrivances how I might secure to myself as much of the gingerbread as would keep good for the next two or three days, and yet none of the rest in manner be wasted. I had a little pair of pocket-compasses, which I usually carried about me for the purpose of making draughts and measurements, at which I was always very ingenious, of the various engines and mechanical inventions in which such a town as Birmingham abounded.

By means of these, and a small penknife which my father had given me, I cut out the one half of the cake, calculating that the remainder would reasonably serve my turn; and subdividing it into many little slices, which were curious to see for the neatness and niceness of their proportion, I sold it out in so many pennyworths to my young companions as served us all the way to Warwick, which is a distance of some twenty miles from this town: and very merry, I assure you, we made ourslves with it, feasting all the way. By this honest stratagem I put double the prime cost of the gingerbread into my purse, and secured as much as I thought would keep good and moist for my next two or three days' eating.

When I told this to my parents on their first visit to me at Warwick, my father (good man), patted me on the cheek, and stroked my head, and seemed as if he could never make enough of me; but my mother unaccountably burst into tears, and said, "it was a very niggardly action," or some such expression, and that "she would rather it would please God to take me"—meaning (God help me) that I should die—"than that she should live to see me grow up *a mean man*," which shows the difference of parent from parent, and how some mothers are more harsh and intolerant to their children than some fathers; when we might expect quite the contrary.

My father, however, loaded me with presents from that time, which made me the envy of my school-fellows. As I felt this growing disposition in them, I naturally sought to avert it by all the means in my power; and from that time I used to eat my little packages of fruit, and other nice things, in a corner, so privately that I was never found out. Once, I remember, I had a huge apple sent me, of that sort which they call *cats'-heads*. I concealed this all day under my pillow; and at night, but not before I had ascertained that my bed-fellow was sound asleep,—which I did by pinching him rather smartly two or three times, which he seemed to perceive no more than a dead person, though once or twice he made a motion as if he would turn, which frightened me,—I say, when I had made all sure, I fell to work upon my apple; and, though it was as big as an ordinary man's two fists, I made shift to get through it before it was time to get up. And a more delicious feast I never made; thinking all night what a good parent I had (I mean my father) to send me so many nice things, when the poor lad that lay by me had no parent or friend in the world to send him anything nice; and thinking of his desolate condition, I munched and munched as silently as I could, that I might not set him a-longing if he overheard me.

And yet, for all this considerateness and attention to other people's feelings, I was never much a favourite with my schoolfellows; which I have often wondered at, seeing that I never defrauded any one of them of the value of a halfpenny, or told stories of them to their master, as some little lying boys would do, but was ready to do any of them all the services in my power, that were consistent with my own well-doing. I think nobody can be expected to go farther than that.

But I am detaining my reader too long in recording my juvenile days. It is time I should go forward to a season when it became natural that I should have some thoughts of marrying, and, as they say, settling in the world. Nevertheless, my reflections on what I may call the boyish period of my life may have their use to some readers. It is pleasant to trace the man in the boy; to observe shoots of generosity in those young years; and to watch the progress of liberal sentiments, and what I may call a genteel way of thinking, which is discernible in some children at a very early age, and usually lays the foundation of all that is praiseworthy in the manly character afterwards.

With the warmest inclinations towards that way of life, and a serious conviction of its superior advantages over a single one, it has been the strange infelicity of my lot never to have entered into the respectable estate of matrimony.

Yet I was once very near it.

I courted a young woman in my twenty-seventh year; for so early I began to feel symptoms of the tender passion! She was well-to-do in the world, as they call it; but yet not such a fortune as, all things considered, perhaps I might have pretended to. It was not my own choice altogether; but my mother very strongly pressed me to it. She was always putting it to me, that I had "comings-in sufficient,"—that I "need not stand upon a portion"; though the young woman, to do her justice, had considerable expectations, which yet did not quite come up to my mark, as I told you before.

My mother had this saying always in her mouth, that I had "money enough"; that it was time I enlarged my housekeeping, and to show a spirit befitting my circumstances. In short, what with her importunities, and my own desires in part co-operating,—for, as I said, I was not yet quite twenty-seven,—a time when the youthful feelings may be pardoned if they show a little impetuosity,—I resolved, I say, upon all these considerations, to set about the business of courting in right earnest. I was a young man then; and having a spice of romance in my character (as the reader has doubtless observed long ago), such as that sex is apt to be taken with, I had reason in no long time to think that my addresses were anything but disagreeable. Certainly the happiest part of a young man's life is the time when he is going a-courting. All the generous impulses are then awake, and he feels a double existence in participating his hopes and wishes with another being.

Return yet again for a brief moment, ye visionary views, transient enchantments! ye moonlight rambles with Cleora in the Silent Walk at Vauxhall (*N.B.*—About a mile from Birmingham, and resembling the gardens of that name near London, only that the price of admission is lower), when the nightingale has suspended her notes in June to listen to our loving discourses, while the moon was overhead! (for we generally used to take our tea at Cleora's mother's before we set out, not so much to save expenses as to avoid the publicity of a repast in the gardens,—coming in much about the time of half-price, as they call it,) ye soft intercommunions of soul, when, exchanging mutual vows, we prattled of coming felicities! The loving disputes we have had under those trees, when this house (planning our future settlement) was rejected, because, though cheap, it was dull; and the other house was given up, because, though agreeably situated, it was too high-rented!—one was too much in the heart of the town, another was too far from business.

These minutiae will seem impertinent to the aged and prudent. I write them only to the young. Young lovers, and passionate as being young (such were Cleora and I then), alone can understand me. After some weeks wasted, as I may now call it, in this sort of amorous colloquy, we at length fixed upon the house in the High Street, No. 203, just vacated by the death of Mr. Hutton of this town, for our future residence. I had all the time lived in lodgings (only renting a shop for business), to be near my mother,—near, I say: not in the same house: for that would have been to introduce confusion into our housekeeping, which it was desirable to keep separate. Oh, the loving wrangles, the endearing differences, I had with Cleora, before we could quite make up our minds to the house that was to receive us!—I pretending, for argument's sake, the rent was too high, and she insisting that the taxes were moderate in proportion; and love at last reconciling us in the same choice. I think at that time, moderately speaking, she might have had anything out of me for asking. I do not, nor shall ever, regret that my character at that time was marked with a tinge of prodigality. Age comes fast enough upon us, and, in its good time, will prune away all that is inconvenient in these excesses. Perhaps it is right that it should do so.

Matters, as I said, were ripening to a conclusion between us, only the house was yet not absolutely taken, some necessary arrangements, which the ardour of my youthful impetuosity could hardly brook at that time (love and youth will be precipitate),—some preliminary arrangements, I say, with the landlord, respecting fixtures, —very necessary things to be considered in a young man about to settle in the world, though not very accordant with the impatient state of my then passions,—some obstacles about the valuation of the fixtures,—had hitherto precluded (and I shall always think providentially) my final closes with his offer; when one of those accidents, which, unimportant in themselves, often arise to give a turn to the most serious intentions of our life, intervened, and put an end at once to my projects of wiving, and of housekeeping.

I was never much given to theatrical entertainments; that is, at no time of my life was I ever what they call a regular play-goer: but on some occasion of a benefit-night, which was expected to be very productive, and indeed turned out so, Cleora expressing a desire to be present, I could do no less than offer, as I did very willingly, to squire her and her mother to the pit. At that time it was not customary in our town for tradesfolk, except some of the very topping ones, to sit, as they now do, in the boxes.

At the time appointed I waited upon the ladies, who had brought with them a young man, a distant relation, whom, it seems, they had invited to be of the party. This a little disconcerted me, as I had about me barely silver enough to pay for our three selves at the door, and did not at first know that their relation had proposed paying for himself. However, to do the young man justice, he not only paid for himself, but for the old lady besides; leaving me only to pay for two, as it were. In our passage to the theatre the notice of Cleora was attracted to some orange wenches that stood about the doors vending their commodities. She was leaning on my arm; and I could feel her every now and then giving me a nudge, as it is called, which I afterwards discovered were hints that I should buy some oranges.

It seems, it is a custom at Birmingham, and perhaps in other places, when a gentleman treats ladies to the play,—especially when a full night is expected, and that the house will be inconveniently warm,—to provide them with this kind of fruit, oranges being esteemed for their cooling property. But how could I guess at that, never having treated ladies to a play before, and being, as I said, quite a novice at entertainments of this kind?

At last, she spoke plain out, and begged that I would buy some of "those oranges," pointing to a particular barrow. But, when I came to examine the fruit, I did not think the quality of it was answerable to the price. In this way I handled several baskets of them; but something in them all displeased me. Some had thin rinds, and some were plainly over-ripe, which is as great a fault as not being ripe enough; and I could not (what they call) make a bargain.

While I stood haggling with the woman, secretly determining to put off my purchase till I should get within the theatre, where I expected we should have better choice, the young man, the cousin (who, it seems had left us without my missing him), came running to us with his pockets stuffed out with oranges, inside and out, as they say. It seems, not liking the look of the barrow-fruit any more than myself, he had slipped away to an eminent fruiterer's, about three doors distant, which I never had the sense to think of, and had laid out a matter of two shillings in some of the best St. Michael's, I think I ever tasted.

What a little hinge, as I said before, the most important affairs in life may turn upon ! The mere inadvertence to the fact that there was an eminent fruiterer's within three doors of us, though we had just passed it without the thought once occurring to me, which he had taken advantage of, lost me the affection of my Cleora. From that time she visibly cooled towards me ; and her partiality was as visibly transferred to this cousin. I was long unable to account for this change in her behaviour ; when one day, accidently discoursing of oranges to my mother, alone, she let drop a sort of reproach to me, as if I had offended Cleora by my *nearness* as she called it, that evening.

Even now, when Cleora has been wedded some years to that same officious relation, as I may call him, I can hardly be persuaded that such a trifle could have been the motive for her inconstancy ; for could she suppose that I would sacrifice my dearest hopes in her to the paltry sum of two shillings, when I was going to treat her to the play, and her mother too (an expense of more than four times that amount), if the young man had not interfered to pay for the latter, as I mentioned ?

But the caprices of the sex are past finding out : and I begin to think my mother was in the right ; for doubtless women know women better than we can pretend to know them.

JAMES MORIER
1780–1849

HAJJI BABA AND THE STOLEN MONEY

My father having died without a will, I was, of course, proclaimed his sole heir without any opposition, and consequently all those who had aspired to be sharers of his property, baulked by my unexpected appearance, immediately withdrew to vent their disappointment in abusing me. They represented me as a wretch devoid of all respect for my parents, as one without religion, an adventurer in the world, and the companion of lûties and wandering dervishes.

As I had no intention of remaining at Ispahan, I treated their endeavours to hurt me with contempt, and consoled myself by giving them a full return of all their scurrility, by expressions which neither they nor their fathers had ever heard—expressions which I had picked up from amongst the illustrious characters with whom I had passed the first years of my youth.

When we were left to ourselves, my mother and I, after having bewailed in sufficiently pathetic language, she the death of a husband, I the loss of a father, the following conversation took place:

"Now tell me, O my mother—for there can be no secrets between us—tell me what was the state of Kerbelai Hassan's concerns. He loved you, and confided in you, and you must therefore be better acquainted with them than any one else."

"What do I know of them, my son?" said she, in great haste, and seeming confusion.

I stopped her, to continue my speech. "You know that, according to the law, his heir is bound to pay his debts: they must be ascertained. Then, the expenses of the funeral are to be defrayed; they will be considerable; and at present I am as destitute of means as on the day you gave me birth. To meet all this, money is necessary, or else both mine and my father's name will be disgraced among men, and my enemies will not fail to overcome me. He must have been reputed wealthy, or else his deathbed would never have been surrounded by that host of blood-suckers and time-servers which have been driven away by my presence. You, my mother, must tell me where he was accustomed to deposit his ready cash; who were, or who are likely to be, his debtors; and what might be his possessions, besides those which are apparent."

"Oh, Allah!" exclaimed she, "what words are these? Your father was a poor, good man, who had neither money nor possessions. Money, indeed! We had dry bread to eat, and that was all! Now and then, after the arrival of a great caravan, when heads to be shaved were plentiful, and his business brisk, we indulged in our dish of rice, and our skewer of kabob, but otherwise we lived like beggars. A bit of bread, a morsel of cheese, an onion, a basin of sour curds—that was our daily fare; and, under these circumstances can you ask me for money, ready money too? There is this house, which you see and know; then his shop, with its furniture; and when I have said that, I have nearly said all. You are just arrived in time, my son, to step into your father's shoes, and take up his business; and *Inshallah*, please God, may your hand be fortunate! may it never cease wagging, from one year's end to the other!"

"This is very strange!" exclaimed I, in my turn. "Fifty years', and more, hard and unceasing toil! and nothing to show for it! This is incredible! We must call in the diviners."

"The diviners?" said my mother, in some agitation; "of what use can they be? They are only called in when a thief is to be discovered. You will not proclaim your mother a thief, Hajji, will you? Go, make inquiries of your friend, and your father's friend, the *âkhon* [schoolmaster]. He is acquainted with the whole of the concerns, and I am sure he will repeat what I have said."

"You do not speak amiss, mother," said I. "The âkhon probably does know what were my father's last wishes, for he appeared to be the principal director in his dying moments; and he may tell me, if money there was left, where it is to be found."

Accordingly I went straightway to seek the old man, whom I found seated precisely in the very same corner of the little parish mosque, surrounded by his scholars, in which some twenty years before I myself had received his instructions. As soon as he saw me he dismissed his scholars, saying that my footsteps were fortunate, and that others, as well as himself, should partake of the pleasure which I was sure to dispense wherever I went.

"Ahi, âkhon," said I, "do not laugh at my beard. My good fortune has entirely forsaken me; and even now, when I had hoped that my destiny, in depriving me of my father, had made up the loss by giving me wealth, I am likely to be disappointed, and to turn out a greater beggar than ever."

"*Allah kerim*, God is merciful," said the schoolmaster; and lifting up his eyes to heaven, whilst he placed his hands on his knees, with their palms uppermost, he exclaimed, " Oh, Allah, whatever is, thou art it." Then addressing himself to me, he said, " Yes, my son, such is the world, and such will it ever be, as long as man shuts not up his heart from all human desires. Want nothing, seek nothing, and nothing will seek you."

" How long have you been a Sûfi," said I, " that you talk after this manner ? I can speak on that subject also, since my evil star led me to Kom, but now I am engrossed with other matters." I then informed him of the object of my visit, and requested him to tell me what he knew of my father's concerns.

Upon this question he coughed, and, making up a face of great wisdom, went through a long string of oaths and professions, and finished by repeating what I had heard from my mother ; namely, that he believed my father to have died possessed of no (*nagd*) ready cash (for that, after all, was the immediate object of my search) ; and what his other property was, he reminded me that I knew as well as himself.

I remained mute for some time with disappointment, and then expressed my surprise in strong terms. My father, I was aware, was too good a Mussulman to have lent out his money upon interest ; for I recollected a circumstance, when I was quite a youth, which proved it. Osman Aga, my first master, wanting to borrow a sum from him, for which he offered an enormous interest, my father put his conscience into the hands of a rigid mollah, who told him that the precepts of the Koran entirely forbade it. Whether since that time he had relaxed his principles, I could not say ; but I was assured that he always set his face against the unlawful practice of taking interest, and that he died as he had lived, a perfect model of a true believer.

I left the mosque in no very agreeable mood, and took my way to the spot where I had made my first appearance in life—namely, my father's shop—turning over in my mind as I went what steps I should take to secure a future livelihood. To remain at Ispahan was out of the question—the place and the inhabitants were odious to me ; therefore, it was only left me to dispose of everything that was now my own, and to return to the capital, which, after all, I knew to be the best market for an adventurer like myself. However, I could not relinquish the thought that my father had died possessed of some ready money, and suspicions would haunt my mind in spite of me, that foul play was going on somewhere or other. I was at a loss to whom to address myself, unknown as I was in the city, and I was thinking of making my case known to the cadi, when, approaching the gate of the caravanserai, I was accosted by the old capiji.

" Peace be unto you, Aga ! " said he ; " may you live many years, and may your abundance increase! My eyes are enlightened by seeing you."

"Are your spirits so well wound up, Ali Mohamed," said I, in return, "that you choose to treat me thus? As for the abundance you talk of, 'tis abundance of grief, for I have none other that I know of. Och!" said I, sighing, "my liver has become water, and my soul has withered up."

"What news is this?" said the old man. "Your father (peace be unto him!) is just dead—you are his heir—you are young, and, *Mashallah!* you are handsome—your wit is not deficient: what do you want more?"

"I am his heir, 'tis true; but what of that—what advantage can accrue to me, when I only get an old mud-built house, with some worn-out carpets, some pots and pans, and decayed furniture, and yonder shop with a brass basin and a dozen of razors? Let me spit upon such an inheritance."

"But where is your money, your ready cash, Hajji? Your father (God be with him!) had the reputation of being as great a niggard of his money as he was liberal of his soap. Everybody knows that he amassed much, and never passed a day without adding to his store."

"That may be true," said I; "but what advantage will that be to me, since I cannot find where it was deposited? My mother says that he had none—the âkhon repeats the same—I am no conjurer to discover the truth. I had it in my mind to go to the cadi."

"To the cadi?" said Ali Mohamed. "Heaven forbid! Go not to him—you might as well knock at the gate of this caravanserai when I am absent, as try to get justice from him, without a heavy fee. No, he sells it by the miscal, at a heavy price, and very light weight does he give after all. He does not turn over one leaf of the Koran until his fingers have been well plated with gold, and if those who have appropriated your father's sacks are to be your opponents, do not you think that they will drain them into the cadi's lap, rather than he should pronounce in your favour?"

"What then is to be done?" said I. "Perhaps the diviners might give me some help."

"There will be no harm in that," answered the doorkeeper. "I have known them make great discoveries during my service in this caravanserai. Merchants have frequently lost their money, and found it again through their means. It was only in the attack of the Turcomans, when much property was stolen, that they were completely at their wits' end. Ah! that was a strange event. It brought much misery on my head; for some were wicked enough to say that I was their accomplice, and, what is more extraordinary, that you were amongst them, Hajji!—for it was on account of your name, which the dog's son made use of to induce me to open the gate, that the whole mischief was produced."

Lucky was it for me that old Ali Mohamed was very dull of sight, or else he would have remarked strange alterations in my features when he made these observations. However, our conference ended by his promising to send me the most expert diviner of Ispahan; "a man," said he, "who would entice a piece of gold out of the earth if buried twenty gez deep, or even if it was hid in the celebrated well of Kashan."

The next morning, soon after the first prayers, a little man came into my room, whom I soon discovered to be the diviner. He was a humpback, with an immense head, with eyes so wonderfully brilliant, and a countenance so intelligent, that I felt he could look through and through me at one glance. He wore a dervish's cap, from under which flowed a profusion of jet-black hair, which, added to a thick bush of a beard, gave an imposing expression to his features. His eyes, which by a quick action of his eyelid (whether real or affected, I know not) twinkled like stars, made the monster, who was not taller than a good bludgeon, look like a little demon.

He began by questioning me very narrowly; made me relate every circumstance of my life—particularly since my return to Ispahan—inquired who were my father's greatest apparent friends and associates, and what my own suspicions led me to conclude. In short, he searched into every particular, with the same scrutiny that a doctor would in tracing and unravelling an intricate disorder.

When he had well pondered over everything that I had unfolded, he then required to be shown the premises which my father principally inhabited. My mother having gone that morning to the bath, I was enabled, unknown to her, to take him into her apartments, where he requested me to leave him to himself, in order that he might obtain a knowledge of the localities necessary to the discoveries which he hoped to make. He remained there a full quarter of an hour, and when he came out requested me to collect those who were in my father's intimacy, and in the habit of much frequenting the house, and that he would return, they being assembled, and begin his operations.

Without saying a word to my mother about the diviner, I requested her to invite her most intimate friends for the following morning, it being my intention to give them a breakfast; and I myself begged the attendance of the âkhon, the capiji, my father's nephew by his first wife, and a brother of my mother, with others who had free entrance into the house.

They came punctually; and when they had partaken of such fare as I could place before them, they were informed of the predicament in which I stood, and that I had requested their attendance to be witnesses to the endeavours of the diviner to discover where my father was wont to keep his money, of the existence of which, somewhere or other, nobody who knew him could doubt. I looked into each man's face as I made this speech, hoping to remark some expression which might throw a light upon my suspicions, but everybody seemed ready to help my investigation, and maintained the most unequivocal innocence of countenance.

At length the dervish, Teez Negah (for that was the name of the conjurer), was introduced, accompanied by an attendant who carried something wrapt up in a handkerchief. Having ordered the women in the anderûn to keep themselves veiled, because they would probably soon be visited by men, I requested the dervish to begin his operations.

He first looked at every one present with great earnestness, but more particularly fixed his basilisk eyes upon the âkhon, who evidently could not stand the scrutiny, but exclaimed "*Allah il Allah!*"—there is but one God,—stroked down his face and beard, and blew first over one shoulder and then over the other, by way of keeping off the evil spirit. Some merriment was raised at his expense; but he did not appear to be in a humour to meet any one's jokes.

After this, the dervish called to his attendant, who from the handkerchief drew forth a brass cup of a plain surface, but written all over with quotations from the Koran, having reference to the crime of stealing, and defrauding the orphan of his lawful property. He was a man of few words, and simply saying, "In the name of Allah, the All-wise, and All-seeing," he placed the cup on the floor, treating it with much reverence, both in touch and in manner.

He then said to the lookers-on, "*Inshallah*, it will lead us at once to the spot where the money of the deceased Kerbelai Hassan (may God show him mercy!) is, or was, deposited."

We all looked at each other, some with expressions of incredulity, others with unfeigned belief, when he bent himself towards the cup, and with little shoves and pats of his hand he impelled it forwards, exclaiming all the time, "See, see, the road it takes. Nothing can stop it. It will go in spite of me. *Mashallah, Mashallah!*"

We followed him until he reached the door of the harem, where we knocked for admittance. After some negotiation it was opened, and there we found a crowd of women (many of whom had only loosely thrown on their veils) waiting with much impatience to witness the feats which this wonderful cup was to perform.

"Make way," said the diviner to the women who stood in his path, as he took his direction towards a corner of the court, upon which the windows of the room opened—"Make way; nothing can stop my guide."

A woman whom I recognised to be my mother, stopped his progress several times, until he was obliged to admonish her, with some bitterness, to keep clear of him.

"Do you not see," said he, "we are on the Lord's business? Justice will be done in spite of the wickedness of man."

At length he reached a distant corner, where it was plain that the earth had been recently disturbed, and there he stopped.

"*Bismillah*, in the name of Allah," said he, "let all present stand around me, and mark what I do." He dug into the ground with his dagger, clawed the soil away with his hands, and discovered a place in which were the remains of an earthen vessel, and the marks near it of there having been another.

"Here," said he, "here the money was, but is no more." Then taking up his cup, he appeared to caress it, and make much of it, calling it his little uncle and his little soul.

Every one stared. All cried out, "*ajaib*," wonderful; and the little humpback was looked upon as a supernatural being.

The capiji, who was accustomed to such discoveries, was the only one who had the readiness to say, "But where is the thief? You have shown us where the game lay, but we want you to catch it for us: the thief and the money, or the money without the thief—that is what we want."

"Softly, my friend," said the dervish to the capiji, "don't jump so soon from the crime to the criminal. We have a medicine for every disorder, although it may take some time to work."

He then cast his eyes upon the company present, twinkling them all the while in quick flashes, and said, "I am sure every one here will be happy to be clear of suspicion, and will agree to what I shall propose. The operation is simple and soon over."

"*Elbettah*," certainly; "*Belli*," yes; "*Een che har est?*" what word is this? was heard to issue from every mouth, and I requested the dervish to proceed.

He called again to his servant, who produced a small bag, whilst he again took the cup under his charge.

"This bag," said the diviner, "contains some old rice. I will put a small handful of it into each person's mouth, which they will forthwith chew. Let those who cannot break it beware, for Eblis is near at hand."

Upon this, placing us in a row, he filled each person's mouth with rice, and all immediately began to masticate. Being the complainant, of course I was exempt from the ordeal; and my mother, who chose to make common cause with me, also stood out of the ranks. The quick-sighted dervish would not allow of this, but made her undergo the trial with the rest, saying, "The property we seek is not yours, but your son's. Had he been your husband, it would be another thing." She agreed to his request, though with bad grace, and then all the jaws were set to wagging, some looking upon it as a good joke, others thinking it a hard trial to the nerves. As fast as each person had ground his mouthful, he called to the dervish and showed the contents of his mouth.

All had now proved their innocence excepting the âkhon and my mother. The former, whose face exhibited the picture of an affected cheerfulness with great nervous apprehension, kept mumbling his rice, and turning it over between his jaws, until he cried out in a querulous tone, " Why do you give me this stuff to chew ? I am old, and have no teeth : it is impossible for me to reduce the grain " ; and then he spat it out. My mother, too, complained of her want of power to break the hard rice, and did the same thing. A silence ensued, which made us all look with more attention than usual upon them, and it was only broken by a time-server of my mother, an old woman, who cried out, " What child's play is this ? Who has ever heard of a son treating his mother with this disrespect, and his old schoolmaster, too ? Shame, shame !—let us go—he is probably the thief himself."

Upon this the dervish said, " Are we fools and asses, to be dealt with in this manner ?—either there was money in that corner, or there was not—either there are thieves in the world, or there are not. This man and this woman," pointing to the âkhon and my mother, " have not done that which all the rest have done. Perhaps they say the truth, they are old, and cannot break the hard grain. Nobody says that they stole the money—they themselves know that best," said he, looking at them through and through ; " but the famous diviner, Hezarfun, he who was truly called the bosom friend to the Great Bear, and the confidant of the planet Saturn,—he who could tell all that a man has ever thought, thinks, or will think,—he hath said that the trial by rice among cowards was the best of all tests of a man's honesty. Now, my friends, from all I have remarked, none of you are slayers of lions, and fear is easily produced among you. However, if you doubt my skill in this instance, I will propose a still easier trial—one which commits nobody, which works like a charm upon the mind, and makes the thief come forward of his own accord, to ease his conscience and purse of its ill-gotten wealth, at one and the same time. I propose the *Hak reezî*, or the heaping up earth. Here in this corner I will make a mound, and will pray so fervently this very night, that, by the blessing of Allah, the Hajji," pointing to me, " will find his money buried in it to-morrow at this hour. Whoever is curious, let them be present, and if something be not discovered, I will give him a miscal of hair from my beard."

He then set to work, and heaped up earth in a corner, whilst the lookers-on loitered about, discussing what they had just seen ; some examining me and the dervish as children of the evil spirit, whilst others again began to think as much of my mother and the schoolmaster. The company then dispersed, most of them promising to return the following morning, at the appointed time, to witness the search into the heap of earth.

I must own that I began now to look upon the restoration of my property as hopeless. The diviner's skill had certainly discovered that money had been buried in my father's house, and he had succeeded in raising ugly suspicions in my mind against two persons whom I felt it to be a sin to suspect; but I doubted whether he could do more.

However, he appeared again on the following morning, accompanied by the capiji, and by several of those who had been present at the former scene. The âkhon, however, did not appear, and my mother was also absent, upon pretext of being obliged to visit a sick friend. We proceeded in a body to the mound, and the dervish having made a holy invocation, he approached it with a sort of mysterious respect.

"Now we shall see," said he, "whether the Gins and the Peris have been at work this night"; and, exclaiming "*Bismillah!*" he dug into the earth with his dagger.

Having thrown off some of the soil, a large stone appeared, and having disengaged that, to the astonishment of all, and to my extreme delight, a canvas bag, well filled, was discovered.

"Oh, my soul! oh, my heart!" exclaimed the humpback, as he seized upon the bag, "you see that the dervish Teez Negah is not a man to lose a hair of his beard. There, there," said he, putting it into my hand, "there is your property: go, and give thanks that you have fallen into my hands, and do not forget my *hak sai* or my commission."

Everybody crowded round me, whilst I broke open the wax that was affixed to the mouth of the bag, upon which I recognised the impression of my father's seal; and eagerness was marked on all their faces as I untied the twine with which it was fastened. My countenance dropped woefully when I found that it contained only silver, for I had made up my mind to see gold. Five hundred reals was the sum of which I became the possessor, out of which I counted fifty, and presented them to the ingenious discoverer of them. "There," said I, "may your house prosper! If I were rich I would give you more: and although this is evidently but a small part of what my father (God be with him!) must have accumulated, still, again I say, may your house prosper, and many sincere thanks to you."

The dervish was satisfied with my treatment of him, and took his leave, and I was soon after left by the rest of the company, the capiji alone remaining. "Famous business we have made of it this morning," said he. "Did I not say that these diviners performed wonders?"

"Yes," said I, "yes, it is wonderful, for I never thought his operations would have come to anything."

Impelled by a spirit of cupidity, now that I had seen money glistening before me, I began to complain that I had received so little, and again expressed to Ali Mohamed my wish of bringing the case before the cadi; "for," said I, "if I am entitled to these five hundred reals, I am entitled to all my father left; and you will acknowledge that this must be but a very small part of his savings."

"Friend," said he, "listen to the words of an old man. Keep what you have got, and be content. In going before the cadi, the first thing you will have to do will be to give of your certain, to get at that most cursed of all property, the uncertain. Be assured that, after having drained you of your four hundred and fifty reals, and having got five hundred from your opponents, you will have the satisfaction to hear him tell you both to 'go in peace, and do not trouble the city with your disputes.' Have not you lived long enough in the world to have learnt this common saying—'Every one's teeth are blunted by acids, except the cadi's, which are by sweets'? The cadi who takes five cucumbers as a bribe will admit any evidence for ten beds of melons."

After some deliberation, I determined to take the advice of the capiji; for it was plain that, if I intended to prosecute any one, it could only be my mother and the âkhon; and to do that, I should raise such a host of enemies, and give rise to such unheard-of scandal, that perhaps I should only get stoned by the populace for my pains.

MARY RUSSELL MITFORD
1787–1855

THE ELECTION

A FEW years back, a gentleman of the name of Danby came to reside in a small decayed borough town—whether in Wiltshire or Cornwall matters not to our story, although in one of those counties the aforesaid town was probably situate, being what is called a close borough, the joint property of two noble families.

Mr. Danby was evidently a man of large fortune, and that fortune as evidently acquired in trade—indeed he made no more secret of the latter circumstance than the former. He built himself a large, square, red house, equally ugly and commodious, just without the town; walled in a couple of acres of ground for a kitchen-garden; kept a heavy one-horse chaise, a stout pony, and a brace of greyhounds; and having furnished his house solidly and handsomely, and arranged his domestic affairs to his heart's content, began to look about amongst his neighbours; scraped acquaintance with the lawyer, the apothecary, and the principal tradesmen; subscribed to the reading-room and the billiard-room; became a member of the bowling-green and the cricket club, and took as lively an interest in the affairs of his new residence as if he had been born and bred in the borough.

Now this interest, however agreeable to himself, was by no means equally conducive to the quiet and comfort of the place. Mr. Danby was a little, square, dark man, with a cocked-up nose, a good-humoured but very knowing smile, a pair of keen black eyes, a loud voluble speech, and a prodigious activity both of mind and body. His very look betokened his character—and that character was one not uncommon among the middle ranks of Englishmen.

In short, besides being, as he often boasted, a downright John Bull, the gentleman was a reformer, zealous and uncompromising as ever attended a dinner at the Crown and Anchor, or made a harangue in Palace Yard. He read Cobbett; had his own scheme for the redemption of tithes; and a plan, which, not understanding, I am sorry I cannot undertake to explain, for clearing off the national debt without loss or injury to anybody.

Besides these great matters, which may rather be termed the theorique than the practique of reform, and which are at least perfectly inoffensive, Mr. Danby condescended to smaller and more worrying observances, and was, indeed, so strict and jealous a guardian of the purity of the corporation, and the incorruptibility of the vestry, that an alderman could not wag a finger, or a churchwarden stir a foot, without being called to account by this vigilant defender of the rights, liberties, and purses of the people.

He was beyond a doubt the most troublesome man in the parish, and that is a wide word. In the matter of reports and inquiries Mr. Hume was but a type of him. He would mingle economy with a parish dinner, and talk of retrenchment at the mayor's feast; brought an action under the Turnpike Act against the clerk and treasurer of the commissioners of the road; commenced a suit in Chancery with the trustees of the charity school; and, finally, threatened to open the borough—that is to say, to support any candidate who should offer to oppose the nominees of the two great families, the one Whig, and the other Tory, who now possessed the two seats in parliament as quietly as their own hereditary estates;—an experiment which recent instances of successful opposition in other places rendered not a little formidable to the noble owners.

What added considerably to the troublesome nature of Mr. Danby's inquisitions was the general cleverness, ability, and information of the individual. He was not a man of classical education, and knew little of books; but with things he was especially conversant. Although very certain that Mr. Danby had been in business, nobody could guess what that business had been. None came amiss to him. He handled the rule and the yard with equal dexterity; astonished the butcher by his insight into the mysteries of fattening and dealing; and the grocer by his familiarity with the sugar and coffee markets; disentangled the perplexities of the confused mass of figures in the parish books with the dexterity of a sworn accountant; and was so great upon points of law, so ready and accurate in quoting reports, cases, and precedents, that he would certainly have passed for a retired attorney, but for the zeal and alertness with which, at his own expense, he was apt to rush into lawsuits.

With so remarkable a genius for turmoil, it is not to be doubted that Mr. Danby, in spite of many excellent and sterling qualities, succeeded in drawing upon himself no small degree of odium. The whole corporation were officially his enemies; but his principal opponent, or rather the person whom he considered as his principal opponent, was Mr. Cardonnel, the rector of the parish, who, besides several disputes pending between them (one especially respecting the proper situation of the church organ, the placing of which harmonious instrument kept the whole town in discord for a twelvemonth), was married to the Lady Elizabeth, sister of the Earl of B., one of the patrons of the borough ; and being, as well as his wife, a very popular and amiable character, was justly regarded by Mr. Danby as one of the chief obstacles to his projected reform. Whilst, however, our reformer was, from the most patriotic motives, doing his best or his worst to dislike Mr. Cardonnel, events of a very different nature were gradually operating to bring them together.

Mr. Danby's family consisted of a wife—a quiet lady-like woman, with very ill-health, who did little else than walk from her bed to her sofa, eat water-gruel and drink soda-water—and of an only daughter, who was, in a word, the very apple of her father's eye.

Rose Danby was indeed a daughter of whom any father might have been proud. Of middle height and exquisite symmetry, with a rich, dark, glowing complexion, a profusion of glossy, curling, raven hair, large affectionate black eyes, and a countenance at once so sweet and so spirited, that its constant expression was like that which a smile gives to other faces.

Her temper and understanding were in exact keeping with such a countenance—playful, gentle, clever, and kind ; and her accomplishments and acquirements of the very highest order. When her father entered on his new residence she had just completed her fifteenth year ; and he, unable longer to dispense with the pleasure of her society, took her from the excellent school near London, at which she had hitherto been placed, and determined that her education should be finished by masters at home.

It so happened, that this little town contained one celebrated artist, a professor of dancing, who kept a weekly academy for young ladies, which was attended by half the families of gentility in the county. M. Le Grand (for the dancing master was a little lively Frenchman) was delighted with Rose. He declared that she was his best pupil, his very best, the best that ever he had in his life.

" Mais voyez, donc, Monsieur ? " said he one day to her father, who would have scorned to know the French for " how d'ye do " ; " Voyez, comme elle met de l'aplomb, de la force, de la nettete, dans ses entrechats ! Qu'elle est leste, et legere, et petrie de graces, la petite ! "

And Mr. Danby, comprehending only that the artist was praising his darling, swore that Monsieur was a good fellow, and returned the compliment after the English fashion, by sending him a haunch of venison the next day.

But M. Le Grand was not the only admirer whom Rose met with at the dancing-school. It chanced that Mr. Cardonnel also had an only daughter, a young person about the same age, bringing up under the eye of her mother, and a constant attendant at the professor's academy. The two girls, nearly of a height, and both good dancers, were placed together as partners; and being almost equally prepossessing in person and manner (for Mary Cardonnel was a sweet, delicate, fair creature, whose mild blue eyes seemed appealing to the kindness of every one they looked upon), took an immediate and lasting fancy to each other; shook hands at meeting and parting, smiled whenever their glances chanced to encounter; and soon began to exchange a few kind and hurried words in the pauses of the dance, and to hold more continuous chat at the conclusion.

And Lady Elizabeth, almost as much charmed with Rose as her daughter, seeing in the lovely little girl everything to like, and nothing to disapprove, encouraged and joined in the acquaintance; attended with a motherly care to her cloaking and shawling; took her home in her own carriage when it rained; and finally waylaid Mr. Danby, who always came himself to fetch his darling, and with her bland and gracious smile requested the pleasure of Miss Danby's company to a party of young people, which she was about to give on the occasion of her daughter's birthday. I am afraid that our sturdy reformer was going to say, No! But Rose's "Oh, papa!" was irresistible; and to the party she went.

After this the young people became every day more intimate. Lady Elizabeth waited on Mrs. Danby, and Mrs. Danby returned the call; but her state of health precluded visiting, and her husband, who piqued himself on firmness and consistency, contrived, though with some violence to his natural kindness of temper, to evade the friendly advances and invitations of the rector.

The two girls, however, saw one another almost every day. It was a friendship like that of Rosalind and Celia, whom, by the way, they severally resembled in temper and character—Rose having much of the brilliant gaiety of the one fair cousin, and Mary the softer and gentler charm of the other. They rode, walked, and sung together; were never happy asunder; played the same music; read the same books; dressed alike; worked for each other; and interchanged their own little property of trinkets and flowers, with a generosity that seemed only emulous which should give most.

At first, Mr. Danby was a little jealous of Rose's partiality to the rectory; but she was so fond of him, so attentive to his pleasures, that he could not find in his heart to check hers; and when, after a long and dangerous illness, with which the always delicate Mary was affected, Mr. Cardonnel went to him, and with tears streaming down his cheeks, told him he believed that, under Providence, he owed his daughter's life to Rose's unwearying care, the father's heart was fairly vanquished; he wrung the good rector's hand, and never grumbled at her long visits again.

Lady Elizabeth, also, had her share in producing this change of feeling, by presenting him in return for innumerable baskets of peaches and melons and hot-house grapes (in the culture of which he was curious) with a portrait of Rose, drawn by herself—a strong and beautiful likeness, with his own favourite greyhound at her feet; a picture which he would not have exchanged for the "Transfiguration."

Perhaps, too, consistent as he thought himself, he was not without an unconscious respect for the birth and station which he affected to despise, and was, at least, as proud of the admiration which his daughter excited in those privileged circles, as of the sturdy independence which he exhibited by keeping aloof from them in his own person. Certain it is, that his spirit of reformation insensibly relaxed, particularly towards the rector; and that he not only ceded the contested point of the organ, but presented a splendid set of pulpit-hangings to the church itself.

Time wore on; Rose had refused half the offers of gentility in the town and neighbourhood; her heart appeared to be invulnerable. Her less affluent and less brilliant friend was generally understood (and as Rose, on hearing the report, did not contradict it, the rumour passed for certainty) to be engaged to a nephew of her mother's, Sir William Frampton, a young gentleman of splendid fortune, who had lately passed much time at his fair place in the neighbourhood.

Time wore on; and Rose was now nineteen, when an event occurred which threatened a grievous interruption to her happiness. The Earl of B.'s member died; his nephew, Sir William Frampton, supported by his uncle's powerful interest, offered himself for the borough; an independent candidate started at the same time; and Mr. Danby felt himself compelled, by his vaunted consistency, to insist on his daughter's renouncing her visits to the rectory, at least until after the termination of the election. Rose wept and pleaded, pleaded and wept, in vain. Her father was obdurate; and she, after writing a most affectionate note to Mary Cardonnel, retired to her own bedroom in very bad spirits, and, perhaps, for the first time in her life, in very bad humour.

About half an hour afterwards, Sir William Frampton and Mr. Cardonnel called at the red house.

"We are come, Mr. Danby," said the rector, "to solicit your interest."

"Nay, nay, my good friend," returned the reformer, "you know that my interest is promised, and that I cannot with any consistency——"

"To solicit your interest with Rose——" resumed his reverence.

"With Rose!" interrupted Mr. Danby.

"Ay—for the gift of her heart and hand—that being, I believe, the suffrage which my good nephew here is most anxious to secure," rejoined Mr. Cardonnel.

"With Rose," again ejaculated Mr. Danby: "why, I thought that your daughter——"

"The gipsy has not told you, then!" replied the rector. "Why, William and she have been playing the parts of Romeo and Juliet for these six months past."

"My Rose!" again exclaimed Mr. Danby. "Why, Rose! Rose! I say!" and the astonished father rushed out of the room, and returned the next minute, holding the blushing girl by the arm. "Rose, do you love this young man?"

"Oh, papa!" said Rose.

"Will you marry him?"

"Oh, papa!"

"Do you wish me to tell him that you will not marry him?"

To this question Rose returned no answer; she only blushed the deeper, and looked down with a half smile. "Take her, then," resumed Mr. Danby; "I see the girl loves you. I can't vote for you, though, for I've promised, and, you know, my good sir, that an honest man's word——"

"I don't want your vote, my dear sir," interrupted Sir William Frampton; "I don't ask for your vote, although the loss of it may cost me my seat, and my uncle his borough. This is the election that I care about, the only election worth caring about. Is it not, my own sweet Rose?—the election, of which the object lasts for life, and the result is happiness. That's the election worth caring about. Is it not, mine own Rose!"

And Rose blushed an affirmative; and Mr. Danby shook his intended son-in-law's hand, until he almost wrung it off, repeating at every moment, "I can't vote for you, for a man must be consistent, but you're the best fellow in the world, and you shall have my Rose. And Rose will be a great lady," continued the delighted father; "my little Rose will be a great lady after all!"

THOMAS INGOLDSBY
(R. H. BARHAM)
1788–1845

THE LADY ROHESIA

THE Lady Rohesia lay on her death-bed !

So said the doctor, and doctors are generally allowed to be judges in these matters ; besides, Doctor Butts was the Court Physician : he carried a crutch-handled staff, with its cross of the blackest ebony —*raison de plus*.

" Is there no hope, Doctor ? " said Beatrice Grey.

" Is there no hope ? " said Everard Ingoldsby.

" Is there no hope ? " said Sir Guy de Montgomeri. He was the Lady Rohesia's husband ; he spoke the last.

The doctor shook his head. He looked at the disconsolate widower *in posse*, then at the hour-glass ; its waning sand seemed sadly to shadow forth the sinking pulse of his patient. Dr. Butts was a very learned man. " *Ars longa, vita brevis !* " said Doctor Butts.

" I am very sorry to hear it," quoth Sir Guy de Montgomeri.

Sir Guy was a brave knight, and a tall ; but he was no scholar.

" Alas ! my poor sister ! " sighed Ingoldsby.

" Alas ! my poor mistress ! " sobbed Beatrice.

Sir Guy neither sighed nor sobbed ; his grief was too deep-seated for outward manifestation.

" And how long, Doctor—— ? " The afflicted husband could not finish the sentence.

Dr. Butts withdrew his hand from the wrist of the dying lady. He pointed to the horologe ; scarcely a quarter of its sand remained in the upper moiety. Again he shook his head ; the eye of the patient waxed dimmer, the rattling in the throat increased.

" What's become of Father Francis ? " whimpered Beatrice.

" The last consolations of the church——" suggested Everard.

A darker shade came over the brow of Sir Guy.

" Where *is* the Confessor ? " continued his grieving brother-in-law.

" In the pantry," cried Marion Hacket pertly, as she tripped downstairs in search of that venerable ecclesiastic ;—" in the pantry, I warrant me." The bower-woman was not wont to be in the wrong ; in the pantry was the holy man discovered—at his devotions.

"*Pax vobiscum!*" said Father Francis, as he entered the chamber of death.

"*Vita brevis!*" retorted Doctor Butts. He was not a man to be browbeat out of his Latin—and by a paltry Friar Minim, too. Had it been a Bishop, indeed, or even a mitred Abbot,—but a miserable Franciscan!

"*Benedicite!*" said the Friar.

"*Ars longa!*" returned the Leech.

Doctor Butts adjusted the tassels of his falling band ; drew his short sad-coloured cloak closer around him ; and, grasping his cross-handled walking-staff, stalked majestically out of the apartment. Father Francis had the field to himself.

The worthy chaplain hastened to administer the last rites of the church. To all appearance he had little time to lose ; as he concluded, the dismal toll of the passing-bell sounded from the belfry tower ;—little Hubert, the bandy-legged sacristan, was pulling with all his might. It was a capital contrivance that same passing-bell, —which of the Urbans or Innocents invented it is a query ; but, whoever he was, he deserved well of his country and of Christendom.

Ah! our ancestors were not such fools, after all, as we, their degenerate children, conceit them to have been. The passing-bell! a most solemn warning to imps of every description, is not to be regarded with impunity ; the most impudent *Succubus* of them all dare as well dip his claws in holy water as come within the verge of its sound. Old Nick himself, if he sets any value at all upon his tail, had best convey himself clean out of hearing, and leave the way open to Paradise. Little Hubert continued pulling with all his might,—and St. Peter began to look out for a customer.

The knell seemed to have some effect even upon the Lady Rohesia ; she raised her head slightly ; inarticulate sounds issued from her lips,—inarticulate, that is, to the profane ears of the laity. Those of Father Francis, indeed, were sharper ; nothing, as he averred, could be more distinct than the words, " A thousand marks to the priory of St. Mary Rouncival."

Now the Lady Rohesia Ingoldsby had brought her husband broad lands and large possessions ; much of her ample dowry, too, was at her own disposal ; and nuncupative wills had not yet been abolished by Acts of Parliament.

" Pious soul!" ejaculated Father Francis. " A thousand marks, she said——"

" If she did, I'll be shot!" said Sir Guy de Montgomeri.

" —A thousand marks!" continued the Confessor, fixing his cold grey eye upon the knight, as he went on heedless of the interruption ; —" a thousand marks ! and as many *Aves* and *Paters* shall be duly said—as soon as the money is paid down."

Sir Guy shrank from the monk's gaze ; he turned to the window, and muttered to himself something that sounded like " Don't you wish you may get it ? "

———

The bell continued to toll. Father Francis had quitted the room, taking with him the remains of the holy oil he had been using for Extreme Unction. Everard Ingoldsby waited on him down stairs.

" A thousand thanks ! " said the latter.

" A thousand marks ! " said the friar.

" A thousand devils ! " growled Sir Guy de Montgomeri, from the top of the landing-place.

But his accents fell unheeded ; his brother-in-law and the friar were gone ; he was left alone with his departing lady and Beatrice Grey.

Sir Guy de Montgomeri stood pensively at the foot of the bed ; his arms were crossed upon his bosom, his chin was sunk upon his breast ; his eyes were filled with tears ; the dim rays of the fading watchlight gave a darker shade to the furrows on his brow, and a brighter tint to the little bald patch on the top of his head—for Sir Guy was a middle-aged gentleman, tall and portly withal, with a slight bend in his shoulders, but that not much ; his complexion was somewhat florid, especially about the nose ; but his lady was *in extremis*, and at this particular moment he was paler than usual.

" Bim ! bome ! " went the bell. The knight groaned audibly ; Beatrice Grey wiped her eye with her little square apron of lace de Malines ; there was a moment's pause, a moment of intense affliction ; she let it fall—all but one corner, which remained between her finger and thumb. She looked at Sir Guy ; drew the thumb and forefinger of her other hand slowly along its border, till they reached the opposite extremity. She sobbed aloud. " So kind a lady ! " said Beatrice Grey.—" So excellent a wife ! " responded Sir Guy.—" So good ! " said the damsel.—" So dear ! " said the knight.—" So pious ! " said she.—" So humble ! " said he.—" So good to the poor ! "—" So capital a manager ! "—" So punctual at matins ! "—" Dinner dished to moment ! "—" So devout ! " said Beatrice.—" So fond of me ! " said Sir Guy.—" And of Father Francis ! "—" What the devil do you mean by that ? " said Sir Guy de Montgomeri.

The knight and the maiden had rung their antiphonic changes on the fine qualities of the departing Lady, like the *Strophe* and *Antistrophe* of a Greek play. The cardinal virtues once disposed of, her minor excellences came under review. She would drown a witch, drink lambs' wool at Christmas, beg Dominie Dumps's boys a holiday, and dine upon sprats on Good Friday! A low moan from the subject of these eulogies seemed to intimate that the enumeration of her good deeds was not altogether lost on her,—that the parting spirit felt and rejoiced in the testimony.

"She was too good for earth!" continued Sir Guy.

"Ye-ye-yes!" sobbed Beatrice.

"I did not deserve her!" said the knight.

"No-o-o-o!" cried the damsel.

"Not but that I made her an excellent husband, and a kind; but she is going, and—and—where, or when, or how—shall I get such another?"

"Not in broad England—not in the whole wide world!" responded Beatrice Grey; "that is, not *just* such another!" Her voice still faltered, but her accents on the whole were more articulate; she dropped the corner of her apron, and had recourse to her handkerchief; in fact, her eyes were getting red—and so was the tip of her nose.

Sir Guy was silent: he gazed for a few moments steadfastly on the face of his lady. The single word, "Another!" fell from his lips like a distant echo; it is not often that the viewless nymph repeats more than is necessary.

"Bim! bome!" went the bell. Bandy-legged Hubert had been tolling for half an hour; he began to grow tired, and St. Peter fidgety.

"Beatrice Grey!" said Sir Guy de Montgomeri, "what's to be done? What's to become of Montgomeri Hall?—and the buttery—and the servants? And what—what's to become of *me*, Beatrice Grey?" There was pathos in his tones, and a solemn pause succeeded. "I'll turn monk myself!" said Sir Guy.

"Monk?" said Beatrice.

"I'll be a Carthusian!" repeated the knight, but in a tone less assured: he relapsed into a reverie. Shave his head!—he did not so much mind that, he was getting rather bald already; but, beans for dinner—and those without butter—and then a horse-hair shirt!

The knight seemed undecided: his eye roamed gloomily around the apartment; it paused upon different objects, but as if it saw them not; its sense was shut, and there was no speculation in its glance: it rested at last upon the fair face of the sympathising damsel at his side, beautiful in her grief.

Her tears had ceased; but her eyes were cast down, mournfully fixed upon her delicate little foot, which was beating the devil's tattoo.

There is no talking to a female when she does not look at you. Sir Guy turned round: he seated himself on the edge of the bed;

and, placing his hand beneath the chin of the lady, turned up her face in an angle of fifteen degrees.

"I don't think I shall take the vows, Beatrice; but what's to become of me? Poor, miserable, old—that is poor, miserable, middle-aged man that I am!—No one to comfort, no one to care for me!" Beatrice's tears flowed afresh, but she opened not her lips. "'Pon my life!" continued he, "I don't believe there is a creature now would care a button if I were hanged to-morrow!"

"Oh! don't say so, Sir Guy!" sighed Beatrice; "you know there's—there's Master Everard, and—and Father Francis—"

"Pish!" cried Sir Guy, testily.

"And—there's your favourite old bitch."

"I am not thinking of old bitches!" quoth Sir Guy de Montgomeri.

Another pause ensued: the knight had released her chin, and taken her hand; it was a pretty little hand, with long taper fingers and filbert-formed nails, and the softness of the palm said little for its owner's industry.

"Sit down, my dear Beatrice," said the knight, thoughtfully; "you must be fatigued with your long watching. Take a seat, my child." Sir Guy did not relinquish her hand; but he sidled along the counterpane, and made room for his companion between himself and the bed-post.

Now this is a very awkward position for two people to be placed in, especially when the right hand of the one holds the right hand of the other: in such an attitude, what the deuce can the gentleman do with his left? Sir Guy closed his till it became an absolute fist, and his knuckles rested on the bed a little in the rear of his companion.

"Another!" repeated Sir Guy, musing; "if, indeed, I could find such another!" He was talking to his thought, but Beatrice Grey answered him.

"There's Madam Fitzfoozle."—"A frump!" said Sir Guy.

"Or the Lady Bumbarton."—"With her hump!" muttered he.

"There's the Dowager——"

"Stop—stop!" said the knight, "stop one moment!" He paused; he was all on the tremble; something seemed rising in his throat, but he gave a great gulp, and swallowed it. "Beatrice," said he, "what think you of"—his voice sank into a most seductive softness,—"what think you of—Beatrice Grey?"

The murder was out: the knight felt infinitely relieved; the knuckles of his left hand unclosed spontaneously; and the arm he had felt such a difficulty in disposing of, found itself—nobody knows how—all at once, encircling the jimp waist of the pretty Beatrice. The young lady's reply was expressed in three syllables. They were,

"Oh, Sir Guy!" The words might be somewhat indefinite, but there was no mistaking the look. Their eyes met; Sir Guy's left arm contracted itself spasmodically: when the eyes meet—at least as theirs met—the lips are very apt to follow the example. The knight had taken one long, loving kiss—nectar and ambrosia! He thought on Doctor Butts and his *repetatur haustus*—a prescription Father Francis had taken infinite pains to translate for him: he was about to repeat it, but the dose was interrupted *in transitu.* Doubtless the adage,

> There's many a slip
> 'Twixt the cup and the lip,

hath reference to medicine. Sir Guy's lip was again all but in conjunction with that of his bride-elect.

It has been hinted already that there was a little round polished patch on the summit of the knight's *pericranium*, from which his locks had gradually receded; a sort of *oasis*—or rather a *Mont Blanc* in miniature, rising above the highest point of vegetation. It was on this little spot, undefended alike by Art and Nature, that at this interesting moment a blow descended, such as we must borrow a term from the Sister Island adequately to describe: it was a "Whack!"

Sir Guy started upon his feet; Beatrice Grey started upon hers: but a single glance to the rear reversed her position,—she fell upon her knees and screamed.

The knight, too, wheeled about, and beheld a sight which might have turned a bolder man to stone. It was She!—the all-but-defunct Rohesia—there she sat, bolt upright!—her eyes no longer glazed with the film of impending dissolution, but scintillating like flint and steel; while in her hand she grasped the bed-staff—a weapon of mickle might, as her husband's bloody coxcomb could now well testify. Words were yet wanting, for the quinsy, which her rage had broken, still impeded her utterance; but the strength and rapidity of her guttural intonations augured well for her future eloquence.

Sir Guy de Montgomeri stood for a while like a man distraught; this resurrection—for such it seemed—had quite overpowered him. "A husband oft-times makes the best physician," says the proverb; he was a living personification of its truth. Still it was whispered he had been content with Dr. Butts; but this lady was restored to bless him for many years. Heavens, what a life he led!

The Lady Rohesia mended apace; her quinsy was cured; the bell was stopped; and little Hubert, the sacristan, kicked out of the chapelry. St. Peter opened his wicket, and looked out; there was nobody there ; so he flung-to the gate in a passion, and went back to his lodge, grumbling at being hoaxed by a runway ring.

Years rolled on. The improvement of Lady Rohesia's temper did not keep pace with that of her health ; and one fine morning Sir Guy de Montgomeri was seen to enter the *porte-cochère* of Durham House, at that time the town residence of Sir Walter Raleigh. Nothing more was ever heard of him ; but a boat full of adventurers was known to have dropped down with the tide that evening to Deptford Hope, where lay the good ship the *Darling*, commanded by Captain Keymis, who sailed next morning on the Virginia voyage.

A brass plate, some eighteen inches long, may yet be seen in Denton chancel, let into a broad slab of Bethersden marble ; it represents a lady kneeling, in her wimple and hood ; her hands are clasped in prayer, and beneath is an inscription in the characters of the age—

'Praie for ye sowle of ye Lady Royse,
And for alle Christen sowles !'

The date is illegible ; but it appears that she survived King Henry the Eighth, and that the dissolution of monasteries had lost St. Mary Rouncival her thousand marks. As for Beatrice Grey, it is well known that she was alive in 1559, and then had virginity enough left to be a maid of honour to " good Queen Bess."

CAPTAIN MARRYAT
1792–1848

S.W. AND BY W. ¾ W.

Jack Littlebrain was, physically considered, as fine grown, and moreover as handsome a boy as ever was seen, but it must be acknowledged that he was not very clever. Nature is, in most instances, very impartial; she has given plumage to the peacock, but, as every one knows, not the slightest ear for music. Throughout the feathered race it is almost invariably the same; the homeliest clad are the finest songsters. Among animals the elephant is certainly the most intelligent, but, at the same time, he cannot be considered as a beauty.

Acting upon this well-ascertained principle, nature imagined that she had done quite enough for Jack when she endowed him with such personal perfection; and did not consider it was at all necessary that he should be very clever; indeed, it must be admitted not only that he was not very clever, but (as the truth must be told) remarkably dull and stupid.

However, the Littlebrains have been for a long while a well-known, numerous, and influential family, so that, if it were possible that Jack could have been taught anything, the means were forthcoming: he was sent to every school in the country; but it was in vain. At every following vacation he was handed over from the one pedagogue to the other, of those whose names were renowned for the Busbian system of teaching by stimulating both ends: he was horsed every day and still remained an ass, and at the end of six months, if he did not run away before that period was over, he was invariably sent back to his parents as incorrigible and unteachable. What was to be done with him? The Littlebrains had always got on in the world, somehow or another, by their interest and connections; but here was one who might be said to have no brains at all. After many pros and cons, and after a variety of consulting letters had passed between the various members of his family, it was decided, that as his maternal uncle, Sir Theophilus Blazers, G.C.B., was at that time second in command in the Mediterranean, he should be sent to sea under his command; the admiral having, in reply to a letter on the subject, answered that it was hard indeed if he did not lick him into some shape or another; and that, at all events, he'd warrant that Jack should be able to box the compass before he had been three months nibbling the ship's biscuit; further, that it was very easy to get over the examination necessary to qualify him for lieutenant, as a turkey and a dozen of brown stout sent in the boat with him on the passing day, as a present to each of the passing captains, would pass him, even if he were as incompetent as a camel (or, as they say at sea, a cable) to pass through the eye of a needle; that having once passed, he would soon have him in command of a fine frigate, with a good nursing first lieutenant; and that if he did not behave himself properly, he would make his signal to come on board of the flag-ship, take him into the cabin, and give him a sound horse-whipping, as other admirals have been known to inflict upon their own sons under similar circumstances. The reader must be aware that, from the tenor of Sir Theophilus' letter, the circumstances which we are narrating must have occurred some fifty years ago.

When Jack was informed that he was to be a midshipman, he looked up in the most innocent way in the world (and innocent he was, sure enough), turned on his heels, and whistled as he went for want of thought. For the last three months he had been at home, and his chief employment was kissing and romping with the maids, who declared him to be the handsomest Littlebrain that the country had ever produced. Our hero viewed the preparations made for his departure with perfect indifference, and wished everybody good-bye with the utmost composure. He was a happy, good-tempered fellow; who never calculated, because he could not; never decided, for he had not wit enough to choose; never foresaw, although he could look straight before him; and never remembered, because he had no memory. The line, "If ignorance is bliss, 'tis folly to be wise," was certainly made especially for Jack; nevertheless he was not totally deficient: he knew what was good to eat or drink, for his taste was perfect, his eyes were very sharp, and he could discover in a moment if a peach was ripe on the wall; his hearing was quick, for he was the first in the school to detect the footsteps of his pedagogue; and he could smell anything savoury nearly a mile off, if the wind lay the right way. Moreover, he knew that if he put his fingers in the fire that he would burn himself; that knives cut severely; that birch tickled; and several other little axioms of this sort which are generally ascertained by children at an early age, but which Jack's capacity had not received until at a much later date. Such as he was, our hero went to sea; his stock in his sea-chest being very abundant, while his stock of ideas was proportionably small.

We will pass over the trans-shipments of Jack until he was

eventually shipped on board the *Mendacious*, then lying at Malta, with the flag of Sir Theophilus Blazers at the fore—a splendid ship carrying 120 guns, and nearly 120 midshipmen of different calibres. (I pass over captain, lieutenant, and ship's company, having made mention of her most valuable qualifications.) Jack was received with a hearty welcome by his uncle, for he came in pudding-time, and was invited to dinner; and the admiral made the important discovery, that if his nephew was a fool in other points, he was certainly no fool at his knife and fork. In a short time his messmates found out that he was no fool at his fists, and his knock-down arguments ended much disputation. Indeed, as the French would say, Jack was perfection in the *physique*, although so very deficient in the *morale*.

But if Pandora's box proved a plague to the whole world, Jack had his individual portion of it, when he was summoned to *box* the compass by his worthy uncle Sir Theophilus Blazers; who, in the course of six months, discovered that he could not make his nephew box it in the three, which he had warranted in his letter; every day our hero's ears were boxed, but the compass never. It required all the cardinal virtues to teach him the cardinal points during the forenoon, and he made a point of forgetting them before the sun went down. Whenever they attempted it (and various were the teachers employed to drive the compass into Jack's head), his head drove round the compass; and try all he could, Jack never could compass it. It appeared, as some people are said only to have one idea, as if Jack could only have one *point* in his head at a time, and to that point he would stand like a well-broken pointer. With him the wind never changed till the next day. His uncle pronounced him to be a fool, but that did not hurt his nephew's feelings; he had been told so too often already.

I have said that Jack had a great respect for good eating and drinking, and, moreover, was blessed with a good appetite: every person has his peculiar fancies, and if there was anything which more titillated the palate and olfactory nerves of our hero, it was a roast goose with sage and onions. Now it so happened, that having been about seven months on board of the *Mendacious*, Jack had one day received a summons to dine with the admiral, for the steward had ordered a roast goose for dinner, and knew not only that Jack was partial to it, but also that Jack was the admiral's nephew, which always goes for something on board of a flag-ship. Just before they were sitting down to table, the admiral wishing to know how the wind was, and having been not a little vexed with the slow progress of his nephew's nautical acquirements, said, "Now, Mr. Littlebrain, go up and bring me down word how the wind is; and mark me, as, when you are sent, nine times out of ten you make a mistake, I shall now bet you five guineas against your dinner that you make a mistake this time : so now be off and we will soon ascertain whether you lose your dinner or I lose my money. Sit down, gentlemen, we will not wait for Mr. Littlebrain."

Jack did not much admire this bet on the part of his uncle, but still less did he like the want of good manners in not waiting for him. He had just time to see the covers removed, to scent a whiff of the goose, and was off.

" The admiral wants to know how the wind is, sir," said Jack to the officer of the watch.

The officer of the watch went to the binnacle, and setting the wind as nearly as he could, replied, " Tell Sir Theophilus that it is *S.W. and by W. ¾ W.*"

" That's one of those confounded long points that I never can remember," cried Jack in despair.

" Then you'll ' get goose,' as the saying is," observed one of the midshipmen.

" No ; I'm afraid that I shan't get any," replied Jack, despondingly. " What did he say, S.W. and by N. ¾ E. ? "

" Not exactly," replied his messmate, who was a good-natured lad, and laughed heartily at Jack's version. " S.W. and by W. ¾ W."

" I never can remember it," cried Jack. " I'm to have five guineas if I do, and no dinner if I don't ; and if I stay here much longer, I shall get no dinner at all events, for they are all terribly peckish, and there will be none left."

" Well, if you'll give me one of the guineas, I'll show you how to manage it," said the midshipman.

" I'll give you two, if you'll only be quick and the goose a'n't all gone," replied Jack.

The midshipman wrote down the point from which the wind blew, at full length, upon a bit of paper, and pinned it to the rim of Jack's hat. " Now," said he, " when you go into the cabin, you can hold your hat so as to read it without their perceiving you."

" Well, so I can ; I never should have thought of that," said Jack.

" You hav'n't wit enough," replied the midshipman.

" Well, I see no wit in the compass," replied Jack.

" Nevertheless, it's full of point," replied the midshipman : " now be quick."

Our hero's eyes served him well if his memory was treacherous ; and as he entered the cabin door he bowed over his hat very politely, and said, as he read it off, " S.W. and by W. ¾ W.," and then he added, without reading at all, " if you please, Sir Theophilus."

" Steward," said the admiral, " tell the officer of the watch to step down."

" How's the wind, Mr. Growler ? "

" S.W. and by W. ¾ W.," replied the officer.

" Then, Mr. Littlebrain, you have won your five guineas, and may now sit down and enjoy your dinner."

Our hero was not slow in obeying the order, and ventured, upon the strength of his success, to send his plate twice for goose. Having eaten their dinner, drunk their wine, and taken their coffee, the officers, at the same time, took the hint which invariably accompanies the latter beverage, made their bows and retreated. As Jack was following his seniors out of the cabin, the admiral put the sum which he had staked into his hands, observing that " it was an ill wind that blew nobody good."

So thought Jack, who, having faithfully paid the midshipman the two guineas for his assistance, was now on the poop keeping his watch, as midshipmen usually do ; that is, stretched out on the signal lockers and composing himself to sleep after the most approved fashion, answering the winks of the stars by blinks of his eyes, until at last he shut them to keep them warm. But, before he had quite composed himself, he thought of the goose and the five guineas. The wind was from the same quarter, blowing soft and mild ; Jack lay in a sort of reverie as it fanned his cheek, for the weather was close and sultry.

" Well," muttered Jack to himself, " I do love that point of the compass, at all events, and I think that I never shall forget S.W. by W. ¾ W. No I never—never liked one before, though——"

" Is that true ? " whispered a gentle voice in his ear ; " do you love ' S.W. and by W. ¾ W.,' and will you, as you say, never forget her ? "

" Why, what's that ? " said Jack, opening his eyes and turning half round on his side.

" It's me—' S.W. and by W. ¾ W.,' that you say you love."

Littlebrain raised himself and looked round ; there was no one on the poop except himself and two or three of the after-guard, who were lying down between the guns.

" Why, who was it that spoke ? " said Jack, much astonished.

" It was the wind you love and who has long loved you," replied the same voice ; " do you wish to see me ? "

" See you—see the wind ?—I've been already sent on that message by the midshipmen," thought Jack.

" Do you love me as you say, and as I love you ? " continued the voice.

" Well, I like you better than any other point of the compass, and I'm sure I never thought I should like one of them," replied Jack.

" That will not do for me ; will you love only me ? "

" I'm not likely to love the others," replied Jack, shutting his eyes again ; " I *hate* them all."

" And love me ? "

" Well, I do love you, that's a fact," replied Jack as he thought of the goose and the five guineas.

" Then look round and you shall see me," said the soft voice.

Jack, who hardly knew whether he was asleep or awake, did at this summons once more take the trouble to open his eyes, and beheld a fairy female figure, pellucid as water, yet apparently possessing substance ; her features were beautifully soft and mild, and her outline trembled and shifted as it were, waving gently to and fro. It smiled sweetly, hung over him, played with his chestnut curls, softly touched his lips with her own, passed her trembling fingers over his cheeks, and its warm breath appeared as if it melted into his. Then it grew more bold—embraced his person, searched into his neck and collar, as if curious to examine him.

Jack felt a pleasure and gratification which he could not well comprehend ; once more the charmer's lips trembled upon his own, now remaining for a moment, now withdrawing, again returning to kiss and kiss again, and once more did the soft voice put the question :

" Do you love me ? "

" Better than goose," replied Jack.

" I don't know who goose may be," replied the fairy form, as she tossed about Jack's waving locks ; " you must love only me, promise me that before I am relieved."

" What, have you got the first watch, as well as me ? " replied Jack.

" I am on duty just now, but I shall not be so long. We southerly winds are never kept long in one place ; some of my sisters will probably be sent here soon."

" I don't understand what you talk about," replied Jack. " Suppose you tell me who you are, and what you are, and I'll do all I can to keep awake ; I don't know how it is, but I've felt more inclined to go to sleep since you have been fanning me about than I did before."

" Then I will remain by your side while you listen to me. I am, as I told you, a wind——"

" That's puzzling," said Jack, interrupting her.

" My name is ' S.W. and by W. $\frac{3}{4}$ W.' "

" Yes, and a very long name it is. If you wish me to remember you, you should have had a shorter one."

This ruffled the wind a little, and she blew rather sharp into the corner of Jack's eye ; however, she proceeded :

" You are a sailor, and of course you know all the winds on the compass by name."

" I wish I did ; but I don't," replied Littlebrain ; " I can recollect you, and not one other."

Again the wind trembled with delight on his lips, and she proceeded: "You know that there are thirty-two points on the compass, and these points are divided into quarters; so that there are, in fact, 128 different winds."

"There are more than I could ever remember; I know that," said Jack.

"Well, we are in all 128. All the winds which have northerly in them are coarse and ugly; all the southerly winds are pretty."

"You don't say so?" replied our hero.

"We are summoned to blow, as required, but the hardest duty generally falls to the northerly winds, as it should do, for they are the strongest; although we southerly winds can blow hard enough when we choose. Our characters are somewhat different. The most unhappy in disposition, and I may say the most malevolent, are the north and easterly winds; the N.W. winds are powerful, but not unkind; the S.E. winds vary, but, at all events, we of the S.W. are considered the mildest and most beneficent. Do you understand me?"

"Not altogether. You're going right round the compass, and I never could make it out, that's a fact. I hear what you say, but I cannot promise to recollect it; I can only recollect S.W. and by W. ¾ W."

"I care only for your recollecting me; if you do that, you may forget all the rest. Now you see we South-Wests are summer winds, and are seldom required but in this season; I have often blown over your ship these last three months, and I always have lingered near you, for I loved you."

"Thank you—now go on, for seven bells have struck some time, and I shall be going to turn in. Is your watch out?"

"No, I shall blow for some hours longer. Why will you leave me—why won't you stay on deck with me?"

"What, stay on deck after my watch is out? No, if I do, blow me! We midshipmen never do that—but I say, why can't you come down with me, and turn in my hammock? It's close to the hatchway, and you can easily do it."

"Well, I will, upon one promise. You say that you love me; now I'm very jealous, for we winds are always supplanting one another. Promise me that you will never mention any other wind in the compass but me; for if you do, they may come to you, and if I hear of it I'll blow the masts out of your ship, that I will."

"You don't say so?" replied Jack, surveying her fragile, trembling form.

"Yes, I will, and on a lee-shore too; so that the ship shall go to pieces on the rocks, and the admiral and every soul on board her be drowned."

"No, you wouldn't, would you?" said our hero, astonished.

"Not if you promise me. Then I'll come to you and pour down your windsails, and dry your washed clothes as they hang on the rigging, and just ripple the waves as you glide along, and hang upon the lips of my dear love, and press him in my arms. Promise me, then, on no account ever to recollect or mention any other wind but me."

"Well, I think I may promise that," replied Jack, "I'm very clever at forgetting; and then you'll come to my hammock, won't you, and sleep with me? You'll be a nice cool bedfellow these warm nights."

"I can't sleep on my watch as midshipmen do; but I'll watch you while you sleep, and I'll fan your cheeks, and keep you cool and comfortable, till I'm relieved."

"And when you go, when will you come again?"

"That I cannot tell—when I'm summoned; and I shall wait with impatience, that you may be sure of."

"There's eight bells," said Jack, starting up; "I must go down and call the officer of the middle watch; but I'll soon turn in, for my relief is not so big as myself, and I can thrash him."

Littlebrain was as good as his word; he cut down his relief, and then thrashed him for venturing to expostulate. The consequence was, that in ten minutes he was in his hammock, and "S.W. and by W. ¾ W." came gently down the hatchway and rested in his arms. Jack soon fell fast asleep, and when he was wakened up the next morning by the quarter-master, his bedfellow was no longer there. A mate inquiring how the wind was, was answered by the quarter-master that they had a fresh breeze from the N.N.W., by which Jack understood that his sweetheart was no longer on duty.

Our hero had passed such a happy night with his soft and kind companion that he could think of nothing else; he longed for her to come again, and, to the surprise of everybody, was now perpetually making inquiries as to the wind which blew. He thought of her continually, and in fact was as much in love with "S.W. and by W. ¾ W." as he possibly could be. She came again—once more did he enjoy her delightful company; again she slept with him in his hammock, and then, after a short stay, she was relieved by another.

We do not intend to accuse the wind of inconstancy, as that was not her fault; nor of treachery, for she loved dearly; nor of violence, for she was all softness and mildness; but we do say that "S. W. and by W. ¾ W." was the occasion of Jack being very often in a scrape, for our hero kept his word; he forgot all other winds, and with him there was no other except his dear "S.W. and by W. ¾ W." It must be admitted of Jack that, at all events, he showed great perseverance, for he stuck to his point.

Our hero would argue with his messmates, for it is not those who are most capable of arguing who are most fond of it ; and, like all arguers not very brilliant, he would flounder and diverge away right and left, just as the flaws of ideas came into his head.

" What nonsense it is your talking that way," would his opponent say ; " why don't you come to the point ? "

" And so I do," cried Jack.

" Well, then, what is your point ? "

" S.W. and by W. ¾ W.," replied our hero.

Who could reply to this ? But in every instance, and through every difficulty, our hero kept his promise, until his uncle, Sir Theophilus, was very undecided whether he should send him home to be locked up in a lunatic asylum, or bring him on in the service to the rank of post-captain. Upon mature consideration, however, as a man in Bedlam is a very useless member of society, and a teetotal non-productive, whereas a captain in the navy is a responsible agent, the admiral came to the conclusion that Littlebrain must follow up his destiny.

At last Jack was set down as the greatest fool in the ship, and was pointed out as such. The ladies observed that such might possibly be the case, but at all events he was the handsomest young man in the Mediterranean fleet. We believe that both parties were correct in their assertions.

Time flies—even a midshipman's time, which does not fly quite so fast as his money—and the time came for Mr. Littlebrain's examination. Sir Theophilus, who now commanded the whole fleet, was almost in despair. How was it possible that a man could navigate a ship with only one quarter point of the compass in his head ?

Sir Theophilus scratched his wig ; and the disposition of the Mediterranean fleet, so important to the country, was altered according to the dispositions of the captains who commanded the ships. In those days there were martinets in the service ; officers who never overlooked an offence, or permitted the least deviation from strict duty ; who were generally hated, but at the same time were most valuable to the service. As for his nephew passing his examination before any of those of the first or second, or even of the third degree, the admiral knew that it was impossible. The consequence was, that one was sent away on a mission to Genoa about nothing ; another to watch for vessels, never expected, off Sardinia ; two more to cruise after a French frigate which had never been built : and thus, by degrees, did the admiral arrange, so as to obtain a set of officers sufficiently pliant to allow his nephew to creep under the gate which barred his promotion, and which he never could have vaulted over. So the signal was made—our hero went on board—his uncle had not forgotten the propriety of a little *douceur* on the occasion ;

and, as the turkeys were all gone, three couple of geese were sent in the same boat, as a present to each of the three passing captains. Littlebrain's heart failed him as he pulled to the ship; even the geese hissed at him, as much as to say, " If you were not such a stupid ass, we might have been left alive in our coops." There was a great deal of truth in that remark, if they did say so.

Nothing could have been made more easy for Littlebrain than his examination. The questions had all been arranged beforehand; and some kind friend had given him all the answers written down. The passing captains apparently suffered from the heat of the weather, and each had his hand on his brow, looking down on the table, at the time that Littlebrain gave his answers, so that of course they did not observe that he was reading them off. As soon as Littlebrain had given his answer, and had had sufficient time to drop his paper under the table, the captains felt better and looked up again.

There were but eight questions for our hero to answer. Seven had been satisfactorily got through; then came the eighth, a very simple one:—" What is your course and distance from Ushant to the Start?" This question having been duly put, the captains were again in deep meditation, shrouding their eyes with the palms of their hands.

Littlebrain had his answer—he looked at the paper. What could be more simple than to reply?—and then the captains would have all risen up, shaken him by the hand, complimented him upon the talent he had displayed, sent their compliments to the commander-in-chief and their thanks for the geese. Jack was just answering, " North——"

" Recollect your promise!" cried a soft voice, which Jack well recollected.

Jack stammered—the captains were mute—and waited patiently.

" I must say it," muttered Jack.

" You shan't," replied the little Wind.

" Indeed I must," said Jack, " or I shall be turned back."

The captains, surprised at this delay and the muttering of Jack, looked up, and one of them gently inquired if Mr. Littlebrain had not dropped his handkerchief or something under the table? And then they again fixed their eyes upon the green cloth.

" If you dare, I'll never see you again," cried " S.W. and by W. ¾ W."—" never come to your hammock—but I'll blow the ship on shore, every soul shall be lost, admiral and all; recollect your promise!"

" Then I shall never pass," replied Jack.

" Do you think that any other point in the compass shall pass you except me?—never! I am too jealous for that. Come now, dearest!" and the Wind again deliciously trembled upon the lips of our hero, who could no longer resist.

"S.W. and by W. ¾ W.," exclaimed Jack firmly.

"You have made a slight mistake, Mr. Littlebrain," said one of the captains. "*Look* again—I meant to say, *think* again."

"S.W. and by W. ¾ W.," again repeated Jack.

"Dearest, how I love you!" whispered the soft Wind.

"Why, Mr. Littlebrain," said one of the captains—for Jack had actually laid the paper down on the table—"what's in the wind now?"

"She's obstinate," replied Jack.

"You appear to be so, at all events," replied the captain. "Pray, try once more."

"I have it!" thought Jack, who tore off the last answer from his paper. "I gained five guineas by that plan once before." He then handed the bit of paper to the passing captain. "I believe that's right, sir," said our hero.

"Yes, that is right; but could you not have said it instead of writing it, Mr. Littlebrain?"

Jack made no reply; his little sweetheart pouted a little, but said nothing; it was an evasion which she did not like. A few seconds of consultation then took place, as a matter of form. Each captain asked of the other if he was perfectly satisfied as to Mr. Littlebrain's capabilities, and the reply was in the affirmative; and they were perfectly satisfied that he was either a fool or a madman. However, as we have had both in the service by way of precedent, Jack was added to the list, and the next day was appointed lieutenant.

Our hero did his duty as lieutenant of the forecastle; and as all the duty of that officer is, when hailed from the quarter-deck, to answer, "*Ay, ay, sir,*" he got on without making many mistakes. And now he was very happy; no one dared to call him a fool except his uncle; he had his own cabin, and many was the time that his dear little "S.W. and by W. ¾ W." would come in by the scuttle and nestle by his side.

"You won't see so much of me soon, dearest," said she, one morning, gravely.

"Why not, my soft one?" replied Jack.

"Don't you recollect that the winter months are coming on?"

"So they are," replied Jack. "Well, I shall long for you back."

And Jack did long, and long very much, for he loved his dear wind and the fine weather which accompanied her. Winter came on, and heavy gales and rain, and thunder and lightning; nothing but double-reefed top-sails and wearing in succession; and our hero walked the forecastle and thought of his favourite wind. The N.E. winds came down furiously, and the weather was bitter cold.

The officers shook the rain and spray off their garments when their watch was over, and called for grog.

" Steward, a glass of grog," cried one ; " and let it be strong."

" The same for me," said Jack ; " only, I'll mix it myself."

Jack poured out the rum till the tumbler was half full.

" Why, Littlebrain," said his messmate, " that is a dose ; that's what we call a regular *Nor-wester*."

" Is it ? " replied Jack. " Well, then, Nor-westers suit me exactly, and I shall stick to them like cobblers' wax."

And during the whole of the winter months our hero showed a great predilection for Nor-westers.

It was in the latter end of February that there was a heavy gale ; it had blown furiously from the northward for three days, and then it paused and panted as if out of breath—no wonder ! And then the wind shifted and shifted again, with squalls and heavy rain, until it blew from every quarter of the compass.

Our hero's watch was over, and he came down and called for a " Nor-wester " as usual.

" How is the wind now ? " asked the first lieutenant of the master, who came down dripping wet.

" S.S.W., but drawing now fast to the westward," said old Spun-yarn.

And so it was ; and it veered round until " S.W. and by W. ¾ W.," with an angry gust, came down the skylight, and blowing strongly into our hero's ear, cried :

" Oh, you false one ! "

" False ! " exclaimed Jack. " What ! you here, and so angry too ? What's the matter ? "

" What's the matter !—do you think I don't know ? What have you been doing ever since I was away, comforting yourself during my absence with *Nor-westers* ? "

" Why, you a'n't jealous of a Nor-wester, are you ? " replied Littlebrain. " I confess I'm rather partial to them."

" What !—this to my face !—I'll never come again, without you promise me that you will have nothing to do with them, and never call for one again. Be quick—I cannot stay more than two minutes ; for it is hard work now, and we relieve quick—say the word."

" Well, then," replied Littlebrain, " you've no objection to *half-and-half* ? "

" None in the world ; that's quite another thing, and has nothing to do with the wind."

" It has, though," thought Jack, " for it gets a man in the wind ; but I won't tell her so ; and," continued he, " you don't mind a raw nip, do you ? "

" No—I care for nothing except a Nor-wester."

"I'll never call for one again," replied Jack; "it is but making my grog a little stronger; in future it shall be *half-and-half*."

"That's a dear! Now I'm off—don't forget me"; and away went the wind in a great hurry.

It was about three months after this short visit, the fleet being off Corsica, that our hero was walking the deck, thinking that he soon should see the object of his affections, when a privateer brig was discovered at anchor a few miles from Bastia. The signal was made for the boats of the fleet to cut her out; and the admiral, wishing that his nephew should distinguish himself somehow, gave him the command of one of the finest boats. Now Jack was as brave as brave could be; he did not know what danger was; he hadn't wit enough to perceive it, and there was no doubt but he would distinguish himself. The boats went on the service. Jack was the very first on board, cheering his men as he darted into the closed ranks of his opponents. Whether it was that he did not think that his head was worth defending, or that he was too busy in breaking the heads of others to look after his own, this is certain, that a tomahawk descended upon it with such force as to bury itself in his skull (and his was a thick skull too). The privateer's men were overpowered by numbers, and then our hero was discovered under a pile of bodies, still breathing heavily. He was hoisted on board and taken into his uncle's cabin; the surgeon shook his head when he had examined that of our hero.

"It must have been a most tremendous blow," said he to the admiral, "to have penetrated——"

"It must have been, indeed," replied the admiral, as the tears rolled down his cheeks; for he loved his nephew.

The surgeon, having done all that his art would enable him to do, left the cabin to attend to the others who were hurt; the admiral also went on the quarter-deck, walking to and fro for an hour in a melancholy mood. He returned to the cabin and bent over his nephew; Jack opened his eyes.

"My dear fellow," said the admiral, "how's your head now?"

"*S.W. and by W.* $\frac{3}{4}$ *W.*," faintly exclaimed our hero, constant in death, as he turned a little on one side and expired.

It was three days afterwards, as the fleet were on a wind making for Malta, that the bell of the ship tolled, and a body, sewed up in a hammock and covered with the Union Jack, was carried to the gangway by the admiral's bargemen. It had been a dull, cloudy day, with little wind; the hands were turned up, the officers and men stood uncovered; the admiral in advance with his arms folded, as the chaplain read the funeral service over the body of our hero,—and as the service proceeded, the sails flapped, for the wind had shifted a little; a motion was made, by the hand of the officer of the watch, to the man at the helm to let the ship go off the wind, that the service might not be disturbed, and a mizzling soft rain descended. The wind had shifted to our hero's much-loved *point*, his fond mistress had come to mourn over the loss of her dearest, and the rain that descended were the tears which she shed at the death of her handsome but not over-gifted lover.

MARY WOLLSTONECRAFT SHELLEY
1797–1851

THE SISTERS OF ALBANO

And near Albano's scarce divided waves
Shine from a sister valley ;—and afar
The Tiber winds, and the broad ocean laves
The Latian coast where sprang the Epic war,
" Arms and the Man," whose re-ascending star
Rose o'er an empire ; but beneath thy right
Tully reposed from Rome ; and where yon bar
Of girding mountains intercepts the sight
The Sabine farm was till'd, the weary bard's delight.

It was to see this beautiful lake that I made my last excursion before quitting Rome. The spring had nearly grown into summer, the trees were all in full but fresh green foliage, the vine-dresser was singing, perched among them, training his vines : the cicala had not yet begun her song, the heats therefore had not commenced ; but at evening the fireflies gleamed among the hills, and the cooing aziolo assured us of what in that country needs no assurance, fine weather for the morrow. We set out early in the morning to avoid the heats, breakfasted at Albano, and till ten o'clock passed our time in visiting the Mosaic, the villa of Cicero, and other curiosities of the place. We reposed during the middle of the day in a tent elevated for us at the hill-top, whence we looked on the hill-embosomed lake, and the distant eminence crowned by a town with its church. Other villages and cottages were scattered among the foldings of mountains, and beyond we saw the deep blue sea of the southern poets, which received the swift and immortal Tiber, rocking it to repose among its devouring waves. The Coliseum falls and the Pantheon decays—the very hills of Rome are perishing—but the Tiber lives for ever, flows for ever, and for ever feeds the land-encircled Mediterranean with fresh waters.

Our summer and pleasure-seeking party consisted of many : to me the most interesting person was the Countess Atanasia D——, who was as beautiful as an imagination of Raphael, and good as the ideal of a poet. Two of her children accompanied her, with animated looks and gentle manners, quiet, yet enjoying. I sat near her, watching the changing shadows of the landscape before us. As the sun descended, it poured a tide of light into the valley of the lake, deluging the deep bank formed by the mountain with liquid gold. The domes and turrets of the far town flashed and gleamed, the trees were dyed in splendour ; two or three slight clouds, which had drunk the radiance till it became their essence, floated golden islets in the lustrous empyrean. The waters, reflecting the brilliancy of the sky and the fire-tinted banks, beamed a second heaven, a second irradiated earth, at our feet. The Mediterranean, gazing on the sun—as the eyes of a mortal bride fail and are dimmed when reflecting her lover's glances—was lost, mixed in his light, till it had become one with him. Long (our souls, like the sea, the hills, and lake, drinking in the supreme loveliness) we gazed, till the too full cup overflowed, and we turned away with a sigh.

At our feet there was a knoll of ground that formed the foreground of our picture ; two trees lay basking against the sky, glittering with the golden light, which like dew seemed to hang amid their branches; a rock closed the prospect on the other side, twined round by creepers, and redolent with blooming myrtle ; a brook, crossed by huge stones, gushed through the turf, and on the fragments of rock that lay about sat two or three persons, peasants, who attracted our attention. One was a hunter, as his gun, lying on a bank not far off, demonstrated ; yet he was a tiller of the soil : his rough straw hat, and his picturesque but coarse dress, belonged to that class. The other was some contadina, in the costume of her country, returning, her basket on her arm, from the village to her cottage home. They were regarding the stores of a pedlar, who with doffed hat stood near: some of these consisted of pictures and prints—views of the country, and portraits of the Madonna. Our peasants regarded these with pleased attention.

" One might easily make a story for that pair," I said : " his gun is a help to the imagination, and we may fancy him a bandit with his contadina love, the terror of all the neighbourhood, except of her, the most defenceless being in it."

" You speak lightly of such a combination," said the lovely countess at my side, " as if it must not in its nature be the cause of dreadful tragedies. The mingling of love with crime is a dread conjunction, and lawless pursuits are never followed without bringing on the criminal, and all allied to him, ineffable misery. I speak with emotion, for your observation reminds me of an unfortunate girl, now one of the Sisters of Charity in the convent of Santa Chiara at Rome, whose unhappy passion for a man such as you mention spread destruction and sorrow widely around her."

I entreated my lovely friend to relate the history of the nun ; for a long time she resisted my entreaties, as not willing to depress the spirit of a party of pleasure by a tale of sorrow. But I urged her, and she yielded. Her sweet Italian phraseology now rings in my ears, and her beautiful countenance is before me. As she spoke, the sun set, and the moon bent her silver horn in the ebbing tide of glory he had left. The lake changed from purple to silver, and the trees, before so splendid, now in dark masses, just reflected from their tops the mild moonlight. The fire-flies flashed among the rocks; the bats circled round us: meanwhile thus commenced the Countess Atanasia:

The nun of whom I speak had a sister older than herself; I can remember them when as children they brought eggs and fruit to my father's villa. Maria and Anina were constantly together. With their large straw hats to shield them from the scorching sun, they were at work in their father's *podere* all day, and in the evening, when Maria, who was the elder by four years, went to the fountain for water, Anina ran at her side. Their cot—the folding of the hill conceals it—is at the lake-side opposite; and about a quarter of a mile up the hill is the rustic fountain of which I speak. Maria was serious, gentle, and considerate; Anina was a laughing, merry little creature, with the face of a cherub. When Maria was fifteen, their mother fell ill, and was nursed at the convent of Santa Chiara at Rome. Maria attended her, never leaving her bedside day or night. The nuns thought her an angel, she deemed them saints: her mother died, and they persuaded her to make one of them; her father could not but acquiesce in her holy intention, and she became one of the Sisters of Charity, the nun-nurses of Santa Chiara. Once or twice a year she visited her home, gave sage and kind advice to Anina, and sometimes wept to part from her; but her piety and her active employments for the sick reconciled her to her fate. Anina was more sorry to lose her sister's society. The other girls of the village did not please her: she was a good child, and worked hard for her father, and her sweetest recompense was the report he made of her to Maria, and the fond praises and caresses the latter bestowed on her when they met.

It was not until she was fifteen that Anina showed any diminution of affection for her sister. Yet I cannot call it diminution, for she loved her perhaps more than ever, though her holy calling and sage lectures prevented her from reposing confidence, and made her tremble lest the nun, devoted to heaven and good works, should read in her eyes, and disapprove of the earthly passion that occupied her. Perhaps a part of her reluctance arose from the reports that were current against her lover's character, and certainly from the disapprobation and even hatred of him that her father frequently expressed. Ill-fated Anina! I know not if in the north your peasants love as ours; but the passion of Anina was entwined with the roots of her being, it was herself: she could die, but not cease to love. The dislike of her father for Domenico made their intercourse clandestine. He was always at the fountain to fill her pitcher, and lift it on her head. He attended the same mass; and when her father went to Albano, Velletri, or Rome, he seemed to learn by instinct the exact moment of his departure, and joined her in the *podere*, labouring with her and for her, till the old man was seen descending the mountain-path on his return. He said he worked for a contadino near Nemi. Anina sometimes wondered that he could spare so much time for her; but his excuses were plausible, and the result too delightful not to blind the innocent girl to its obvious cause.

Poor Domenico! the reports spread against him were too well founded: his sole excuse was that his father had been a robber before him, and he had spent his early years among these lawless men. He had better things in his nature, and yearned for the peace of the guiltless. Yet he could hardly be called guilty, for no dread crime stained him; nevertheless, he was an outlaw and a bandit, and now that he loved Anina these names were the stings of an adder to pierce his soul. He would have fled from his comrades to a far country, but Anina dwelt amid their very haunts. At this period also, the police established by the French government, which then possessed Rome, made these bands more alive to the conduct of their members, and rumours of active measures to be taken against those who occupied the hills near Albano, Nemi, and Velletri, caused them to draw together in tighter bonds. Domenico would not, if he could, desert his friends in the hour of danger.

On a *festa* at this time—it was towards the end of October—Anina strolled with her father among the villagers, who all over Italy make holiday, by congregating and walking in one place. Their talk was entirely of the *laddri* and the French, and many terrible stories were related of the extirpation of banditti in the kingdom of Naples, and the mode by which the French succeeded in their undertaking was minutely described. The troops scoured the country, visiting one haunt of the robbers after the other, and dislodging them, tracked them, as in those countries they hunt the wild beasts of the forest, till drawing the circle narrower, they enclosed them in one spot. They then drew a cordon round the place, which they guarded with the utmost vigilance, forbidding any to enter it with provisions, on pain of instant death. And as this menace was rigorously executed, in a short time the besieged bandits were starved into a surrender. The French troops were now daily expected, for they had been seen at Velletri and Nemi; at the same time it was affirmed that several outlaws had taken up their abode at Rocca Giovane, a deserted village on the summit of one of these hills, and it was supposed that they would make that place the scene of their final retreat.

The next day, as Anina worked in the *podere*, a party of French horse passed by along the road that separated her garden from the lake. Curiosity made her look at them ; and her beauty was too great not to attract : their observations and address soon drove her away—for a woman in love consecrates herself to her lover, and deems the admiration of others to be profanation. She spoke to her father of the impertinence of these men, and he answered by rejoicing at their arrival and the destruction of the lawless bands that would ensue. When, in the evening, Anina went to the fountain, she looked timidly around, and hoped that Domenico would be at his accustomed post, for the arrival of the French destroyed her feeling of security. She went rather later than usual, and a cloudy evening made it seem already dark ; the wind roared among the trees, bending hither and thither even the stately cypresses ; the waters of the lake were agitated into high waves, and dark masses of thunder-cloud lowered over the hill-tops, giving a lurid tinge to the landscape. Anina passed quickly up the mountain-path : when she came in sight of the fountain, which was rudely hewn in the living rock, she saw Domenico leaning against a projection of the hill, his hat drawn over his eyes, his *tabaro* fallen from his shoulders, his arms folded in an attitude of dejection. He started when he saw her ; his voice and phrases were broken and unconnected ; yet he never gazed on her with such ardent love, nor solicited her to delay her departure with such impassioned tenderness.

" How glad I am to find you here ! " she said : " I was fearful of meeting one of the French soldiers : I dread them even more than the banditti."

Domenico cast a look of eager inquiry on her, and then turned away, saying, " Sorry am I that I shall not be here to protect you. I am obliged to go to Rome for a week or two. You will be faithful, Anina mia ; you will love me, though I never see you more ? "

The interview, under these circumstances, was longer than usual : he led her down the path till they nearly came in sight of her cottage; still they lingered : a low whistle was heard among the myrtle underwood at the lake side ; he started ; it was repeated, and he answered it by a similar note : Anina, terrified, was about to ask what this meant, when, for the first time, he pressed her to his heart, kissed her roseate lips, and, with a muttered " Carissima addio," left her, springing down the bank ; and as she gazed in wonder, she thought she saw a boat cross a line of light made by the opening of a cloud. She stood long absorbed in reverie, wondering and remembering with thrilling pleasure the quick embrace and impassioned farewell of her lover. She delayed so long that her father came to seek her.

Each evening after this Anina visited the fountain at the Ave Maria ; he was not there ; each day seemed an age ; and incomprehensible fears occupied her heart. About a fortnight after, letters arrived from Maria. They came to say that she had been ill of the malaria fever, that she was now convalescent, but that change of air was necessary for her recovery, and that she had obtained leave to spend a month at home at Albano. She asked her father to come the next day to fetch her. These were pleasant tidings for Anina ; she resolved to disclose everything to her sister, and during her long visit she doubted not but that she would contrive her happiness. Old Andrea departed the following morning, and the whole day was spent by the sweet girl in dreams of future bliss. In the evening Maria arrived, weak and wan, with all the marks of that dread illness about her ; yet, as she assured her sister, feeling quite well.

As they sat at their frugal supper several villagers came in to inquire for Maria ; but all their talk was of the French soldiers and the robbers, of whom a band of at least twenty was collected in Rocca Giovane, strictly watched by the military.

" We may be grateful to the French," said Andrea, " for this good deed : the country will be rid of these ruffians."

" True, friend," said another ; " but it is horrible to think what these men suffer ; they have, it appears, exhausted all the food they brought with them to the village, and are literally starving. They have not an ounce of macaroni among them ; and a poor fellow who was taken and executed yesterday was a mere anatomy ; you could tell every bone in his skin."

" There was a sad story the other day," said another, " of an old man from Nemi, whose son, they say, is among them at Rocca Giovane : he was found within the lines with some *baccalà* under his *pastrano*, and shot on the spot."

" There is not a more desperate gang," observed the first speaker, " in the states and the regno put together. They have sworn never to yield but upon good terms : to secure these, their plan is to waylay passengers and make prisoners, whom they keep as hostages for mild treatment from the government. But the French are merciless ; they are better pleased that the bandits wreak their vengeance on these poor creatures than spare one of their lives."

" They have captured two persons already," said another ; " and there is old Betta Tossi half frantic, for she is sure her son is taken : he has not been at home these ten days."

" I should rather guess," said an old man, " that he went there with good will : the young scapegrace kept company with Domenico Baldi of Nemi."

" No worse company could he have kept in the whole country," said Andrea : " Domenico is the bad son of a bad race. Is he in the village with the rest ? "

" My own eyes assured me of that," replied the other. " When I was up the hill with eggs and fowls to the piquette there, I saw the branches of an ilex move ; the poor fellow was weak, perhaps, and could not keep his hold ; presently he dropt to the ground ; every musket was levelled at him, but he started up and was away like a hare among the rocks. Once he turned, and then I saw Domenico as plainly, though thinner, poor lad, by much than he was, as plainly as I now see——Santa Virgine ! what is the matter with Nina ? "

She had fainted ; the company broke up, and she was left to her sister's care. When the poor child came to herself she was fully aware of her situation, and said nothing, except expressing a wish to retire to rest. Maria was in high spirits at the prospect of her long holiday at home, but the illness of her sister made her refrain from talking that night, and blessing her, as she said good-night, she soon slept. Domenico starving !—Domenico trying to escape and dying through hunger was the vision of horror that wholly possessed poor Anina. At another time the discovery that her lover was a robber might have inflicted pangs as keen as those which she now felt ; but this at present made a faint impression, obscured by worse wretchedness. Maria was in a deep and tranquil sleep. Anina rose, dressed herself silently, and crept down stairs. She stored her market-basket with what food there was in the house, and, unlatching the cottage-door, issued forth, resolved to reach Rocca Giovane and to administer to her lover's dreadful wants. The night was dark, but this was favourable, for she knew every path and turn of the hills, every bush and knoll of ground between her home and the deserted village which occupies the summit of that hill : you may see the dark outline of some of its houses about two hours' walk from her cottage. The night was dark, but still ; the libeccio brought the clouds below the mountain-tops, and veiled the horizon in mist ; not a leaf stirred ; her footsteps sounded loud in her ears, but resolution overcame fear. She had entered yon ilex grove, her spirits rose with her success, when suddenly she was challenged by a sentinel : no time for escape ; fear chilled her blood ; her basket dropped from her arm ; its contents rolled out on the ground ; the soldier fired his gun and brought several others around him ; she was made prisoner.

In the morning, when Maria awoke, she missed her sister from her side. I have overslept myself, she thought, and Nina would not disturb me. But when she came down stairs and met her father, and Anina did not appear, they began to wonder. She was not in the *podere* ; two hours passed, and then Andrea went to seek her.

Entering the near village, he saw the contadini crowding together, and a stifled exclamation of " Ecco il padre ! " told him that some evil had betided. His first impression was that his daughter was drowned ; but the truth, that she had been taken by the French carrying provisions within the forbidden line, was still more terrible. He returned in frantic desperation to his cottage, first to acquaint Maria with what had happened and then to ascend the hill to save his child from her impending fate. Maria heard his tale with horror ; but an hospital is a school in which to learn self-possession and presence of mind. " Do you remain, my father," she said : " I will go. My holy character will awe these men, my tears move them : trust me ; I swear that I will save my sister." Andrea yielded to her superior courage and energy.

The nuns of Santa Chiara when out of their convent do not usually wear their monastic habit, but dress simply in a black gown. Maria, however, had brought her nun's habiliments with her, and thinking thus to impress the soldiers with respect, she now put it on. She received her father's benediction, and asking that of the Virgin and the saints, she departed on her expedition. Ascending the hill, she was soon stopped by the sentinels. She asked to see their commanding officer, and being conducted to him, she announced herself as the sister of the unfortunate girl who had been captured the night before. The officer, who had received her with carelessness, now changed countenance ; his serious look frightened Maria, who clasped her hands, exclaiming, " You have not injured the child ? she is safe ? "

" She is safe—now," he replied with hesitation ; " but there is no hope of pardon."

" Holy Virgin, have mercy on her ! what will be done to her ? "

" I have received strict orders ; in two hours she dies."

" No ! no ! " exclaimed Maria impetuously, " that cannot be ! you cannot be so wicked as to murder a child like her."

" She is old enough, madame," said the officer, " to know that she ought not to disobey orders ; mine are so strict that were she but nine years old, she dies."

These terrible words stung Maria to fresh resolution : she entreated for mercy ; she knelt ; she vowed that she would not depart without her sister ; she appealed to Heaven and the saints. The officer, though cold-hearted, was good natured and courteous, and he assured her with the utmost gentleness that her supplications were of no avail ; that were the criminal his own daughter he must enforce his orders. As a sole concession, he permitted her to see her sister. Despair inspired the nun with energy ; she almost ran up the hill, outspeeding her guide ; they crossed a folding of the hills to a little sheep-cot, where sentinels paraded before the door.

There was no glass to the windows, so the shutters were shut, and when Maria first went in from the bright daylight she hardly saw the slight figure of her sister leaning against the wall, her dark hair fallen below her waist, her head sunk on her bosom, over which her arms were folded. She started wildly as the door opened, saw her sister, and sprung with a piercing shriek into her arms.

They were left alone together: Anina uttered a thousand frantic exclamations, beseeching her sister to save her, and shuddering at the near approach of her fate. Maria had felt herself, since their mother's death, the natural protectress and support of her sister, and she never deemed herself so called on to fulfil this character as now that the trembling girl clasped her neck, her tears falling on her cheeks and her choked voice entreating her to save her. The thought—O could I suffer instead of you! was in her heart, and she was about to express it, when it suggested another idea, on which she was resolved to act. First she soothed Anina by her promises, then glanced round the cot; they were quite alone: she went to the window, and through a crevice saw the soldiers conversing at some distance. "Yes, dearest sister," she cried, "I will—I can save you—quick—we must change dresses—there is no time to be lost!—you must escape in my habit."

"And you remain to die?"

"They dare not murder the innocent, a nun! Fear not for me—I am safe."

Anina easily yielded to her sister, but her fingers trembled; every string she touched she entangled. Maria was perfectly self-possessed, pale, but calm. She tied up her sister's long hair, and adjusted her veil over it so as to conceal it; she unlaced her bodice, and arranged the folds of her own habit on her with the greatest care; then, more hastily, she assumed the dress of her sister, putting on, after a lapse of many years her native contadina costume. Anina stood by, weeping and helpless, hardly hearing her sister's injunctions to return speedily to their father, and under his guidance seek sanctuary. The guard now opened the door. Anina clung to her sister in terror, while she, in soothing tones, entreated her to calm herself.

The soldier said they must delay no longer, for the priest had arrived to confess the prisoner.

To Anina the idea of confession associated with death was terrible; to Maria it brought hope. She whispered in a smothered voice, "The priest will protect me—fear not—hasten to our father!"

Anina almost mechanically obeyed: weeping with her handkerchief placed unaffectedly before her face, she passed the soldiers; they closed the door on the prisoner, who hastened to the window and saw her sister descend the hill with tottering steps, till she was lost behind some rising ground. The nun fell on her knees—cold dew bathed her brow, instinctively she feared: the French had shown small respect for the monastic character; they destroyed the convents and desecrated the churches. Would they be merciful to her, and spare the innocent? Alas! was not Anina innocent also? Her sole crime had been disobeying an arbitrary command, and she had done the same.

"Courage!" cried Maria; "perhaps I am fitter to die than my sister is. Gesu, pardon me my sins, but I do not believe that I shall outlive this day!"

In the meantime, Anina descended the hill slowly and tremblingly. She feared discovery, she feared for her sister, and above all, at the present moment, she feared the reproaches and anger of her father. By dwelling on this last idea, it became exaggerated into excessive terror, and she determined, instead of returning to her home, to make a circuit among the hills, to find her way by herself to Albano, where she trusted to find protection from her pastor and confessor. She avoided the open paths, and following rather the direction she wished to pursue than any beaten road, she passed along nearer to Rocca Giovane than she anticipated. She looked up at its ruined houses and bell-less steeple, straining her eyes to catch a glimpse of him, the author of all her ills. A low but distinct whistle reached her ear, not far off; she started—she remembered that on the night when she last saw Domenico a note like that had called him from her side; the sound was echoed and re-echoed from other quarters; she stood aghast, her bosom heaving, her hands clasped. First she saw a dark and ragged head of hair, shadowing two fiercely gleaming eyes, rise from beneath a bush. She screamed, but before she could repeat her scream three men leapt from behind a rock, secured her arms, threw a cloth over her face, and hurried her up the acclivity. Their talk, as she went along, informed her of the horror and danger of her situation.

Pity, they said, that the holy father and some of his red stockings did not command the troops: with a nun in their hands, they might obtain any terms. Coarse jests passed as they dragged their victim towards their ruined village. The paving of the street told her when they arrived at Rocca Giovane, and the change of atmosphere that they entered a house. They unbandaged her eyes: the scene was squalid and miserable, the walls ragged and black with smoke, the floor strewn with offals and dirt; a rude table and broken bench was all the furniture; and the leaves of Indian corn, heaped high in one corner, served, it seemed for a bed, for a man lay on it, his head buried in his folded arms. Anina looked round on her savage hosts: their countenances expressed every variety of brutal ferocity now rendered more dreadful from gaunt famine and suffering.

"O there is none who will save me!" she cried. The voice startled the man who was lying on the floor; he leapt up—it was Domenico: Domenico, so changed, with sunk cheeks and eyes, matted hair, and looks whose wildness and desperation differed little from the dark countenances around him. Could this be her lover?

His recognition and surprise at her dress led to an explanation. When the robbers first heard that their prey was no prize, they were mortified and angry; but when she related the danger she had incurred by endeavouring to bring them food, they swore with horrid oaths that no harm should befall her, but that if she liked she might make one of them in all honour and equality. The innocent girl shuddered. "Let me go," she cried; "let me only escape and hide myself in a convent for ever!"

Domenico looked at her in agony. "Yes, poor child," he said, "go, save yourself: God grant no evil befall you; the ruin is too wide already." Then turning eagerly to his comrades, he continued: "You hear her story. She was to have been shot for bringing food to us: her sister has substituted herself in her place. We know the French; one victim is to them as good as another: Maria dies in their hands. Let us save her. Our time is up; we must fall like men, or starve like dogs: we have still ammunition, still some strength left. To arms! let us rush on the poltroons, free their prisoner, and escape or die!"

There needed but an impulse like this to urge the outlaws to desperate resolves. They prepared their arms with looks of ferocious determination. Domenico, meanwhile, led Anina out of the house, to the verge of the hill, inquiring whither she intended to go. On her saying, to Albano, he observed, "That were hardly safe; be guided by me, I entreat you: take these piastres, hire the first conveyance you find, hasten to Rome, to the convent of Santa Chiara: for pity's sake, do not linger in this neighbourhood."

"I will obey your injunctions, Domenico," she replied, "but I cannot take your money; it has cost you too dear: fear not, I shall arrive safely at Rome without that ill-fated silver."

Domenico's comrades now called loudly to him: he had no time to urge his request; he threw the despised dollars at her feet.

"Nina, adieu for ever," he said: "may you love again more happily!"

"Never!" she replied. "God has saved me in this dress; it were sacrilege to change it: I shall never quit Santa Chiara."

Domenico had led her a part of the way down the rock; his comrades appeared at the top, calling to him.

"Gesu save you!" cried he: "reach the convent—Maria shall join you there before night. Farewell!" He hastily kissed her hand, and sprang up the acclivity to rejoin his impatient friends.

The unfortunate Andrea had waited long for the return of his children. The leafless trees and bright clear atmosphere permitted every object to be visible, but he saw no trace of them on the hill-side ; the shadows of the dial showed noon to be passed, when, with uncontrollable impatience, he began to climb the hill, towards the spot where Anina had been taken. The path he pursued was in part the same that this unhappy girl had taken on her way to Rome. The father and daughter met : the old man saw the nun's dress, and saw her unaccompanied : she covered her face with her hands in a transport of fear and shame ; but when, mistaking her for Maria, he asked in a tone of anguish for l is youngest darling, her arms fell ; she dared not raise her eyes, which streamed with tears.

" Unhappy girl ! " exclaimed Andrea, " where is your sister ? "

She pointed to the cottage prison, now discernible near the summit of a steep acclivity. " She is safe," she replied : " she saved me ; but they dare not murder her."

" Heaven bless her for this good deed," exclaimed the old man, fervently ; " but you hasten on your way, and I will go in search of her."

Each proceeded on an opposite path. The old man wound up the hill, now in view, and now losing sight of the hut where his child was captive ; he was aged, and the way was steep. Once, when the closing of the hill hid the point towards which he for ever strained his eyes, a single shot was fired in that direction ; his staff fell from his hands, his knees trembled and failed him ; several minutes of dead silence elapsed before he recovered himself sufficiently to proceed : full of fears he went on, and at the next turn saw the cot again. A party of soldiers were on the open space before it, drawn up in a line as if expecting an attack. In a few moments from above them shots were fired, which they returned, and the whole was enveloped and veiled in smoke. Still Andrea climbed the hill, eager to discover what had become of his child : the firing continued quick and hot. Now and then, in the pauses of musketry and the answering echoes of the mountains, he heard a funereal chant ; presently, before he was aware, at a turning of the hill, he met a company of priests and contadini, carrying a large cross and a bier. The miserable father rushed forward with frantic impatience ; the awe-struck peasants set down their load—the face was uncovered, and the wretched man fell senseless on the corpse of his murdered child.

The countess Atanasia paused, overcome by the emotions inspired by the history she related. A long pause ensued : at length one of the party observed, " Maria, then, was the sacrifice to her goodness."

"The French," said the countess, "did not venerate her holy vocation; one peasant girl to them was the same as another. The immolation of any victim suited their purpose of awe-striking the peasantry. Scarcely, however, had the shot entered her heart, and her blameless spirit been received by the saints in Paradise, when Domenico and his followers rushed down the hill to avenge her and themselves. The contest was furious and bloody; twenty French soldiers fell, and not one of the banditti escaped, Domenico, the foremost of the assailants, being the first to fall."

I asked, "And where are now Anina and her father?"

"You may see them, if you will," said the countess, "on your return to Rome. She is a nun of Santa Chiara. Constant acts of benevolence and piety have inspired her with calm and resignation. Her prayers are daily put up for Domenico's soul, and she hopes, through the intercession of the Virgin, to rejoin him in the other world.

"Andrea is very old; he has outlived the memory of his sufferings, but he derives comfort from the filial attentions of his surviving daughter. But when I look at his cottage on this lake, and remember the happy laughing face of Anina among the vines, I shudder at the recollection of the passion that has made her cheeks pale, her thoughts for ever conversant with death, her only wish to find repose in the grave."

MARY WOLLSTONECRAFT SHELLEY

THE FALSE RHYME

On a fine July day, the fair Margaret, Queen of Navarre, then on a visit to her royal brother, had arranged a rural feast for the morning following, which Francis declined attending. He was melancholy; and the cause was said to be some lover's quarrel with a favourite dame. The morrow came, and dark rain and murky clouds destroyed at once the schemes of the courtly throng. Margaret was angry, and she grew weary: her only hope for amusement was in Francis, and he had shut himself up—an excellent reason why she should the more desire to see him. She entered his apartment: he was standing at the casement, against which the noisy shower beat, writing with a diamond on the glass. Two beautiful dogs were his sole companions. As Queen Margaret entered, he hastily let down the silken curtain before the window, and looked a little confused.

"What treason is this, my liege," said the queen, "which crimsons your cheek? I must see the same."

"It is treason," replied the king, "and therefore, sweet sister, thou mayest not see it."

This the more excited Margaret's curiosity, and a playful contest ensued: Francis at last yielded: he threw himself on a huge high-backed settee; and as the lady drew back the curtain with an arch smile, he grew grave and sentimental as he reflected on the cause which had inspired his libel against all womankind.

"What have we here?" cried Margaret: "nay, this is *lèse majesté*—

Souvent femme varie,
Bien fou qui s'y fie!

Very little change would greatly amend your couplet:—would it not run better thus—

Souvent homme varie,
Bien folle qui s'y fie?

I could tell you twenty stories of man's inconstancy."

"I will be content with one true tale of woman's fidelity," said

Francis drily ; " but do not provoke me. I would fain be at peace with the soft Mutabilities, for thy dear sake."

" I defy your Grace," replied Margaret rashly, " to instance the falsehood of one noble and well-reputed dame."

" Not even Emilie de Lagny ? " asked the King.

This was a sore subject for the Queen. Emilie had been brought up in her own household, the most beautiful and the most virtuous of her maids of honour. She had long loved the Sire de Lagny, and their nuptials were celebrated with rejoicings but little ominous of the result. De Lagny was accused but a year after of traitorously yielding to the Emperor a fortress under his command, and he was condemned to perpetual imprisonment. For some time Emilie seemed inconsolable, often visiting the miserable dungeon of her husband, and suffering on her return from witnessing his wretchedness such paroxysms of grief as threatened her life. Suddenly, in the midst of her sorrow, she disappeared ; and inquiry only divulged the disgraceful fact, that she had escaped from France, bearing her jewels with her, and accompanied by her page, Robinet Leroux. It was whispered that, during their journey, the lady and the stripling often occupied one chamber ; and Margaret, enraged at these discoveries, commanded that no further quest should be made for her lost favourite.

Taunted now by her brother, she defended Emilie, declaring that she believed her to be guiltless, even going so far as to boast that within a month she would bring proof of her innocence.

" Robinet was a pretty boy," said Francis, laughing.

" Let us make a bet," cried Margaret : " if I lose, I will bear this vile rhyme of thine as a motto to my shame to my grave ; if I win——"

" I will break my window, and grant thee whatever boon thou askest."

The result of this bet was long sung by troubadour and minstrel. The Queen employed a hundred emissaries—published rewards for any intelligence of Emilie—all in vain. The month was expiring, and Margaret would have given many bright jewels to redeem her word. On the eve of the fatal day, the jailor of the prison in which the Sire de Lagny was confined sought an audience of the Queen ; he brought her a message from the knight to say, that if the Lady Margaret would ask his pardon as her boon, and obtain from her royal brother that he might be brought before him, her bet was won. Fair Margaret was very joyful, and readily made the desired promise. Francis was unwilling to see his false servant, but he was in high good humour, for a cavalier had that morning brought intelligence of a victory over the Imperialists. The messenger himself was lauded in the despatches as the most fearless and bravest knight in

France. The King loaded him with presents, only regretting that a vow prevented the soldier from raising his visor or declaring his name.

That same evening, as the setting sun shone on the lattice on which the ungallant rhyme was traced, Francis reposed on the same settee, and the beautiful Queen of Navarre, with triumph in her bright eyes, sat beside him. Attended by guards, the prisoner was brought in; his frame was attenuated by privation, and he walked with tottering steps. He knelt at the feet of Francis, and uncovered his head; a quantity of rich golden hair then escaping, fell over the sunken cheeks and pallid brow of the suppliant.

"We have treason here!" cried the King: "sir jailor, where is your prisoner?"

"Sire, blame him not," said the soft faltering voice of Emilie; "wiser men than he have been deceived by woman. My dear lord was guiltless of the crime for which he suffered. There was but one mode to save him: I assumed his chains—he escaped with poor Robinet Leroux in my attire—he joined your army: the young and gallant cavalier who delivered the despatches to your Grace, whom you overwhelmed with honours and reward, is my own Enguerrard de Lagny. I waited but for his arrival with testimonials of his innocence to declare myself to my lady, the Queen. Has she not won her bet? And the boon she asks——"

"Is de Lagny's pardon," said Margaret, as she also knelt to the King: "spare your faithful vassal, sire, and reward this lady's truth."

Francis first broke the false-speaking window, then he raised the ladies from their supplicatory posture.

In the tournament given to celebrate this "Triumph of Ladies," the Sire de Lagny bore off every prize; and surely there was more loveliness in Emilie's faded cheek, more grace in her emaciated form—types as they were of truest affection—than in the prouder bearing and fresher complexion of the most brilliant beauty in attendance on the courtly festival.

THOMAS HOOD
1799–1845

A TALE OF TERROR

THE following story I had from the lips of a well-known Aeronaut, and nearly in the same words.

It was on one of my ascents from Vauxhall, and a gentleman of the name of Mavor had engaged himself as a companion in my aerial excursion. But when the time came his nerves failed him, and I looked vainly round for the person who was to occupy the vacant seat in the car. Having waited for him till the last possible moment, and the crowd in the gardens becoming impatient, I prepared to ascend alone ; and the last cord that attached me to the earth was about to be cast off, when suddenly a strange gentleman pushed forward and volunteered to go up with me into the clouds. He pressed the request with so much earnestness that, having satisfied myself, by a few questions, of his respectability and received his promise to submit in every point to my directions, I consented to receive him in lieu of the absentee ; whereupon he stepped with evident eagerness and alacrity into the machine. In another minute we were rising above the trees ; and in justice to my companion I must say, that in all my experience no person at a first ascent had ever shown such perfect coolness and self-possession. The sudden rise of the machine, the novelty of the situation, the real and exaggerated dangers of the voyage, and the cheering of the spectators are apt to cause some trepidation, or at any rate excitement, in the boldest individuals ; whereas the stranger was as composed and comfortable as if he had been sitting quite at home in his own library chair. A bird could not have seemed more at ease, or more in its element, and yet he solemnly assured me, upon his honour, that he had never been up before in his life. Instead of exhibiting any alarm at our great height from the earth, he evinced the liveliest pleasure whenever I emptied one of my bags of sand, and even once or twice urged me to part with more of the ballast. In the meantime, the wind, which was very light, carried us gently along in a north-east direction, and the day being particularly bright and clear, we enjoyed a delightful bird's-eye view of the great metropolis and the surrounding country. My companion listened with great interest while I pointed out to him the various objects over which we passed, till I happened casually to observe that the balloon must be directly over Hoxton. My fellow-traveller then for the first time betrayed some uneasiness, and anxiously inquired whether I thought he could be recognised by any one at our then distance from the earth. It was, I told him, quite impossible. Nevertheless he continued very uneasy, frequently repeating, "I hope they don't see," and entreating me earnestly to discharge more ballast. It then flashed upon me for the first time that his offer to ascend with me had been a whim of the moment, and that he feared the being seen at that perilous elevation by any member of his own family. I therefore asked him if he resided at Hoxton, to which he replied in the affirmative ; urging again, and with great vehemence, the emptying of the remaining sandbags.

This, however, was out of the question, considering the altitude of the balloon, the course of the wind, and the proximity of the sea-coast. But my comrade was deaf to these reasons ; he insisted on going higher, and on my refusal to discharge more ballast deliberately pulled off and threw his hat, coat, and waistcoat overboard.

" Hurrah, that lightened her ! " he shouted ; " but it's not enough yet," and he began unloosening his cravat.

" Nonsense," said I, " my good fellow, nobody can recognise you at this distance, even with a telescope."

" Don't be too sure of that," he retorted rather simply ; " they have sharp eyes at Miles's."

" At where ? "

" At Miles's Madhouse ! "

Gracious Heaven !—the truth flashed upon me in an instant. I was sitting in the frail car of a balloon, at least a mile above the earth with a Lunatic ! The horrors of the situation, for a minute, seemed to deprive me of my own senses. A sudden freak of a distempered fancy, a transient fury, the slightest struggle might send us both, at a moment's notice, into eternity ! In the meantime the Maniac, still repeating his insane cry of " higher, higher, higher," divested himself, successively, of every remaining article of clothing, throwing each portion, as soon as taken off, to the winds. The inutility of remonstrance, or rather the probability of its producing a fatal irritation, kept me silent during these operations : but judge of my terror when, having thrown his stockings overboard, I heard him say, " We are not yet high enough by ten thousand miles—one of us must throw out the other."

To describe my feelings at this speech is impossible. Not only the awfulness of my position, but its novelty, conspired to bewilder me, for certainly no flight of imagination—no, not the wildest nightmare dream—had ever placed me in so desperate and forlorn a situation. It was horrible, horrible! Words, pleadings, remonstrances were useless, and resistance would be certain destruction. I had better have been unarmed, in an American Wilderness, at the mercy of a savage Indian! And now, without daring to stir a hand in opposition, I saw the Lunatic deliberately heave first one and then the other bag of ballast from the car, the balloon, of course, rising with proportionate rapidity. Up, up, up it soared—to an altitude I had never even dared to contemplate; the earth was lost to my eyes, and nothing but the huge clouds rolled beneath us! The world was gone, I felt, for ever! The Maniac, however, was still dissatisfied with our ascent, and again began to mutter.

"Have you a wife and children?" he asked abruptly.

Prompted by a natural instinct, and with a pardonable deviation from truth, I replied that I was married, and had fourteen young ones who depended on me for their bread!

"Ha! ha! ha!" laughed the Maniac, with a sparkling of his eyes that chilled my very marrow. "I have three hundred wives and five thousand children; and if the balloon had not been so heavy by carrying double, I should have been home to them by this time."

"And where do they live?" I asked, anxious to gain time by any question that first occurred to me.

"In the moon," replied the Maniac; "and when I have lightened the car, I shall be there in no time."

I heard no more, for suddenly approaching me, and throwing his arms round my body——

MRS. CATHERINE GRACE GORE
1799–1861

EHRENBREITSTEIN

In the course of the campaigns immediately following the French Revolution the fortress of Ehrenbreitstein, on the banks of the Rhine, experienced, on more than one occasion, the unequal fortunes of war ; and was compelled to submit to the superior force, or superior skill, of a conquering army. After the passage of the French troops under Hoche, effected at Weisse Thurm, in 1797, a blockade, which endured until the peace of Leoben, harassed its devoted garrison. It was then abandoned to the possession of the troops of the Elector of Mayence ; and although the little town of Thal, situated at its base, had been sacrificed in the course of the siege, Coblentz, whose position on the opposite bank, at the confluence of the Moselle with the Rhine, derives its best security from the fortress, was thus restored to tranquillity, and a hope of happier times.

The confusion of an ill-disciplined and inexperienced army had indeed rendered abortive to the Rhenish shores those local advantages by which they ought to have been secured from devastation ; and the prolonged disorganisation and disunion prevalent in the adjacent provinces had, by the most impolitic inconsistency, embarrassed every branch of public business, and while agriculture was driven from the ravaged plains, and commerce from the ensanguined waves of the Rhine, civil discord had embroiled the citizens of almost every town of mark along its course.

But affairs were now beginning to wear a more promising aspect. The Congress of Rastadt had already opened its negotiations, and despair on one side, and exhaustion or weariness on the other, had succeeded in cooling the heat of those national feuds which had brought the ruinous footsteps of advancing and retreating armies to trample the bosom of an afflicted country. That there were some among its sons over-eager to avenge the deep scars thus inflicted, the murder of the French deputies at the very gates of Rastadt terribly attests.

It chanced that some days previous to the opening of the Congress, a French noble—the Count D'Aubigny—with his wife and son, had been arrested, on their return to their native country, by the authorities of Coblentz; who, judging from the passports and papers in his possession that he had high influence, and an important connection with the Directory, secured him in the fortress of Ehrenbreitstein as a valuable hostage for the interests of their city.

The Count, who had sought safety in emigration during the short supremacy of one of the earlier and more furious factions of the republic, had been recently recalled to fill an appointment of dignity and honour under the new government. Galling as it was to his feelings to be thus thwarted and restrained upon the very threshold of France, yet his trust in the efficacy of an appeal which he had forwarded to the Congress prevented him from giving way to the natural impatience of his mind. A deeper feeling, however—a feeling of horror and desperation—soon superseded his irritation and regrets: a body of French troops presented itself before the fortress, menacing its garrison and luckless inhabitants with all the horrors of a protracted siege.

It was in vain that D'Aubigny recalled to his own mind, and whispered to his fair companion, that the fortress was bomb-proof and casemated with unequal art; and still more vain were his entreaties to Colonel Faber, its brave but sturdy commandant, that his wife and child might be conveyed under a flag of truce to Coblentz. The colonel, to whom his prisoner was both nationally and individually an object of distrust, persisted that the interest of his command forbade the concession.

"Your ladies of France," said he, "God give them grace!—are too nimble-tongued to be trusted in an enemy's camp, and Moritz Faber will scarcely be tempted to enable the fair Countess to carry tidings of the nakedness of the land, and of the impoverished resources of the fort, unto a band which bears the tri-coloured rag as its ensign, and treachery as its password. No, no!—abide in the old eagle's nest. Our galleries are a surety from your friends in the valley; and when our provisions fail—which fail they shall ere I yield the charge committed to my hand unto a gang of marauding cut-throats—the Countess and her son shall honourably share our fare and our famine. Perhaps the plea of a lady's sufferings may more promptly disperse your gentle countrymen yonder, who write themselves *preux chevaliers*, than falconet or culverin!"

Count D'Aubigny, finding persuasion fruitless, and knowing that resistance might even less avail him, could only pray, that either the return of his own *estafette* from Rastadt, or of that despatched by Colonel Faber, might bring a mandate of intelligence between the besieging and besieged. A few days sufficed to show him, and the expiration of several weeks tended most horribly to prove, that the fortress had been surprised in an hour of security and consequent destitution; he looked tremblingly to the result, and marked the daily diminution of their apportionment of provisions, with a sense of dread he dared not reveal to his companions in misfortune.

If any woman, however, could be gifted to receive with fortitude an announcement of evil, severe as that anticipated by the Count, it was Eveline—his lovely and most beloved wife: for her mind was as firm and elevated in its character as her demeanour and disposition were femininely gentle: and her attachment to the young Eugene, the son of D'Aubigny by a former marriage, partook of a conscientious devotion to his interests, such as the mere tenderness of maternal love could not have alone suggested.

It was for him—it was for that fair boy, who had loved her so fondly—that her first apprehensions of the horror of their position became terrible to her mind. Eugene was frail and delicate, and had been nurtured with the softest tending; he had attained neither the strength of body nor mind essential to the endurance of an evil from which his high condition might have seemed to secure him; and his parents, for they were equally so in affection for the child, had not courage to forewarn and inure him to the approaching calamity.

They saw him from the first reject with silent but evident loathing the coarse food tendered for his support. They marked his soft cheek grow wan under the deprivation, his little voice gradually weaken, his step bound less playfully along the rude pavement of their chamber; and they looked into each other's faces with fearful eyes as they first noted the change; but dared not interrogate the boy, or utter one audible comment. Soon, however, fatally soon, the miserable fact became too loudly a matter of comment in the garrison for even the child to remain in ignorance of their threatened destiny. Day after day passed, and brought nothing but sights of death and sounds of lamentation; and the wasting strength of the prisoners rendered their minds still more susceptible of terror and despair; but neither their wants nor the murmurs of the soldiery could influence by the weight of a feather the stern determination of the commandant to yield but in his hour of death.

Let those who limit their consciousness of the pangs of hunger by the loss of an occasional meal, which may have rendered restless their luxurious couch, affect to underrate the agonies of starvation, and to attemper according to Adam Smith's theory of morality their arguments for the indecency of bewailing a vulgar lack of food. But the actual sense of famine,—the gnawing, irritating sense, which confuses the ears with strange sounds—the body with sickness—the heart with perturbation—the head with dizzy bewilderment—these are sufferings which defy the mastery of mental fortitude!

D'Aubigny was the first to give utterance to his feelings, for they were solely urged by the suppressed torments he was condemned to witness. " My Eveline," said he, " my sweet, my heavenly-minded wife, could I have believed when I sought your hand, amid the lofty pomp of your high estate, that I should but win it to share in the horrors of my evil destiny—could I have dreamed, when I wept my first glad tears over this boy's cradle, that I should live to wish him unborn—to see him perish—slowly—horribly——"

" Hush ! D'Aubigny, he sleeps ; his head hath sunk upon my knee."

" No ! mother," said the boy very faintly, " I am not sleeping ; I am listening quietly to my kind father's voice."

" It is exhaustion ! by the God of mercy ! it is exhaustion which hath bowed his head ! " exclaimed the Count, taking his son into his arms and gazing with an indescribable thrill upon his attenuated countenance, then rushing forwards in despite of the outcry and resistance of the various sentries, he forced himself into the presence of Colonel Faber, still straining his child to his bosom.

" Look at him ! " said he, with a voice broken by sobs ; " 'tis my only child,—look upon him,—and if you have the heart of a man, deny not my petition. It is not yet too late,—send him from Ehrenbreitstein."

" It cannot be," answered Faber resolutely, although the manifest condition of the lovely boy brought a deep flush even to his temples. " I will give him up my own share of provision with pleasure, Count D'Aubigny ; but not a living soul must leave the fortress !—I am deeply responsible to my country : and the famishing condition of my soldiers—*my children*—might otherwise prompt me to desert a trust which the Congress of Rastadt appear so little interested to protect. My duty, sir, is one of sternness ; I *cannot* grant your request."

" Do not weep, father," murmured the child faintly, " I never saw tears of thine before ; do not let them fall for Eugene. I *will* be better ; I *will* feed heartily on the food we can still procure ;—do not weep, father."

And with an effort mighty at his age the child did indeed force between his lips the loathsome morsels which fell scantily to their share. Every domestic animal within the walls had been sacrificed ; and the obscene flesh of dogs and horses had become a delicacy beyond the soldiers' power of purchase ! and on such revolting aliments did Eveline force herself to feed, in order to entice and deceive the boy's enfeebled appetite. But all would not do ;—already many of the least hardy of the garrison had fallen a sacrifice to want of wholesome food ;—and the failing strength and tremulous lips of Eugene and his mother proclaimed that they were soon to follow. Yes, they were dying of starvation !

Again the Count attempted to move the feelings of Faber in their behalf; but he no longer bore denial with resignation. Moved beyond his patience, he raved, threatened, and even attempted violence; and as the scene had many witnesses, the commandant felt it due to himself to punish the offender with solitary confinement.

"Thus, too," thought the staunch old soldier, "I shall spare this unfortunate parent the misery of looking upon sufferings which he cannot alleviate."

The wretched chamber inhabited by the Countess D'Aubigny was situated in one of the loftiest and most secure towers of the fortress; and when the sun, which had lost its power to cheer the desponding prisoners, dawned through the arrow-slits on the day succeeding that of D'Aubigny's imprisonment, Eveline rose to drag her failing, quivering limbs towards the morning air, and resting her head beside the narrow opening, looking down upon the blue, glassy, dancing, *free* waters of the Rhine, that rippled far, far below the fortress, and prayed that they might rise and overwhelm her. But she instantly reproved the thought, as she had already done the proposal of her husband, that they should anticipate their inevitable and horrible end.

"This child," she had replied, "is a sacred deposit in our hands; we have no right to leave him orphaned, to his sorrow; and you could not—no! you could not attempt *his* little life!"

"What seest thou yonder, mother?" faltered the boy, whom her movement had disturbed, but who was now too weak to approach the *soupirail* for refreshment.

"I see Heaven's mighty sunshine, dear Eugene, bright as if it shone upon no human misery. I see the white city of Coblentz, backed by its green plantations, and sending up the smoke of a thousand hearths. Beside them there is happiness, Eugene,—smiles and food, child,—and with *us* abideth nought save trust in the mercy of God. Think upon it—think, beloved child, that we shall soon be free from pain and grief!"

"I cannot, think, mother; my head swims strangely. But there is still feeling in my heart,—and it is all for thee and for my father."

"Eugene, should we survive this peril, and thou hast the strength of youth in thy favour, let this remembrance become a pledge for the tender mercies of thy future life; so that the poor and the hungry may not plead to thee in vain."

"Mother, thy words reach not my failing ears; draw nearer, mother, for I would die with my hand in thine."

On that very day the destines of the fortress were accomplished; and the sacrifice which had been made was made in vain:—the fiat of the Congress of Rastadt commanded the brave Faber to open its gates to the enemy of his country. The noble brother of Eveline

D'Aubigny, whose anxiety for her liberation had motived in a great measure the blockade of Ehrenbreitstein, was the first to rush into the chamber of the captive. No living thing stirred there. The boy had died first, for his face was covered and his limbs composed; and Eveline—if the fair wasted thing which lay beside him might claim that name—had perished in the effort of executing that last duty!

DOUGLAS JERROLD
1803–1857

THE TRAGEDY OF THE TILL

Told by the Hermit of Bellyfulle

" It is a strange tale, but it hath the recommendation of brevity. Some folks may see nothing in it but tricksiness of an extravagant spirit ; and some, perchance, may pluck a heart of meaning out of it. However, be it as it may, you shall hear it, sir.

" There was a man called Isaac Pugwash, a dweller in a miserable slough of London, a squalid denizen of one of the foul nooks of that city of Plutus. He kept a shop, which, though small as a cabin, was visited as granary and store-house by half the neighbourhood. All the creature-comforts of the poor—from bread to that questionable superfluity, small-beer—were sold by Isaac. Strange it was that with such a trade Pugwash grew not rich. He had many bad debts, and of all shopkeepers was most unfortunate in false coin. Certain it is he had neither eye not ear for bad money. Counterfeit semblances of majesty beguiled him out of bread and butter, and cheese, and red herring, just as readily as legitimate royalty struck at the Mint. Malice might impute something of this to the political principles of Pugwash, who, as he had avowed himself again and again, was no lover of a monarchy.

" Nevertheless, I cannot think Pugwash had so little regard for the countenance of majesty as to welcome it as readily when silvered copper as when sterling silver. No, a wild foolish enthusiast was Pugwash, but in the household matter of good and bad money he had very wholesome prejudices. He had a reasonable wish to grow rich, yet was entirely ignorant of the by-ways and short-cuts to wealth. He would have sauntered through life with his hands in his pockets and a daisy in his mouth ; and dying with just enough in his house to pay the undertaker, would have thought himself a fortunate fellow ; he was, in the words of Mrs. Pugwash, such a careless, foolish, dreaming creature. He was cheated every hour by a customer of some kind ; and yet to deny credit to anybody—he would as soon have denied the wife of his bosom. His customers knew the weakness and failed not to exercise it.

" To be sure, now and then, fresh from conjugal counsel, he would refuse to add a single herring to a debtor's score ; no, he would not be sent to the workhouse by anybody. A quarter of an hour after, the denied herring, with an added small loaf, was given to the little girl sent to the shop by the rejected mother, —' he couldn't bear to see poor children wanting anything.'

" Pugwash had another unprofitable weakness. He was fond of what he called nature, though in his dim, close shop he could give her but a stifling welcome. Nevertheless, he had the earliest primroses on his counter,—' they threw,' he said, ' such a nice light about the place.' A sly, knavish customer presented Issaac with a pot of polyanthuses, and, won by the flowery gift, Pugwash gave the donor ruinous credit. The man with wall-flowers regularly stopped at Isaac's shop, and for only sixpence Pugwash would tell his wife he had made the place a Paradise. ' If we can't go to nature, Sally, isn't it a pleasant thing to be able to bring nature to us ? '

" Whereupon Mrs. Pugwash would declare that a man with at least three children to provide for had no need to talk of nature. Nevertheless, the flower-man made his weekly call. Though at many a house the penny could not every week be spared to buy a hint, a look of nature for the darkened dwellers, Isaac, despite of Mrs. Pugwash, always purchased. It is a common thing, an old familiar cry," said the Hermit—" to see the poor man's florist, to hear his loud-voiced invitation to take his nosegays, his penny-roots ; and yet is it a call, a conjuration of the heart of man overlaboured and desponding—walled in by the gloom of a town—divorced from the fields and their sweet healthful influences—almost shut out from the sky that reeks in vapour over him ;—it is a call that tells him there are things of the earth beside food and covering to live for ; and that God in His great bounty hath made them for all men. Is it not so ? " asked the Hermit.

" Most certainly," we answered ; " it would be the very sinfulness of avarice to think otherwise."

" Why, sir," said the Hermit, benevolently smiling, " thus considered, the loud-lunged city bawler of roots and flowers becomes a high benevolence, a peripatetic priest of nature. Adown dark lanes and miry alleys he takes sweet remembrances—touching records of the loveliness of earth, that with their bright looks and balmy odours cheer and uplift the dumpish heart of man ; that make his soul stir within him, and acknowledge the beautiful. The penny, the ill-spared penny—for it would buy a wheaten roll—the poor housewife pays for root of primrose, is her offering to the hopeful loveliness of nature ; is her testimony of the soul struggling with the blighting, crushing circumstance of sordid earth, and sometimes yearning towards earth's sweetest aspects. Amidst the violence, the coarseness, and the suffering that may surround and defile the wretched there must be moments when the heart escapes, craving for the innocent and lovely; when the soul makes for itself even of a flower a comfort and a refuge."

The Hermit paused a moment, and then in blither voice resumed. "But I have strayed a little from the history of our small tradesman, Pugwash. Well, sir, Isaac for some three or four years kept on his old way, his wife still prophesying in loud and louder voice the inevitable workhouse. He would so think and talk of nature when he should mind his shop; he would so often snatch a holiday to lose it in the fields, when he should take stock and balance his books. What was worse, he every week lost more and more by bad money. With no more sense than a buzzard, as Mrs. Pugwash said, for a good shilling, he was the victim of those laborious folks who make their money with a fine independence of the state, out of their own materials. It seemed the common compact of a host of coiners to put off their base-born offspring upon Isaac Pugwash; who, it must be confessed, bore the loss and the indignity like a Christian martyr.

"At last, however, the spirit of the man was stung. A guinea, as Pugwash believed of statute gold, was found to be of little less value than a brass button. Mrs. Pugwash clamoured and screamed as though a besieging foe was in her house; and Pugwash himself felt that further patience would be pusillanimity. Whereupon, sir, what think you Isaac did? Why, he suffered himself to be driven by the voice and vehemence of his wife to a conjurer, who in a neighbouring attic was a sideral go-between to the neighbourhood—a vender of intelligence from the stars to all who sought and duly fee'd him. This magician would declare to Pugwash the whereabout of the felon coiner, and—the thought was anodyne to the hurt mind of Isaac's wife—the knave would be law-throttled.

"With sad indignant spirit did Isaac Pugwash seek Father Lotus; for so, sir, was the conjurer called. He was none of your common wizards. Oh no! he left it to the mere quack-salvers and mountebanks of his craft to take upon them a haggard solemnity of look, and to drop monosyllables, heavy as bullets, upon the ear of the questioner. The mighty and magnificent hocuspocus of twelvepenny magicians was scorned by Lotus. There was nothing in his look or manner that showed him the worse for keeping company with spirits: on the contrary, perhaps, the privileges he enjoyed of them served to make him only the more blithe and jocund. He might have passed for a gentleman, at once easy and cunning in the law; his sole knowledge, that of labyrinthine sentences made expressly to wind poor common sense on parchment. He had an eye like a snake, a constant smile upon his lip, a cheek coloured like an apple, and an activity of movement wide away from the solemnity of the conjurer.

He was a small eel-figured man of about sixty, dressed in glossy black, with silver buckles and flowing periwig.

"It was impossible not to have a better opinion of sprites and demons seeing that so nice, so polished a gentleman was their especial pet. And then his attic had no mystic circle, no curtain of black, no death's head, no mummy of apocryphal dragon—the vulgar catchpennies of fortune-telling trader. There was not even a pack of cards to elevate the soul of man into the regions of the mystic world. No, the room was plainly yet comfortably set out. Father Lotus reposed in an easy chair, nursing a snow-white cat upon his knee; now tenderly patting the creature with one hand, and now turning over a little Hebrew volume with the other. If a man wished to have dealings with sorry demons, could he desire a nicer little gentleman than Father Lotus to make the acquaintance for him? In a few words Isaac Pugwash told his story to the smiling magician. He had, amongst much other bad money, taken a counterfeit guinea; could Father Lotus discover the evil-doer?

"'Yes, yes, yes,' said Lotus, smiling, 'of course—to be sure; but that will do but little: in your present state—but let me look at your tongue.' Pugwash obediently thrust the organ forth. 'Yes, yes, as I thought. 'Twill do you no good to hang the rogue; none at all. What we must do is this—we must cure you of the disease.'

"'Disease!' cried Pugwash. 'Bating the loss of my money, I was never better in all my days.'

"'Ha! my poor man,' said Lotus, 'it is the benevolence of nature that she often goes on, quietly breaking us up, ourselves knowing no more of the mischief than a girl's doll when the girl rips up its seams. Your malady is of the perceptive organs. Leave you alone and you'll sink to the condition of a baboon.'

"'God bless me!' cried Pugwash.

"'A jackass with sense to choose a thistle from a toadstool will be a reasoning creature to you! for consider, my poor soul,' said Lotus in a compassionate voice, 'in this world of tribulation we inhabit, consider what a benighted nincompoop is man if he cannot elect a good shilling from a bad one.'

"'I have not a sharp eye for money,' said Pugwash modestly. 'It's a gift, sir; I'm assured it's a gift.'

"'A sharp eye! An eye of horn,' said Lotus. 'Never mind, I can remedy all that; I can restore you to the world and to yourself. The greatest physicians, the wisest philosophers have, in the profundity of their wisdom, made money the test of wit. A man is believed mad; he is a very rich man, and his heir has very good reason to believe him lunatic; whereupon the heir, the madman's careful friend, calls about the sufferer a company of wizards to sit in judgment on the suspected brain and report a verdict thereupon.

Well, ninety-nine times out of the hundred, what is the first question put, as test of reason ? Why, a question of money. The physician, laying certain pieces of current coin in his palm, asks of the patient their several value. If he answer truly, why truly there is hope ; but if he stammer or falter at the coin, the verdict runs, and wisely runs, mad—incapably mad.'

" 'I'm not so bad as that,' said Pugwash, a little alarmed.

" 'Don't say how you are—it's presumption in any man,' cried Lotus. 'Nevertheless, be as you may, I'll cure you if you'll give attention to my remedy.'

" 'I'll give my whole soul to it,' exclaimed Pugwash.

" 'Very good, very good ; I like your earnestness, but I don't want all your soul,' said Father Lotus, smiling—'I want only part of it : that, if you confide in me, I can take from you with no danger. Ay, with less peril than the pricking of a whitlow. Now, then, for examination. Now, to have a good stare at this soul of yours.' Here Father Lotus gently removed the white cat from his knee, for he had been patting her all the time he talked, and turned full round upon Pugwash. 'Turn out your breeches' pockets,' said Lotus ; and the tractable Pugwash immediately displayed the linings. 'So ! ' cried Lotus, looking narrowly at the brown holland whereof they were made—'very bad, indeed ; very bad ; never knew a soul in a worse state in all my life.'

" Pugwash looked at his pockets and then at the conjurer : he was about to speak, but the fixed earnest look of Father Lotus held him in respectful silence.

" 'Yes, yes,' said the wizard, still eyeing the brown holland, 'I can see it all ; a vagabond soul ; a soul wandering here and there like a pauper without a settlement ; a ragamuffin soul.'

" Pugwash found confidence and breath. 'Was there ever such a joke ? ' he cried ; 'know a man's soul by the linings of his breeches' pockets ! ' and Pugwash laughed, albeit uncomfortably.

" Father Lotus looked at the man with philosophic compassion. 'Ha, my good friend ! ' he said, 'that all comes of your ignorance of moral anatomy.'

" 'Well, but, Father Lotus——'

" 'Peace,' said the wizard, 'and answer me. You'd have this soul of yours cured ? '

" 'If there's anything the matter with it,' answered Pugwash. 'Though not of any conceit I speak it, yet I think it as sweet and as healthy a soul as the souls of my neighbours. I never did wrong to anybody.'

" 'Pooh ! ' cried Father Lotus.

" 'I never denied credit to the hungry,' continued Pugwash.

" 'Fiddle-de-dee ! ' said the wizard very nervously.

" 'I never laid out a penny in law upon a customer; I never refused small-beer to——'

" 'Silence!' cried Father Lotus; 'don't offend philosophy by thus bragging of your follies. You are in a perilous condition; still you may be saved. At this very moment, I much fear it, gangrene has touched your soul: nevertheless, I can separate the sound from the mortified parts and start you new again as though your lips were first wet with mother's milk.'

" Pugwash merely said—for the wizard began to awe him—'I'm very much obliged to you.'

" 'Now,' said Lotus, 'answer a few questions and then I'll proceed to the cure. What do you think of money?'

" 'A very nice thing,' said Pugwash, 'though I can do with as little of it as most folks.'

" Father Lotus shook his head. 'Well, and the world about you?'

" 'A beautiful world,' said Pugwash; 'only the worst of it is, I can't leave the shop as often as I would to enjoy it. I'm shut in all day long, I may say, a prisoner to brick-dust, herrings, and bacon. Sometimes, when the sun shines and the cobbler's lark over the way sings as if he'd split his pipe, why then, do you know, I do so long to get into the fields; I do hunger for a bit of grass like any cow.'

" The wizard looked almost hopelessly on Pugwash. 'And that's your religion and business? Infidel of the counter! Saracen of the till! However—patience,' said Lotus, 'and let us conclude.—And the men and women of the world, what do you think of them?'

" 'God bless 'em, poor souls!' said Pugwash. 'It's a sad scramble some of 'em have, isn't it?'

" 'Well,' said the conjurer, 'for a tradesman, your soul is in a wretched condition. However, it is not so hopelessly bad that I may not yet make it profitable to you. I must cure it of its vagabond desires and above all make it respectful of money. You will take this book.' Here Lotus took a little volume from a cupboard and placed it in the hand of Pugwash. 'Lay it under your pillow every night for a week, and on the eighth morning let me see you.'

" 'Come, there's nothing easier than that,' said Pguwash with a smile, and reverently putting the volume in his pocket—(the book was closed by metal clasps, curiously chased)—he descended the garret stairs of the conjurer.

" On the morning of the eighth day Pugwash again stood before Lotus.

" 'How do you feel now?' asked the conjurer with a knowing look.

" 'I haven't opened the book—'tis just as I took it,' said Pugwash, making no further answer.

" 'I know that,' said Lotus; 'the clasps be thanked for your ignorance.' Pugwash slightly coloured; for, to say the truth, both he and his wife had vainly pulled and tugged and fingered and coaxed the clasps that they might look upon the necromantic page. 'Well, the book has worked,' said the conjurer; 'I have it.'

" 'Have it! what?' asked Pugwash.

" 'Your soul,' answered the sorcerer. 'In all my practice,' he added gravely, 'I never had a soul come into my hands in worse condition.'

" 'Impossible!' cried Pugwash. 'If my soul is, as you say, in your own hands, how is it that I'm alive? How is it that I can eat, drink, sleep, walk, talk, do everything, just like anybody else?'

" 'Ha!' said Lotus, 'that's a common mistake. Thousands and thousands would swear, ay, as they'd swear to their own noses, that they have their souls in their own possession; bless you,' and the conjurer laughed maliciously, 'it's a popular error. Their souls are altogether out of 'em.'

" 'Well,' said Pugwash, 'if it's true that you have, indeed, my soul, I should like to have a look at it.'

" 'In good time,' said the conjurer; 'I'll bring it to your house and put it in its proper lodging. In another week I'll bring it to you; 'twill then be strong enough to bear removal.'

" 'And what am I to do all the time without it?' asked Pugwash in a tone of banter. 'Come,' said he, still jesting, 'if you really have my soul, what's it like—what's its colour; if indeed souls have colours?'

" 'Green—green as a grasshopper when it first came into my hands,' said the wizard; 'but 'tis changing daily. More: it was a skipping, chirping, giddy soul; 'tis every hour mending. In a week's time, I tell you, it will be fit for the business of the world.'

" 'And pray, good father—for the matter has till now escaped me—what am I to pay you for this pain and trouble, for this precious care of my miserable soul?'

" 'Nothing,' answered Lotus, 'nothing whatever. The work is too nice and precious to be paid for; I have a reward you dream not of for my labour. Think you that men's immortal souls are to be mended like iron pots, at tinker's price? Oh, no! they who meddle with souls go for higher wages.'

"After further talk Pugwash departed, the conjurer promising to bring him home his soul at midnight that night week. It seemed strange to Pugwash, as the time passed on, that he never seemed to miss his soul; that, in very truth, he went through the labours of the day with even better gravity than when his soul possessed him. And more: he began to feel himself more at home in his shop; the cobbler's lark over the way continued to sing, but awoke in Isaac's heart no thought of the fields: and then for flowers and plants, why, Isaac began to think such matters fitter the thoughts of children and foolish girls than the attention of grown men with the world before them. Even Mrs. Pugwash saw an alteration in her husband; and though to him she said nothing, she returned thanks to her own sagacity that made him seek the conjurer.

"At length the night arrived when Lotus had promised to bring home the soul of Pugwash. He sent his wife to bed, and sat with his eyes upon the Dutch clock, anxiously awaiting the conjurer. Twelve o'clock struck, and at the same moment Father Lotus smote the door-post of Isaac Pugwash.

"'Have you brought it?' asked Pugwash.

"'Or wherefore should I come?' said Lotus. 'Quick; show a light to the till, that your soul may find itself at home.'

"'The till!' cried Pugwash; 'what the devil should my soul do in the till?'

"'Speak not irreverently,' said the conjurer, 'but show a light.'

"'May I live for ever in darkness if I do!' cried Pugwash.

"'It is no matter,' said the conjurer: and then he cried, 'Soul, to your earthly dwelling-place! Seek it—you know it.' Then turning to Pugwash, Lotus said, 'It is all right. Your soul's in the till.'

"'How did it get there?' cried Pugwash in amazement.

"'Through the slit in the counter,' said the conjurer; and ere Pugwash could speak again the conjurer had quitted the shop.

"For some minutes Pugwash felt himself afraid to stir. For the first time in his life he felt himself ill at ease, left as he was with no other company save his own soul. He at length took heart and went behind the counter that he might see if his soul was really in the till. With trembling hand he drew the coffer, and there, to his amazement, squatted like a tailor, upon a crown-piece, did Pugwash behold his own soul, which cried out to him in notes no louder than a cricket's—'How are you? *I* am comfortable.' It was a strange yet pleasing sight to Pugwash to behold what he felt to be his own soul embodied in a figure no bigger than the top joint of his thumb. There it was, a stark-naked thing with the precise features of Pugwash; albeit the complexion was of a yellower hue. 'The conjurer said it was green,' cried Pugwash: 'as I live, if that be my soul—and I begin to feel a strange odd love for it—it is yellow as a guinea. Ha! ha! Pretty, precious, darling soul!' cried Pugwash as the creature took up every piece of coin in the till and rang it with such a look of rascally cunning that sure I am Pugwash would in past times have hated the creature for the trick.

"But every day Pugwash became fonder and fonder of the creature in the till: it was to him such a counsellor and such a blessing. Whenever the old flower-man came to the door, the soul of Pugwash from the till would bid him pack with his rubbish : if a poor woman —an old customer it might be—begged for the credit of a loaf, the Spirit of the Till, calling through the slit in the counter, would command Pugwash to deny her. More : Pugwash never again took a bad shilling. No sooner did he throw the pocket-piece down upon the counter than the voice from the till would denounce its worthlessness. And the soul of Pugwash never quitted the till. There it lived, feeding upon the colour of money, and capering, and rubbing its small scoundrel hands in glee as the coin dropped—dropped in. In time the soul of Pugwash grew too big for so small a habitation, and then Pugwash moved his soul into an iron box; and some time after he sent his soul to his banker's—the thing had waxed so big and strong on gold and silver."

"And so," said we, "the man flourished, and the conjurer took no wages for all he did to the soul of Pugwash ?"

"Hear the end," said the Hermit. "For some time it was a growing pleasure to Pugwash to look at his soul, as it always was with the world-buying metals. At length he grew old, very old; and every day his soul grew uglier. Then he hated to look upon it; and then his soul would come to him and grin its deformity at him. Pugwash died, almost as rich as an Indian king; but he died, shrieking in his madness to be saved from the terrors of his own soul."

"And such the end," we said; "such the Tragedy of the Till ? A strange romance."

"Romance," said the Sage of Bellyfulle; "sir, 'tis a story true as life. For at this very moment how many thousands, blind and deaf to the sweet looks and voice of nature, live and die with their souls in a Till ?"

DOUGLAS JERROLD

JACQUES COCAST, THE HUNCHBACK PHILOSOPHER

"THANK God for my hunch!" cried Jacques Cocast, then eleven years old, and escaped from the pitying hands of Martin Fleau the miller, who, casting a compassionate glance at Cocast's unseemly load, exclaimed:

"Well, the saints have burthened thee enough—go, I wouldn't beat a hunchback."

"Thank God for my hunch!" were the grateful words of the apple-stealing Jacques, and he followed his lighter-heeled companions, who, on the first alarm, had scampered safely off from the miller's orchard, leaving the deformed co-mate to the vengeance of the despoiled. The miller, as we have shown, was merciful, and Jacques Cocast, the hunchback, went his way unbruised.

Jacques Cocast grew up, the living plaything of the boys of the village. He was their drudge, their jest, their scapegoat. His good-humour turned bitterness itself to merriment, and with at times the tears starting to his eyes he would laugh them down, and without knowing it play the practical philosopher.

"Out, ye imp of deformity!" cried Cocast's stepmother at least once a day; whereupon Jacques, to the increasing ire of his father's wife, would meekly cry:

"Thank God for my hunch!"

Left to himself, now spurned, and now at least endured by his growing companions, Jacques Cocast made a friend of his book, and found the exceeding reward of such friendship. He could read, write, and cypher to the shame of many of his seniors. Jacques Cocast's father took sudden pride in his own misshapen flesh, and Cocast's wife stormed at her stepson with increasing vigour.

The notary wanted a clerk. All eyes were turned upon Jacques as the very lad for the office. The notary himself condescended to canvass the pretensions of Jacques to the dignity. Already Jacques felt himself installed, when a slim, fair-haired, pink-complexioned youth was preferred to Cocast, the notary's wife having pithily informed her obedient husband that his house should be no dwelling-place for a hunchback.

Jacques Cocast sighed as he turned from the notary's door, and his heart beat heavily as he crawled to his paternal home. In two or three days, however, the hunchback smiled and laughed as before, and the clerkship was forgotten in sweet communings with his book.

Some four years passed on,—when oh, shame to the notary's wife—shame to the fair-haired youth—the faithless woman fled from the bosom of her husband, taking with her in her flight her husband's clerk! Great was the consternation throughout the village—loud and deep the revilings of every honest spouse. Jacques Cocast joined in no abuse; but with a fine charity for the inexperience of youth, with even a tenderness towards the sin of the unfaithful wife, and considering within himself the subtle powers of the tempter, he felt grateful for his escape, and breathed his gratitude in his wonted syllables:

"Thank God for my hunch!"

Jacques Cocast was now a painstaking, philosophic tailor; and from no high elevation than his shop-board could look down on many of the vanities of human life. He was now twenty, and increasing years had only served to mellow his rich heart and make him feel a lessening load upon his shoulders. Jacques would make one at all village holidays, led thereto by his own light-heartedness, and of late, furthermore urged to each festival by the blue eyes of Félicité, the baker's daughter.

Luckless Jacques Cocast! Fly the sweet perdition! You know not the falsehood of those azure lights—the venom of that pouting, pulpy lip; Félicité laughs with a witch's laugh at the love of the hunchback—whilst he, poor innocent—exalted, sublimated by his passion, lives in an atmosphere of balm and sun—vaults like a grasshopper about the earth, and gives his heart and soul to the tyranny that rejoices him. Jacques Cocast knew not vanity. He would clothe himself in the humblest weed, and then think that the best wardrobe which drew to itself the least notice. Now was it otherwise. The eyes of Félicité had smiled upon the tailor, and Jacques Cocast should henceforth be the best and the most critical customer of Jacques Cocast. If Félicité had looked with favour on his body, he would take the hitherto despised article under his future care and habit it worthy of her who had elected it as her own. As for his hump, that was gone, yea, vanished, melted in the sunlight of Félicité's eyes. With these rejoicing thoughts Jacques Cocast would array himself finely as the finest caterpillar; his vestments now barred, and spotted, and burnished with a hundred hues. And as he basked in the smiles of Félicité, the baker's wicked daughter would laugh in her hollow heart and the folks of the village would confidentially clap their fingers to their noses and wink towards the tailor.

For a month or more was Jacques Cocast the blissful Adam of this fool's paradise. For a full month did he breathe Elysium. At length the eyes of Jacques Cocast were opened and he saw his forlornness. It was the day of a *ducasse*. In the pride of his heart, and in all the glory of his trade, did the hunchback array himself to dance with Félicité, the baker's daughter. She had of late been so loving, so complying, so tender! The next dance might be at their own wedding. At all events, how they would dance on the coming Sunday! He, the hunchback, buoyed by his loving heart, would foot it so lightly that not a blade of grass should bend beneath him—not a dew-drop be scattered by his mercurial toe.

The dancers are assembled. The fiddles sound. Jacques Cocast, in all the glory of a new suit, burning like a peacock in a conflict of colours, and in the triumph of a gladdened soul, advances to lead out Félicité, the baker's daughter. Already he has his hand upon her hand when a gigantic thumb and finger with vice-like power grips the nose of Jacques Cocast and whirls him from his partner. A laugh that drowns the fiddles bursts from the merry-makers. Jacques Cocast, with lightning in his eyes, and all the blood in his body rushing to his nose, looked for his assailant.

Hercule Grossetête, a rival of six feet, French measure, with fierce eyes and parrot nose, glaring and protruding from between raven whiskers, with arms akimbo, stands before the tailor. Nevertheless, the soul of Jacques Cocast is mighty, and he is meditating how he may best spring upon the giant and tear his iron heart from his body, when—oh, ye daughters of Eve! oh, ye rosy wickednesses, ye honied poisons!—Félicité, the baker's daughter, advanced to Hercule, and curtseying, and putting her hand in his—in his hand, yet warm from the outraged nose of her doating lover, signified that she was ready to dance, that she had looked with eyes of favour on the punishment of the tailor. Then sank the heart of Jacques Cocast. He quitted the scene of his past happiness, and in an agony of despair wandered, a very lunatic.

Foolish Jacques Cocast! Who would pity the despair of a hunchback? Who compassionate a love-broken heart, if accompanied by overladen shoulders? What is a beautiful sentiment with a straight backed, comely man, is a thing for a jest, an excellent joke with a hunchback. And so, Jacques Cocast, go home. Sleep not in the fields at nights. Lie not under the window of the baker's daughter, and waste not away until, as you complain, your head has grown too little for your hat,—but up, man, and to your comfortable abode. Shave yourself, change your linen, leap upon your shop-board, thread your needle, heat your goose, and defy love! A friendly

Genius whispered some such advice to Jacques Cocast, for ere a month had passed, the tailor had once more taken to his sober attire, was seated smiling at his work, and if a thought of the cruel baker's daughter would sometimes intrude, he would banish the unwelcome guest by the very vehemence of stitching.

Months passed away, and the time of drawing for the conscription arrived. Mothers looked anxious—plighted maidens would sigh frequently and look with tender gaze upon their future husband—the young men would laugh, laugh louder than was their wont to hush the secret care that preyed upon them. But what was the conscription, with the banishment, the danger, the wounds and death combined in the word to Jacques Cocast ? He was a hunchback. His shoulders were exempt by nature from a knapsack. He was not a comely morsel for glory ; he was not worthy of the powder and shot bestowed upon prettier men. No, he was secure in his deformity ; his heart started not at the muttering of the beaten sheepskin. Hence Jacques Cocast, without one throb, save for the fate of some old acquaintance, might linger about the town-hall of the arrondissement, and learn the fortune of his fellow-villagers.

The day of drawing came. There was the shriek of triumph as one sprang into his mother's arms—as his sister clung about his neck—as his plighted wife, and *now* their wedding-day was certain—there were bursts of joy and tears of happiness as the exempt sprang among the crowd ; and there were cries of despair, and sobbings as among breaking hearts as the new conscripts told the fate that tore them from their homes.

"Thank God for my hunch ! " cried Jacques Cocast twenty times as he saw the wretchedness of the conscript soldier.

Among those drawn to wear future laurels was Hercule Grossetête. He looked savage as a snubbed ogre ; and the baker's beautiful daughter hung on his arm, and was crying her heart out, and vowing between her sobs that for the sake of her dear Hercule she would try to live and die a maid : and Hercule, with his fancy listening to the whistling bullets, smiled vacantly on the magnanimity of Félicité, and bade Heaven help her in all her trials.

And did the heart of Jacques Cocast rejoice at this ? By no means—he felt no triumph at the calamity of Grossetête—no pleasure at the grief of his fair, false baker's daughter ; but with a gush of gratitude he exclaimed :

"Thank God for my hunch ! "

Hercule Grossetête went to the wars. Fortune, that had heaped such obloquy upon the shoulders of Cocast, had fitted Grossetête for the dignity of a grenadier. He quitted the village, left the baker's daughter, and was soon marching, and perhaps day-dreaming of pillage and epaulettes. We know not what struggles Félicité endured to keep her pledge to Hercule; they must have been severe and manifold; for it was at least six months after the departure of her grenadier that she wedded the son of the village grocer, the grocer father opportunely dying and leaving his stock and business to his only son. All the world—that is, all the village—believed in the conjugal bliss of the grocer and his wife. Pierre Chandelles was so meek, so gentle a soul, any woman must be happy with him.

Again, Félicité was always the sweetest-tempered girl: there had been curious tales of her sudden passion, but such tales had been trumped up by the ugliest girls of the village.

Three months had passed since Pierre and Félicité were one; and Jacques Cocast—for in the magnanimity of his soul he did not withdraw his custom from Pierre on account of his wife; besides, Pierre's was the only shop in the village—modestly tapped a sou on Pierre's counter, it being the intention of the tailor to dispense that coin in beeswax. Suddenly there was a noise within; Jacques recognised the voice of Félicité, albeit he had never before heard it at so high a pitch. Another minute, and Pierre rushes into the shop followed by his wife, who, heedless of the wants of a customer, heedless of the cries of her husband, demolished an earthen pipkin, unluckily in her hand, upon her lord and sovereign's head. No sheep ever bled with more meekness than did Pierre Chandelles the grocer.

"What did you want?" asked Pierre, with still a vigilant eye to business.

"I'll call again when your wounds are dressed," said Jacques Cocast; "in the meantime, thank God for my hunch!"

Years went on, and Jacques Cocast gathered about him the small comforts of the world, and keeping the spirit of his youth, was blithe as a bird.

One autumn evening, wandering a mile or two on the road from the village, and thinking he knew not upon what, Jacques Cocast was suddenly startled in his reflections by a loud voice.

"For the love of the saints, if you have it, give me a pinch of snuff."

The prayer proceeded from a blind soldier, seated on a tree felled near the roadside.

"With all my heart," cried Cocast. "Here, empty my box."

"Alas, good sir!" said the soldier, "look at me again."

Cocast looked and saw that the man had lost both his arms.

"You must, indeed, *give* me the snuff," said the soldier.

"With all my heart, I say again," cried Cocast, and with the most delicate care he supplied the nostrils of the mutilated veteran.

"Good Heavens!" suddenly exclaimed Cocast, "why, you are Hercule Grossetête."

"I am," answered the soldier. "And what have you to say to that?"

"What!" Jacques Cocast, looking at the eyeless, armless victim of glory, could only say:

"*Thank God for my hunch!*"

Almost all men have a hunch of some kind. Let them, with Jacques Cocast, thank God for it.

BENJAMIN DISRAELI
1804–1881

A TRUE STORY

When I was a young boy I had delicate health, and was somewhat of a pensive and contemplative turn of mind: it was my delight in the long summer evenings to slip away from my noisy and more robust companions, that I might walk in the shade of a venerable wood, my favourite haunt, and listen to the cawing of the old rooks, who seemed as fond of this retreat as I was.

One evening I sat later than usual, though the distant sound of the cathedral clock had more than once warned me to my home. There was a stillness in all nature that I was unwilling to disturb by the least motion.

From this reverie I was suddenly startled by the sight of a tall, slender female who was standing by me, looking sorrowfully and steadily in my face. She was dressed in white, from head to foot, in a fashion I had never seen before; her garments were unusually long and flowing, and rustled as she glided through the low shrubs near me as if they were made of the richest silk. My heart beat as if I was dying, and I knew not that I could have stirred from the spot; but she seemed so very mild and beautiful, I did not attempt it. Her pale brown hair was braided round her head, but there were some locks that strayed upon her neck; and altogether she looked like a lovely picture, but not like a living woman. I closed my eyes forcibly with my hands, and when I looked again she had vanished.

I cannot exactly say why I did not on my return speak of this beautiful appearance, nor why, with a strange mixture of hope and fear, I went again and again to the same spot that I might see her. She always came, and often in the storm and the plashing rain, that never seemed to touch or to annoy her, and looked sweetly at me, and silently passed on; and though she was so near to me, that once the wind lifted those light straying locks, and I felt them against my cheek, yet I never could move or speak to her. I fell ill; and when I recovered my mother closely questioned me of the tall lady, of whom, in the height of my fever, I had so often spoken.

I cannot tell you what a weight was taken from my boyish spirits when I learnt that this was no apparition, but a most lovely woman; not young, though she had kept her young looks, for the grief which had broken her heart seemed to have spared her beauty.

When the rebel troops were retreating after their total defeat, in that very wood I was so fond of, a young officer, unable any longer to endure the anguish of his wounds, sunk from his horse, and laid himself down to die. He was found there by the daughter of Sir Henry R——, and conveyed by a trusty domestic to her father's mansion. Sir Henry was a loyalist; but the officer's desperate condition excited his compassion, and his many wounds spoke a language a brave man could not misunderstand. Sir Henry's daughter with many tears pleaded for him, and pronounced that he should be carefully and secretly attended. And well she kept that promise, for she waited upon him (her mother being long dead) for many weeks, and anxiously watched for the first opening of eyes, that, languid as he was, looked brightly and gratefully upon his young nurse.

You may fancy better than I can tell you, as he slowly recovered, all the moments that were spent in reading, and low-voiced singing, and gentle playing on the lute, and how many fresh flowers were brought to one whose wounded limbs would not bear him to gather them for himself, and how calmly the days glided on in the blessedness of returning health and in that sweet silence so carefully enjoined him.

I will pass by this to speak of one day, which, bright and pleasanter than others, did not seem more bright or more lovely than the looks of the young maiden, as she gaily spoke of "a little festival" which (though it must bear an unworthier name) she meant really to give in honour of her guest's recovery; "and it is time, lady," said he, "for that guest so tended and so honoured, to tell you his whole story, and speak to you of one who will help him to thank you; may I ask you, fair lady, to write a little billet for me, which even in these times of danger I may find some means to forward?"

To his mother, no doubt, she thought, as with light steps and a lighter heart she seated herself by his couch, and smilingly bade him dictate; but, when he said "My dear wife," and lifted up his eyes to be asked for more, he saw before him a pale statue, that gave him one look of utter despair, and fell, for he had no power to help her, heavily at his feet.

Those eyes never truly reflected the pure soul again, or answered by answering looks the fond enquiries of her poor old father.

She lived to be as I saw her,—sweet and gentle, and delicate always; but reason returned no more. She visited till the day of her death the spot where she first saw that young soldier, and dressed herself in the very clothes that he said so well became her.

SAMUEL WARREN
1807–1877

THE RESURRECTIONIST

My gentle reader—start not at learning that I have been, in my time, a resurrectionist! Let not this appalling word, this humiliating confession, conjure up in your fancy a throng of vampire-like images and associations, or earn your "Physician's" dismissal from your hearts and hearths. It is your own groundless fears, my fair trembler!—your own superstitious prejudices—that have driven me, and will drive many others of my brethren, to such dreadful doings as those hereafter detailed. Come, come—let us have one word of reason between us on the abstract question—and then for my tale. You expect us to cure you of disease, and yet deny us the only means of learning *how*! You would have us bring you the ore of skill and experience, yet forbid us to break the soil or sink a shaft! Is this fair, *fair* reader? Is this reasonable?

What I am now going to describe was my first and last exploit in the way of body-stealing. It was a grotesque if not a ludicrous scene, and occurred during the period of my "walking the hospitals," as it is called, which occupied the two seasons immediately after my leaving Cambridge. A young and rather interesting female was admitted a patient at the hospital I attended; her case baffled all our skill, and her symptoms even defied diagnosis. *Now*, it seemed an enlargement of the heart—now, an ossification—then this, that, and the other; and at last it was plain we knew nothing at all about the matter—no, not even whether her disorder was organic or functional, primary or symptomatic—or whether it *was* really the heart that was at fault. She received no benefit at all under the fluctuating schemes of treatment we pursued, and at length fell into dying circumstances. As soon as her friends were apprised of her situation, and had an inkling of our intention to open the body, they insisted on removing her immediately from the hospital, that she might "die at home."

In vain did Sir —— and his dressers expostulate vehemently with them, and represent, in exaggerated terms, the imminent peril attending such a step. Her two brothers avowed their apprehension of our designs, and were inflexible in exercising their right of removing their sister. I used all my rhetoric on the occasion, but in vain; and at last said to the young men, " Well, if you are afraid only of our *dissecting* her, we can get hold of her, if we are so disposed, as easily if she die with you as with us."

" Well—we'll *troy* that, measter," replied the elder, while his Herculean fist oscillated somewhat significantly before my eyes. The poor girl was removed accordingly to her father's house, which was at a certain village about five miles from London, and survived her arrival scarcely ten minutes! We soon contrived to receive intelligence of the event; and as I and Sir ——'s two dressers had taken great interest in the case throughout, and felt intense curiosity about the real nature of the disease, we met together and entered into a solemn compact, that, come what might, we would have her body out of the ground. A trusty spy informed us of the time and exact place of the girl's burial; and on expressing to Sir —— our determination about the matter, he patted me on the back, saying, " Ah, my fine fellow!—IF you have SPIRIT enough—dangerous," etc. etc.

Was it not skilfully said? The baronet further told us, he felt himself so curious about the matter that if fifty pounds would be of use to us in furthering our purpose, they were at our service. It needed not this, nor a glance at the *éclat* with which the successful issue of the affair would be attended among our fellow-students, to spur our resolves.

The notable scheme was finally adjusted at my rooms in the Borough. M—— and E——, Sir ——'s dressers, and myself, with an experienced "*grab*"—that is to say, a *professional* resurrectionist—were to set off from the Borough about nine o'clock the next evening—which would be the third day after the burial—in a glass coach provided with all " appliances and means to boot." During the day, however, our friend the grab suffered so severely from an overnight's excess as to disappoint us of his invaluable assistance. This unexpected *contretempts* nearly put an end to our project; for the few other grabs we knew were absent on *professional tours*! Luckily, however, I bethought me of a poor Irish porter—a sort of " ne'er-do-weel" hanger-on at the hospital—whom I had several times hired to go on errands. This man I sent for to my room, and, in the presence of my two coadjutors, persuaded, threatened, and bothered into acquiescence, promising him half-a-guinea for his evening's work—and as much whisky as he could drink prudently. As Mr. Tip—that was the name he went by—had some personal acquaintance with the sick grab, he succeeded in borrowing his chief tools; with which, in a sack large enough to contain our expected prize, he repaired to my rooms about nine o'clock, while the coach was standing at the door. Our Jehu had received a quiet douceur in addition to the hire of himself and coach.

As soon as we had exhibited sundry doses of Irish cordial to our friend Tip—under the effects of which he became quite " bouncible," and *ranted* about the feat he was to take a prominent part in—and equipped ourselves in our worst clothes, and white top-coats, we entered the vehicle—four in number—and drove off. The weather had been exceedingly capricious all the evening—moonlight, rain, thunder, and lightning, fitfully alternating. The only thing we were anxious about was the darkness, to shield us from all possible observation. I must own that, in analysing the feelings that prompted me to undertake and go through with this affair, the mere love of adventure operated quite as powerfully as the wish to benefit the cause of anatomical science. A midnight expedition to the tombs !—It took our fancy amazingly ; and then Sir ——'s cunning hint about the " danger "—and our " spirit " !

The garrulous Tip supplied us with amusement all the way down—rattle, rattle, rattle, incessantly ; but as soon as we had arrived at that part of the road where we were to stop, and caught sight of —— church, with its hoary steeple—glistening in the fading moonlight, as though it were standing sentinel over the graves around it, one of which we were going so rudely to violate—Tip's spirits began to falter a little. He said little—and that at intervals.

To be very candid with the reader, *none* of us felt over-much at our ease. Our expedition began to wear a somewhat hare-brained aspect, and to be environed with formidable contingencies which we had not taken sufficiently into our calculations. What, for instance, if the two stout fellows, the brothers, should be out watching their sister's grave ? They were not likely to stand on much ceremony with us. And then the manual difficulties ! E—— was the only one of us that had ever assisted at the exhumation of a body—and the rest of us were likely to prove but bungling workmen. However, we had gone too far to think of retreating. We none of us *spoke* our suspicions, but the silence that reigned within the coach was tolerably significant. In contemplation, however, of some such contingency we had put a bottle of brandy in the coach pocket ; and before we drew up, had all four of us drunk pretty deeply of it. At length the coach turned down a by-lane to the left, which led directly to the churchyard wall ; and after moving a few steps down it, in order to shelter our vehicle from the observation of highway passengers, the coach stopped, and the driver opened the door.

" Come, Tip," said I, " out with you."

" Get out, did you say, sir ? To be sure I will—Och ! to be sure I will." But there was small show of alacrity in his movements as he descended the steps ; for while I was speaking I was interrupted by the solemn clangour of the church clock announcing the hour of midnight. The sounds seemed to *warn* us against what we were going to do.

" 'Tis a cowld night, yer honours," said Tip, in an undertone, as we successively alighted, and stood together, looking up and down the dark lane, to see if anything was stirring but ourselves. " 'Tis a cowld night—and—and—and," he stammered.

" Why, you cowardly old scoundrel," grumbled M——, " are you frightened already ? What's the matter, eh ? Hoist up the bag on your shoulders directly, and lead the way down the lane."

" Och, but yer honours—och ! by the mother that bore me, but 'tis a murtherous cruel thing, I'm thinking, to wake the poor cratur from her last sleep."

He said this so querulously, that I began to entertain serious apprehensions, after all, of his defection ; so I insisted on his taking a little more brandy, by way of bringing him up to par. It was of no use, however. His reluctance increased every moment—and it even dispirited *us*. I verily believe the turning of a straw would have decided us all on jumping into the coach again, and returning home without accomplishing our errand. Too many of the students, however, were apprised of our expedition, for us to think of terminating it so ridiculously. As it were by mutual consent, we stood and paused a few moments, about half-way down the lane. M—— whistled with infinite spirit and distinctness ; E—— remarked to me that he always " thought a churchyard at midnight was the gloomiest object imaginable " ; and I talked about *business*— " soon be over "—" shallow grave "—etc. etc.

" Confound it—what if those two brothers of hers SHOULD be there ? " said M—— abruptly, making a dead stop, and folding his arms on his breast.

" Powerful fellows, both of them ! " muttered E——. We resumed our march—when Tip, our advanced guard—a title he earned by anticipating our steps about three inches—suddenly stood still, let down the bag from his shoulders, elevated both hands in a listening attitude, and exclaimed, " Whisht !—whisht !—By my soul, *what* was that ? "

We all paused in silence, looking palely at one another—but could hear nothing except the drowsy flutter of a bat wheeling away from us a little overhead.

" Fait—an' wasn't it somebody *spaking* on the far side o' the hedge I heard ? " whispered Tip.

" Poh—stuff, you idiot ! " I exclaimed, losing my temper. " Come, M—— and E——, it's high time we had done with all this cowardly nonsense ; and if we mean really to *do* anything, we must make haste. 'Tis past twelve—day breaks about four—and it is coming on wet, you see." Several large drops of rain, pattering heavily among the leaves and branches, corroborated my words, by announcing a coming shower, and the air was sultry enough to warrant the expectation of a thunderstorm. We therefore buttoned up our greatcoats to the chin, and hurried on to the churchyard wall, which ran across the bottom of the lane. This wall we had to climb over to get into the churchyard, and it was not a very high one.

Here Tip annoyed us again. I told him to lay down his bag, mount the wall, and look over into the yard, to see whether all was clear before us; and, as far as the light would enable him, to look about for a new-made grave. Very reluctantly he complied, and contrived to scramble to the top of the wall. He had hardly time, however, to peer over into the churchyard, when a fluttering streak of lightning flashed over us, followed, in a second or two, by a loud burst of thunder! Tip fell in an instant to the ground, like a cockchafer shaken from an elm-tree, and lay crossing himself, and muttering paternosters. We could scarcely help laughing at the manner in which he tumbled down, simultaneously with the flash of lightning. "Now, look ye, gintlemen," said he, still squatting on the ground, "do you mane to give the poor cratur Christian burial, when ye've done wid her? An' will you put her back again as ye found her? 'Case, if you won't, blood an' oons"——

"Hark ye now, Tip," said I sternly, taking out one of a brace of *empty* pistols I had put into my greatcoat pocket, and presenting it to his head, "we have hired you on this business, for the want of a better, you wretched fellow! and if you give us any more of your nonsense, by —— I'll send a bullet through your brain! Do you hear me, Tip?"

"Och, aisy, aisy wid ye! don't murther me! Bad luck to me that I ever cam wid ye! Och, and if ivver I live to die, won't I see and bury my ould body out o' the rache of all the docthers in the world? If I don't, divel burn me!" We all laughed aloud at Tip's truly Hibernian expostulation.

"Come, sir, mount! over with you!" said we, helping to push him upwards. "Now, drop this bag on the other side," we continued, giving him the sack that contained our implements. We all three of us then followed, and alighted safely in the churchyard. It poured with rain; and, to enhance the dreariness and horrors of the time and place, flashes of lightning followed in quick succession, shedding a transient awful glare over the scene, revealing the white tombstones, the ivy-grown venerable church, and our own figures, a shivering group, come on an unhallowed errand! I perfectly well recollect the lively feelings of apprehension—"the compunctious visitings of remorse"—which the circumstances called forth in my own breast, and which, I had no doubt, were shared by my companions.

As no time, however, was to be lost, I left the group, for an instant, under the wall to search out the grave. The accurate instructions I had received enabled me to pitch on the spot with little difficulty; and I returned to my companions, who immediately followed me to the scene of operations. We had no umbrellas, and our greatcoats were saturated with wet; but the brandy we had recently taken did us good service, by exhilarating our spirits and especially those of Tip. He untied the sack in a twinkling, and shook out the hoes and spades, etc.; and taking one of the latter himself, he commenced digging with such energy that we had hardly prepared ourselves for work before he had cleared away nearly the whole of the mound. The rain soon abated, and the lightning ceased for a considerable interval, though thunder was heard occasionally grumbling sullenly in the distance, as if expressing anger at our unholy doings—at least I felt it so. The pitchy darkness continued, so that we could scarcely see one another's figures. We worked on in silence, as fast as our spades could be got into the ground; taking it in turns, two by two, as the grave would not admit of more. On—on—on we worked till we had hollowed out about three feet of earth. Tip then hastily joined together a long iron screw or borer, which he thrust into the ground, for the purpose of ascertaining the depth at which the coffin yet lay from us.

To our vexation, we found a distance of three feet remained to be got through.

"Sure, and by the soul of St. Patrick, but we'll not be done by the morning!" said Tip, as he threw down the instrument and resumed his spade.

We were all discouraged. Oh, how earnestly I wished myself at home, in my snug little bed in the Borough! How I cursed the Quixotism that had led me into such an undertaking! I had no time, however, for reflection, as it was my turn to relieve one of the diggers; so into the grave I jumped, and worked away as lustily as before. While I was thus engaged, a sudden noise, close to our ears, so startled me, that I protest I thought I should have dropped down dead in the grave I was robbing.

I and my fellow-digger let fall our spades, and all four stood still for a second or two in an ecstasy of fearful apprehension. We could not see more than a few inches around us, but heard the grass trodden by approaching feet! They proved to be those of an ass, that was turned at night into the churchyard, and had gone on eating his way towards us; and, while we were standing in mute expectation of what was to come next, opened on us with an astounding hee-haw! hee-haw! hee-haw! Even after we had discovered the ludicrous nature of the interruption, we were too agitated to laugh. The brute was actually close upon us, and had *given tongue* from under poor Tip's elbow, having approached him from behind as he stood leaning on his spade. Tip started suddenly backward against the animal's head, and fell down.

Away sprang the jackass, as much confounded as Tip, kicking and scampering like a mad creature among the tombstones, and hee-hawing incessantly, as if a hundred devils had got into it for the purpose of discomfiting us. I felt so much fury and fear lest the noise should lead to our discovery I could have killed the brute if it had been within my reach, while Tip stammered, in an affrightened whisper—" Och, the baste ! Och, the baste ! The big black divel of a baste ! The murtherous, thundering " —— and a great many epithets of the same sort. We gradually recovered from the agitation which this provoking interruption had occasioned ; and Tip, under the promise of two bottles of whisky as soon as we arrived safe at home with our prize, renewed his exertions, and dug with such energy that we soon cleared away the remainder of the superincumbent earth, and stood upon the bare lid of the coffin. The grapplers, with ropes attached to them, were then fixed in the sides and extremities, and we were in the act of raising the coffin, when the sound of a human voice, accompanied with footsteps, fell on our startled ears. We heard both distinctly, and crouched down close over the brink of the grave, awaiting in breathless suspense a corroboration of our fears. After a pause of two or three minutes, however, finding that the sounds were not renewed, we began to breathe freer, persuaded that our ears must have deceived us.

Once more we resumed our work, succeeded in hoisting up the coffin—not without a slip, however, which nearly precipitated it down again to the bottom, with all four of us upon it—and depositing it on the graveside. Before proceeding to use our screws or wrenches, we once more looked and listened, and listened and looked ; but neither seeing nor hearing anything we set to work, prized off the lid in a twinkling, and a transient glimpse of moonlight disclosed to us the shrouded inmate—all white and damp. I removed the face-cloth, and unpinned the cap, while M—— loosed the sleeves from the wrists. Thus were we engaged, when E——, who had hold of the feet, ready to lift them out, suddenly let them go—gasped, " Oh, my God ! there they are ! " and placed his hand on my arm. He shook like an aspen leaf. I looked towards the quarter whither his eyes were directed, and, sure enough, saw the figure of a man—if not two—moving stealthily towards us. " Well, we're discovered, that's clear," I whispered as calmly as I could.

" We shall be murdered ! " groaned E——.

" Lend me one of the pistols you have with you," said M—— resolutely ; " by ——, I'll have a shot for my life, however ! "

As for poor Tip, who had heard every syllable of this startling colloquy, and himself seen the approaching figures, he looked at me in silence, the image of black horror! I could have laughed even then, to see his staring black eyes—his little cocked ruby-tinted nose—his chattering teeth.

"Hush—hush!" said I, cocking my pistol, while M—— did the same; for none but myself knew that they were unloaded. To add to our consternation, the malignant moon withdrew the small scantling of light she had been doling out to us, and sank beneath a vast cloud, "black as Erebus," but not before we had caught a glimpse of two more figures moving towards us in an opposite direction. "Surrounded!" two of us muttered in the same breath. We all rose to our feet, and stood together, not knowing what to do—unable in the darkness to see one another distinctly. Presently we heard a voice say, in a subdued tone, "Where are they? where? *Sure* I saw them! Oh, there they are. Halloa—halloa!"

That was enough—the signal of our flight. Without an instant's pause, or uttering another syllable, off we sprung, like small-shot from a gun's mouth, all of us in different directions, we knew not whither. I heard the report of a gun—mercy on me! and pelted away, scarcely knowing what I was about, dodging among the graves—now coming full-butt against a plaguy tombstone, then tumbling on the slippery grass—while some one followed close at my heels, panting and puffing, but whether friend or foe I knew not.

At length I stumbled against a large tombstone; and, finding it open at the two ends, crept under it, resolved there to abide the issue. At the moment of my ensconcing myself the sound of the person's footsteps who had followed me suddenly ceased. I heard a splashing sound, then a kicking and scrambling, a faint stifled cry of "Ugh—oh ugh!" and all was still. Doubtless it must be one of my companions, who had been wounded. What could I do, however? I did not know in what direction he lay—the night was pitch-dark—and if I crept from my hiding-place, for all I knew, I might be shot myself. I shall never forget that hour—no, never! There was I, squatting like a tod on the wet grass and weeds, not daring to do more than breathe! Here was a predicament! I could not conjecture how the affair would terminate.

Was I to lie where I was till daylight, that then I might step into the arms of my captors? What was become of my companions? While turning these thoughts in my mind, and wondering that all was so quiet, my ear caught the sound of the splashing of water, apparently at but a yard or two's distance, mingled with the sounds of a half-smothered human voice—"Ugh! ugh! Och, murther! murther! murther!"—another splash—"and isn't it dead, and drowned, and kilt I am"——

Whew! *Tip* in trouble, thought I, not daring to speak. Yes—

it was poor Tip, I afterwards found—who had followed at my heels, scampering after me as fast as fright could drive him, till his career was unexpectedly ended by his tumbling—souse—head over heels, into a newly-opened grave in his path, with more than a foot of water in it. There the poor fellow remained, after recovering from the first shock of his fall, not daring to utter a word for some time, lest he should be discovered—straddling over the water with his toes and elbows stuck into the loose soil on each side, to support him. This was his interesting position, as he subsequently informed me, at the time of uttering the sounds which first attracted my attention. Though not aware of his situation at the time, I was almost choked with laughter as he went on with his soliloquy, somewhat in this strain :—

"Och, Tip, ye ould divel! Don't it sarve ye right, ye fool? Ye villainous ould coffin-robber! Won't ye burn for this hereafter, ye sinner? Ulaloo! When ye are dead yourself, may ye be trated like that poor cratur—and yourself alive to see it! Och, hubbaboo! hubbaboo! Isn't it sure that I'll be drowned, an' then it's kilt I'll be!" A loud splash, and a pause for a few moments, as if he were readjusting his footing—"Och! an' I'm catching my dith of cowld! Fait, an' it's a divel a drop o' the two bottles o' whisky I'll ever see—Och, och, och!"—another splash—"och, an' isn't this uncomfortable! Murther and oons!—if ever I come out of this—sha'n't I be dead before I do?"

"Tip—Tip—Tip!" I whispered in a low tone. There was a dead silence. "Tip, Tip, where are you? What's the matter, eh?" No answer; but he muttered in a low tone to himself—"*Where am I!* by my soul! Isn't it dead, and kilt, and drowned, and murthered I am—that's all!"

"Tip—Tip—Tip!" I repeated, a little louder.

"Tip, indeed! Fait, ye may call, bad luck to ye—whoever ye are—but it's divel a word I'll be after spaking to ye."

"Tip, you simpleton! It's I—Mr. ——."

In an instant there was a sound of jumping and splashing, as if surprise had made him slip from his standing again, and he called out, "Whoo! whoo! an' is't you, sweet Mr. ——! What is the matter wid ye? Are ye kilt? Where are they all? Have they taken ye away, every mother's son of you?" he asked eagerly, in a breath.

"Why, what are *you* doing, Tip? Where are *you*?"

"Fait, an' it's being *washed* I am, in the feet, and in the queerest *tub* your honour ever saw!" A noise of scuffling not many yards off, silenced us both in an instant.

Presently I distinguished the voice of E——, calling out, "Help, M——!" (my name)—"Where are you?" The noise increased, and seemed nearer than before. I crept from my lurking place, and aided at Tip's resurrection, when both of us hurried towards the spot whence the sound came. By the faint moonlight I could just see the outlines of two figures violently struggling and grappling together. Before I could come up to them both fell down, locked in each other's arms, rolling over each other, grasping one another's collars, gasping and panting as if in mortal struggle. The moon suddenly emerged, and who do you think, reader, was E——'s antagonist ? Why, the person whose appearance had so discomfited and affrighted us all—OUR COACHMAN.

That worthy individual, alarmed at our protracted stay, had, contrary to our injunctions, left his coach to come and search after us. He it was whom we had seen stealing towards us ; his step—his voice had alarmed us, for he could not see us distinctly enough to discover whether we were his fare or not. He was on the point of whispering my name, it seems—when we must all have understood one another—when lo ! we all started off in the manner which has been described ; and he himself, not knowing that he was the reason of it, had taken to his heels, and fled for his life ! He supposed we had fallen into a sort of ambuscade. He happened to hide himself behind the tombstone next but one to that which sheltered E——. Finding all quiet, he and E——, as if by mutual consent, were groping from their hiding-places, when they unexpectedly fell foul of one another—each too affrighted to speak—and hence the scuffle.

After this satisfactory dénouement we all repaired to the grave's mouth, and found the corpse and coffin precisely as we had left them. We were not many moments in taking out the body, stripping it, and thrusting it into the sack we had brought. We then tied the top of the sack, carefully deposited the shroud, etc., in the coffin, re-screwed down the lid—fearful, impious mockery !—and consigned it once more to its resting-place, Tip scattering a handful of earth on the lid, and exclaiming reverently—" An' may the Lord forgive us for what we have done to ye ! " The coachman and I then took the body between us to the coach, leaving M——, and E——, and Tip to fill up the grave.

Our troubles were not yet ended, however. Truly it seemed as though Providence were throwing every obstacle in our way. Nothing went right. On reaching the spot where we had left the coach, behold it lay several yards farther in the lane, tilted into the ditch—for the horses, being hungry, and left to themselves, in their anxiety to graze on the verdant bank of the hedge, had contrived to overturn the vehicle in the ditch—and one of the horses was kicking vigorously when we came up—the whole body off the ground—and resting on that of his companion. We had considerable difficulty in righting the coach, as the horses were inclined to be obstreperous. We succeeded, however—deposited our unholy spoil within, turned the horses' heads towards the high road, and then, after enjoining Jehu to keep his place on the box, I went to see how my companions were getting on. They had nearly completed their task, and told me that "shovelling *in* was surprisingly easier than shovelling *out*!"

We took great pains to leave everything as neat and as nearly resembling what we found it as possible, in order that our visit might not be suspected. We then carried away each our own tools, and hurried as fast as possible to our coach, for the dim twilight had already stolen a march upon us, devoutly thankful that, after so many interruptions, we had succeeded in effecting our object.

It was broad daylight before we reached town, and a wretched coach company we looked, all wearied and dirty—Tip especially, who nevertheless snored in the corner as comfortably as if he had been warm in his bed. I heartily resolved with him, on leaving the coach, that it should be "the devil's own dear self only that should timpt me out again *body-snatching*!"

MRS. GASKELL
1810–1865

THE SQUIRE'S STORY

IN the year 1769 the little town of Barford was thrown into a state of great excitement by the intelligence that a gentleman (and "quite the gentleman," said the landlord of the George Inn) had been looking at Mr. Clavering's old house. This house was neither in the town nor in the country. It stood on the outskirts of Barford, on the roadside leading to Derby. The last occupant had been a Mr. Clavering—a Northumberland gentleman of good family—who had come to live in Barford while he was but a younger son; but when some elder branches of the family died, he had returned to take possession of the family estate. The house of which I speak was called the White House, from its being covered with a greyish kind of stucco. It had a good garden to the back, and Mr. Clavering had built capital stables, with what were then considered the latest improvements. The point of good stabling was expected to let the house, as it was in a hunting county; otherwise it had few recommendations. There were many bedrooms; some entered through others, even to the number of five, leading one beyond the other; several sitting-rooms of the small and poky kind, wainscoted round with wood, and then painted a heavy slate colour; one good dining-room, and a drawing-room over it, both looking into the garden, with pleasant bow-windows.

Such was the accommodation offered by the White House. It did not seem to be very tempting to strangers, though the good people of Barford rather piqued themselves on it, as the largest house in the town; and as a house in which "townspeople" and "county people" had often met at Mr. Clavering's friendly dinners. To appreciate this circumstance of pleasant recollection, you should have lived some years in a little country town, surrounded by gentlemen's seats. You would then understand how a bow or a courtesy from a member of a county family elevates the individuals who receive it almost as much, in their own eyes, as the pair of blue garters fringed with silver did Mr. Bickerstaff's ward. They trip lightly on air for a whole day afterwards. Now Mr. Clavering was gone, where could town and county mingle ?

I mention these things that you may have an idea of the desirability of the letting of the White House in the Barfordites' imagination ; and to make the mixture thick and slab, you must add for yourselves the bustle, the mystery, and the importance which every little event either causes or assumes in a small town ; and then, perhaps, it will be no wonder to you that twenty ragged little urchins accompanied the " gentleman " aforesaid to the door of the White House ; and that, although he was above an hour inspecting it under the auspices of Mr. Jones, the agent's clerk, thirty more had joined themselves on to the wondering crowd before his exit, and awaited such crumbs of intelligence as they could gather before they were threatened or whipped out of hearing distance. Presently out came the " gentleman " and the lawyer's clerk. The latter was speaking as he followed the former over the threshold. The gentleman was tall, well-dressed, handsome ; but there was a sinister cold look in his quick-glancing, light blue eye, which a keen observer might not have liked. There were no keen observers among the boys and ill-conditioned gaping girls. But they stood too near ; inconveniently close ; and the gentleman, lifting up his right hand, in which he carried a short riding-whip, dealt one or two sharp blows to the nearest, with a look of savage enjoyment on his face as they moved away whimpering and crying. An instant after, his expression of countenance had changed.

" Here ! " said he, drawing out a handful of money, partly silver, partly copper, and throwing it into the midst of them. " Scramble for it ! fight it out, my lads ! Come this afternoon, at three, to the George, and I'll throw you out some more."

So the boys hurrahed for him as he walked off with the agent's clerk. He chuckled to himself, as over a pleasant thought. " I'll have some fun with those lads," he said ; " I'll teach 'em to prowling and prying about me. I'll tell you what I'll do. I'll make the money so hot in the fire-shovel that it shall burn their fingers. You come and see the faces and the howling. I shall be very glad if you will dine with me at two ; and by that time I may have made up my mind respecting the house."

Mr. Jones, the agent's clerk, agreed to come to the George at two, but, somehow, he had a distaste for his entertainer. Mr. Jones would not like to have said, even to himself, that a man with a purse full of money, who kept many horses, and spoke familiarly of noblemen—above all, who thought of taking the White House—could be anything but a gentleman ; but still the uneasy wonder as to who this Mr. Robinson Higgins could be, filled the clerk's mind long after Mr. Higgins, Mr. Higgins's servants, and Mr. Higgins's stud had taken possession of the White House.

The White House was re-stuccoed (this time of a pale yellow colour), and put into thorough repair by the accommodating and delighted landlord; while his tenant seemed inclined to spend any amount of money on internal decorations, which were showy and effective in their character, enough to make the White House a nine days' wonder to the good people of Barford. The slate-coloured paints became pink, and were picked out with gold; the old-fashioned banisters were replaced by newly gilt ones; but, above all, the stables were a sight to be seen. Since the days of the Roman Emperor never was there such provision made for the care, the comfort, and the health of horses. But every one said it was no wonder, when they were led through Barford, covered up to their eyes, but curving their arched and delicate necks, and prancing with short high steps, in repressed eagerness.

Only one groom came with them; yet they required the care of three men. Mr. Higgins, however, preferred engaging two lads out of Barford; and Barford highly approved of his preference. Not only was it kind and thoughtful to give employment to the lounging lads themselves, but they were receiving such a training in Mr. Higgins's stables as might fit them for Doncaster or Newmarket.

The district of Derbyshire in which Barford was situated was too close to Leicestershire not to support a hunt and a pack of hounds. The master of the hounds was a certain Sir Harry Manley, who was *aut* a huntsman *aut nullus*. He measured a man by the "length of his fork," not by the expression of his countenance or the shape of his head. But, as Sir Harry was wont to observe, there was such a thing as too long a fork, so his approbation was withheld until he had seen a man on horseback; and if his seat there was square and easy, his hand light, and his courage good, Sir Harry hailed him as a brother.

Mr. Higgins attended the first meet of the season, not as a subscriber but as an amateur. The Barford huntsmen piqued themselves on their bold riding; and their knowledge of the country came by nature; yet this new strange man, whom nobody knew, was in at the death, sitting on his horse, both well breathed and calm, without a hair turned on the sleek skin of the latter, supremely addressing the old huntsman as he hacked off the tail of the fox; and he, the old man, who was testy even under Sir Harry's slightest rebuke, and flew out on any other member of the hunt that dared to utter a word against his sixty years' experience as stable-boy, groom, poacher, and what not—he, old Isaac Wormeley, was meekly listening to the wisdom of this stranger, only now and then giving one of his quick, up-turning, cunning glances, not unlike the sharp o'er-canny looks of the poor deceased Reynard, round whom the hounds were howling, unadmonished by the short whip, which was now tucked into Wormeley's well-worn pocket.

When Sir Harry rode into the copse—full of dead brushwood and wet tangled grass—and was followed by the members of the hunt, as one by one they cantered past, Mr. Higgins took off his cap and bowed—half deferentially, half insolently—with a lurking smile in the corner of his eye at the discomfited looks of one or too of the laggards.

" A famous run, sir," said Sir Harry. " The first time you have hunted in our country ; but I hope we shall see you often."

" I hope to become a member of the hunt, sir," said Mr. Higgins.

" Most happy—proud, I'm sure, to receive so daring a rider among us. You took the Cropper-gate, I fancy ; while some of our friends here "—scowling at one or two cowards by way of finishing his speech. " Allow me to introduce myself—master of the hounds." He fumbled in his waistcoat pocket for the card on which his name was formally inscribed. " Some of our friends here are kind enough to come home with me to dinner ; might I ask for the honour ? "

" My name is Higgins," replied the stranger, bowing low. " I am only lately come to occupy the White House at Barford, and I have not as yet presented my letters of introduction."

" Hang it ! " replied Sir Harry ; " a man with a seat like yours, and that good brush in your hand, might ride up to any door in the county (I'm a Leicestershire man !) and be a welcome guest. Mr. Higgins, I shall be proud to become better acquainted with you over my dinner-table."

Mr. Higgins knew pretty well how to improve the acquaintance thus begun. He could sing a good song, tell a good story, and was well up in practical jokes ; with plenty of that keen worldly sense, which seems like an instinct in some men, and which in this case taught him on whom he might play off such jokes, with impunity from their resentment, and with a security of applause from the more boisterous, vehement, or prosperous. At the end of twelve months Mr. Robinson Higgins was, out-and-out, the most popular member of the Barford hunt ; had beaten all the others by a couple of lengths, as his first patron, Sir Harry, observed one evening, when they were just leaving the dinner-table of an old hunting squire in the neighbourhood.

" Because, you know," said Squire Hearn, holding Sir Harry by the button—" I mean, you see, this young spark is looking sweet upon Catherine ; and she's a good girl, and will have ten thousand pounds down, the day she's married, by her mother's will ; and—excuse me, Sir Harry—but I should not like my girl to throw herself away."

Though Sir Harry had a long ride before him, and but the early and short light of a new moon to take it in, his kind heart was so much touched by Squire Hearn's trembling, tearful anxiety, that he stopped and turned back into the dining-room to say, with more asseverations than I care to give :

" My good Squire, I may say I know that man pretty well by this time, and a better fellow never existed. If I had twenty daughters he should have the pick of them."

Squire Hearn never thought of asking the grounds for his old friend's opinion of Mr. Higgins ; it had been given with too much earnestness for any doubts to cross the old man's mind as to the possibility of its not being well founded. Mr. Hearn was not a doubter, or a thinker, or suspicious by nature ; it was simply love for Catherine, his only daughter, that prompted his anxiety in this case ; and, after what Sir Harry had said, the old man could totter with an easy mind, though not with very steady legs, into the drawing-room, where his bonny, blushing daughter Catherine and Mr. Higgins stood close together on the hearth-rug—he whispering, she listening with downcast eyes.

She looked so happy, so like what her dead mother had looked when the Squire was a young man, that all his thought was how to please her most. His son and heir was about to be married, and bring his wife to live with the Squire ; Barford and the White House were not distant an hour's ride ; and, even as these thoughts passed through his mind, he asked Mr. Higgins if he could not stay all night—the young moon was already set—the roads would be dark—and Catherine looked up with a pretty anxiety, which, however, had not much doubt in it, for the answer.

With every encouragement of this kind from the old Squire, it took everybody rather by surprise when one morning it was discovered that Miss Catherine Hearn was missing ; and when, according to the usual fashion in such cases, a note was found, saying that she had eloped with " the man of her heart," and gone to Gretna Green, no one could imagine why she could not quietly have stopped at home and been married in the parish church. She had always been a romantic, sentimental girl ; very pretty and very affectionate, and very much spoiled, and very much wanting in common sense. Her indulgent father was deeply hurt at this want of confidence in his never-varying affection ; but when his son came, hot with indignation from the Baronet's (his future father-in-law's house, where every form of law and of ceremony was to accompany his own impending marriage), Squire Hearn pleaded the cause of the young couple with imploring cogency, and protested that it was a piece of spirit in his daughter, which he admired and was proud of.

However, it ended with Mr. Nathaniel Hearn's declaring that he and his wife would have nothing to do with his sister and her husband.

"Wait till you've seen him, Nat!" said the old Squire, trembling with his distressful anticipations of family discord; "he's an excuse for any girl. Only ask Sir Harry's opinion of him."

"Confound Sir Harry! So that a man sits his horse well, Sir Harry cares nothing about anything else. Who is this man—this fellow? Where does he come from? What are his means? Who are his family?"

"He comes from the south—Surrey or Somersetshire, I forget which; and he pays his way well and liberally. There's not a tradesman in Barford but says he cares no more for money than for water; he spends like a prince, Nat. I don't know who his family are, but he seals with a coat of arms, which may tell you if you want to know—and he goes regularly to collect his rents from his estates in the south. Oh, Nat! if you would but be friendly, I should be as well pleased with Kitty's marriage as any father in the county."

Mr. Nathaniel Hearn gloomed, and muttered an oath or two to himself. The poor old father was reaping the consequences of his weak indulgence to his two children. Mr. and Mrs. Nathaniel Hearn kept apart from Catherine and her husband; and Squire Hearn durst never ask them to Levison Hall, though it was his own house. Indeed, he stole away as if he were a culprit whenever he went to visit the White House; and if he passed a night there, he was fain to equivocate when he returned home the next day; an equivocation which was well interpreted by the surly, proud Nathaniel. But the younger Mr. and Mrs. Hearn were the only people who did not visit at the White House.

Mr. and Mrs. Higgins were decidedly more popular than their brother and sister-in-law. She made a very pretty, sweet-tempered hostess, and her education had not been such as to make her intolerant of any want of refinement in the associates who gathered round her husband. She had gentle smiles for townspeople as well as county people; and unconsciously played an admirable second in her husband's project of making himself universally popular.

But there is some one to make ill-natured remarks, and draw ill-natured conclusions from very simple premises, in every place; and in Barford this bird of ill-omen was a Miss Pratt. She did not hunt—so Mr. Higgins's admirable riding did not call out her admiration. She did not drink—so the well-selected wines, so lavishly dispensed among his guests, could never mollify Miss Pratt. She could not bear comic songs, or buffo stories—so, in that way, her approbation was impregnable. And these three secrets of popularity constituted Mr. Higgins's great charm.

Miss Pratt sat and watched. Her face looked immovably grave

at the end of any of Mr. Higgins's best stories; but there was a keen, needle-like glance of her unwinking little eyes, which Mr. Higgins felt rather than saw, and which made him shiver, even on a hot day, when it fell upon him. Miss Pratt was a dissenter, and, to propitiate this female Mordecai, Mr. Higgins asked the dissenting minister whose services she attended, to dinner; kept himself and his company in good order; gave a handsome donation to the poor of the chapel.

All in vain—Miss Pratt stirred not a muscle more of her face towards graciousness; and Mr. Higgins was conscious that, in spite of all his open efforts to captivate Mr. Davis, there was a secret influence on the other side, throwing in doubts and suspicions, and evil interpretations of all he said or did. Miss Pratt, the little, plain old maid, living on eighty pounds a year, was the thorn in the popular Mr. Higgins's side, although she had never spoken one uncivil word to him; indeed, on the contrary, had treated him with a stiff and elaborate civility.

The thorn—the grief to Mrs. Higgins was this. They had no children! Oh! how she would stand and envy the careless, busy motion of half a dozen children; and then, when observed, move on with a deep, deep sigh of yearning regret. But it was as well.

It was noticed that Mr. Higgins was remarkably careful of his health. He ate, drank, took exercise, rested, by some secret rules of his own; occasionally bursting into an excess, it is true, but only on rare occasions—such as when he returned from visiting his estates in the south, and collecting his rents. That unusual exertion and fatigue—for there were no stage-coaches within forty miles of Barford, and he, like most country gentlemen of that day, would have preferred riding if there had been—seemed to require some strange excess to compensate for it; and rumours went through the town that he shut himself up, and drank enormously for some days after his return. But no one was admitted to these orgies.

One day—they remembered it well afterwards—the hounds met not far from the town; and the fox was found in a part of the wild heath, which was beginning to be enclosed by a few of the more wealthy townspeople, who were desirous of building themselves houses rather more in the country than those they had hitherto lived in.

Among these the principal was a Mr. Dudgeon, the attorney of Barford, and the agent for all the county families about. The firm of Dudgeon had managed the leases, the marriage-settlements, and the wills of the neighbourhood for generations. Mr. Dudgeon's father had the responsibility of collecting the landowners' rents just as the present Mr. Dudgeon had at the time of which I speak: and as his son and his son's son have done since. Their business was an hereditary estate to them; and with something of the old feudal feeling was mixed a kind of proud humility at their position towards the squires whose family secrets they had mastered, and the mysteries of whose fortunes and estates were better known to the Messrs. Dudgeon than to themselves.

Mr. John Dudgeon had built himself a house on Wildbury Heath—a mere cottage, as he called it; but though only two storeys high, it spread out far and wide, and workpeople from Derby had been sent for on purpose to make the inside as complete as possible. The gardens too were exquisite in arrangement, if not very extensive; and not a flower was grown in them but of the rarest species.

It must have been somewhat of a mortification to the owner of this dainty place when, on the day of which I speak, the fox, after a long race, during which he had described a circle of many miles, took refuge in the garden; but Mr. Dudgeon put a good face on the matter when a gentleman hunter, with the careless insolence of the squires of those days and that place, rode across the velvet lawn, and tapping at the window of the dining-room with his whip-handle, asked permission—no! that is not it—rather, informed Mr. Dudgeon of their intention—to enter his garden in a body, and have the fox unearthed. Mr. Dudgeon compelled himself to smile assent, with the grace of a masculine Griselda; and then he hastily gave orders to have all that the house afforded of provision set out for luncheon, guessing rightly enough that a six hours' run would give even homely fare an acceptable welcome.

He bore without wincing the entrance of the dirty boots into his exquisitely clean rooms; he only felt grateful for the care with which Mr. Higgins strode about, laboriously and noiselessly moving on the tip of his toes, as he reconnoitred the rooms with a curious eye.

"I'm going to build a house myself, Dudgeon; and, upon my word, I don't think I could take a better model than yours."

"Oh! my poor cottage would be too small to afford any hints for such a house as you would wish to build, Mr. Higgins," replied Mr. Dudgeon, gently rubbing his hands nevertheless at the compliment.

"Not at all! not at all! Let me see. You have dining-room, drawing-room"—he hesitated, and Mr. Dudgeon filled up the blank as he expected.

"Four sitting-rooms and the bedrooms. But allow me to show you over the house. I confess I took some pains in arranging it, and, though far smaller than what you would require, it may, nevertheless, afford you some hints."

So they left the eating gentlemen with their mouths and their plates quite full, and the scent of the fox overpowering that of the hasty rashers of ham; and they carefully inspected all the ground-floor rooms. Then Mr. Dudgeon said:

"If you are not tired, Mr. Higgins—it is rather my hobby, so you must pull me up if you are—we will go upstairs, and I will show you my sanctum."

Mr. Dudgeon's sanctum was the centre room, over the porch, which formed a balcony, and which was carefully filled with choice flowers in pots. Inside, there were all kinds of elegant contrivances for hiding the real strength of all the boxes and chests required by the particular nature of Mr. Dudgeon's business: for although his office was in Barford, he kept (as he informed Mr. Higgins) what was the most valuable here, as being safer than an office which was locked up and left every night.

But, as Mr. Higgins reminded him with a sly poke in the side, when next they met, his own house was not over-secure. A fortnight after the gentlemen of the Barford hunt lunched there, Mr. Dudgeon's strong-box—in his sanctum upstairs, with the mysterious spring-bolt to the window invented by himself, and the secret of which was only known to the inventor and a few of his most intimate friends, to whom he had proudly shown it;—this strong-box, containing the collected Christmas rents of half a dozen landlords (there was then no bank nearer than Derby), was rifled; and the secretly rich Mr. Dudgeon had to stop his agent in his purchases of paintings by Flemish artists, because the money was required to make good the missing rents.

The Dogberries and Verges of those days were quite incapable of obtaining any clue to the robber or robbers; and though one or two vagrants were taken up and brought before Mr. Dunover and Mr. Higgins, the magistrates who usually attended in the court-room at Barford, there was no evidence brought against them, and after a couple of nights' durance in the lock-ups they were set at liberty. But it became a standing joke with Mr. Higgins to ask Mr. Dudgeon, from time to time, whether he would recommend him a place of safety for his valuables; or if he had made any more inventions lately for securing houses from robbers.

About two years after this time—about seven years after Mr. Higgins had been married—one Tuesday evening, Mr. Davis was sitting reading the news in the coffee-room of the George Inn. He belonged to a club of gentlemen who met there occasionally to play at whist, to read what few newspapers and magazines were published in those days, to chat about the market at Derby, and prices all over the country.

This Tuesday night it was a black frost; and few people were in the room. Mr. Davis was anxious to finish an article in the *Gentleman's Magazine*; indeed, he was making extracts from it, intending to answer it, and yet unable with his small income to purchase a copy. So he stayed late; it was past nine, and at ten o'clock the room was closed.

But while he wrote, Mr. Higgins came in. He was pale and haggard with cold; Mr. Davis, who had had for some time sole possession of the fire, moved politely on one side, and handed to the new-comer the sole London newspaper which the room afforded.

Mr. Higgins accepted it, and made some remark on the intense coldness of the weather; but Mr. Davis was too full of his article, and intended reply, to fall into conversation readily. Mr. Higgins hitched his chair nearer to the fire, and put his feet on the fender, giving an audible shudder. He put the newspaper on one end of the table near him, and sat gazing into the red embers of the fire, crouching down over them as if his very marrow were chilled. At length he said:

"There is no account of the murder at Bath in that paper?"

Mr. Davis, who had finished taking his notes, and was preparing to go, stopped short, and asked:

"Has there been a murder at Bath? No! I have not seen anything of it—who was murdered?"

"Oh! it was a shocking, terrible murder!" said Mr. Higgins, not raising his look from the fire, but gazing on with his eyes dilated till the whites were seen all round them. "A terrible, terrible murder! I wonder what will become of the murderer? I can fancy the red glowing centre of that fire—look and see how infinitely distant it seems, and how the distance magnifies it into something awful and unquenchable."

"My dear sir, you are feverish; how you shake and shiver!" said Mr. Davis, thinking privately that his companion had symptoms of fever, and that he was wandering in his mind.

"Oh, no!" said Mr. Higgins, "I am not feverish. It is the night which is so cold."

And for a time he talked with Mr. Davis about the article in the *Gentleman's Magazine*, for he was rather a reader himself, and could take more interest in Mr. Davis's pursuits than most of the people at Barford. At length it drew near to ten, and Mr. Davis rose up to go home to his lodgings.

"No, Davis, don't go. I want you here. We will have a bottle of port together, and that will put Saunders into good humour. I want to tell you about this murder," he continued, dropping his voice, and speaking hoarse and low. "She was an old woman, and he killed her, sitting reading her Bible by her own fireside!" He looked at Mr. Davis with a strange searching gaze, as if trying to find some sympathy in the horror which the idea presented to him.

"Who do you mean, my dear sir? What is this murder you are so full of? No one has been murdered here."

"No, you fool! I tell you it was in Bath!" said Mr. Higgins, with sudden passion; and then calming himself to most velvet-smoothness of manner, he laid his hand on Mr. Davis's knee, there, as they sat by the fire, and gently detaining him, began the narration of the crime he was so full of; but his voice and manner were constrained to a stony quietude: he never looked in Mr. Davis's face; once or twice, as Mr. Davis remembered afterwards, his grip tightened like a compressing vice.

"She lived in a small house in a quiet old-fashioned street, she and her maid. People said she was a good old woman; but for all that she hoarded and hoarded, and never gave to the poor. Mr. Davis, it is wicked not to give to the poor—wicked—wicked, is it not? I always give to the poor, for once I read in the Bible that 'Charity covereth a multitude of sins.' The wicked old woman never gave, but hoarded her money, and saved, and saved. Some one heard of it; I say she threw a temptation in his way, and God will punish her for it. And this man—or it might be a woman, who knows?—and this person—heard also that she went to church in the mornings, and her maid in the afternoons; and so—while the maid was at church, and the street and the house quite still, and the darkness of a winter afternoon coming on—she was nodding over the Bible—and that, mark you! is a sin, and one that God will avenge sooner or later; and a step came in the dusk up the stair, and that person I told you of stood in the room. At first he—no! At first, it is supposed—for, you understand, all this is mere guess-work—it is supposed that he asked her civilly enough to give him her money, or to tell him where it was; but the old miser defied him, and would not ask for mercy and give up her keys, even when he threatened her, but looked him in the face as if he had been a baby—Oh, God! Mr. Davis, I once dreamt when I was a little innocent boy that I should commit a crime like this, and I wakened up crying; and my mother comforted me—that is the reason I tremble so now—that and the cold, for it is very very cold!"

"But did he murder the old lady?" asked Mr. Davis. "I beg your pardon, sir, but I am interested by your story."

"Yes! he cut her throat; and there she lies yet in her quiet little parlour, with her face upturned and all ghastly white, in the middle of a pool of blood. Mr. Davis, this wine is no better than water; I must have some brandy!"

Mr. Davis was horror-struck by the story, which seemed to have fascinated him as much as it had done his companion.

"Have they got any clue to the murderer?" said he. Mr. Higgins drank down half a tumber of raw brandy before he answered.

"No! no clue whatever. They will never be able to discover him, and I should not wonder—Mr. Davis—I should not wonder if he repented after all, and did bitter penance for his crime; and if so—will there be mercy for him at the last day?"

"God knows!" said Mr. Davis, with solemnity. "It is an awful story," continued he, rousing himself; "I hardly like to leave this warm light room and go out into the darkness after hearing it. But it must be done," buttoning on his great-coat—"I can only say I hope and trust they will find out the murderer and hang him.—If you'll take my advice, Mr. Higgins, you'll have your bed warmed, and drink a treacle-posset just the last thing; and, if you'll allow me, I'll send you my answer to Philologus before it goes up to old Urban."

The next morning Mr. Davis went to call on Miss Pratt, who was not very well; and by way of being agreeable and entertaining, he related to her all he had heard the night before about the murder at Bath; and really he made a very pretty connected story out of it, and interested Miss Pratt very much in the fate of the old lady—partly because of a similarity in their situations; for she also privately hoarded money, and had but one servant, and stopped at home alone on Sunday afternoons to allow her servant to go to church.

"And when did all this happen?" she asked.

"I don't know if Mr. Higgins named the day; and yet I think it must have been on this very last Sunday."

"And to-day is Wednesday. Ill news travels fast."

"Yes, Mr. Higgins thought it might have been in the London newspaper."

"That it could never be. Where did Mr. Higgins learn all about it?"

"I don't know, I did not ask; I think he only came home yesterday; he had been south to collect his rents, somebody said."

Miss Pratt grunted. She used to vent her dislike and suspicions of Mr. Higgins in a grunt whenever his name was mentioned.

"Well, I sha'n't see you for some days. Godfrey Merton has asked me to go and stay with him and his sister; and I think it will do me good. Besides," added she, "these winter evenings—and these murderers at large in the country—I don't quite like living with only Peggy to call to in case of need."

Miss Pratt went to stay with her cousin, Mr. Merton. He was an active magistrate, and enjoyed his reputation as such. One day he came in, having just received his letters.

"Bad account of the morals of your little town here, Jessy!" said he, touching one of his letters. "You've either a murderer among you, or some friend of a murderer. Here's a poor old lady at Bath had her throat cut last Sunday week; and I've a letter from the Home Office, asking to lend them 'my very efficient aid,' as they are pleased to call it, towards finding out the culprit. It seems he must have been thirsty, and of a comfortable jolly turn; for before going to his horrid work he tapped a barrel of ginger wine the old lady had set by to work; and he wrapped the spigot round with a piece of a letter taken out of his pocket, as may be supposed; and this piece of a letter was found afterwards; there are only these letters on the outside, '*ns, Esq., -arford, -egworth,*' which some one has ingeniously made out to mean Barford, near Kegworth. On the other side there is some allusion to a racehorse, I conjecture, though the name is singular enough: 'Church-and-King-and-down-with-the-Rump.'"

Miss Pratt caught at this name immediately; it had hurt her feelings as a dissenter only a few months ago, and she remembered it well.

"Mr. Nat Hearn has—or had (as I am speaking in the witness-box, as it were, I must take care of my tenses)—a horse with that ridiculous name."

"Mr. Nat Hearn," repeated Mr. Merton, making a note of the intelligence; then he recurred to his letter from the Home Office again.

"There is also a piece of a small key, broken in the futile attempt to open a desk—well, well. Nothing more of consequence. The letter is what we must rely upon."

"Mr. Davis said that Mr. Higgins told him——" Miss Pratt began.

"Higgins!" exclaimed Mr. Merton, "*ns*. Is it Higgins, the blustering fellow that ran away with Nat Hearn's sister?"

"Yes!" said Miss Pratt. "But though he has never been a favourite of mine——"

"*ns*," repeated Mr. Merton. "It is too horrible to think of; a member of the hunt—kind old Squire Hearn's son-in-law! Who else have you in Barford with names that end in *ns*?"

"There's Jackson, and Higginson, and Blenkinsop, and Davis, and Jones. Cousin! One thing strikes me—how did Mr. Higgins know all about it to tell Mr. Davis on Tuesday what had happened on Sunday afternoon?"

There is no need to add much more. Those curious in lives of the highwaymen may find the name of Higgins as conspicuous among those annals as that of Claude Duval. Kate Hearn's husband collected his rents on the highway, like many another "gentleman" of the day; but, having been unlucky in one or two of his adventures, and hearing exaggerated accounts of the hoarded wealth of the old lady at Bath, he was led on from robbery to murder, and was hanged for his crime at Derby in 1775.

He had not been an unkind husband; and his poor wife took lodgings in Derby to be near him in his last moments—his awful last moments. Her old father went with her everywhere, but into her husband's cell ; and wrung her heart by constantly accusing himself of having promoted her marriage with a man of whom he knew so little. He abdicated his squireship in favour of his son Nathaniel. Nat was prosperous, and the helpless silly father could be of no use to him ; but to his widowed daughter the foolish old man was all in all ; her knight, her protector, her companion—her most faithful loving companion. Only he ever declined assuming the office of her counsellor—shaking his head sadly, and saying :

" Ah ! Kate, Kate ! if I had had more wisdom to have advised thee better, thou need'st not have been an exile here in Brussels, shrinking from the sight of every English person as if they knew thy story."

I saw the White House not a month ago ; it was to let, perhaps for the twentieth time since Mr. Higgins occupied it ; but still the tradition goes in Barford that once upon a time a highwayman lived there, and amassed untold treasures ; and that the ill-gotten wealth yet remains walled up in some unknown concealed chamber ; but in what part of the house no one knows.

MRS. GASKELL

THE HALF-BROTHERS

My mother was twice married. She never spoke of her first husband, and it is only from other people that I have learnt what little I know about him. I believe she was scarcely seventeen when she was married to him: and he was barely one-and-twenty. He rented a small farm up in Cumberland, somewhere towards the sea-coast; but he was perhaps too young and inexperienced to have the charge of land and cattle; anyhow, his affairs did not prosper, and he fell into ill-health, and died of consumption before they had been three years man and wife, leaving my mother a young widow of twenty, with a little child only just able to walk, and the farm on her hands for four years more by the lease, with half the stock on it dead, or sold off one by one to pay the more pressing debts, and with no money to purchase more, or even to buy the provisions needed for the small consumption of every day. There was another child coming, too; and sad and sorry, I believe, she was to think of it.

A dreary winter she must have had in her lonesome dwelling, with never another near it for miles around; her sister came to bear her company, and they two planned and plotted how to make every penny they could raise go as far as possible. I can't tell you how it happened that my little sister, whom I never saw, came to sicken and die; but, as if my poor mother's cup was not full enough, only a fortnight before Gregory was born the little girl took ill of scarlet fever, and in a week she lay dead.

My mother was, I believe, just stunned with this last blow. My aunt has told me that she did not cry; Aunt Fanny would have been thankful if she had; but she sat holding the poor wee lassie's hand, and looking in her pretty, pale, dead face, without so much as shedding a tear. And it was all the same, when they had to take her away to be buried. She just kissed the child, and sat her down in the window-seat to watch the little black train of people (neighbours—my aunt, and one far-off cousin, who were all the friends they could muster) go winding away amongst the snow, which had fallen thinly over the country the night before.

When my aunt came back from the funeral, she found my mother in the same place, and as dry-eyed as ever. So she continued until after Gregory was born; and, somehow, his coming seemed to loosen the tears, and she cried day and night, day and night, till my aunt and the other watcher looked at each other in dismay, and would fain have stopped her if they had but known how. But she bade them let her alone, and not be over-anxious, for every drop she shed eased her brain, which had been in a terrible state before for want of the power to cry. She seemed after that to think of nothing but her new little baby; she hardly appeared to remember either her husband or her little daughter that lay dead in Brigham churchyard—at least so Aunt Fanny said; but she was a great talker, and my mother was very silent by nature, and I think Aunt Fanny may have been mistaken in believing that my mother never thought of her husband and child just because she never spoke about them.

Aunt Fanny was older than my mother, and had a way of treating her like a child; but, for all that, she was a kind, warm-hearted creature, who thought more of her sister's welfare than she did of her own; and it was on her bit of money that they principally lived, and on what the two could earn by working for the great Glasgow sewing-merchants. But by-and-by my mother's eyesight began to fail. It was not that she was exactly blind, for she could see well enough to guide herself about the house, and to do a good deal of domestic work; but she could no longer do fine sewing and earn money. It must have been with the heavy crying she had had in her day, for she was but a young creature at this time, and as pretty a young woman, I have heard people say, as any on the country-side.

She took it sadly to heart that she could no longer gain anything towards the keep of herself and her child. My Aunt Fanny would fain have persuaded her that she had enough to do in managing their cottage and minding Gregory; but my mother knew that they were pinched, and that Aunt Fanny herself had not as much to eat, even of the commonest kind of food, as she could have done with; and as for Gregory, he was not a strong lad, and needed, not more food—for he always had enough, whoever went short—but better nourishment, and more flesh-meat.

One day—it was Aunt Fanny who told me all this about my poor mother, long after her death—as the sisters were sitting together, Aunt Fanny working, and my mother hushing Gregory to sleep, William Preston, who was afterwards my father, came in.

He was reckoned an old bachelor; I suppose he was long past forty, and he was one of the wealthiest farmers thereabouts, and had known my grandfather well, and my mother and my aunt in their more prosperous days. He sat down, and began to twirl his hat by way of being agreeable; my Aunt Fanny talked, and he listened and looked at my mother. But he said very little, either on that visit, or on many another that he paid before he spoke out what had been the real purpose of his calling so often all along, and from the very first time he came to their house.

One Sunday, however, my Aunt Fanny stayed away from church, and took care of the child, and my mother went alone. When she came back, she ran straight upstairs, without going into the kitchen to look at Gregory or speak any word to her sister, and Aunt Fanny heard her cry as if her heart was breaking; so she went up and scolded her right well through the bolted door, till at last she got her to open it. And then she threw herself on my aunt's neck, and told her that William Preston had asked her to marry him, and had promised to take good charge of her boy, and to let him want for nothing, neither in the way of keep nor of education, and that she had consented.

Aunt Fanny was a good deal shocked at this; for, as I have said, she had often thought that my mother had forgotten her first husband very quickly, and now here was proof positive of it, if she could so soon think of marrying again. Besides, as Aunt Fanny used to say, she herself would have been a far more suitable match for a man of William Preston's age than Helen, who, though she was a widow, had not seen her four-and-twentieth summer.

However, as Aunt Fanny said, they had not asked her advice; and there was much to be said on the other side of the question. Helen's eyesight would never be good for much again, and as William Preston's wife she would never need to do anything, if she chose to sit with her hands before her; and a boy was a great charge to a widowed mother; and now there would be a decent, steady man to see after him. So, by-and-by, Aunt Fanny seemed to take a brighter view of the marriage than did my mother herself, who hardly ever looked up, and never smiled after the day when she promised William Preston to be his wife. But much as she had loved Gregory before, she seemed to love him more now. She was continually talking to him when they were alone, though he was far too young to understand her moaning words, or give her any comfort, except by his caresses.

At last William Preston and she were wed; and she went to be mistress of a well-stocked house, not above half an hour's walk from where Aunt Fanny lived. I believe she did all that she could to please my father; and a more dutiful wife, I have heard him himself say, could never have been. But she did not love him, and he soon found it out. She loved Gregory, and she did not love him.

Perhaps, love would have come in time, if he had been patient enough to wait; but it just turned him sour to see how her eye brightened and her colour came at the sight of that little child, while for him who had given her so much, she had only gentle words as cold as ice. He got to taunt her with the difference in her manner, as if that would bring love: and he took a positive dislike to Gregory,—he was so jealous of the ready love that always gushed out like a spring of fresh water when he came near. He wanted her to love him more, and perhaps that was all well and good; but he wanted her to love her child less, and that was an evil wish.

One day, he gave way to his temper, and cursed and swore at Gregory, who had got into some mischief, as children will; my mother made some excuse for him; my father said it was hard enough to have to keep another man's child, without having it perpetually held up in its naughtiness by his wife, who ought to be always in the same mind that he was; and so from little they got to more; and the end of it was, that my mother took to her bed before her time, and I was born that very day.

My father was glad, and proud, and sorry, all in a breath; glad and proud that a son was born to him; and sorry for his poor wife's state, and to think how his angry words had brought it on. But he was a man who liked better to be angry than sorry, so he soon found out that it was all Gregory's fault, and owed him an additional grudge for having hastened my birth.

He had another grudge against him before long. My mother began to sink the day after I was born. My father sent to Carlisle for doctors, and would have coined his heart's blood into gold to save her, if that could have been; but it could not.

My Aunt Fanny used to say sometimes, that she thought that Helen did not wish to live, and so just let herself die away without trying to take hold on life; but when I questioned her, she owned that my mother did all the doctors bade her do, with the same sort of uncomplaining patience with which she had acted through life. One of her last requests was to have Gregory laid in her bed by my side, and then she made him take hold of my little hand. Her husband came in while she was looking at us so, and when he bent tenderly over her to ask her how she felt now, and seemed to gaze on us two little half-brothers, with a grave sort of kindliness, she looked up in his face and smiled, almost her first smile at him; and such a sweet smile! as more besides Aunt Fanny have said.

In an hour she was dead. Aunt Fanny came to live with us. It was the best thing that could be done. My father would have been glad to return to his old mode of bachelor life, but what could he do with two little children? He needed a woman to take care of him, and who so fitting as his wife's elder sister? So she had the charge of me from my birth; and for a time I was weakly, as was but natural, and she was always beside me, night and day watching over me, and my father nearly as anxious as she. For his land had come down from father to son for more than three hundred years, and he would have cared for me merely as his flesh and blood that was to inherit the land after him.

But he needed something to love, for all that, to most people, he was a stern, hard man, and he took to me as, I fancy, he had taken to no human being before—as he might have taken to my mother, if she had had no former life for him to be jealous of. I loved him back again right heartily. I loved all around me, I believe, for everybody was kind to me. After a time, I overcame my original weakliness of constitution, and was just a bonny, strong-looking lad whom every passer-by noticed, when my father took me with him to the nearest town.

At home I was the darling of my aunt, the tenderly-beloved of my father, the pet and plaything of the old domestic, the " young master " of the farm-labourers, before whom I played many a lordly antic, assuming a sort of authority which sat oddly enough, I doubt not, on such a baby as I was.

Gregory was three years older than I. Aunt Fanny was always kind to him in deed and in action, but she did not often think about him, she had fallen so completely into the habit of being engrossed by me, from the fact of my having come into her charge as a delicate baby. My father never got over his grudging dislike to his stepson, who had so innocently wrestled with him for the possession of my mother's heart. I mistrust me, too, that my father always considered him as the cause of my mother's death and my early delicacy ; and utterly unreasonable as this may seem, I believe my father rather cherished his feeling of alienation to my brother as a duty, than strove to repress it.

Yet not for the world would my father have grudged him anything that money could purchase. That was, as it were, in the bond when he had wedded my mother. Gregory was lumpish and loutish, awkward and ungainly, marring whatever he meddled in, and many a hard word and sharp scolding did he get from the people about the farm, who hardly waited till my father's back was turned before they rated the stepson.

I am ashamed—my heart is sore to think how I fell into the fashion of the family, and slighted my poor orphan step-brother. I don't think I ever scouted him, or was wilfully ill-natured to him ; but the habit of being considered in all things, and being treated as something uncommon and superior, made me insolent in my prosperity, and I exacted more than Gregory was always willing to grant, and then, irritated, I sometimes repeated the disparaging words I had heard others use with regard to him, without fully understanding their meaning. Whether he did or not I cannot tell. I am afraid he did. He used to turn silent and quiet—sullen and sulky, my father thought it ; stupid, Aunt Fanny used to call it.

But every one said he was stupid and dull, and this stupidity and dulness grew upon him. He would sit without speaking a word, sometimes, for hours; then my father would bid him rise and do some piece of work, maybe, about the farm. And he would take three or four tellings before he would go. When we were sent to school, it was all the same. He could never be made to remember his lessons; the schoolmaster grew weary of scolding and flogging, and at last advised my father just to take him away, and set him to some farmwork that might not be above his comprehension. I think he was more gloomy and stupid than ever after this, yet he was not a cross lad; he was patient and good-natured, and would try to do a kind turn for any one, even if they had been scolding or cuffing him not a minute before. But very often his attempts at kindness ended in some mischief to the very people he was trying to serve, owing to his awkward, ungainly ways.

I suppose I was a clever lad; at any rate, I always got plenty of praise; and was, as we called it, the cock of the school. The schoolmaster said I could learn anything I chose, but my father, who had no great learning himself, saw little use in much for me, and took me away betimes, and kept me with him about the farm. Gregory was made into a kind of shepherd, receiving his training under old Adam, who was nearly past his work. I think old Adam was almost the first person who had a good opinion of Gregory. He stood to it that my brother had good parts, though he did not rightly know how to bring them out; and, for knowing the bearings of the Fells, he said he had never seen a lad like him. My father would try to bring Adam round to speak of Gregory's faults and shortcomings; but, instead of that, he would praise him twice as much as soon as he found out what was my father's object.

One winter-time, when I was about sixteen, and Gregory nineteen, I was sent by my father on an errand to a place about seven miles distant by the road, but only about four by the Fells. He bade me return by the road, whichever way I took in going, for the evenings closed in early, and were often thick and misty; besides which, old Adam, now paralytic and bedridden, foretold a downfall of snow before long.

I soon got to my journey's end, and soon had done my business; earlier by an hour, I thought, than my father had expected, so I took the decision of the way by which I would return into my own hands, and set off back again over the Fells, just as the first shades of evening began to fall. It looked dark and gloomy enough; but everything was so still that I thought I should have plenty of time to get home before the snow came down.

Off I set at a pretty quick pace. But night came on quicker. The right path was clear enough in the daytime, although at several points two or three exactly similar diverged from the same place; but when there was a good light, the traveller was guided by the sight of distant objects,—a piece of rock,—a fall in the ground—which were quite invisible to me now. I plucked up a brave heart, however, and took what seemed to me the right road. It was wrong, however, and led me whither I knew not, but to some wild boggy moor where the solitude seemed painful, intense, as if never footfall of man had come thither to break the silence.

I tried to shout,—with the dimmest possible hope of being heard—rather to reassure myself by the sound of my own voice; but my voice came husky and short, and yet it dismayed me; it seemed so weird and strange in that noiseless expanse of black darkness. Suddenly the air was filled thick with dusky flakes, my face and hands were wet with snow. It cut me off from the slightest knowledge of where I was, for I lost every idea of the direction from which I had come, so that I could not even retrace my steps; it hemmed me in, thicker, thicker, with a darkness that might be felt. The boggy soil on which I stood quaked under me if I remained long in one place, and yet I dared not move far.

All my youthful hardiness seemed to leave me at once. I was on the point of crying, and only very shame seemed to keep it down. To save myself from shedding tears, I shouted—terrible, wild shouts for bare life they were. I turned sick as I paused to listen; no answering sound came but the unfeeling echoes. Only the noiseless, pitiless snow kept falling thicker, thicker—faster, faster! I was growing numb and sleepy. I tried to move about, but I dared not go far, for fear of the precipices which, I knew, abounded in certain places on the Fells. Now and then, I stood still and shouted again; but my voice was getting choked with tears, as I thought of the desolate, helpless death I was to die, and how little they at home, sitting round the warm, red, bright fire, wotted what was become of me,—and how my poor father would grieve for me—it would surely kill him—it would break his heart, poor old man! Aunt Fanny too—was this to be the end of all her cares for me?

I began to review my life in a strange kind of vivid dream, in which the various scenes of my few boyish years passed before me like visions. In a pang of agony, caused by such remembrance of my short life, I gathered up my strength and called out once more, a long, despairing, wailing cry, to which I had no hope of obtaining any answer, save from the echoes around, dulled as the sound might be by the thickened air.

To my surprise, I heard a cry—almost as long, as wild as mine—so wild that it seemed unearthly, and I almost thought it must be the voice of some of the mocking spirits of the Fells, about whom I had heard so many tales. My heart suddenly began to beat fast and loud. I could not reply for a minute or two. I nearly fancied I had lost the power of utterance.

Just at this moment a dog barked. Was it Lassie's bark—my brother's collie?—an ugly enough brute, with a white, ill-looking face, that my father always kicked whenever he saw it, partly for its own demerits, partly because it belonged to my brother. On such occasions, Gregory would whistle Lassie away, and go off and sit with her in some outhouse.

My father had once or twice been ashamed of himself, when the poor collie had yowled out with the suddenness of the pain, and had relieved himself of his self-reproach by blaming my brother, who, he said, had no notion of training a dog, and was enough to ruin any collie in Christendom with his stupid way of allowing them to lie by the kitchen fire. To all which Gregory would answer nothing, nor even seem to hear, but go on looking absent and moody. Yes! there again! It was Lassie's bark! Now or never! I lifted up my voice and shouted "Lassie! Lassie! For God's sake, Lassie!"

Another moment, and the great white-faced Lassie was curving and gambolling with delight round my feet and legs, looking, however, up in my face with her intelligent, apprehensive eyes, as if fearing lest I might greet her with a blow, as I had done oftentimes before. But I cried with gladness, as I stooped down and patted her. My mind was sharing in my body's weakness, and I could not reason, but I knew that help was at hand. A grey figure came more and more distinctly out of the thick, close-pressing darkness. It was Gregory wrapped in his maud.

"Oh, Gregory!" said I, and I fell upon his neck, unable to speak another word. He never spoke much, and made me no answer for some little time. Then he told me we must move, we must walk for the dear life—we must find our road home, if possible; but we must move or we should be frozen to death.

"Don't you know the way home?" asked I.

"I thought I did when I set out, but I am doubtful now. The snow blinds me, and I am feared that in moving about just now I have lost the right gait homewards."

He had his shepherd's staff with him, and by dint of plunging it before us at every step we took—clinging close to each other, we went on safely enough, as far as not falling down any of the steep rocks, but it was slow, dreary work. My brother, I saw, was more guided by Lassie and the way she took than anything else, trusting to her instinct. It was too dark to see far before us; but he called her back continually, and noted from what quarter she returned, and shaped our slow steps accordingly. But the tedious motion scarcely kept my very blood from freezing. Every bone, every fibre in my body seemed first to ache, and then to swell, and then to turn numb with the intense cold. My brother bore it better than I, from having been more out upon the hills. He did not speak, except to call Lassie. I strove to be brave, and not complain; but now I felt the deadly fatal sleep stealing over me.

"I can go no farther," I said, in a drowsy tone. I remember I suddenly became dogged and resolved. Sleep I would, were it only for five minutes. If death were to be the consequence, sleep I would. Gregory stood still. I suppose he recognised the peculiar phase of suffering to which I had been brought by the cold.

"It is of no use," said he, as if to himself. "We are no nearer home than we were when we started, as far as I can tell. Our only chance is in Lassie. Here! roll thee in my maud, lad, and lay thee down on this sheltered side of this bit of rock. Creep close under it, lad, and I'll lie by thee, and strive to keep the warmth in us. Stay! hast gotten aught about thee they'll know at home?"

I felt him unkind thus to keep me from slumber, but on his repeating the question, I pulled out my pocket-handkerchief, of some showy pattern, which Aunt Fanny had hemmed for me—Gregory took it, and tied it round Lassie's neck.

"Hie thee, Lassie, hie thee home!" And the white-faced, ill-favoured brute was off like a shot in the darkness. Now I might lie down—now I might sleep. In my drowsy stupor I felt that I was being tenderly covered up by my brother; but what with I neither knew nor cared—I was too dull, too selfish, too numb to think and reason, or I might have known that in that bleak bare place there was naught to wrap me in, save what was taken off another. I was glad enough when he ceased his cares and lay down by me. I took his hand.

"Thou canst not remember, lad, how we lay together thus by our dying mother. She put thy small, wee hand in mine—I reckon she sees us now; and belike we shall soon be with her. Anyhow, God's will be done."

"Dear Gregory," I muttered, and crept nearer to him for warmth. He was talking still, and again about our mother, when I fell asleep. In an instant—or so it seemed—there were many voices about me—many faces hovering round me—the sweet luxury of warmth was stealing into every part of me. I was in my own little bed at home. I am thankful to say, my first word was "Gregory?"

A look passed from one to another—my father's stern old face strove in vain to keep its sternness; his mouth quivered, his eyes filled slowly with unwonted tears.

"I would have given him half my land—I would have blessed him as my son,—oh God! I would have knelt at his feet, and asked him to forgive my hardness of heart."

I heard no more. A whirl came through my brain, catching me

back to death. I came slowly to my consciousness, weeks afterwards. My father's hair was white when I recovered, and his hands shook as he looked into my face.

We spoke no more of Gregory. We could not speak of him ; but he was strangely in our thoughts. Lassie came and went with never a word of blame ; nay, my father would try to stroke her, but she shrank away ; and he, as if reproved by the poor dumb beast, would sigh, and be silent and abstracted for a time.

Aunt Fanny—always a talker—told me all. How, on that fatal night, my father, irritated by my prolonged absence, and probably more anxious than he cared to show, had been fierce and imperious, even beyond his wont, to Gregory : had upbraided him with his father's poverty, his own stupidity which made his services good for nothing—for so, in spite of the old shepherd, my father always chose to consider them.

At last, Gregory had risen up, and whistled Lassie out with him—poor Lassie, crouching underneath his chair for fear of a kick or a blow. Some time before, there had been some talk between my father and my aunt respecting my return ; and when Aunt Fanny told me all this, she said she fancied that Gregory might have noticed the coming storm, and gone out silently to meet me. Three hours afterwards, when all were running about in wild alarm, not knowing whither to go in search of me—not even missing Gregory, or heeding his absence, poor fellow—poor, poor fellow !—Lassie came home, with my handkerchief tied round her neck. They knew and understood, and the whole strength of the farm was turned out to follow her, with wraps, and blankets, and brandy, and everything that could be thought of. I lay in chilly sleep, but still alive, beneath the rock that Lassie guided them to. I was covered over with my brother's plaid, and his thick shepherd's coat was carefully wrapped round my feet. He was in his shirt-sleeves—his arm thrown over me—a quiet smile (he had hardly ever smiled in life) upon his still, cold face.

My father's last words were, " God forgive me my hardness of heart towards the fatherless child ! "

And what marked the depth of his feeling of repentance, perhaps more than all, considering the passionate love he bore my mother, was this : we found a paper of directions after his death, in which he desired that he might lie at the foot of the grave in which, by his desire, poor Gregory had been laid with OUR MOTHER.

WILLIAM MAKEPEACE THACKERAY

1811–1863

DENNIS HAGGARTY'S WIFE

THERE was an odious Irishwoman and her daughter who used to frequent the "Royal Hotel" at Leamington some years ago, and who went by the name of Mrs. Major Gam. Gam had been a distinguished officer in his Majesty's service, whom nothing but death and his own amiable wife could overcome. The widow mourned her husband in the most becoming bombazeen she could muster, and had at least half an inch of lampblack round the immense visiting-tickets which she left at the houses of the nobility and gentry her friends.

Some of us, I am sorry to say, used to call her Mrs. Major Gammon; for if the worthy widow had a propensity, it was to talk largely of herself and family (of her own family, for she held her husband's very cheap), and of the wonders of her paternal mansion, Molloyville, county of Mayo. She was of the Molloys of that county; and though I never heard of the family before, I have little doubt, from what Mrs. Major Gam stated, that they were the most ancient and illustrious family of that part of Ireland. I remember there came down to see his aunt a young fellow with huge red whiskers and tight nankeens, a green coat, and an awful breastpin, who, after two days' stay at the Spa, proposed marriage to Miss S——, or, in default, a duel with her father; and who drove a flash curricle with a bay and a grey, and who was presented with much pride by Mrs. Gam as Castlereagh Molloy of Molloyville. We all agreed that he was the most insufferable snob of the whole season, and were delighted when a bailiff came down in search of him.

Well, this is all I know personally of the Molloyville family; but at the house, if you met the Widow Gam, and talked on any subject in life, you were sure to hear of it. If you asked her to have pease at dinner, she would say, "Oh, sir, after the pease at Molloyville, I really don't care for any others—do I, dearest Jemima? We always had a dish in the month of June, when my father gave his head gardener a guinea (we had three at Molloyville), and sent him with his compliments and a quart of pease to our neighbour, dear Lord Marrowfat. What a sweet place Marrowfat Park is! isn't it, Jemima?" If a carriage passed by the window, Mrs. Major Gammon would be sure to tell you that there were three carriages at Molloyville—"the barouche, the chawiot, and the covered cyar." In the same manner she would favour you with the number and names of the footmen of the establishment; and on a visit to Warwick Castle (for this bustling woman made one in every party of pleasure that was formed from the hotel), she gave us to understand that the great walk by the river was altogether inferior to the principal avenue of Molloyville Park. I should not have been able to tell so much about Mrs. Gam and her daughter, but that, between ourselves, I was particularly sweet upon a young lady at the time, whose papa lived at the "Royal," and was under the care of Dr. Jephson.

The Jemima appealed to by Mrs. Gam in the above sentence was, of course, her daughter, apostrophised by her mother, "Jemima, my soul's darling!" or "Jemima, my blessed child!" or, "Jemima, my own love!" The sacrifices that Mrs. Gam had made for that daughter were, she said, astonishing. The money she had spent in masters upon her, the illnesses through which she had nursed her, the ineffable love the mother bore her, were only known to Heaven, Mrs. Gam said. They used to come into the room with their arms round each other's waists; at dinner, between the courses, the mother would sit with one hand locked in her daughter's; and if only two or three young men were present at the time, would be pretty sure to kiss her Jemima more than once during the time whilst the bohea was poured out.

As for Miss Gam, if she was not handsome, candour forbids me to say she was ugly. She was neither one no t'other. She was a person who wore ringlets and a band round her forehead; she knew four songs, which became rather tedious at the end of a couple of months' acquaintance; she had excessively bare shoulders; she inclined to wear numbers of cheap ornaments, rings, brooches, *ferronnières*, smelling-bottles, and was always, we thought, very smartly dressed: though old Mrs. Lynx hinted that her gowns and her mother's were turned over and over again, and that her eyes were almost put out by darning stockings.

These eyes Miss Gam had very large, though rather red and weak, and used to roll them about at every eligible unmarried man in the place. But though the widow subscribed to all the balls; though she hired a fly to go to the meet of the hounds; though she was constant at church, and Jemima sang louder than any person there except the clerk; and though, probably, any person who made her a happy husband would be invited down to enjoy the three footmen, gardeners, and carriages at Molloyville, yet no English gentleman was found sufficiently audacious to propose. Old Lynx used to say that the pair had been at Tunbridge, Harrogate, Brighton, Ramsgate, Cheltenham, for this eight years past; where they had met, it seemed, with no better fortune. Indeed, the widow looked rather high for her blessed child; and as she looked with the contempt which no small number of Irish people feel upon all persons who get their bread by labour or commerce, and as she was a person whose energetic manners, costume, and brogue were not much to the taste of quiet English country gentlemen, Jemima—sweet, spotless flower—still remained on her hands, a thought withered, perhaps, and seedy.

Now at this time the 120th Regiment was quartered at Weedon Barracks, and with the corps was a certain Assistant-Surgeon Haggarty, a large, lean, tough, raw-boned man, with big hands, knock-knees, and carroty whiskers, and, withal, as honest a creature as ever handled a lancet. Haggarty, as his name imports, was of the very same nation as Mrs. Gam; and, what is more, the honest fellow had some of the peculiarities which belonged to the widow, and bragged about his family almost as much as she did. I do not know of what particular part of Ireland they were kings, but monarchs they must have been, as have been the ancestors of so many thousand Hibernian families; but they had been men of no small consideration in Dublin, "where my father," Haggarty said, "is as well known as King William's statue, and where he 'rowls his carriage, too,' let me tell ye."

Hence, Haggarty was called by the wags "Rowl the carriage," and several of them made inquiries of Mrs. Gam regarding him. "Mrs. Gam, when you used to go up from Molloyville to the Lord-Lieutenant's balls, and had your town-house in Fitzwilliam Square, used you to meet the famous Doctor Haggarty in society?"

"Is it Surgeon Haggarty of Gloucester Street, ye mean? The black Papist! D'ye suppose that the Molloys would sit down to table with a creature of that sort?"

"Why, isn't he the most famous physician in Dublin, and doesn't he rowl his carriage there?"

"The horrid wretch! He keeps a shop, I tell ye, and sends his sons out with the medicine. He's got four of them off into the army—Ulick and Phil, and Terence and Denny; and now it's Charles that takes out the physic. But how should I know about these odious creatures? Their mother was a Burke, of Burke's Town, County Cavan, and brought Surgeon Haggarty two thousand pounds. She was a Protestant, and I am surprised how she could have taken up with a horrid, odious, Popish apothecary!"

From the extent of the widow's information, I am led to suppose that the inhabitants of Dublin are not less anxious about their neighbours than are the natives of English cities; and I think it is very probable that Mrs. Gam's account of the young Haggartys who carried out the medicine is perfectly correct, for a lad in the 120th made a caricature of Haggarty coming out of a chemist's shop with an oil-cloth basket under his arm, which set the worthy surgeon in such a fury that there would have been a duel between him and the ensign could the fiery doctor have had his way.

Now Dionysius Haggarty was of an exceedingly inflammable temperament, and it chanced that of all the invalids, the visitors, the young squires of Warwickshire, the young manufacturers from Birmingham, the young officers from the barracks—it chanced, unluckily for Miss Gam and himself, that he was the only individual who was in the least smitten by her personal charms. He was very tender and modest about his love, however; for it must be owned that he respected Mrs. Gam hugely, and fully admitted, like a good simple fellow as he was, the superiority of that lady's birth and breeding to his own. How could he hope that he, a humble assistant-surgeon, with a thousand pounds his Aunt Kitty left him for all his fortune—how could he hope that one of the race of Molloyville would ever condescend to marry him?

Inflamed, however, by love, and inspired by wine, one day, at a picnic at Kenilworth, Haggarty, whose love and raptures were the talk of the whole regiment, was induced by his waggish comrades to make a proposal in form.

"Are you aware, Mr. Haggarty, that you are speaking to a Molloy?" was all the reply majestic Mrs. Gam made when, according to the usual formula, the fluttering Jemima referred her suitor to "mamma." She left him with a look which was meant to crush the poor fellow to earth; she gathered up her cloak and bonnet, and precipitately called for her fly. She took care to tell every single soul in Leamington that the son of the odious Papist apothecary had had the audacity to propose for her daughter (indeed, a proposal, coming from whatever quarter it may, does no harm), and left Haggarty in a state of extreme depression and despair.

His down-heartedness, indeed, surprised most of his acquaintances in and out of the regiment; for the young lady was no beauty, and a doubtful fortune, and Dennis was a man outwardly of an unromantic turn, who seemed to have a great deal more liking for beef-steak and whisky-punch than for women, however fascinating.

But there is no doubt this shy, uncouth, rough fellow had a warmer and more faithful heart hid within him than many a dandy who is as handsome as Apollo. I, for my part, never can understand why a man falls in love, and heartily give him credit for so doing never mind with what or whom. *That* I take to be a point quite as much beyond an individual's own control as the catching of the small-pox or the colour of his hair. To the surprise of all, Assistant-Surgeon Dionysius Haggarty was deeply and seriously in love; and I am told that one day he very nearly killed the before-mentioned young ensign with a carving-knife for venturing to make a second caricature representing Lady Gammon and Jemima in a fantastical park, surrounded by three gardeners, three carriages, three footmen, and the covered cyar. He would have no joking concerning them. He became moody and quarrelsome of habit. He was for some time much more in the surgery and hospital than in the mess. He gave up the eating, for the most part, of those vast quantities of beef and pudding for which his stomach had used to afford such ample and swift accommodation; and when the cloth was drawn, instead of taking twelve tumblers, and singing Irish melodies as he used to do in a horrible cracked yelling voice, he would retire to his own apartment, or gloomily pace the barrack-yard, or madly whip and spur a grey mare he had on the road to Leamington, where his Jemima (although invisible for him) still dwelt.

The season at Leamington coming to a conclusion by the withdrawal of the young fellows who frequented that watering-place, the Widow Gam retired to her usual quarters for the other months of the year. Where these quarters were, I think we have no right to ask; for I believe she had quarrelled with her brother at Molloyville, and, besides, was a great deal too proud to be a burden on anybody.

Not only did the widow quit Leamington, but very soon afterwards the 120th received its marching orders, and left Weedon and Warwickshire. Haggarty's appetite was by this time partially restored; but his love was not altered, and his humour was still morose and gloomy. I am informed that at this period of his life he wrote some poems relative to his unhappy passion—a wild set of verses of several lengths, and in his handwriting, being discovered upon a sheet of paper in which a pitch-plaster was wrapped up, which Lieutenant and Adjutant Wheezer was compelled to put on for a cold.

Fancy, then, three years afterwards, the surprise of all Haggarty's acquaintances on reading in the public papers the following announcement:—

"Married, at Monkstown, on the 12th instant, Dionysius Haggarty, Esq., of H.M. 120th Foot, to Jemima Amelia Wilhelmina Molloy, daughter of the late Major Lancelot Gam, R.M., and granddaughter of the late, and niece of the present, Burke Bodkin Blake Molloy, Esq., Molloyville, County Mayo."

"Has the course of true love at last begun to run smooth?" thought I, as I laid down the paper, and the old times, and the old leering, bragging widow, and the high shoulders of her daughter, and the jolly days with the 120th, and Dr. Jephson's one-horse chaise, and the Warwickshire hunt, and—and Louisa S——, but never mind *her*—came back to my mind. "Has that good-natured, simple fellow at last met with his reward? Well, if he has not to marry the mother-in-law, too, he may get on well enough."

Another year announced the retirement of Assistant-Surgeon Haggarty from the 120th, where he was replaced by Assistant-Surgeon Angus Rothsay Leech, a Scotchman, probably, with whom I have not the least acquaintance, and who has nothing whatever to do with this little history.

Still more years passed on, during which time I will not say that I kept a constant watch upon the fortunes of Mr. Haggarty and his lady; for, perhaps, if the truth were known, I never thought for a moment about them, until one day, being at Kingstown, near Dublin, dawdling on the beach and staring at the Hill of Howth, as most people at that watering-place do, I saw coming towards me a tall gaunt man, with a pair of bushy red whiskers, of which I thought I had seen the like in former years, and a face which could be no other than Haggarty's. It was Haggarty, ten years older than when we last met, and greatly more grim and thin. He had on one shoulder a young gentleman in a dirty tartan costume, and a face exceedingly like his own peeping from under a battered plume of black feathers, while with his other hand he was dragging a light green go-cart, in which reposed a female infant of some two years old. Both were roaring with great power of lungs.

As soon as Dennis saw me, his face lost the dull, puzzled expression which had seemed to characterise it. He dropped the pole of the go-cart from one hand and his son from the other, and came jumping forward to greet me with all his might, leaving his progeny roaring in the road.

"Bless my sowl," says he, "sure it's Fitz-Boodle! Fitz, don't you remember me? Dennis Haggarty of the 120th? Leamington, you know?—Molloy, my boy, hould your tongue and stop your screeching, and Jemima's, too; d'ye hear?—Well, it does good to sore eyes to see an old face. How fat you're grown, Fitz; and were ye ever in Ireland before? and a'n't ye delighted with it? Confess, now, isn't it beautiful?"

This question regarding the merits of their country, which I have remarked is put by most Irish persons, being answered in a satisfactory manner, and the shouts of the infants appeased from an apple-stall hard by, Dennis and I talked of old times; and I congratulated him on his marriage with the lovely girl whom we all admired, and hoped he had a fortune with her, and so forth. His appearance, however, did not bespeak a great fortune. He had an old grey hat, short old trousers, an old waistcoat with regimental buttons, and patched Blucher boots, such as are not usually sported by persons in easy life.

"Ah!" says he, with a sigh, in reply to my queries, "times are changed since them days, Fitz-Boodle. My wife's not what she was—the beautiful creature you knew her.—Molloy, my boy, run off in a hurry to your mamma, and tell her an English gentleman is coming home to dine;—for you'll dine with me, Fitz, in course?" And I agreed to partake of that meal; though Master Molloy altogether declined to obey his papa's orders with respect to announcing the stranger.

"Well, I must announce you myself," says Haggarty, with a smile. "Come, it's just dinner-time, and my little cottage is not a hundred yards off." Accordingly, we all marched in procession to Dennis's little cottage, which was one of a row and a half of one-storied houses, with little courtyards before them, and mostly with very fine names on the door-posts of each. "Surgeon Haggarty" was emblazoned on Dennis's gate, on a stained green copper-plate; and, not content with this, on the door-post above the bell was an oval with the inscription of "New Molloyville." The bell was broken, of course; the court, or garden path, was mouldy, weedy, seedy; there were some dirty rocks, by way of ornament, round a faded grass-plot in the centre; some clothes and rags hanging out of most part of the windows of New Molloyville, the immediate entrance to which was by a battered scraper, under a broken trellis-work, up which a withered creeper declined any longer to climb.

"Small, but snug," says Haggarty. "I'll lead the way, Fitz. Put your hat on the flower-pot there, and turn to the left into the drawing-room." A fog of onions and turf-smoke filled the whole of the house, and gave signs that dinner was not far off. Far off? You could hear it frizzling in the kitchen, where the maid was also endeavouring to hush the crying of a third refractory child. But as we entered, all three of Haggarty's darlings were in full war.

"Is it you, Dennis?" cried a sharp raw voice, from a dark corner in the drawing-room to which we were introduced, and in which a dirty tablecloth was laid for dinner, some bottles of porter and a cold mutton-bone being laid out on a rickety grand piano hard by. "Ye're always late, Mr. Haggarty. Have you brought the whisky from Nowlan's? I'll go bail ye've not now."

"My dear, I've brought an old friend of yours and mine to take pot-luck with us to-day," said Dennis.

"When is he to come?" said the lady. At which speech I was rather surprised, for I stood before her.

"Here he is, Jemima, my love," answered Dennis, looking at me. "Mr. Fitz-Boodle; don't you remember him in Warwickshire, darling?"

"Mr. Fitz-Boodle! I am very glad to see him," said the lady, rising and curtseying with much cordiality.

Mrs. Haggarty was blind!

Mrs. Haggarty was not only blind, but it was evident that small-pox had been the cause of her loss of vision. Her eyes were bound with a bandage, her features were entirely swollen, scarred, and distorted by the horrible effects of the malady. She had been knitting in a corner when we entered, and was wrapped in a very dirty bed-gown. Her voice to me was quite different from that in which she addressed her husband. She spoke to Haggarty in broad Irish: she addressed me in that most odious of all languages—Irish-English, endeavouring to the utmost to disguise her brogue, and to speak with the true dawdling *distingué* English air.

"Are you long in I-a-land?" said the poor creature in this accent. "You must faind it a sad ba'ba'ous place, Mr. Fitz-Boodle, I'm shu-ah! It was vary kaind of you to come upon us *en famille*, and accept a dinner *sans cérémonie*.—Mr. Haggarty, I hope you'll put the waine into aice; Mr. Fitz-Boodle must be melted with this hot weathah."

For some time she conducted the conversation in this polite strain, and I was obliged to say, in reply to a query of hers, that I did not find her the least altered, though I should never have recognised her but for this rencontre. She told Haggarty with a significant air to get the wine from the cellah, and whispered to me that he was his own butlah; and the poor fellow, taking the hint, scudded away into the town for a pound of veal cutlets and a couple of bottles of wine from the tavern.

"Will the childhren get their potatoes and butther here?" said a barefoot girl, with long black hair flowing over her face, which she thrust in at the door.

"Let them sup in the nursery, Elizabeth, and send—ah! Edwards to me."

"Is it cook you mane, ma'am?" said the girl.

"Send her at once!" shrieked the unfortunate woman; and the noise of frying presently ceasing, a hot woman made her appearance, wiping her brows with her apron, and asking, with an accent decidedly Hibernian, what the misthress wanted.

"Lead me up to my dressing-room, Edwards; I really am not fit to be seen in this dishabille by Mr. Fitz-Boodle."

"Fait' I can't!" says Edwards. "Sure the masther's out at the butcher's, and can't look to the kitchen-fire ! "

" Nonsense, I must go ! " cried Mrs. Haggarty ; and so Edwards, putting on a resigned air, and giving her arm and face a further rub with her apron, held out her arm to Mrs. Dennis, and the pair went upstairs.

She left me to indulge my reflections for half an hour, at the end of which period she came downstairs dressed in an old yellow satin, with the poor shoulders exposed just as much as ever. She had mounted a tawdry cap, which Haggarty himself must have selected for her. She had all sorts of necklaces, bracelets, and ear-rings in gold, in garnets, in mother-of-pearl, in ormolu. She brought in a furious savour of musk, which drove the odours of onions and turf-smoke before it ; and she waved across her wretched, angular, mean, scarred features an old cambric handkerchief with a yellow lace border.

" And so you would have known me anywhere, Mr. Fitz-Boodle ? " said she, with a grin that was meant to be most fascinating. " I was sure you would ; for though my dreadful illness deprived me of my sight, it is a mercy that it did not change my features or complexion at all ! "

This mortification had been spared the unhappy woman ; but I don't know whether, with all her vanity, her infernal pride, folly, and selfishness, it was charitable to leave her in her error.

Yet why correct her ? There is a quality in certain people which is above all advice, exposure, or correction. Only let a man or woman have DULNESS sufficient, and they need bow to no extant authority. A dullard recognises no betters ; a dullard can't see that he is in the wrong ; a dullard has no scruples of conscience, no doubts of pleasing, or succeeding, or doing right—no qualms for other people's feelings, no respect but for the fool himself. How can you make a fool perceive that he is a fool ? Such a personage can no more see his own folly than he can see his own ears. And the great quality of dulness is to be unalterably contented with itself. What myriads of souls are there of this admirable sort—selfish, stingy, ignorant, passionate, brutal ; bad sons, mothers, fathers, never known to do kind actions !

To pause, however, in this disquisition, which was carrying us far off Kingstown, New Molloyville, Ireland—nay, into the wide world wherever Dulness inhabits—let it be stated that Mrs. Haggarty, from my brief acquaintance with her and her mother, was of the order of persons just mentioned. There was an air of conscious merit about her, very hard to swallow along with the infamous dinner poor Dennis managed, after much delay, to get on the table. She did not fail to invite me to Molloyville, where she said her cousin would be charmed to see me ; and she told me almost as many anecdotes about that place as her mother used to impart in former days. I observed, moreover, that Dennis cut her the favourite pieces of the beef-steak, that she ate thereof with great gusto, and that she drank with similar eagerness of the various strong liquors at table. " We Irish ladies are all fond of a leetle glass of punch," she said, with a playful air ; and Dennis mixed her a powerful tumbler of such violent grog as I myself could swallow only with some difficulty. She talked of her suffering a great deal, of her sacrifices, of the luxuries to which she had been accustomed before marriage—in a word, of a hundred of those themes on which some ladies are in the custom of enlarging when they wish to plague some husbands.

But honest Dennis, far from being angry at this perpetual, wearisome, impudent recurrence to her own superiority, rather encouraged the conversation than otherwise. It pleased him to hear his wife discourse about her merits and family splendours. He was so thoroughly beaten down and henpecked that he, as it were, gloried in his servitude, and fancied that his wife's magnificence reflected credit on himself. He looked towards me, who was half sick of the woman and her egotism, as if expecting me to exhibit the deepest sympathy, and flung me glances across the table as much as to say, " What a gifted creature my Jemima is, and what a fine fellow I am to be in possession of her ! " When the children came down she scolded them, of course, and dismissed them abruptly (for which circumstance, perhaps, the writer of these pages was not in his heart very sorry) ; and, after having sat a preposterously long time, left us, asking whether we would have coffee there or in her boudoir.

" Oh ! here, of course," said Dennis, with rather a troubled air ; and in about ten minutes the lovely creature was led back to us again by " Edwards," and the coffee made its appearance. After coffee her husband begged her to let Mr. Fitz-Boodle hear her voice. " He longs for some of his old favourites."

" No ! *do* you ? " said she, and was led in triumph to the jingling old piano, and with a screechy, wiry voice sung those very abominable old ditties which I had heard her sing at Leamington ten years back.

Haggarty, as she sang, flung himself back in his chair delighted. Husbands always are, and with the same song—one that they have heard when they were nineteen years old, probably ; most Englishmen's tunes have that date, and it is rather affecting, I think, to hear an old gentleman of sixty or seventy quavering the old ditty that was fresh when *he* was fresh and in his prime. If he has a musical wife, depend on it he thinks her old songs of 1788 are better than any he has heard since—in fact he has heard *none* since. When the old couple are in high good-humour, the old gentleman will take the old lady round the waist, and say, " My dear, do sing me one of your own songs" ; and she sits down and sings with her old voice, and, as she sings, the roses of her youth bloom again for a moment. Ranelagh resuscitates, and she is dancing a minuet in powder and a train.

This is another digression. It was occasioned by looking at poor Dennis's face while his wife was screeching (and, believe me, the former was the most pleasant occupation). Bottom tickled by the fairies could not have been in greater ecstasies. He thought the music was divine ; and had further reason for exulting in it, which was, that his wife was always in a good-humour after singing, and never would sing but in that happy frame of mind. Dennis had hinted so much in our little colloquy during the ten minutes of his lady's absence in the "boudoir" ; so, at the conclusion of each piece, we shouted "Bravo !" and clapped our hands like mad.

Such was my insight into the life of Surgeon Dionysius Haggarty and his wife ; and I must have come upon him at a favourable moment too, for poor Dennis has spoken subsequently of our delightful evening at Kingstown, and evidently thinks to this day that his friend was fascinated by the entertainment there. His inward economy was as follows : he had his half-pay, a thousand pounds, about a hundred a year that his father left, and his wife had sixty pounds a year from the mother—which the mother, of course, never paid. He had no practice, for he was absorbed in attention to his Jemima and the children, whom he used to wash, to dress, to carry out, to walk, or to ride, as we have seen, and who could not have a servant, as their dear blind mother could never be left alone. Mrs. Haggarty, a great invalid, used to lie in bed till one, and have breakfast, and hot luncheon there. A fifth part of his income was spent in having her wheeled about in a chair, by which it was his duty to walk daily for an allotted number of hours. Dinner would ensue, and the amateur clergy, who abound in Ireland, and of whom Mrs. Haggarty was a great admirer, lauded her everywhere as a model of resignation and virtue, and praised beyond measure the admirable piety with which she bore her sufferings.

Well, every man to his taste. It did not certainly appear to me that *she* was the martyr of the family.

"The circumstances of my marriage with Jemima," Dennis said to me in some after-conversations we had on this interesting subject, "were the most romantic and touching you can conceive. You saw what an impression the dear girl had made upon me when we were at Weedon ; for from the first day I set eyes on her, and heard her sing her delightful song of 'Dark-eyed Maiden of Araby,' I felt, and said to Turniquet of ours that very night, that *she* was the dark-eyed maid of Araby for *me*—not that she was, you know, for she was born in Shropshire. But I felt that I had seen the woman who was to make me happy or miserable for life. You know how I proposed for her at Kenilworth, and how I was rejected, and how I almost shot myself in consequence—no, you don't know that, for I said nothing about it to any one; but I can tell you it was a very near thing, and a very lucky thing for me I didn't do it, for—would you believe it?—the dear girl was in love with me all the time."

"Was she really?" said I, who recollected that Miss Gam's love of those days showed itself in a very singular manner; but the fact is, when women are most in love they most disguise it.

"Over head and ears in love with poor Dennis," resumed that worthy fellow, "who'd ever have thought it? But I have it from the best authority, from her own mother, with whom I'm not over and above good friends now; but of this fact she assured me, and I'll tell you when and how.

"We were quartered at Cork three years after we were at Weedon, and it was our last year at home; and a great mercy that my dear girl spoke in time, or where should we have been *now*? Well, one day, marching home from parade, I saw a lady seated at an open window by another who seemed an invalid; and the lady at the window, who was dressed in the profoundest mourning, cried out with a scream, 'Gracious heavens! it's Mr. Haggarty of the 120th.'

"'Sure I know that voice,' says I to Whiskerton.

"'It's a great mercy you don't know it a deal too well,' says he; 'it's Lady Gammon. She's on some husband-hunting scheme, depend on it, for that daughter of hers. She was at Bath last year on the same errand, and at Cheltenham the year before, where, Heaven bless you! she's as well known as the "Hen and Chickens."'

"'I'll thank you not to speak disrespectfully of Miss Jemima Gam,' said I to Whiskerton; 'she's of one of the first families in Ireland, and whoever says a word against a woman I once proposed for, insults me—do you understand?'

"'Well, marry her, if you like,' says Whiskerton, quite peevish; 'marry her, and be hanged!'

"Marry her! the very idea of it set my brain a-whirling, and made me a thousand times more mad than I am by nature.

"You may be sure I walked up the hill to the parade-ground that afternoon, and with a beating heart, too. I came to the widow's house. It was called 'New Molloyville,' as this is. Wherever she takes a house for six months, she calls it 'New Molloyville'; and has had one in Mallow, in Bandon, in Sligo, in Castlebar, in Fermoy, in Drogheda, and the deuce knows where besides. But the blinds were down, and though I thought I saw somebody behind 'em, no notice was taken of poor Denny Haggarty, and I paced up and down all mess-time in hopes of catching a glimpse of Jemima, but in vain.

The next day I was on the ground again ; I was just as much in love as ever, that's the fact. I'd never been in that way before, look you ; and when once caught, I knew it was for life.

" There's no use in telling you how long I beat about the bush, but when I *did* get admittance to the house (it was through the means of young Castlereagh Molloy, whom you may remember at Leamington, and who was at Cork for the regatta, and used to dine at our mess, and had taken a mighty fancy to me)—when I *did* get into the house, I say, I rushed *in medias res* at once. I couldn't keep myself quiet ; my heart was too full.

" Oh, Fitz ! I shall never forget the day—the moment I was inthrojuiced into the dthrawing-room " (as he began to be agitated, Dennis's brogue broke out with greater richness than ever ; but though a stranger may catch, and repeat from memory, a few words, it is next to impossible for him to *keep up a conversation* in Irish, so that we had best give up all attempts to imitate Dennis). " When I saw old Mother Gam," said he, " my feelings overcame me all at once. I rowled down on the ground, sir, as if I'd been hit by a musket-ball. ' Dearest madam,' says I, ' I'll die if you don't give me Jemima.'

" ' Heavens, Mr. Haggarty ! ' says she, ' how you seize me with surprise !—Castlereagh, my dear nephew, had you not better leave us ? ' and away he went, lighting a cigar, and leaving me still on the floor.

" ' Rise, Mr. Haggarty,' continued the widow. ' I will not attempt to deny that this constancy towards my daughter is extremely affecting, however sudden your present appeal may be. I will not attempt to deny that, perhaps, Jemima may have a similar feeling ; but, as I said, I never could give my daughter to a Catholic.'

" ' I'm as good a Protestant as yourself, ma'am,' says I ; ' my mother was an heiress, and we were all brought up her way.'

" ' That makes the matter very different,' says she, turning up the whites of her eyes. ' How could I ever have reconciled it to my conscience to see my blessed child married to a Papist ? How could I ever have taken him to Molloyville ? Well, this obstacle being removed, *I* must put myself no longer in the way between two young people. *I* must sacrifice myself, as I always have when my darling girl was in question. You shall see her, the poor dear, lovely, gentle sufferer, and learn your fate from her own lips.'

" ' The sufferer, ma'am,' says I ; ' has Miss Gam been ill ? '

" ' What ! haven't you heard ? ' cried the widow. ' Haven't you heard of the dreadful illness which so nearly carried her from me ? For nine weeks, Mr. Haggarty, I watched her day and night without taking a wink of sleep—for nine weeks she lay trembling between death and life ; and I paid the doctor eighty-three guineas. She is restored now, but she is the wreck of the beautiful creature she was. Suffering, and, perhaps, *another disappointment*—but we won't mention that *now*—have so pulled her down. But I will leave you, and prepare my sweet girl for this strange, this entirely unexpected visit.'

"I won't tell you what took place between me and Jemima, to whom I was introduced as she sat in the darkened room, poor sufferer! nor describe to you with what a thrill of joy I seized (after groping about for it) her poor, emaciated hand. She did not withdraw it; I came out of that room an engaged man, sir; and *now* I was enabled to show her that I had always loved her sincerely, for there was my will made three years back in her favour—that night she refused me, as I told ye. I would have shot myself, but they'd have brought me in *non compos*, and my brother Mick would have contested the will; and so I determined to live, in order that she might benefit by my dying. I had but a thousand pounds then; since that my father has left me two more. I willed every shilling to her, as you may fancy, and settled it upon her when we married, as we did soon after. It was not for some time that I was allowed to see the poor girl's face, or indeed was aware of the horrid loss she had sustained. Fancy my agony, my dear fellow, when I saw that beautiful wreck!"

There was something not a little affecting to think, in the conduct of this brave fellow, that he never once, as he told his story, seemed to allude to the possibility of his declining to marry a woman who was not the same as the woman he loved, but that he was quite as faithful to her now as he had been when captivated by the poor, tawdry charms of the silly Miss of Leamington. It was hard that such a noble heart as this should be flung away upon yonder foul mass of greedy vanity. Was it hard, or not, that he should remain deceived in his obstinate humility, and continue to admire the selfish, silly being whom he had chosen to worship?

"I should have been appointed surgeon of the regiment," continued Dennis, "soon after, when it was ordered abroad to Jamaica, where it now is. But my wife would not hear of going, and said she would break her heart if she left her mother. So I retired on half-pay, and took this cottage; and in case any practice should fall in my way—why, there is my name on the brass plate, and I'm ready for anything that comes. But the only case that ever *did* come was one day when I was driving my wife in the chaise; and another, one night, of a beggar with a broken head. My wife makes me a present of a baby every year, and we've no debts; and between you and me and the post, as long as my mother-in-law is out of the house, I'm as happy as I need be."

"What! you and the old lady don't get on well?" said I.

" I can't say we do ; it's not in nature, you know," said Dennis, with a faint grin. " She comes into the house and turns it topsy-turvy. When she's here, I'm obliged to sleep in the scullery. She's never paid her daughter's income since the first year, though she brags about her sacrifices as if she had ruined herself for Jemima ; and besides, when she's here, there's a whole clan of the Molloys, horse, foot, and dragoons, that are quartered upon us, and eat me out of house and home."

" And is Molloyville such a fine place as the widow described it ? " asked I, laughing, and not a little curious.

" Oh, a mighty fine place entirely ! " said Dennis. " There's the oak park of two hundred acres, the finest land ye ever saw, only they've cut all the wood down. The garden in the old Molloy's time, they say, was the finest ever seen in the west of Ireland ; but they've taken all the glass to mend the house windows : and small blame to them either. There's a clear rent-roll of three and fifty hundred a year, only it's in the hand of receivers ; besides other debts, on which there is no land security."

" Your cousin-in-law, Castlereagh Molloy, won't come into a large fortune ? "

" Oh, he'll do very well," said Dennis. " As long as he can get credit, he's not the fellow to stint himself. Faith, I was fool enough to put my name to a bit of paper for him, and as they could not catch him in Mayo, they laid hold of me at Kingstown here. And there was a pretty-to-do. Didn't Mrs. Gam say I was ruining her family, that's all ! I paid it by instalments (for all my money is settled on Jemima) ; and Castlereagh, who's an honourable fellow, offered me any satisfaction in life. Anyhow, he couldn't do more than *that*."

" Of course not ; and now you're friends ? "

" Yes, and he and his aunt have had a tiff, too ; and he abuses her properly, I warrant ye. He says that she carried about Jemima from place to place, and flung her at the head of every unmarried man in England a'most—my poor Jemima, and she all the while dying in love with me ! As soon as she got over the small-pox—she took it at Fermoy : God bless her ! I wish I'd been by to be her nurse-tender—as soon as she was rid of it, the old lady said to Castlereagh, ' Castlereagh, go to the bar'cks, and find out in the Army List where the 120th is.' Off she came to Cork hot foot. It appears that while she was ill, Jemima's love for me showed itself in such a violent way that her mother was overcome, and promised that, should the dear child recover, she would try and bring us together. Castlereagh says she would have gone after us to Jamaica."

" I have no doubt she would," said I.

" Could you have a stronger proof of love than that ? " cried

Dennis. " My dear girl's illness and frightful blindness have, of course, injured her health and her temper. She cannot in her position look to the children, you know, and so they come under my charge for the most part ; and her temper is unequal, certainly. But you see what a sensitive, refined, elegant creature she is, and may fancy that she's often put out by a rough fellow like me."

Here Dennis left me, saying it was time to go and walk out the children ; and I think his story has matter of some wholesome reflection in it for bachelors who are about to change their condition, or may console some who are mourning their celibacy. Marry, gentlemen, if you like ; leave your comfortable dinner at the club for cold mutton and curl-papers at your home ; give up your books or pleasures, and take to yourselves wives and children ; but think well on what you do first, as I have no doubt you will after this advice and example. Advice is always useful in matters of love ; men always take it ; they always follow other people's opinions, not their own ; they always profit by example. When they see a pretty woman, and feel the delicious madness of love coming over them, they always stop to calculate her temper, her money, their own money, or suitableness for the married life. . . . Ha, ha, ha ! Let us fool in this way no more. I have been in love forty-three times with all ranks and conditions of women, and would have married every time if they would have let me. How many wives had King Solomon, the wisest of men ? And is not that story a warning to us that Love is master of the wisest ? It is only fools who defy him.

I must come, however, to the last, and perhaps the saddest, part of poor Denny Haggarty's history. I met him once more, and in such a condition as made me determine to write this history.

In the month of June last I happened to be at Richmond, a delightful little place of retreat ; and there, sunning himself upon the terrace, was my old friend of the 120th. He looked older, thinner, poorer, and more wretched than I had ever seen him. " What ! you have given up Kingstown ? " said I, shaking him by the hand.

" Yes," says he.

" And is my lady and your family here at Richmond ? "

" No," says he, with a sad shake of the head, and the poor fellow's hollow eyes filled with tears.

" Good heavens, Denny ! what's the matter ? " said I. He was squeezing my hand like a vice as I spoke.

" They've LEFT me ! " he burst out with a dreadful shout of passionate grief—a horrible scream which seemed to be wrenched out of his heart. " Left me ! " said he, sinking down on a seat, and clenching his great fists, and shaking his lean arms wildly. " I'm a wise man now, Mr. Fitz-Boodle. Jemima has gone away from me ; and yet you know how I loved her, and how happy we were ! I've got nobody now ; but I'll die soon, that's one comfort, and to think it's she that'll kill me after all ! "

The story, which he told me with a wild and furious lamentation such as is not known among men of our cooler country, and such as I don't like now to recall, was a very simple one. The mother-in-law had taken possession of the house, and had driven him from it. His property at his marriage was settled on his wife. She had never loved him, and told him this secret at last, and drove him out of doors with her selfish scorn and ill-temper. The boy had died ; the girls were better, he said, brought up among the Molloys than they could be with him ; and so he was quite alone in the world, and was living, or rather dying, on forty pounds a year.

His troubles are very likely over by this time. The two fools who caused his misery will never read this history of him—*they* never read godless stories in magazines ; and I wish, honest reader, that you and I went to church as much as they do. These people are not wicked *because* of their religious observances, but *in spite* of them. They are too dull to understand humility, too blind to see a tender and simple heart under a rough ungainly bosom. They are sure that all their conduct towards my poor friend here has been perfectly righteous, and that they have given proofs of the most Christian virtue. Haggarty's wife is considered by her friends as a martyr to a savage husband, and her mother is the angel that has come to rescue her. All they did was to cheat him and desert him. And safe in that wonderful self-complacency with which the fools of this earth are endowed, they have not a single pang of conscience for their villainy towards him, and consider their heartlessness as a proof and consequence of their spotless piety and virtue.

WILLIAM MAKEPEACE THACKERAY

A GAMBLER'S DEATH

ANYBODY who was at C—— school some twelve years since must recollect Jack Attwood. He was the most dashing lad in the place, with more money in his pocket than belonged to the whole fifth form, in which we were companions.

When he was about fifteen, Jack suddenly retreated from C——; and presently we heard that he had a commission in a cavalry regiment, and was to have a great fortune from his father when that old gentleman should die. Jack himself came to confirm these stories a few months after, and paid a visit to his old school-chums. He had laid aside his little school-jacket and inky corduroys, and now appeared in such a splendid military suit as won the respect of all of us. His hair was dripping with oil; his hands were covered with rings; he had a dusky down over his upper lip, which looked not unlike a moustache; and a multiplicity of frogs and braiding on his surtout, which would have sufficed to lace a field-marshal. When old Swishtail, the usher, passed in his seedy black coat and gaiters, Jack gave him such a look of contempt as set us all a-laughing. In fact, it was his turn to laugh now; for he used to roar very stoutly, some months before, when Swishtail was in the custom of belabouring him with his great cane.

Jack's talk was all about the regiment, and the fine fellows in it: how he had ridden a steeplechase with Captain Boldero, and licked him at the last hedge; and how he had very nearly fought a duel with Sir George Grig, about dancing with Lady Mary Slamken at a ball. "I soon made the baronet know what it was to deal with a man of the N—th," said Jack. "Dammee, sir, when I lugged out my barkers, and talked of fighting across the mess-room table, Grig turned as pale as a sheet, or as——"

"Or as you used to do, Attwood, when Swishtail hauled you up," piped out little Hicks, the foundation-boy.

It was beneath Jack's dignity to thrash anybody now but a grown-up baronet; so he let off little Hicks, and passed over the general titter which was raised at his expense. However, he entertained us with his histories about lords and ladies, and so-and-so "of ours," until we thought him one of the greatest men in his Majesty's service, and until the school-bell rung, when, with a heavy heart, we got our books together and marched in to be whacked by old Swishtail. I promise you, he revenged himself on us for Jack's contempt of him. I got that day at least twenty cuts to my share, which ought to have belonged to Cornet Attwood of the N—th Dragoons.

When we came to think more coolly over our quondam schoolfellow's swaggering talk and manner, we were not quite so impressed by his merits as at his first appearance among us. We recollected how he used, in former times, to tell us great stories, which were so monstrously improbable that the smallest boy in the school would scout at them; how often we caught him tripping in facts, and how unblushingly he admitted his little errors on the score of veracity. He and I, though never great friends, had been close companions. I was Jack's form-fellow (we fought with amazing emulation for the *last* place in the class); but still I was rather hurt at the coolness of my old comrade, who had forgotten all our former intimacy in his steeplechases with Captain Boldero and his duel with Sir George Grig.

Nothing more was heard of Attwood for some years. A tailor one day came down to C——, who had made clothes for Jack in his schooldays, and furnished him with regimentals. He produced a long bill for one hundred and twenty pounds and upwards, and asked where news might be had of his customer. Jack was in India, with his regiment, shooting tigers and jackals, no doubt. Occasionally, from that distant country some magnificent rumour would reach us of his proceedings. Once I heard that he had been called to a court-martial for unbecoming conduct; another time, that he kept twenty horses, and won the gold plate at the Calcutta races. Presently, however, as the recollections of the fifth form wore away, Jack's image disappeared likewise, and I ceased to ask or think about my college chum.

A year since, as I was smoking my cigar in the "Estaminet du Grand Balcon"—an excellent smoking-shop, where the tobacco is unexceptionable, and the Hollands of singular merit—a dark-looking, thick-set man, in a greasy well-cut coat, with a shabby hat cocked on one side of his dirty face, took the place opposite me, at the little marble table, and called for brandy. I did not much admire the impudence or the appearance of my friend, nor the fixed stare with which he chose to examine me. At last, he thrust a great greasy hand across the table, and said, "Titmarsh, do you forget your old friend Attwood?"

I confess my recognition of him was not so joyful as on the day, ten years earlier, when he had come, bedizened with lace and gold rings, to see us at C—— school. A man, in the tenth part of a century, learns a deal of worldly wisdom, and his hand, which goes naturally forward to seize the gloved finger of a millionaire, or a milor, draws instinctively back from a dirty fist, encompassed by a ragged wrist-band and a tattered cuff. But Attwood was in nowise so backward, and the iron squeeze with which he shook my passive paw proved that he was either very affectionate or very poor. You, my dear sir, who are reading this history, know very well the great art of shaking hands. Recollect how you shook Lord Dash's hand the other day, and how you shook *off* poor Blank when he came to borrow five pounds of you.

However, the genial influence of the Hollands speedily dissipated anything like coolness between us; and, in the course of an hour's conversation, we became almost as intimate as when we were suffering together under the ferule of old Swishtail. Jack told me that he had quitted the army in disgust; and that his father, who was to leave him a fortune, had died ten thousand pounds in debt. He did not touch upon his own circumstances; but I could read them in his elbows, which were peeping through his old frock. He talked a great deal, however, of runs of luck, good and bad; and related to me an infallible plan for breaking all the play-banks in Europe—a great number of old tricks. And a vast quantity of gin-punch was consumed on the occasion; so long, in fact, did our conversation continue, that (I confess it with shame) the sentiment, or something stronger, quite got the better of me, and I have, to this day, no sort of notion how our palaver concluded. Only, on the next morning, I did not possess a certain five-pound note which on the previous evening was in my sketch-book (by far the prettiest drawing, by the way, in the collection); but there, instead, was a strip of paper, thus inscribed:

I O U
Five Pounds. John Attwood,
Late of the N—th Dragoons.

I suppose Attwood borrowed the money, from this remarkable and ceremonious acknowledgment on his part. Had I been sober, I would just as soon have lent him the nose on my face, for, in my then circumstances, the note was of much more consequence to me.

As I lay cursing my ill fortune, and thinking how on earth I should manage to subsist for the next two months, Attwood burst into my little garret—his face strangely flushed—singing and shouting as if it had been the night before. "Titmarsh," cried he, "you are my preserver! my best friend! Look here, and here, and here!" And at every word Mr. Attwood produced a handful of gold, or a glittering heap of five-franc pieces, or a bundle of greasy, dusky bank-notes, more beautiful than either silver or gold. He had won thirteen thousand francs after leaving me, at midnight, in my garret. He separated my poor little all, of six pieces, from this shining and imposing collection; and the passion of envy entered my soul. I felt far more anxious now than before, although starvation was then staring me in the face; I hated Attwood for *cheating* me out of all this wealth. Poor fellow! it had been better for him had he never seen a shilling of it.

However, a grand breakfast at the Café Anglais dissipated my chagrin; and I will do my friend the justice to say that he nobly shared some portion of his good fortune with me. As far as the creature comforts were concerned, I feasted as well as he, and never was particular as to settling my share of the reckoning.

Jack now changed his lodgings, had cards with "Captain Attwood" engraved on them, and drove about a prancing cab-horse as tall as the giraffe at the Jardin des Plantes; he had as many frogs on his coat as in the old days, and frequented all the flash restaurateurs' and boarding-houses of the capital. Madame de Saint Laurent, and Madame la Baronne de Vaudrey, and Madame la Comtesse de Don Jonville, ladies of the highest rank, who keep a *société choisie*, and condescend to give dinners at five francs a head, vied with each other in their attentions to Jack. His was the wing of the fowl, and the largest portion of the Charlotte-Russe; his was the place at the *écarté* table, where the countess would ease him nightly of a few pieces, declaring that he was the most charming cavalier—*la fleur d'Albion*. Jack's society, it may be seen, was not very select; nor, in truth, were his inclinations; he was a careless, dare-devil, Macheath kind of fellow, who might be seen daily with a wife on each arm.

It may be supposed that, with the life he led, his five hundred pounds of winnings would not last him long. Nor did they. But for some time his luck never deserted him, and his cash, instead of growing lower, seemed always to maintain a certain level. He played every night.

Of course, such a humble fellow as I could not hope for a continued acquaintance and intimacy with Attwood. He grew overbearing and cool, I thought. At any rate, I did not admire my situation as his follower and dependant, and left his grand dinner for a certain ordinary where I could partake of five capital dishes for ninepence. Occasionally, however, Attwood favoured me with a visit, or gave me a drive behind his great cab-horse. He had formed a whole host of friends besides. There was Fips, the barrister (Heaven knows what he was doing at Paris!); and Gortz, the West Indian, who was there on the same business; and Flapper, a medical student: all these three I met one night at Flapper's rooms, where Jack was invited, and a great "spread" was laid in honour of him.

Jack arrived rather late. He looked pale and agitated; and

though he ate no supper, he drank raw brandy in such a manner as made Flapper's eyes wink: the poor fellow had but three bottles, and Jack bid fair to swallow them all. However, the West Indian generously remedied the evil; and producing a napoleon, we speedily got the change for it in the shape of four bottles of champagne.

Our supper was uproariously harmonious. Fips sang "The Good Old English Gentleman"; Jack, "The British Grenadiers"; and your humble servant, when called upon, sang that beautiful ditty, "When the Bloom is on the Rye," in a manner that drew tears from every eye—except Flapper's, who was asleep, and Jack's, who was singing "The Bay of Biscay O," at the same time. Gortz and Fips were all the time lunging at each other with a pair of single-sticks, the barrister having a very strong notion that he was Richard the Third. At last Fips hits the West Indian such a blow across his sconce that the other grew furious; he seized a champagne bottle (which was, providentially, empty), and hurled it across the room at Fips. Had that celebrated barrister not bowed his head at the moment, the Queen's Bench would have lost one of its most eloquent practitioners.

Fips stood as straight as he could; his cheek was pale with wrath. "M-m-ister Go-gortz," he said, "I always heard you were a blackguard; now I can pr-pr-peperove it.—Flapper, your pistols! Every ge-ge-genlmn knows what I mean."

Young Mr. Flapper had a small pair of pocket-pistols, which the tipsy barrister had suddenly remembered, and with which he proposed to sacrifice the West Indian. Gortz was nothing loth, but was quite as valorous as the lawyer.

Attwood, who, in spite of his potations, seemed the soberest man of the party, had much enjoyed the scene, until this sudden demand for the weapons. "Pshaw!" said he eagerly, "don't give these men the means of murdering each other. Sit down, and let us have another song." But they would not be still; and Flapper forthwith produced his pistol-case, and opened it, in order that the duel might take place on the spot. There were no pistols there! "I beg your pardon," said Attwood, looking much confused; "I—I took the pistols home with me to clean them!"

I don't know what there was in his tone, or in the words, but we were sobered all of a sudden. Attwood was conscious of the singular effect produced by him, for he blushed, and endeavoured to speak of other things. But we could not bring our spirits back to the mark again, and soon separated for the night. As we issued into the street, Jack took me aside and whispered, "Have you a napoleon, Titmarsh, in your purse?" Alas! I was not so rich. My reply was, that I was coming to Jack, only in the morning, to borrow a similar sum.

He did not make any reply, but turned away homeward. I never heard him speak another word.

. . . .

Two mornings after (for none of our party met on the day succeeding the supper), I was awakened by my porter, who brought a pressing letter from Mr. Gortz:

"DEAR T.,—I wish you would come over here to breakfast. There's a row about Attwood.—Yours truly, SOLOMON GORTZ."

I immediately set forward to Gortz's; he lived in the Rue du Heldes, a few doors from Attwood's new lodging. If the reader is curious to know the house in which the catastrophe of this history took place, he has but to march some twenty doors down from the Boulevard des Italiens, when he will see a fine door, with a naked Cupid shooting at him from the hall, and a Venus beckoning him up the stairs. On arriving at the West Indian's, at about mid-day (it was a Sunday morning), I found that gentleman in his dressing-gown, discussing, in the company of Mr. Fips, a large plate of *bifteck aux pommes*.

"Here's a pretty row!" said Gortz, quoting from his letter. "Attwood's off;—have a bit of beefsteak?"

"What do you mean?" exclaimed I, adopting the familiar phraseology of my acquaintances. "Attwood off?—has he cut his stick?"

"Not bad," said the feeling and elegant Fips—"not such a bad guess, my boy; but he has not exactly *cut his stick.*"

"What then?"

"*Why, his throat.*" The man's mouth was full of bleeding beef as he uttered this gentlemanly witticism.

I wish I could say that I was myself in the least affected by the news. I did not joke about it, like my friend Fips—this was more for propriety's sake than for feeling's—but for my old school acquaintance, the friend of my early days, the merry associate of the last few months, I own, with shame, that I had not a tear or a pang. In some German tale there is an account of a creature most beautiful and bewitching, whom all men admire and follow; but this charming and fantastic spirit only leads them, one by one, into ruin, and then leaves them. The novelist, who describes her beauty, says that his heroine is a fairy, and *has no heart.* I think the intimacy which is begotten over the wine-bottle is a spirit of this nature. I never knew a good feeling come from it, or an honest friendship made by it; it only entices men and ruins them; it is only a phantom of friendship and feeling, called up by the delirious blood, and the wicked spells of the wine.

But to drop this strain of moralising (in which the writer is not too anxious to proceed, for he cuts in it a most pitiful figure), we passed sundry criticisms upon poor Attwood's character; expressed our horror at his death—which sentiment was fully proved by Mr. Fips, who declared that the notion of it made him feel quite faint, and was obliged to drink a large glass of brandy; and, finally, we agreed that we would go and see the poor fellow's corpse, and witness, if necessary, his burial.

Flapper, who had joined us, was the first to propose this visit. He said he did not mind the fifteen francs which Jack owed him for billiards, but he was anxious to *get back his pistol*. Accordingly, we sallied forth, and speedily arrived at the hotel which Attwood inhabited still. He had occupied, for a time, very fine apartments in this house; and it was only on arriving there that day that we found he had been gradually driven from his magnificent suite of rooms *au premier*, to a little chamber in the fifth storey. We mounted, and found him. It was a little shabby room, with a few articles of rickety furniture, and a bed in an alcove. The light from the one window was falling full upon the bed and the body. Jack was dressed in a fine lawn shirt—he had kept it, poor fellow, *to die in*, for in all his drawers and cupboards there was not a single article of clothing; he had pawned everything by which he could raise a penny—desk, books, dressing-case, and clothes; and not a single halfpenny was found in his possession.[1]

He was lying with one hand on his breast, the other falling towards the ground. There was an expression of perfect calm on the face, and no mark of blood to stain the side towards the light. On the other side, however, there was a great pool of black blood, and in it the pistol: it looked more like a toy than a weapon to take away the life of this vigorous young man. In his forehead, at the side, was a small black wound; Jack's life had passed through it; it was little bigger than a mole.

. . . .

"Regardez un peu," said the landlady, "messieurs, il m'a gâté trois matelas, et il me doit quarante quatre francs."

This was all his epitaph: he had spoiled three mattresses, and owed the landlady four-and-forty francs. In the whole world there was not a soul to love him or lament him. We, his friends, were looking at his body more as an object of curiosity, watching it with a kind of interest with which one follows the fifth act of a tragedy, and leaving it with the same feeling with which one leaves the theatre when the play is over and the curtain is down.

[1] In order to account for these trivial details, the reader must be told that the story is, for the chief part, a fact. The letter was likewise a copy from one found in the manner described.

Beside Jack's bed, on his little " table de nuit," lay the remains of his last meal, and an open letter, which we read. It was from one of his suspicious acquaintances of former days, and ran thus :

" Où es-tu, cher Jack ? *why you not come and see me*—tu me dois de l'argent, entends-tu ?—un chapeau, une cachemire, *a box of the Play.* Viens demain soir, je t'attendrai *at eight o'clock,* Passage des Panoramas. *My Sir is at his country.* Adieu à demain.
" Samedi." " FIFINE."

. . . .

I shuddered as I walked through this very Passage des Panoramas, in the evening. The girl was there, pacing to and fro, and looking in the countenance of every passer-by, to recognise Attwood. " ADIEU À DEMAIN ! "—there was a dreadful meaning in the words, which the writer of them little knew. " Adieu à demain ! "—the morrow was come, and the soul of the poor suicide was now in the presence of God. I dare not think of his fate ; for, except in the fact of his poverty and desperation, was he worse than any of us, his companions who had shared his debauches, and marched with him up to the very brink of the grave ?

There is but one more circumstance to relate regarding poor Jack —his burial ; it was of a piece with his death.

He was nailed into a paltry coffin and buried, at the expense of the arrondissement, in a nook of the burial-place beyond the Barrière de l'Etoile. They buried him at six o'clock of a bitter winter's morning, and it was with difficulty that an English clergyman could be found to read a service over his grave. The three men who have figured in this history acted as Jack's mourners ; and as the ceremony was to take place so early in the morning, these men sat up the night through, *and were almost drunk* as they followed his coffin to its resting-place.

MORAL

" When we turned out in our greatcoats," said one of them afterwards, " reeking of cigars and brandy-and-water, d——e, sir, we quite frightened the old buck of a parson ; he did not much like our company." After the ceremony was concluded, these gentlemen were very happy to get home to a warm and comfortable breakfast, and finished the day royally at Frascati's.

WILLIAM MAKEPEACE THACKERAY

A LITTLE DINNER IN BITTLESTONE STREET

In that noble romance called *Ten Thousand a Year*, I remember a profoundly pathetic description of the Christian manner in which the hero, Mr. Aubrey, bore his misfortunes. After making a display of the most florid and grandiloquent resignation, and quitting his country mansion, the writer supposes Aubrey to come to town in a post-chaise and pair sitting bodkin probably between his wife and sister. It is about seven o'clock, carriages are rattling about, knockers are thundering, and tears bedim the fine eyes of Kate and Mrs. Aubrey as they think that in happier times at this hour—their Aubrey used formerly to go out to dinner to the houses of the aristocracy his friends. This is the gist of the passage—the elegant words I forget. But the noble, noble sentiment I shall always cherish and remember. What can be more sublime than the notion of a great man's relatives in tears about—his dinner? With a few touches, what author ever more happily described a Snob?

We were reading the passage lately at the house of my friend, Raymond Gray, Esquire, Barrister-at-Law, an ingenuous youth without the least practice, but who has luckily a great share of good spirits, which enables him to bide his time, and bear laughingly his humble position in the world. Meanwhile, until it is altered, the stern laws of necessity and the expenses of the Northern Circuit oblige Mr. Gray to live in a very tiny mansion in a very queer small square in the airy neighbourhood of Gray's Inn.

What is the more remarkable is, that Gray has a wife there. Mrs. Gray was a Miss Harley Baker: and I suppose I need not say *that* is a respectable family. Allied to the Cavendishes, the Oxfords, the Marrybones, they still, though rather *déchus* from their original splendour, hold their heads as high as any. Mrs. Harley Baker, I know, never goes to church without John behind to carry her prayer-book; nor will Miss Welbeck, her sister, walk twenty yards a shopping without the protection of Figby, her sugar-loaf page; though the old lady is as ugly as any woman in the parish, and as tall and whiskery as a Grenadier. The astonishment is, how Emily Harley Baker could have stooped to marry Raymond Gray. She, who was the prettiest and proudest of the family; she, who refused Sir Cockle Byles, of the Bengal Service; she, who turned up her little nose at Essex Temple, Q.C., and connected with the noble house of Albyn; she, who had but £4000 *pour tout potage*, to marry a man who had scarcely as much more. A scream of wrath and indignation was uttered by the whole family when they heard of this *mésalliance*. Mrs. Harley Baker never speaks of her daughter now but with tears in her eyes, and as a ruined creature. Miss Welbeck says, " I consider that man a villain," and has denounced poor good-natured Mrs. Perkins as a swindler, at whose ball the young people met for the first time.

Mr. and Mrs. Gray, meanwhile, live in Gray's Inn Lane, aforesaid, with a maid-servant and a nurse, whose hands are very full, and in a most provoking and unnatural state of happiness. They have never once thought of crying about their dinner, like the wretchedly puling and Snobbish womankind of my favourite Snob Aubrey, of *Ten Thousand a Year*; but, on the contrary, accept such humble victuals as Fate awards them with a most perfect and thankful good grace—nay, actually have a portion for a hungry friend at times—as the present writer can gratefully testify.

I was mentioning these dinners, and some admirable lemon puddings which Mrs. Gray makes, to our mutual friend the great Mr. Goldmore, the East India Director, when that gentleman's face assumed an expression of almost apoplectic terror, and he gasped out, " What! Do they give dinners? " He seemed to think it a crime and a wonder that such people should dine at all, and that it was their custom to huddle round their kitchen fire over a bone and a crust. Whenever he meets them in society, it is a matter of wonder to him (and he always expresses his surprise very loud) how the lady can appear decently dressed, and the man have an unpatched coat to his back. I have heard him enlarge upon this poverty before the whole room at the Conflagrative Club, to which he and I and Gray have the honour to belong.

We meet at the Club on most days. At half-past four, Goldmore arrives in St. James's Street, from the City, and you may see him reading the evening papers in the bow window of the Club which enfilades Pall Mall—a large plethoric man, with a bunch of seals in a large bow-windowed light waistcoat. He has large coat-tails, stuffed with agents' letters and papers about companies of which he is a Director. His seals jingle as he walks. I wish I had such a man for an uncle, and that he himself were childless. I would love and cherish him, and be kind to him.

At six o'clock in the full season, when all the world is in St. James's Street, and the carriages are cutting in and out among the cabs on the stand, and the tufted dandies are showing their listless faces out of White's; and you see respectable grey-headed gentlemen waggling their heads to each other through the plate-glass windows of Arthur's: and the red-coats wish to be Briarean, so as to hold all the gentlemen's horses; and that wonderful red-coated royal porter is sunning himself before Marlborough House;—at the noon of London time, you see a light-yellow carriage with black horses, and a coachman in a tight floss-silk wig, and two footmen in powder and white and yellow liveries, and a large woman inside in shot silk, a poodle, and a pink parasol, which drives up to the gate of the Conflagrative, and the page goes and says to Mr. Goldmore (who is perfectly aware of the fact, as he is looking out of the windows with about forty other Conflagrative bucks), "Your carriage, sir." G. wags his head. "Remember, eight o'clock precisely," says he to Mulligatawney, the other East India Director, and ascending the carriage plumps down by the side of Mrs. Goldmore for a drive in the Park, and then home to Portland Place. As the carriage whirls off, all the young bucks in the Club feel a secret elation. It is a part of their establishment, as it were. That carriage belongs to their Club, and their Club belongs to them. They follow the equipage with interest; they eye it knowingly as they see it in the Park. But halt! we are not come to the Club Snobs yet. O my brave Snobs, what a flurry there will be among you when those papers appear!

Well, you may judge from the above description what sort of a man Goldmore is. A dull and pompous Leadenhall Street Crœsus, good-natured withal, and affable—cruelly affable. "Mr. Goldmore can never forget," his lady used to say, "that it was Mrs. Gray's grandfather who sent him to India; and though that young woman has made the most imprudent marriage in the world, and has left her station in society, her husband seems an ingenious and laborious young man, and we shall do everything in our power to be of use to him." So they used to ask the Grays to dinner twice or thrice in a season, when, by way of increasing the kindness, Buff, the butler, is ordered to hire a fly to convey them to and from Portland Place.

Of course I am much too good-natured a friend of both parties not to tell Gray of Goldmore's opinion regarding him, and the Nabob's astonishment at the idea of the briefless barrister having any dinner at all. Indeed, Goldmore's saying became a joke against Gray amongst us wags at the Club, and we used to ask him when he tasted meat last? whether we should bring him home something from dinner? and cut a thousand other mad pranks with him in our facetious way.

One day, then, coming home from the Club, Mr. Gray conveyed to his wife the astounding information that he had asked Goldmore to dinner.

" My love," says Mrs. Gray, in a tremor, " how could you be so cruel ? Why, the dining-room won't hold Mrs. Goldmore."

" Make your mind easy, Mrs. Gray, her ladyship is in Paris. It is only Crœsus that's coming, and we are going to the play afterwards —to Sadler's Wells. Goldmore said at the Club that he thought Shakespeare was a great dramatic poet, and ought to be patronised ; whereupon, fired with enthusiasm, I invited him to our banquet."

" Goodness gracious ! what *can* we give him for dinner ? He has two French cooks ; you know Mrs. Goldmore is always telling us about them ; and he dines with Aldermen every day."

> " A plain leg of mutton, my Lucy,
> I prythee get ready at three ;
> Have it tender, and smoking, and juicy,
> And what better meat can there be ? "

says Gray, quoting my favourite poet.

" But the cook is ill ; and you know that horrible Pattypan, the pastrycook's——"

" Silence, Frau ! " says Gray, in a deep-tragedy voice. " *I* will have the ordering of this repast. Do all things as I bid thee. Invite our friend Snob here to partake of the feast. Be mine the task of procuring it."

" Don't be expensive, Raymond," says his wife.

" Peace, thou timid partner of the briefless one. Goldmore's dinner shall be suited to our narrow means. Only do thou in all things my commands." And seeing by the peculiar expression of the rogue's countenance that some mad waggery was in preparation, I awaited the morrow with anxiety.

Punctual to the hour—(by the way, I cannot omit here to mark down my hatred, scorn, and indignation towards those miserable Snobs who come to dinner at nine, when they are asked at eight, in order to make a sensation in the company. May the loathing of honest folks, the back-biting of others, the curses of cooks, pursue these wretches, and avenge the society on which they trample !)— Punctual, I say, to the hour of five, which Mr. and Mrs. Raymond Gray had appointed, a youth of an elegant appearance, in a neat evening dress, whose trim whiskers indicated neatness, whose light step denoted activity (for in sooth he was hungry, and always is at the dinner hour, whatsoever that hour may be), and whose rich golden hair, curling down his shoulders, was set off by a perfectly new four-and-ninepenny silk hat, was seen wending his way down Bittlestone Street, Bittlestone Square, Gray's Inn. The person in question, I need not say, was Mr. Snob. *He* was never late when invited to dine. But to proceed with my narrative:

Although Mr. Snob may have flattered himself that he made a sensation as he strutted down Bittlestone Street with his richly gilt-knobbed cane (and indeed I vow I saw heads looking at me from Miss Squilsby's, the brass-plated milliner opposite Raymond Gray's, who has three silver-paper bonnets, and two fly-blown French prints of fashion in the window), yet what was the emotion produced by my arrival compared to that with which the little street thrilled, when at five minutes past five the floss-wigged coachman, the yellow hammer-cloth and flunkies, the black horses and blazing silver harness of Mr. Goldmore whirled down the street! It is a very little street, of very little houses, most of them with very large brass plates like Miss Squilsby's. Coal-merchants, architects, and surveyors, two surgeons, a solicitor, a dancing-master, and of course several house-agents, occupy the houses—little two-storeyed edifices with little stucco porticoes. Goldmore's carriage overtopped the roof almost; the first floors might shake hands with Crœsus as he lolled inside; all the windows of those first floors thronged with children and women in a twinkling. There was Mrs. Hammerly in curl-papers; Mrs. Saxby with her front awry; Mr. Wriggles peering through the gauze curtains, holding the while his hot glass of rum-and-water—in fine, a tremendous commotion in Bittlestone Street, as the Goldmore carriage drove up to Mr. Raymond Gray's door.

"How kind it is of him to come with *both* the footmen!" says little Mrs. Gray, peeping at the vehicle too. The huge domestic, descending from his perch, gave a rap at the door which almost drove in the building. All the heads were out; the sun was shining; the very organ-boy paused; the footman, the coach, and Goldmore's red face and white waistcoat were blazing in splendour. The herculean plushed one went back to open the carriage-door.

Raymond Gray opened his—in his shirt-sleeves.

He ran up to the carriage. "Come in, Goldmore," he says. "Just in time, my boy. Open the door Whatdyecallum, and let your master out,"—and Whatdyecallum obeyed mechanically, with a face of wonder and horror, only to be equalled by the look of stupefied astonishment which ornamented the purple countenance of his master.

"Wawt taim will you please have the *cage*, sir," says Whatdyecallum, in that peculiar, unspellable, inimitable, flunkyfied pronunciation which forms one of the chief charms of existence.

"Best have it to the theatre, at night," Gray exclaims; "it is but a step from here to the Wells, and we can walk there. I've got tickets for all. Be at Sadler's Wells at eleven."

"Yes, at eleven," exclaims Goldmore perturbedly, and walks with a flurried step into the house, as if he were going to execution (as indeed he was, with that wicked Gray as a Jack Ketch over him). The carriage drove away, followed by numberless eyes from door-steps and balconies ; its appearance is still a wonder in Bittlestone Street.

"Go in there, and amuse yourself with Snob," says Gray, opening the little drawing-room door. "I'll call out as soon as the chops are ready. Fanny's below, seeing to the pudding."

"Gracious mercy !" says Goldmore to me, quite confidentially, "How could he ask us ? I really had no idea of this—this utter destitution."

"Dinner, dinner !" roars out Gray from the dining-room, whence issued a great smoking and frying ; and entering that apartment we find Mrs. Gray ready to receive us, and looking perfectly like a Princess who, by some accident, had a bowl of potatoes in her hand, which vegetables she placed on the table. Her husband was meanwhile cooking mutton-chops on a gridiron over the fire.

"Fanny has made the roly-poly pudding," says he ; "the chops are my part. Here's a fine one ; try this, Goldmore." And he popped a fizzing cutlet on that gentleman's plate. What words, what notes of exclamation can describe the nabob's astonishment ? The table-cloth was a very old one, darned in a score of places. There was mustard in a tea-cup, a silver fork for Goldmore—all ours were iron.

"I wasn't born with a silver spoon in my mouth," says Gray gravely. "That fork is the only one we have. Fanny has it generally."

"Raymond !" cries Mrs. Gray, in an imploring voice.

"She was used to better things, you know : and I hope one day to get her a dinner service. I'm told the electro-plate is uncommonly good. Where the deuce *is* that boy with the beer ? And now," said he, springing up, "I'll be a gentleman." And so he put on his coat, and sate down quite gravely, with four fresh mutton chops which he had by this time broiled.

"We don't have meat every day, Mr. Goldmore," he continued, "and it's a treat to me to get a dinner like this. You little know, you gentlemen of England, who live at home at ease, what hardships briefless barristers endure."

"Gracious mercy !" says Mr. Goldmore.

"Where's the half-and-half ? Fanny, go over to the Keys and get the beer. Here's sixpence." And what was our astonishment when Fanny got up as if to go !

"Gracious mercy ! let *me*," cries Goldmore.

" Not for worlds, my dear sir. She's used to it. They wouldn't serve you as well as they serve her. Leave her alone. Law bless you ! " Raymond said with astounding composure. And Mrs. Gray left the room, and actually came back with a tray on which there was a pewter flagon of beer. Little Polly (to whom, at her christening, I had the honour of presenting a silver mug, *ex officio*), followed with a couple of tobacco pipes, and the queerest roguish look in her round little chubby face.

" Did you speak to Tapling about the gin, Fanny, my dear ? " Gray asked, after bidding Polly put the pipes on the chimney-piece, which that little person had some little difficulty in reaching— " The last was turpentine, and even your brewing didn't make good punch of it. You would hardly suspect, Goldmore, that my wife, a Harley Baker, would ever make gin-punch ? I think my mother-in-law would commit suicide if she saw her."

" Don't be always laughing at mamma, Raymond," says Mrs. Gray.

" Well, well, she wouldn't die, and I *don't* wish she would. And you don't make gin-punch, and you don't like it either—and—Goldmore, do you drink your beer out of the glass, or out of the pewter ? "

" Gracious mercy ! " ejaculates Crœsus once more, as little Polly, taking the pot with both her little bunches of hands, offers it smiling to that astonished Director.

And so, in a word, the dinner commenced, and was presently ended in a similar fashion. Gray pursued his unfortunate guest with the most queer and outrageous description of his struggles, misery, and poverty. He described how he cleaned the knives when they were first married ; and how he used to drag the children in a little cart ; how his wife could toss pancakes ; and what parts of his dress she made. He told Tibbits, his clerk (who was in fact the functionary who had brought the beer from the public-house, which Mrs. Fanny had fetched from the neighbouring apartment)—to fetch " the bottle of port wine," when the dinner was over ; and told Goldmore as wonderful a history about the way in which that bottle of wine had come into his hands, as any of his former stories had been. When the repast was all over, and it was near time to move to the play, and Mrs. Gray had retired, and we were sitting ruminating rather silently over the last glasses of port, Gray suddenly breaks the silence by slapping Goldmore on the shoulder, and saying, " Now, Goldmore, tell me something."

" What ? " asks Crœsus.

" Haven't you had a good dinner ? "

Goldmore started, as if a sudden truth had just dawned upon him. He *had* had a good dinner ; and didn't know it until then. The three mutton chops consumed by him were best of the mutton kind :

the potatoes were perfect of their order; as for the roly-poly, it was too good. The porter was frothy and cool, and the port wine was worthy of the gills of a bishop. I speak with ulterior views; for there is more in Gray's cellar.

"Well," says Goldmore, after a pause, during which he took time to consider the momentous question Gray put to him—"'Pon my word—now you say so—I—I have—I really have had a monsous good dinnah—monsous good, upon my ward! Here's your health, Gray, my boy, and your amiable lady; and when Mrs. Goldmore comes back, I hope we shall see you more in Portland Place." And with this the time came for the play, and we went to see Mr. Phelps at Sadler's Wells.

The best of this story (for the truth of every word of which I pledge my honour) is, that after this banquet, which Goldmore enjoyed so, the honest fellow felt a prodigious compassion and regard for the starving and miserable giver of the feast, and determined to help him in his profession. And being a Director of the newly established Antibilious Life Assurance Company, he has had Gray appointed standing Counsel, with a pretty annual fee; and only yesterday, in an appeal from Bombay (Buckmuckjee Bobbachee *v.* Ramchowder-Bahawder) in the Privy Council, Lord Brougham complimented Mr. Gray, who was in the case, on his curious and exact knowledge of the Sanscrit language.

Whether he knows Sanscrit or not, I can't say; but Goldmore got him the business; and so I cannot help having a lurking regard for that pompous old Bigwig.

WILLIAM MAKEPEACE THACKERAY

THE PRINCESS'S TRAGEDY

I WAS walking with my Lady Lyndon in the Rotunda at Ranelagh It was in the year 1790; the emigration from France had already commenced, the old counts and marquises were thronging to our shores: not starving and miserable, as one saw them a few years afterwards, but unmolested as yet, and bringing with them some token of their national splendour. I was walking with Lady Lyndon, who, proverbially jealous and always anxious to annoy me, spied out a foreign lady who was evidently remarking me, and of course asked who was the hideous fat Dutch-woman who was leering at me so? I knew her not in the least. I felt I had seen the lady's face somewhere (it was now, as my wife said, enormously fat and bloated); but I did not recognise in the bearer of that face one who had been among the most beautiful women in Germany in her day.

It was no other than Madame de Liliengarten, the mistress, or, as some said, the morganatic wife, of the old Duke of X——, Duke Victor's father. She had left X—— a few months after the elder duke's demise, had gone to Paris, as I heard, where some unprincipled adventurer had married her for her money; but, however, had always retained her quasi-royal title, and pretended, amidst the great laughter of the Parisians who frequented her house, to the honours and ceremonial of a sovereign's widow. She had a throne erected in her state-room, and was styled by her servants and those who wished to pay court to her, or borrow money from her, "Altesse." Report said she drank rather copiously—certainly her face bore every mark of that habit, and had lost the rosy, frank, good-humoured beauty which had charmed the sovereign who had ennobled her.

Although she did not address me in the circle at Ranelagh, I was at this period as well known as the Prince of Wales, and she had no difficulty in finding my house in Berkeley Square; whither a note was next morning despatched to me. "An old friend of Monsieur de Balibari," it stated (in extremely bad French), "is anxious to see the Chevalier again and to talk over old happy times. Rosina de

Liliengarten (can it be that Redmond Balibari has forgotten her ?) will be at her house in Leicester Fields all the morning, looking for one who would never have passed her by *twenty years* ago."

Rosina of Liliengarten it was, indeed—such a full-blown Rosina I have seldom seen. I found her in a decent first-floor in Leicester Fields (the poor soul fell much lower afterwards) drinking tea, which had somehow a very strong smell of brandy in it ; and after salutations, which would be more tedious to recount than they were to perform, and after further straggling conversation, she gave me briefly the following narrative of the events in X——, which I may well entitle the " Princess's Tragedy."

" You remember Monsieur de Geldern, the Police Minister. He was of Dutch extraction, and, what is more, of a family of Dutch Jews. Although everybody was aware of this blot in his scutcheon, he was mortally angry if ever his origin was suspected ; and made up for his father's errors by outrageous professions of religion and the most austere practices of devotion. He visited church every morning, confessed once a week, and hated Jews and Protestants as much as an inquisitor could do. He never lost an opportunity of proving his sincerity, by persecuting one or the other whenever occasion fell in his way.

" He hated the princess mortally ; for her highness in some whim had insulted him with his origin, caused pork to be removed from before him at table, or injured him in some such silly way ; and he had a violent animosity to the old Baron de Magny, both in his capacity of Protestant, and because the latter in some haughty mood had publicly turned his back upon him as a sharper and a spy. Perpetual quarrels were taking place between them in council ; where it was only the presence of his august master that restrained the baron from publicly and frequently expressing the contempt which he felt for the officer of police.

" Thus Geldern had hatred as one reason for ruining the princess, and it is my belief he had a stronger motive still—interest. You remember whom the duke married, after the death of his first wife ? —a princess of the house of F——. Geldern built his fine palace two years after, and, as I feel convinced, with the money which was paid to him by the F—— family for forwarding the match.

" To go to Prince Victor and report to his highness a case which everybody knew, was not by any means Geldern's desire. He knew the man would be ruined for ever in the prince's estimation who carried him intelligence so disastrous. His aim, therefore, was to leave the matter to explain itself to his highness ; and, when the time was ripe, he cast about for a means of carrying his point. He had spies in the houses of the elder and younger Magny ; but this you know, of course, from your experience of Continental customs. We had spies over each other. Your black (Zamar, I think, was his name) used to give me reports every morning; and I used to entertain the dear old duke with stories of you and your uncle practising picquet and dice in the morning, and with your quarrels and intrigues. We levied similar contributions on everybody in X——, to amuse the dear old man. Monsieur de Magny's valet used to report both to me and Monsieur de Geldern.

"I knew of the fact of the emerald being in pawn; and it was out of my exchequer that the poor princess drew the funds which were spent upon the odious Löwe, and the still more worthless young chevalier. How the princess could trust the latter as she persisted in doing, is beyond my comprehension; but there is no infatuation like that of a woman in love: and you will remark, my dear Monsieur de Balibari, that our sex generally fix upon a bad man."

"Not always, madam," I interposed; "your humble servant has created many such attachments."

"I do not see that that affects the truth of the proposition," said the old lady drily, and continued her narrative. "The Jew who held the emerald had had many dealings with the princess, and at last was offered a bribe of such magnitude that he determined to give up the pledge. He committed the inconceivable imprudence of bringing the emerald with him to X——, and waited on Magny, who was provided by the princess with the money to redeem the pledge, and was actually ready to pay it.

"Their interview took place in Magny's own apartments, when his valet overheard every word of their conversation. The young man, who was always utterly careless of money when it was in his possession, was so easy in offering it, that Löwe rose in his demands, and had the conscience to ask double the sum for which he had previously stipulated.

"At this the chevalier lost all patience, fell on the wretch, and was for killing him; when the opportune valet rushed in and saved him. The man had heard every word of the conversation between the disputants, and the Jew ran flying with terror into his arms; and Magny, a quick and passionate, but not a violent man, bade the servant lead the villain downstairs, and thought no more of him.

"Perhaps he was not sorry to be rid of him, and to have in his possession a large sum of money, 4000 ducats, with which he could tempt fortune once more; as you know he did at your table that night."

"Your ladyship went halves, madam," said I; "and you know how little I was the better for my winnings."

"The man conducted the trembling Israelite out of the palace, and no sooner had seen him lodged at the house of one of his brethren, where he was accustomed to put up, than he went away to the office of his Excellency the Minister of Police, and narrated every word of the conversation which had taken place between the Jew and his master.

"Geldern expressed the greatest satisfaction at his spy's prudence and fidelity. He gave him a purse of twenty ducats, and promised to provide for him handsomely: as great men do sometimes promise to reward their instruments; but you, Monsieur de Balibari, know how seldom those promises are kept. 'Now, go and find out,' said Monsieur de Geldern, 'at what time the Israelite proposes to return home again, or whether he will repent and take the money.' The man went on this errand. Meanwhile, to make matters sure, Geldern arranged a play-party at my house, inviting you thither with your bank, as you may remember; and finding means, at the same time, to let Maxime de Magny know that there was to be faro at Madame de Liliengarten's. It was an invitation the poor fellow never neglected."

I remembered the facts and listened on, amazed at the artifice of the infernal Minister of Police.

"The spy came back from his message to Löwe, and stated that he had made inquiries among the servants of the house where the Heidelberg banker lodged, and that it was the latter's intention to leave X—— that afternoon. He travelled by himself, riding an old horse, exceedingly humbly attired, after the manner of his people.

"'Johann,' said the Minister, clapping the pleased spy upon the shoulder, 'I am more and more pleased with you. I have been thinking, since you left me, of your intelligence, and the faithful manner in which you have served me; and shall soon find an occasion to place you according to your merits. Which way does this Israelitish scoundrel take?'

"'He goes to R—— to-night.'

"'And must pass by the Kaiserwald. Are you a man of courage, Johann Kerner?'

"'Will your Excellency try me?' said the man, his eyes glittering: 'I served through the Seven Years' War, and was never known to fail there.'

"'Now, listen. The emerald must be taken from that Jew: in the very keeping it the scoundrel has committed high treason. To the man who brings me that emerald I swear I will give five hundred louis. You understand why it is necessary that it should be restored to her highness. I need say no more.'

"'You shall have it to-night, sir,' said the man. 'Of course your Excellency will hold me harmless in case of accident.'

"'Psha!' answered the Minister; 'I will pay you half the money beforehand; such is my confidence in you. Accident's impossible, if you take your measures properly. There are four leagues of wood; the Jew rides slowly. It will be night before he can reach, let us say, the old Powder-Mill in the wood. What's to prevent you from putting a rope across the road, and dealing with him there? Be back with me this evening at supper. If you meet any of the patrol, say "foxes are loose,"—that's the word for to-night. They will let you pass them without questions.'

"The man went off quite charmed with his commission; and when Magny was losing his money at our faro-table, his servant waylaid the Jew at the spot named the Powder-Mill, in the Kaiserwald. The Jew's horse stumbled over a rope which had been placed across the road; and, as the rider fell groaning to the ground, Johann Kerner rushed out on him, masked, and pistol in hand, and demanded his money. He had no wish to kill the Jew, I believe, unless his resistance should render extreme measures necessary.

"Nor did he commit any such murder; for, as the yelling Jew roared for mercy, and his assailant menaced him with a pistol, a squad of patrol came up, and laid hold of the robber and the wounded man.

"Kerner swore an oath. 'You have come too soon,' said he to the sergeant of the police. '*Foxes are loose.*' 'Some are caught,' said the sergeant, quite unconcerned; and bound the fellow's hands with the rope which he had stretched across the road to entrap the Jew. He was placed behind a policeman on a horse; Löwe was similarly accommodated, and the party thus came back into the town as the night fell.

"They were taken forthwith to the police quarter; and, as the chief happened to be there, they were examined by his Excellency in person. Both were rigorously searched; the Jew's papers and cases taken from him: the jewel was found in a private pocket. As for the spy, the Minister, looking at him angrily, said, 'Why, this is the servant of Chevalier de Magny, one of her highness's equerries!' and, without hearing a word in exculpation from the poor frightened wretch, ordered him into close confinement.

"Calling for his horse, he then rode to the prince's apartments at the palace, and asked for an instant audience. When admitted, he produced the emerald. 'This jewel,' said he, 'has been found on the person of a Heidelberg Jew, who has been here repeatedly of late, and has had many dealings with her highness's equerry, the Chevalier de Magny. This afternoon the chevalier's servant came from his master's lodgings, accompanied by the Hebrew; was heard to make inquiries as to the route the man intended to take on his way homewards; followed him, or preceded him rather, and was found in the act of rifling his victim by my police in the Kaiserwald. The man will confess nothing; but, on being searched, a large sum in gold was found on his person; and though it is with the utmost pain that I can bring myself to entertain such an opinion, and to implicate a gentleman of the character and name of Monsieur de Magny, I do submit that our duty is to have the chevalier examined relative to the affair. As Monsieur de Magny is in her highness's private service, and in her confidence, I have heard, I would not venture to apprehend him without your highness's permission.'

"The prince's Master of the Horse, a friend of the old Baron de Magny, who was present at the interview, no sooner heard the strange intelligence, than he hastened away to the old general with the dreadful news of his grandson's supposed crime. Perhaps his highness himself was not unwilling that his old friend and tutor in arms should have the chance of saving his family from disgrace; at all events, Monsieur de Hengst, the Master of the Horse, was permitted to go off to the baron undisturbed, and break to him the intelligence of the accusation pending over the unfortunate chevalier.

"It is possible that he expected some such dreadful catastrophe, for, after hearing Hengst's narrative (as the latter afterwards told me), he only said, 'Heaven's will be done!' for some time refused to stir a step in the matter, and then only by the solicitation of his friend was induced to write the letter which Maxime de Magny received at our play-table.

"Whilst he was there, squandering the princess's money, a police visit was paid to his apartments, and a hundred proofs, not of his own guilt with respect to the robbery, but of his guilty connection with the princess, were discovered there,—tokens of her giving, passionate letters from her, copies of his own correspondence to his young friends at Paris,—all of which the Police Minister perused, and carefully put together under seal for his highness, Prince Victor. I have no doubt he perused them, for, on delivering them to the hereditary prince, Gelder said that, *in obedience to his highness's orders*, he had collected the chevalier's papers; but he need not say that, on his honour, he (Geldern) himself had never examined the documents. His difference with Messieurs de Magny was known; he begged his highness to employ any other official person in the judgment of the accusation brought against the young chevalier.

"All these things were going on while the chevalier was at play. A run of luck—you had great luck in those days, Monsieur de Balibari—was against him. He stayed and lost his 4000 ducats. He received his uncle's note, and, such was the infatuation of the wretched gambler, that, on receipt of it, he went down to the courtyard, where the horse was in waiting, absolutely took the money which the poor old gentleman had placed in the saddle-holsters, brought it upstairs, played it, and lost it; and when he issued from the room to fly, it was too late: he was placed in arrest at the bottom of my staircase, as you were upon entering your own home.

"Even when he came in under the charge of the soldiery, sent to arrest him, the old general, who was waiting, was overjoyed to see him, and flung himself into the lad's arms, and embraced him: it was said, for the first time in many years. 'He is here, gentlemen,' he sobbed out,—'thank God he is not guilty of the robbery!' and then sank back in a chair in a burst of emotion; painful, it was said by those present, to witness on the part of a man so brave, and known to be so cold and stern.

"'Robbery!' said the young man, 'I swear before heaven I am guilty of none!' and a scene of most touching reconciliation passed between them, before the unhappy young man was led from the guard-house into the prison which he was destined never to quit.

"That night the duke looked over the papers which Geldern had brought to him. It was at a very early stage of the perusal, no doubt, that he gave orders for your arrest; for you were taken at midnight, Magny at ten o'clock; after which time the old Baron de Magny had seen his highness, protesting of his grandson's innocence, and the prince had received him most graciously and kindly. His highness said he had no doubt the young man was innocent; his birth and his blood rendered such a crime impossible; but suspicion was too strong against him; he was known to have been that day closeted with the Jew; to have received a very large sum of money which he squandered at play, and of which the Hebrew had doubtless been the lender,—to have despatched his servant after him, who inquired the hour of the Jew's departure, lay in wait for him, and rifled him. Suspicion was so strong against the chevalier, that common justice required his arrest; and, meanwhile, until he cleared himself, he should be kept in not dishonourable durance, and every regard had for his name, and the services of his honourable grandfather. With this assurance, and with a warm grasp of the hand, the prince left old General de Magny that night; and the veteran retired to rest, almost consoled and confident in Maxime's eventual and immediate release.

"But in the morning, before daybreak, the prince, who had been reading papers all night, wildly called to the page, who slept in the next room across the door, bade him get horses, which were always kept in readiness in the stables, and, flinging a parcel of letters into a box, told the page to follow him on horseback with these. The young man (Monsieur de Weissenborn) told this to a young lady who was then of my household, and who is now Madame de Weissenborn, and a mother of a score of children.

"The page described that never was such a change seen as in his august master in the course of that single night. His eyes were blood-shot, his face livid, his clothes were hanging loose about him, and he who had always made his appearance on parade as precisely dressed as any sergeant of his troops, might have been seen galloping through the lonely streets at early dawn without a hat, his unpowdered hair streaming behind him, like a madman.

"The page, with the box of papers, clattered after his master,—it was no easy task to follow him; and they rode from the palace to the town, and through it to the general's quarter. The sentinels at the door were scared by the strange figure that rushed up to the general's gate, and, not knowing him, crossed bayonets, and refused him admission. 'Fools,' said Weissenborn, 'it is the prince!' And, jangling at the bell, as if for an alarm of fire, the door was at length opened by the porter, and his highness ran up to the general's bed-chamber, followed by the page with the box.

"'Magny—Magny,' roared the prince, thundering at the closed door, 'get up!' And to the queries of the old man from within, answered, 'It is I—Victor—the prince!—get up!' And presently the door was opened by the general in his *robe-de-chambre*, and the prince entered. The page brought in the box, and was bidden to wait without, which he did; but there led from Monsieur de Magny's bedroom into his ante-chamber two doors, the great one which formed the entrance into his room, and a smaller one which led, as the fashion is with our houses abroad, into the closet which communicates with the alcove where the bed is. The door of this was found by M. de Weissenborn to be open, and the young man was thus enabled to hear and see everything which occurred within the apartment.

"The general, somewhat nervously, asked what was the reason of so early a visit from his highness; to which the prince did not for a while reply, further than by staring at him rather wildly, and pacing up and down the room.

"At last he said, 'Here is the cause!' dashing his fist on the box; and, as he had forgotten to bring the key with him, he went to the door for a moment, saying, 'Weissenborn perhaps has it'; but, seeing over the stove one of the general's *couteaux-de-chasse*, he took it down, and said, 'That will do,' and fell to work to burst the red trunk open with the blade of the forest-knife. The point broke, and he gave an oath, but continued haggling on with the broken blade, which was better suited to his purpose than the long, pointed knife, and finally succeeded in wrenching open the lid of the chest.

"'What is the matter?' said he, laughing. 'Here's the matter:—read that!—here's more matter, read that!—here's more—no, not that; that's somebody else's picture—but here's hers! Do you know that, Magny? My wife's—the princess's!' Why did you and your cursed race ever come out of France, to plant your infernal wickedness wherever your feet fell, and to ruin honest German homes ? What have you and yours ever had from my family but confidence and kindness ? We gave you a home when you had none, and here's our reward ! ' and he flung a parcel of papers down before the old general ; who saw the truth at once :—he had known it long before, probably, and sunk down on his chair, covering his face.

" The prince went on gesticulating, and shrieking almost. ' If a man injured you so, Magny, before you begot the father of that gambling, lying villain yonder, you would have known how to revenge yourself. You would have killed him ! Yes, would have killed him. But who's to help me to my revenge ? I've no equal. I can't meet that dog of a Frenchman,—that pimp from Versailles,—and kill him, as if he had played the traitor to one of his own degree.'

" ' The blood of Maxime de Magny,' said the old gentleman, proudly, ' is as good as that of any prince in Christendom.'

" ' Can I take it ? ' cried the prince : ' you know I can't. I can't have the privilege of any other gentleman of Europe. What am I to do ? Look here, Magny : I was wild when I came here : I didn't know what to do. You've served me for thirty years ; you've saved my life twice : they are all knaves and harlots about my poor old father here—no honest men or women—you are the only one—you saved my life : tell me what am I to do ? ' Thus, from insulting Monsieur de Magny, the poor distracted prince fell to supplicating him ; and, at last, fairly flung himself down, and burst out in an agony of tears.

" Old Magny, one of the most rigid and cold of men on common occasions, when he saw this outbreak of passion on the prince's part, became, as my informant has described to me, as much affected as his master. The old man, from being cold and high, suddenly fell, as it were, into a whimpering querulousness of extreme old age. He lost all sense of dignity : he went down on his knees, and broke out into all sorts of wild, incoherent attempts at consolation ; so much so, that Weissenborn said he could not bear to look at the scene, and actually turned away from the contemplation of it.

" But, from what followed in a few days, we may guess the results of the long interview. The prince, when he came away from the conversation with his old servant, forgot his fatal box of papers and sent the page back for them. The general was on his knees praying in the room when the young man entered, and only stirred and looked round wildly as the other removed the packet. The prince rode away to his hunting-lodge at three leagues from X——, and three days after that Maxime de Magny died in prison ; having made a confession that he was engaged in an attempt to rob the

Jew, and that he had made away with himself, ashamed of his dishonour.

"But it is not known that it was the general himself who took his grandson poison; it was said even that he shot him in the prison. This, however, was not the case. General de Magny carried his grandson the draught which was to carry him out of the world; represented to the wretched youth that his fate was inevitable; that it would be public and disgraceful unless he chose to anticipate the punishment, and so left him. But *it was not of his own accord*, and not until he had used *every* means of escape, as you shall hear, that the unfortunate being's life was brought to an end.

"As for General de Magny, he quite fell into imbecility a short time after his grandson's death, and my honoured duke's demise. After his highness the prince married the Princess Mary of F——, as they were walking in the English park together they once met old Magny riding in the sun on the easy-chair, in which he was carried commonly abroad after his paralytic fits. 'This is my wife, Magny,' said the prince, affectionately, taking the veteran's hand; and he added, turning to his princess, 'General de Magny saved my life during the Seven Years' War.'

"'What, you've taken her back again?' said the old man. 'I wish you'd send me back my poor Maxime.' He had quite forgotten the death of the poor Princess Olivia, and the prince, looking very dark indeed, passed away.

"And now," said Madame de Liliengarten, "I have only one more gloomy story to relate to you—the death of the Princess Olivia. It is even more horrible than the tale I have just told you." With which preface the old lady resumed her narrative.

"The kind, weak princess's fate was hastened, if not occasioned, by the cowardice of Magny. He found means to communicate with her from his prison, and her highness, who was not in open disgrace yet (for the duke, out of regard to the family, persisted in charging Magny with only robbery), made the most desperate efforts to relieve him, and to bribe the gaolers to effect his escape. She was so wild that she lost all patience and prudence in the conduct of any schemes she may have had for Magny's liberation; for her husband was inexorable, and caused the chevalier's prison to be too strictly guarded for escape to be possible. She offered the state jewels in pawn to the court banker; who of course was obliged to decline the transaction. She fell down on her knees, it is said, to Geldern, the Police Minister, and offered him heaven knows what as a bribe. Finally, she came screaming to my poor dear duke, who, with his age, diseases, and easy habits, was quite unfit for scenes of so violent a nature; and who, in consequence of the excitement created in his august bosom by her frantic violence and grief, had a fit in which I very nigh lost him. That his dear life was brought to an untimely end by these transactions I have not the slightest doubt ; for the Strasbourg pie, of which they said he died, never, I am sure, could have injured him, but for the injury which his dear gentle heart received from the unusual occurrences in which he was forced to take a share.

" All her highness's movements were carefully, though not ostensibly, watched by her husband, Prince Victor ; who, waiting upon his august father, sternly signified to him that if his highness (*my* duke) should dare to aid the princess in her efforts to release Magny, he, Prince Victor, would publicly accuse the princess and her paramour of high treason, and take measures with the Diet for removing his father from the throne, as incapacitated to reign. Hence, interposition on our part was vain, and Magny was left to his fate.

" It came, as you are aware, very suddenly. Geldern, Police Minister, Hengst, Master of the Horse, and the colonel of the prince's guard, waited upon the young man in his prison two days after his grandfather had visited him there and left behind him the phial of poison which the criminal had not the courage to use. And Geldern signified to the young man that unless he took of his own accord the laurel-water provided by the elder Magny, more violent means of death would be instantly employed upon him, and that a file of grenadiers was in waiting in the courtyard to despatch him. Seeing this, Magny, with the most dreadful self-abasement, after dragging himself round the room on his knees, from one officer to another, weeping and screaming with terror, at last desperately drank off the potion, and was a corpse in a few minutes. Thus ended this wretched young man.

" His death was made public in the *Court Gazette* two days after, the paragraph stating that Monsieur de M——, struck with remorse for having attempted the murder of the Jew, had put himself to death by poison in prison ; and a warning was added to all young noblemen of the duchy to avoid the dreadful sin of gambling, which had been the cause of the young man's ruin, and had brought upon the grey hairs of one of the noblest and most honourable of the servants of the duke irretrievable sorrow.

" The funeral was conducted with decent privacy, the General de Magny attending it. The carriage of the two dukes and all the first people of the court made their calls upon the general afterwards. He attended parade as usual the next day on the Arsenal Place, and Duke Victor, who had been inspecting the building, came out of it leaning on the brave old warrior's arm. He was particularly gracious to the old man, and told his officers the oft-repeated story how at Rosbach, when the X—— contingent served with the troops of the unlucky Soubise, the general had thrown himself in the way of a French dragoon who was pressing hard upon his highness in the rout, had received the blow intended for his master, and killed the assailant. And he alluded to the family motto of 'Magny sans tache,' and said, 'It had always been so with his gallant friend and tutor in arms.' This speech affected all present very much, with the exception of the old general, who only bowed and did not speak; but when he went home he was heard muttering, 'Magny sans tache, Magny sans tache!' and was attacked with paralysis that night, from which he never more than partially recovered.

"The news of Maxime's death had somehow been kept from the princess until now: a *Gazette* even being printed without the paragraph containing the account of his suicide; but it was at length, I know not how, made known to her. And when she heard it, her ladies tell me, she screamed and fell, as if struck dead; then sat up wildly and raved like a madwoman, and was then carried to her bed, where her physician attended her, and where she lay of a brain-fever. All this while the prince used to send to make inquiries concerning her; and from his giving orders that his castle of Schlangenfels should be prepared and furnished, I make no doubt it was his intention to send her into confinement thither; as had been done with the unhappy sister of his Britannic Majesty at Zell.

"She sent repeatedly to demand an interview with his highness; which the latter declined, saying that he would communicate with her highness when her health was sufficiently recovered. To one of her passionate letters he sent back for reply a packet, which, when opened, was found to contain the emerald that had been the cause round which all this dark intrigue moved.

"Her highness at this time became quite frantic; vowed in the presence of all her ladies that one lock of her darling Maxime's hair was more precious to her than all the jewels in the world; rang for her carriage, and said she would go and kiss his tomb; proclaimed the murdered martyr's innocence, and called down the punishment of heaven, the wrath of her family, upon his assassin. The prince, on hearing these speeches (they were all, of course, regularly brought to him), is said to have given one of his dreadful looks (which I remember now), and to have said, 'This cannot last much longer.'

"All that day and the next the Princess Olivia passed in dictating the most passionate letters to the prince her father, to the Kings of France, Naples, and Spain, her kinsmen, and to all other branches of her family, calling upon them in the most incoherent terms to protect her against the butcher and assassin her husband, assailing his person in the maddest terms of reproach, and at the same time confessing her love for the murdered Magny. It was in vain that those ladies who were faithful to her pointed out to her the inutility of these letters, the dangerous folly of the confessions which they made; she insisted upon writing them, and used to give them to her second robe-woman, a Frenchwoman (her highness always affectioned persons of that nation), who had the key of her cassette, and carried every one of these epistles to Geldern.

"With the exception that no public receptions were held, the ceremony of the princess's establishment went on as before. Her ladies were allowed to wait upon her and perform their usual duties about her person. The only men admitted were, however, her servants, her physician and chaplain; and one day when she wished to go into the garden, a heyduc, who kept the door, intimated to her highness that the prince's orders were that she should keep her apartments.

"They abut, as you remember, upon the landing of the marble staircase of Schloss X——; the entrance to Prince Victor's suite of rooms being opposite the princess's on the same landing. This space is large, filled with sofas and benches, and the gentlemen and officers who waited upon the duke used to make a sort of antechamber of the landing-place, and pay their court to his highness there, as he passed out, at eleven o'clock to parade. At such a time, the heyducs within the princess's suite of rooms used to turn out with their halberts and present to Prince Victor—the same ceremony being performed on his own side, when pages came out and announced the approach of his highness. The pages used to come out and say, 'The prince, gentlemen!' and the drums beat in the hall, and the gentlemen rose, who were waiting on the benches that ran along the balustrade.

As if fate impelled her to her death, one day the princess, as her guards turned out, and she was aware that the prince was standing as was his wont, on the landing, conversing with his gentlemen (in the old days he used to cross to the princess's apartment and kiss her hand)—the princess, who had been anxious all the morning, complaining of heat, insisting that all the doors of the apartments should be left open; and giving tokens of an insanity which I think was now evident, rushed wildly at the doors when the guards passed out, flung them open, and before a word could be said, or her ladies could follow her, was in presence of Duke Victor, who was talking as usual on the landing: placing herself between him and the stair, she began apostrophizing him with frantic vehemence:

"'Take notice, gentlemen!' she screamed out, 'that this man is a murderer and a liar; that he lays plots for honourable gentlemen, and kills them in prison! Take notice, that I too am in prison, and fear the same fate: the same butcher who killed Maxime de Magny may, any night, put the knife to my throat. I appeal to you, and to all the kings of Europe, my royal kinsmen. I demand to be set free from this tyrant and villain, this liar and traitor! I adjure you all, as gentlemen of honour, to carry these letters to my relatives, and say from whom you had them!' and with this the unhappy lady began scattering letters about among the astonished crowd.

"'*Let no man stoop!*' cried the prince, in a voice of thunder. 'Madame de Gleim, you should have watched your patient better. Call the princess's physicians: her highness's brain is affected. Gentlemen, have the goodness to retire.' And the prince stood on the landing as the gentlemen went down the stairs, saying fiercely to the guard, 'Soldier, if she moves, strike with your halbert!' on which the man brought the point of his weapon to the princess's breast; and the lady, frightened, shrank back and re-entered her apartments. 'Now, Monsieur de Weissenborn,' said the prince, 'pick up all those papers': and the prince went into his own apartments, preceded by his pages, and never quitted them until he had seen every one of the papers burnt.

"The next day the *Court Gazette* contained a bulletin signed by the three physicians, stating that 'her highness the Hereditary Princess laboured under inflammation of the brain, and had passed a restless and disturbed night.' Similar notices were issued day after day. The services of all her ladies, except two, were dispensed with. Guards were placed within and without her doors; her windows were secured, so that escape from them was impossible: and you know what took place ten days after. The church-bells were ringing all night, and the prayers of the faithful asked for a person *in extremis*. A *Gazette* appeared in the morning, edged with black, and stating that the high and mighty Princess Olivia Maria Ferdinanda, consort of his Serene Highness Victor Louis Emanuel, Hereditary Prince of X——, had died in the evening of the 24th of January 1769.

"But do you know *how* she died, sir? That, too, is a mystery. Weissenborn, the page, was concerned in this dark tragedy; and the secret was so dreadful, that never, believe me, till Prince Victor's death did I reveal it.

"After the fatal *esclandre* which the princess had made, the prince sent for Weissenborn, and binding him by the most solemn adjuration to secrecy (he only broke it to his wife many years after: indeed, there is no secret in the world that women cannot know if they will), despatched him on the following mysterious commission.

"'There lives,' said his highness, 'on the Kehl side of the river, opposite to Strasbourg, a man whose residence you will easily find out from his name, which is *Monsieur de Strasbourg*. You will make your inquiries concerning him quietly, and without occasioning any remark; perhaps you had better go into Strasbourg for the purpose, where the person is quite well known. You will take with you any comrade on whom you can perfectly rely: the lives of both, remember, depend on your secrecy. You will find out some period when Monsieur de Strasbourg is alone, or only in company of the domestic who lives with him: (I myself visited the man by accident on my return from Paris five years since, and hence am induced to send for him now, in my present emergency). You will have your carriage waiting at his door at night; and you and your comrade will enter his house masked; and present him with a purse of a hundred louis; promising him double that sum on his return from his expedition. If he refuse, you must use force and bring him; menacing him with instant death should he decline to follow you. You will place him in the carriage with the blinds drawn, one or other of you never losing sight of him the whole way, and threatening him with death if he discover himself or cry out. You will lodge him in the Old Tower here, where a room shall be prepared for him; and his work being done, you will restore him to his home in the same speed and secrecy with which you brought him from it.'

" Such were the mysterious orders Prince Victor gave his page; and Weissenborn, selecting for his comrade in the expedition Lieutenant Bartenstein, set out on his strange journey.

" All this while the palace was hushed, as if in mourning; the bulletins in the *Court Gazette* appeared, announcing the continuance of the princess's malady; and though she had but few attendants, strange and circumstantial stories were told regarding the progress of her complaint. She was quite wild. She had tried to kill herself. She had fancied herself to be I don't know how many different characters. Expresses were sent to her family informing them of her state, and couriers despatched *publicly* to Vienna and Paris to procure the attendance of physicians skilled in treating diseases of the brain. That pretended anxiety was all a feint: it was never intended that the princess should recover.

" The day on which Weissenborn and Bartenstein returned from their expedition, it was announced that her highness the princess was much worse; that night the report through the town was that she was at the agony: and that night the unfortunate creature was endeavouring to make her escape.

" She had unlimited confidence in the French chamber-woman who attended her, and between her and this woman the plan of escape was arranged. The princess took her jewels in a casket; a private door, opening from one of her rooms and leading into the outer gate, it was said, of the palace, was discovered for her; and a letter was brought to her, purporting to be from the duke her father-in-law, and stating that a carriage and horses had been provided, and would take her to B——: the territory where she might communicate with her family and be safe.

" The unhappy lady, confiding in her guardian, set out on the expedition. The passages wound through the walls of the modern part of the palace and abutted in effect at the old Owl Tower, as it was called, on the outer wall: the tower was pulled down afterwards, and for good reason.

" At a certain place the candle, which the chamber-woman was carrying, went out; and the princess would have screamed with terror, but her hand was seized, and a voice cried, 'Hush!' The next minute a man in a mask (it was the duke himself) rushed forward, gagged her with a handkerchief, her hands and legs were bound, and she was carried swooning with terror into a vaulted room, where she was placed by a person there waiting, and tied in an arm-chair. The same mask who had gagged her, came and bared her neck and said, 'It had best be done now she has fainted.'

" Perhaps it would have been as well; for though she recovered from her swoon, and her confessor, who was present, came forward and endeavoured to prepare her for the awful deed which was about to be done upon her, and for the state into which she was about to enter, when she came to herself it was only to scream like a maniac, to curse the duke as a butcher and tyrant, and to call upon Magny, her dear Magny.

" At this the duke said, quite calmly, 'May God have mercy on her sinful soul!' He, the confessor, and Geldern, who were present, went down on their knees; and, as his highness dropped his handkerchief, Weissenborn fell down in a fainting fit; while *Monsieur de Strasbourg*, taking the back hair in his hand, separated the shrieking head of Olivia from her miserable, sinful body. May heaven have mercy upon her soul!"

. . . .

This was the story told by Madame de Liliengarten, and the reader will have no difficulty in drawing from it that part which affected myself and my uncle; who, after six weeks of arrest, were set at liberty, but with orders to quit the duchy immediately: indeed, with an escort of dragoons to conduct us to the frontier. What property we had we were allowed to sell and realise in money; but none of our play debts were paid to us; and all my hopes of the Countess Ida were thus at an end.

When Duke Victor came to the throne, which he did when, six months after, apolexy carried off the old sovereign his father, all the good old usages of X—— were given up,—play forbidden; the opera and ballet sent to the right-about; and the regiments which the old duke had sold recalled from their foreign service: with them came my countess's beggarly cousin the ensign, and he married her. I don't know whether they were happy or not. It is certain that a woman of such a poor spirit did not merit any very high degree of pleasure.

The now reigning Duke of X—— himself married four years after his first wife's demise, and Geldern, though no longer Police Minister, built the grand house of which Madame de Liliengarten spoke. What became of the minor actors in the great tragedy, who knows? Only Monsieur de Strasbourg was restored to his duties. Of the rest,—the Jew, the chamber-woman, the spy on Magny, I know nothing. Those sharp tools with which great people cut out their enterprises are generally broken in the using: nor did I ever hear that their employers had much regard for them in their ruin.

WILLIAM MAKEPEACE THACKERAY

"DIMOND CUT DIMOND"

From the Memoirs of Chawles Jeames Yellowplush

THE name of my nex master was, if posbil, still more elygant and youfonious than that of my fust. I now found myself boddy servant to the Honrabble Halgernon Percy Deuceace, youngest and fifth son of the Earl of Crabs.

Halgernon was a barrystir—that is, he lived in Pump Cort, Temple; a wulgar naybrood, witch praps my readers don't no. Suffiz it to say, it's on the confines of the citty, and the chosen aboad of the lawyers of this metrappolish.

When I say that Mr. Deuceace was a barrystir, I don't mean that he went sesshums or surcoats (as they call 'em), but simply that he kep chambers, lived in Pump Cort, and looked out for a commitionarship, or a revisinship, or any other place that the Wig guvvyment could give him. His father was a Wig pier (as the landriss told me), and had been a Toary pier. The fack is, his lordship was so poar that he would be anythink or nothink, to get provisions for his sons and an inkum for himself.

I phansy that he aloud Halgernon two hundred a year; and it would have been a very comforable maintenants, only he knever paid him.

Owever, the young genlmn was a genlmn, and no mistake; he got his allowents of nothink a year, and spent it in the most honrabble and fashnabble manner. He kept a kab—he went to Holmax—and Crockfud's—he moved in the most xquizzit suckles, and trubbld the law boox very little, I can tell you. Those fashnabble gents have ways of getten money witch comman pipple doant understand.

Though he only had a therd floar in Pump Cort, he lived as if he had the welth of Cresas. The tenpun notes floo abowt as common as haypince—clarrit and shampang was at his house as vulgar as gin; and verry glad I was, to be sure, to be a valley to a zion of the nobillaty.

Deuceace had, in his sittin-room, a large pictur on a sheet of paper. The names of his family was wrote on it ; it was wrote in the shape of a tree, a-groin out of a man-in-armer's stomick, and the names were on little plates among the bows. The pictur said that the Deuceaces kem into England in the year 1066, along with William Conqueruns. My master called it his podygree. I do bleev it was because he had this pictur, and because he was the *Honrabble* Deuceace, that he mannitched to live as he did. If he had been a common man, you'd have said he was no better than a swinler. It's only rank and buth that can warrant such singularities as my master show'd. For it's no use disgysing it—the Honrabble Halgernon was a GAMBLER. For a man of wulgar family, it's the wust trade that can be ; for a man of common feelinx of honesty, this profession is quite imposbil ; but for a real thoroughbread genlmn, it's the esiest and most prophetable line he can take.

It may praps appear curious that such a fashnable man should live in the Temple ; but it must be recklected that it's not only lawyers who live in what's called the Ins of Cort. Many batchylers, who have nothink to do with lor, have here there loginx ; and many sham barrysters, who never put on a wig and gownd twise in their lives, kip apartments in the Temple, instead of Bon Street, Pickledilly, or other fashnabble places.

Frinstance, on our stairkis (so these houses are called) there was 8 sets of chamberses, and only 3 lawyers. These was bottom floar, Screwson, Hewson, and Jewson, attorneys ; fust floar, Mr. Sergeant Flabber—opsite, Mr. Counslor Bruffy ; and secknd pair, Mr. Haggerstony, an Irish counslor, praktising at the Old Baly, and lickwise what they call reporter to the *Morning Post* nyouspapper. Opsite him was wrote—

MR. RICHARD BLEWITT ;

and on the thud floar, with my master, lived one Mr. Dawkins.

This young fellow was a new comer into the Temple, and unlucky it was for him too—he'd better have never been born ; for it's my firm apinion that the Temple ruined him—that is, with the help of my master and Mr. Dick Blewitt, as you shall hear.

Mr. Dawkins, as I was gave to understand by his young man, had jest left the Universary of Oxford, and had a pretty little fortn of his own—six thousand pound or so—in the stox. He was jest of age, an orfin who had lost his father and mother ; and having distinkwished hisself at Collitch, where he gained seffral prices, was come to town to push his fortn, and study the barryster's bisness.

Not bein of a very high fammly hisself—indeed, I've heard say his father was a chismonger, or something of that lo sort—Dawkins was glad to find his old Oxford friend, Mr. Blewitt, younger son to rich Squire Blewitt, of Listershire, and to take rooms so near him.

Now, tho' there was a considdrable intimacy between me and Mr. Blewitt's gentleman, there was scarcely any betwixt our masters—mine being too much of the aristoxy to associate with one of Mr. Blewitt's sort. Blewitt was what they call a bettin man; he went reglar to Tattlesall's, kep a pony, wore a white hat, a blue berd's-eye handkercher, and a cut-away coat. In his manners he was the very contrary of my master, who was a slim, ellygant man as ever I see; he had very white hands, rayther a sallow face, with sharp dark ise, and small wiskus neatly trimmed and as black as Warren's jet; he spoke very low and soft; he seemed to be watchin the person with whom he was in convysation, and always flatterd everybody. As for Blewitt, he was quite of another sort. He was always swearin, singing, and slappin people on the back, as hearty as posbill. He seemed a merry, careless, honest cretur, whom one would trust with life and soul. So thought Dawkins, at least; who, though a quiet young man, fond of his boox, novvles, Byron's poems, floot-playing, and such-like scientafic amusemints, grew hand in glove with honest Dick Blewitt, and soon after with my master, the Honrabble Halgernon. Poor Daw! he thought he was making good connexions and real friends: he had fallen in with a couple of the most etrocious swinlers that ever lived.

Before Mr. Dawkins's arrivial in our house, Mr. Deuceace had barely condysended to speak to Mr. Blewitt; it was only about a month after that suckumstance that my master, all of a sudding, grew very friendly with him. The reason was pretty clear—Deuceace *wanted him*. Dawkins had not been an hour in master's company before he knew that he had a pidgin to pluck.

Blewitt knew this too, and bein very fond of pidgin, intended to keep this one entirely to himself. It was amusing to see the Honrabble Halgernon manuvring to get this pore bird out of Blewitt's clause, who thought he had it safe. In fact, he'd brought Dawkins to these chambers for that very porpus, thinking to have him under his eye, and strip him at leisure.

My master very soon found out what was Mr. Blewitt's game. Gamblers know gamblers, if not by instink, at least by reputation; and though Mr. Blewitt moved in a much lower spear than Mr. Deuceace, they knew each other's dealins and caracters puffickly well.

"Charles, you scoundrel," said Deuceace to me one day (he always spoak in that kind way), "who is this person that has taken the opsit chambers, and plays the flute so industrusly?"

"It's Mr. Dawkins, a rich young gentleman from Oxford, and a great friend of Mr. Blewittses, sir," says I; "they seem to live in each other's rooms."

Master said nothink, but he *grin'd*—my eye, how he did grin! Not the fowl find himself could snear more satannickly.

I knew what he meant :—

Imprimish. A man who plays the floot is a simpleton.

Secknly. Mr. Blewitt is a raskle.

Thirdmo. When a raskle and a simpleton is always together, and when the simpleton is *rich*, one knows pretty well what will come of it.

I was but a lad in them days, but I knew what was what, as well as my master ; it's not gentlemen only that's up to snough. Law bless us ! there was four of us on this stairkes, four as nice young men as you ever see—Mr. Bruffy's young man, Mr. Dawkinses, Mr. Blewitt's, and me ; and we knew what our masters was about as well as they did theirselfs. Frinstance, I can say this for *myself*, there wasn't a paper in Deuceace's desk or drawer, not a bill, a note, or mimerandum, which I hadn't read as well as he : with Blewitt's it was the same—me and his young man used to read 'em all. There wasn't a bottle of wine that we didn't get a glass out of, nor a pound of sugar that we didn't have some lumps of it. We had keys to all the cubbards ; we pipped into all the letters that kem and went ; we pored over all the bill-files ; we'd the best pickens out of the dinners, the livvers of the fowls, the force-mit balls out of the soup, the eggs from the sallit. As for the coals and candles, we left them to the landrisses. You may call this robry. Nonsince ! it's only our rights ; a suvvant's purquizzits is as sacred as the laws of Hengland.

Well, the long and short of it is this. Richard Blewitt, esquire, was sityouated as follows :—He'd an incum of three hunderd a year from his father. Out of this he had to pay one hunderd and, ninety for money borrowed by him at collidge, seventy for chambers, seventy more for his hoss, aty for his suvvant on bord wagis, and about three hunderd and fifty for a sepparat establishmint in the Regency Park ; besides this, his pockit-money, say a hunderd, his eatin, drinkin, and wine-marchant's bill, about two hunderd moar. So that you see he laid by a pretty handsome sum at the end of the year.

My master was diffrent ; and being a more fashnabble man than Mr. B., in course he owed a deal more money. There was fust :—

Account *contray*, at Crockford's	£3,711	0	0
Bills of xchange and I. O. U.'s (but he didn't pay these in most cases)	4,963	0	0
21 tailors' bills, in all	1,306	11	9
3 hossdealers' do.	402	0	0
2 coachbilder	506	0	0
Bills contracted at Cambritch	2,193	6	8
Sundries	987	10	0
	£14,069	8	5

I give this as a curosity—pipple doant know how in many cases fashnabble life is carried on; and to know even what a real gnlmn *owes* is somethink instructif and agreeable.

But to my tail. The very day after my master had made the inquiries concerning Mr. Dawkins, witch I mentioned already, he met Mr. Blewitt on the stairs; and byoutiffle it was to see how this gnlmn, who had before been almost cut by my master, was now received by him. One of the sweatest smiles I ever saw was now vizzable on Mr. Deuceace's countenance. He held out his hand, covered with a white kid glove, and said in the most frenly tone of vice posbill, "What! Mr. Blewitt? It is an age since we met. What a shame that such near naybors should see each other so seldom!"

Mr. Blewitt, who was standing at his door, in a pe-green dressing-gown, smoakin a segar, and singin a hunting coarus, looked surprised, flattered, and then suspicious.

"Why, yes," says he, "it is, Mr. Deuceace, a long time."

"Not, I think, since we dined at Sir George Hookey's. By the-bye, what an evening that was—hay, Mr. Blewitt? What wine! what capital songs! I recollect your 'Mayday in the morning'—cuss me, the best comick song I ever heard. I was speaking to the Duke of Doncaster about it only yesterday. You know the duke, I think?"

Mr. Blewitt said, quite surly, "No, I don't."

"Not know him!" cries master; "why, hang it, Blewitt, he knows *you*; as every sporting man in England does, I should think. Why, man, your good things are in everybody's mouth at Newmarket."

And so master went on chaffin Mr. Blewitt. That gnlmn at fust answered him quite short and angry; but, after a little more flummery, he grew as pleased as posbill, took in all Deuceace's flatry and bleeved all his lies. At last the door shut, and they both went into Mr. Blewitt's chambers together.

Of course I can't say what past there; but in an hour master kem up to his own room as yaller as mustard, and smellin sadly of backo-smoke. I never see any genlmn more sick than he was; *he'd been smoakin seagars* along with Blewitt. I said nothink, in course, tho I'd often heard him xpress his horrow of backo, and knew very well he would as soon swallow pizon as smoke. But he wasn't a chap to do a thing without a reason: if he'd been smoakin, I warrant he had smoaked to some porpus.

I didn't hear the convysation between 'em; but Mr. Blewitt's man did: it was—"Well, Mr. Blewitt, what capital seagars! Have you one for a friend to smoak?" (The old fox, it wasn't only the *seagars* he was a-smoakin!) "Walk in," says Mr. Blewitt; and they began a chaffin together—master very ankshous about the young gintleman who had come to live in our chambers, Mr. Dawkins, and always coming back to that subject, saying that people on the same stairkis ot to be frenly; how glad he'd be, for his part, to know Mr. Dick Blewitt, and *any friend of his*, and so on. Mr. Dick, howsever, seamed quite aware of the trap laid for him. "I really don't no this Dawkins," says he: "he's a chismonger's son, I hear; and tho I've exchanged visits with him, I doant intend to continyou the acquaintance, not wishin to assoshate with that kind of pipple." So they went on, master fishin, and Mr. Blewitt not wishin to take the hook at no price.

"Confound the vulgar thief!" muttard my master, as he was laying on his sophy, after being so very ill; "I've poisoned myself with his infernal tobacco, and he has foiled me. The cursed swindling boor! he thinks he'll ruin this poor cheesemonger, does he? I'll step in, and *warn* him."

I thought I should bust a-laffin when he talked in this style. I knew very well what his "warning" meant—lockin the stable-door, but stealin the hoss fust.

Next day, his strattygam for becoming acquainted with Mr. Dawkins we exicuted; and very pritty it was.

Besides potry and the floote, Mr. Dawkins, I must tell you, had some other parshallities—wiz., he was very fond of good eatin and drinkin. After doddling over his music and boox all day, this young genlmn used to sally out of evenings, dine sumptiously at a tavern, drinkin all sots of wine along with his friend Mr. Blewitt. He was a quiet young fellow enough at fust; but it was Mr. B. who (for his own porpuses, no doubt) had got him into this kind of life. Well, I needn't say that he who eats a fine dinner, and drinks too much overnight, wants a bottle of soda-water, and a gril, praps, in the morning. Such was Mr. Dawkinses case; and reglar almost as twelve o'clock came, the waiter from "Dix Coffy-House" was to be seen on our stairkis, bringing up Mr. D.'s hot breakfast.

No man would have thought there was anything in such a trifling cirkumstance; master did, though, and pounced upon it like a cock on a barlycorn.

He sent me out to Mr. Morell's in Pickledilly, for wot's called a Strasbug-pie—in French, a "*patty defau graw.*" He takes a card, and nails it on the outside case (patty defaw graws come generally in a round wooden box, like a drumb); and what do you think he writes on it? why, as follos:—"*For the Honourable Algernon Percy Deauceace, &c., &c., &c. With Prince Talleyrand's compliments.*"

Prince Tallyram's complimints, indeed! I laff when I think of it, still, the old surpint! He *was* a surpint, that Deuceace, and no mistake.

Well, by a most extrornary piece of ill-luck, the nex day punctially as Mr. Dawkinses brexfas was coming *up* the stairs, Mr.

Halgernon Percy Deuceace was going *down*. He was as gay as a lark, humming an Oppra tune, and twizzting round his head his hevy gold-headed cane. Down he went very fast, and by a most unlucky axdent struck his cane against the waiter's tray, and away went Mr. Dawkinses gril, kayann, kitchup, soda-water and all! I can't think how my master should have choas such an exact time; to be sure, his windo looked upon the cort, and he could see every one who came into our door.

As soon as the axdent had took place, master was in such a rage as, to be sure, no man ever was in before: he swore at the waiter in the most dreddfle way; he threatened him with his stick, and it was only when he see that the waiter was raythera bigger man than hisself that he was in the least pazzyfied. He returned to his own chambres; and John, the waiter, went off for more gril to Dixes Coffy-House.

"This is a most unlucky axdent, to be sure, Charles," says master to me, after a few minits paws, during witch he had been and wrote a note, put it into an anvelope, and sealed it with his bigg seal of arms. "But stay—a thought strikes me—take this note to Mr. Dawkins, and that pye you brought yesterday; and hearkye, you scoundrel, if you say where you got it I will break every bone in your skin!"

These kind of prommises were among the few which I knew him to keep; and as I loved boath my skinn and my boans, I carried the noat, and of cors said nothink. Waiting in Mr. Dawkinses chambus for a few minnits, I returned to my master with an anser. I may as well give both of these documence, of which I happen to have taken coppies.

I

THE HON. A. P. DEUCEACE TO T. S. DAWKINS, ESQ.

TEMPLE, *Tuesday*.

"Mr. DEUCEACE presents his compliments to Mr. Dawkins, and begs at the same time to offer his most sincere apologies and regrets for the accident which has just taken place.

"May Mr. Deuceace be allowed to take a neighbour's privilege, and to remedy the evil he has occasioned to the best of his power? If Mr. Dawkins will do him the favour to partake of the contents of the accompanying case (from Strasburg direct, and the gift of a friend, on whose taste as a gourmand Mr. Dawkins may rely), perhaps he will find that it is not a bad substitute for the *plat* which Mr. Deuceace's awkwardness destroyed.

"It will also, Mr. Deuceace is sure, be no small gratification to the original donor of the *pâté*, when he learns that it has fallen into the hands of so celebrated a *bon vivant* as Mr. Dawkins.

"T. S. Dawkins, Esq., etc., etc., etc."

II

FROM T. S. DAWKINS, ESQ., TO THE HON. A. P. DEUCEACE.

" Mr. Thomas Smith Dawkins presents his grateful compliments to the Hon. Mr. Deuceace, and accepts with the greatest pleasure Mr. Deuceace's generous proffer.

" It would be one of the *happiest moments* of Mr. Smith Dawkins's life if the Hon. Mr. Deuceace would *extend his generosity* still further, and condescend to partake of the repast which his *munificent politeness* has furnished.

" Temple, *Tuesday*."

Many and many a time, I say, have I grin'd over these letters, which I had wrote from the original by Mr. Bruffy's copyin clark. Deuceace's flam about Prince Tallyram was puffickly successful. I saw young Dawkins blush with delite as he red the note ; he toar up for or five sheets before he composed the answer to it, which was as you red abuff, and roat in a hand quite trembling with pleasyer. If you could but have seen the look of triumph in Deuceace's wicked black eyes when he read the noat ! I never see a deamin yet, but I can phansy 1, a-holding a writhing soal on his pitch-fork, and smilin like Deuceace. He dressed himself in his very best clothes, and in he went, after sending me over to say that he would xcept with pleasyour Mr. Dawkins's invite.

The pie was cut up, and a most frenly conversation begun betwixt the two genlmin. Deuceace was quite captivating. He spoke to Mr. Dawkins in the most respeckful and flatrin manner—agread in everythink he said—prazed his taste, his furniter, his coat, his classick nolledge, and his playin on the floot ; you'd have thought, to hear him, that such a polygon of exlens as Dawkins did not breath—that such a modist, sinsear, honrabble genlmn as Deuceace was to be seen nowhere xcept in Pump Cort. Poor Daw was complitly taken in. My master said he'd introduce him to the Duke of Doncaster, and Heaven knows how many nobs more, till Dawkins was quite intawsicated with pleasyour. I know as a fac (and it pretty well shows the young genlmn's carryter) that he went that very day and ordered 2 new coats, on porpos to be introjuiced to the lords in.

But the best joak of all was at last. Singin, swagrin, and swarink, up stares came Mr. Dick Blewitt. He flung open Mr. Dawkins's door, shouting out, " Daw, my old buck, how are you ? " when, all of a sudden, he sees Mr. Deuceace : his jor dropt, he turned chocky white, and then burnin red, and looked as if a stror would knock him down. " My dear Mr. Blewitt," says my master, smiling and offring his hand, " how glad I am to see you ! Mr. Dawkins and I were just talking about your pony ! Pray sit down."

Blewitt did. And now was the question, who should sit the other out; but, law bless you, Mr. Blewitt was no match for my master: all the time he was fidgetty, silent, and sulky; on the contry, master was charmin. I never herd such a flo of conversatin, or so many wittacisms as he uttered. At last, completely beat, Mr. Blewitt took his leaf; that instant master followed him, and passin his arm through that of Mr. Dick, led him into our chambers, and began talkin to him in the most affabl and affeckshnat manner.

But Dick was too angry to listen: at last, when master was telling him some long story about the Duke of Doncaster, Blewitt burst out,—

"A plague on the Duke of Doncaster! Come, come, Mr. Deuceace, don't you be running your rigs upon me; I an't the man to be bamboozl'd by long-winded stories about dukes and duchesses. You think I don't know you; every man knows you and your line of country. Yes, you're after young Dawkins there, and think to pluck him; but you shan't—no, by ——, you shan't." (The reader must recklect that the oaths which interspussed Mr. B's convysation I have lift out.) Well, after he'd fired a wolley of em, Mr. Deuceace spoke as cool as possbill.

"Heark ye, Blewitt. I know you to be one of the most infernal thieves and scoundrels unhung. If you attempt to hector with me, I will cane you; if you want more, I'll shoot you; if you meddle between me and Dawkins, I will do both. I know your whole life, you miserable swindler and coward. I know you have already won two hunderd pounds of this lad, and want all. I will have half, or you never shall have a penny." It's quite true that master knew things; but how was the wonder.

I couldn't see Mr B..'s face during this dialogue, bein on the wrong side of the door; but there was a considdrable paws after thuse complymints had passed between the two genlmn—one walkin quickly up and down the room; tother, angry and stupid, sittin down, and stampin with his foot.

"Now listen to this, Mr. Blewitt," continues master at last. "If you're quiet, you shall half this fellow's money; but venture to win a shilling from him in my absence or without my consent, and you do it at your peril."

"Well, well, Mr. Deuceace," cried Dick, it's very hard, and I must say not fair: the game was of my startin, and you've no right to interfere with my friend."

"Mr. Blewitt, you are a fool! You professed yesterday not to know this man, and I was obliged to find him out for myself. I should like to know by what law of honour I am bound to give him up to you."

It was charmin to hear this pair of raskles talkin about *honour*. I declare I could have found it in my heart to warn young Dawkins of the precious way in which these chaps were going to serve him. But if *they* didn't know what honour was, *I* did; and never, never did I tell tails about my masters when in their sarvice—*out*, in cors, the hobligation is no longer binding.

Well, the nex day there was a gran dinner at our chambers—white soop, turbit, and lobstir sos; saddil of Scoch muttn, grous, and M'Arony; wines, shampang, hock, maderia, a bottle of poart, and ever so many of clarrit. The compny presint was three—wiz., the Honrabble A. P. Deuceace, R. Blewitt, and Mr. Dawkins, Exquires. My i, how we genlmn in the kitchin did enjy it! Mr. Blewittes man eat so much grous (when it was brot out of the parlor) that I reely thought he would be sik; Mr. Dawkinses genlmn (who was only abowt 13 years of age) grew so il with M'Arony and plumb-puddn as to be obleeged to take sefral of Mr. D's pils, which ½ kild him. But this is all promiscuous: I an't talkin of the survants now, but the masters.

Would you bleeve it? After dinner and praps 8 bottles of wine between the 3, the genlm sat down to *écarty*. It's a game where only 2 plays, and where, in coarse, when there's only 3, one looks on.

Fust they playd crown pints, and a pound the bett. At this game they were wonderful equill; and about suppertime (when grilled am, more shampang, devld biskits, and other things, was brot in) the play stood thus: Mr. Dawkins had won 2 pounds; Mr. Blewitt, 30 shillings; the Honrabble Mr. Deuceace having lost £3 10*s*. After the devvle and the shampang the play was a little higher. Now it was pound pints, and five pound the bet. I thought, to be sure, after hearing the complymints between Blewitt and master in the morning, that now poor Dawkins's time was come.

Not so: Dawkins won always, Mr. B. betting on his play, and giving him the very best of advice. At the end of the evening (which was abowt five o'clock the nex morning) they stopt. Master was counting up the skore on a card.

"Blewitt," says he, "I've been unlucky. I owe you—let me see—yes, five-and-forty pounds!"

"Five-and-forty," says Blewitt, "and no mistake!"

"I will give you a cheque," says the honrabble genlmn.

"Oh, don't mention it, my dear sir!" But master got a grate. sheet of paper, and drew him a check on Messeers. Pump, Algit and Co., his bankers.

"Now," says master, "I've got to settle with you, my dear Mr. Dawkins. If you had backd your luck, I should have owed you a very handsome sum of money. *Voyons*, thirteen points at a pound—it is easy to calculate"; and drawin out his puss, he clinked over the table 13 goolden suverings, which shon till they made my eyes wink.

So did pore Dawkinses, as he put out his hand, all trembling, and drew them in.

"Let me say," added master, "let me say (and I've had some little experience) that you are the very best *écarté* player with whom I ever sat down."

Dawkinses eyes glistened as he put the money up, and said, "Law, Deuceace, you flatter me."

Flatter him! I should think he did. It was the very think which master ment.

"But mind you, Dawkins," continyoud he, "I must have my revenge; for I'm ruined—positively ruined—by your luck."

"Well, well," says Mr. Thomas Smith Dawkins, as pleased as if he had gained a millium, "shall it be to-morrow?—Blewitt, what say you?"

Mr. Blewitt agreed, in course. My master, after a little demurring, consented too. "We'll meet," says he, "at your chambers. But mind, my dear fello, not too much wine: I can't stand it at any time, especially when I have to play *écarté* with *you*."

Pore Dawkins left our rooms as happy as a prins. "Here, Charles," says he, and flung me a sovring. Pore fellow, pore fellow! I knew what was a-comin!

But the best of it was, that these 13 sovrings which Dawkins won, *master had borrowed them from Mr. Blewitt!* I brought 'em, with 7 more, from that young genlmn's chambers that very morning, for since his interview with master, Blewitt had nothing to refuse him.

Well, shall I continue the tail? If Mr. Dawkins had been the least bit wiser, it would have taken him six months befoar he lost his money; as it was, he was such a confunded ninny that it took him a very short time to part with it.

Nex day (it was Thursday, and master's acquaintance with Mr. Dawkins had only commenced on Tuesday), Mr. Dawkins, as I said, gev his party—dinner at 7. Mr. Blewitt and the two Mr. D.'s as befoar. Play begins at 11. This time I knew the bisness was pretty serious, for we suvvants was packed off to bed at 2 o'clock. On Friday I went to chambers: no master—he kem in for 5 minutes at about 12, made a little toilet, ordered more devvles and soda-water, and back again he went to Mr. Dawkins's.

They had dinner there at 7 again; but nobody seamed to eat, for all the vittls came out to us genlmn: they had in more wine though, and must have drunk at least 2 dozen in the 36 hours.

At ten o'clock, however, on Friday night, back my master came to his chambers. I saw him as I never saw him before—namly, reglar drunk. He staggered about the room, he danced, he hickipd, he swoar, he flung me a heap of silver, and, finely, he sunk down exosted on his bed ; I pullin off his boots and close, and making him comfrabble.

When I had removed his garmints, I did what it's the duty of every servant to do—I emtied his pockets, and looked at his pockit-book and all his letters : a number of axdents have been prevented that way.

I found there, among a heap of things, the following pretty dockyment :—

> I. O. U.
> £4700.
> THOMAS SMITH DAWKINS.
> *Friday, 16th January.*

There was another bit of paper of the same kind—" I.O.U. four hundred pounds.—Richard Blewitt " ; but this, in corse, ment nothink.

. . . . .

Nex mornin, at nine, master was up, and as sober as a judg. He drest, and was off to Mr. Dawkins. At 10 he ordered a cab, and the two genlmn went together.

" Where shall he drive, sir ? " says I.

" Oh, tell him to drive to THE BANK."

Pore Dawkins, his eyes red with remors and sleepliss drunkenniss, gave a shudder and a sob, as he sunk back in the wehicle ; and they drove on.

That day he sold out every hapny he was worth, xcept five hundred pounds.

. . . . .

Abowt 12 master had returned, and Mr. Dick Blewitt came stridin up the stairs with a sollum and important hair.

" Is your master at home ? " says he.

" Yes, sir," says I ; and in he walks—I, in coars, with my ear to the keyhole, listning with all my mite.

" Well," says Blewitt, " we maid a pretty good night of it, Mr. Deuceace. Yu've settled, I see, with Dawkins."

" Settled ! " says master. " Oh, yes—yes—I've settled with him."

" Four thousand seven hundred, I think ? "

" About that—yes."

" That makes my share—let me see—two thousand three hundred and fifty ; which I'll thank you to fork out."

"Upon my word—why—Mr. Blewitt," says master, "I don't really understand what you mean."

"*You don't know what I mean!*" says, Blewitt, in an axent such as I never before heard—"you don't know what I mean! Did you not promise me that we were to go shares? Didn't I lend you twenty sovereigns the other night to pay our losings to Dawkins? Didn't you swear, on your honour as a gentleman, to give me half of all that might be won in this affair?"

"Agreed, sir," says Deuceace; "agreed."

"Well, sir, and now what have you to say!"

"Why, *that I don't intend to keep my promise!* You infernal fool and ninny! do you suppose I was labouring for *you*? Do you fancy I was going to the expense of giving a dinner to that jackass yonder, that you should profit by it? Get away, sir! Leave the room, sir! Or, stop—here—I will give you four hundred pounds—your own note of hand, sir, for that sum, if you will consent to forget all that has passed between us, and that you have never known Mr. Algernon Deuceace."

I've seen pipple angery before now, but never any like Blewitt. He stormed, groaned, belloed, swoar! At last he fairly began blubbring—now cussing and nashing his teeth, now praying dear Mr. Deuceace to grant him mercy.

At last master flung open the door (Heavn bless us! it's well I didn't tumble hed over eells into the room), and said, "Charles, show the gentleman downstairs!" My master looked at him quite steddy. Blewitt slunk down, as misrabble as any man I ever see. As for Dawkins, Heaven knows where he was!

. . . .

"Charles," says my master to me, about an hour afterwards, "I'm going to Paris; you may come, too, if you please."

CHARLES DICKENS
1812–1870

THE BAGMAN'S STORY

ONE winter's evening, about five o'clock, just as it began to grow dusk, a man in a gig might have been seen urging his tired horse along the road which leads across Marlborough Downs, in the direction of Bristol. I say he might have been seen, and I have no doubt he would have been, if anybody but a blind man had happened to pass that way; but the weather was so bad, and the night so cold and wet, that nothing was out but the water, and so the traveller jogged along in the middle of the road, lonesome and dreary enough. If any bagman of that day could have caught sight of the little neck-or-nothing sort of gig, with a clay-coloured body and red wheels, and the vixenish, ill-tempered, fast-going bay mare, that looked like a cross between a butcher's horse and a two-penny post-office pony, he would have known at once that this traveller could have been no other than Tom Smart, of the great house of Bilson and Slum, Cateaton Street, City. However, as there was no bagman to look on, nobody knew anything at all about the matter; and so Tom Smart and his clay-coloured gig with the red wheels, and the vixenish mare with the fast pace, went on together, keeping the secret among them: and nobody was a bit the wiser.

There are many pleasanter places, even in this dreary world, than Marlborough Downs when it blows hard; and if you throw in beside, a gloomy winter's evening, a miry and sloppy road, and a pelting fall of heavy rain, and try the effect, by way of experiment, in your own proper person, you will experience the full force of this observation.

The wind blew—not up the road or down it, though that's bad enough, but sheer across it, sending the rain slanting down like the lines they used to rule in the copybooks at school, to make the boys slope well. For a moment it would die away, and the traveller would begin to delude himself into the belief that, exhausted with its previous fury, it had quietly lain itself down to rest, when, whoo! he would hear it growling and whistling in the distance, and on it would come rushing over the hill-tops, and sweeping along the plain, gathering sound and strength as it drew nearer, until it dashed with a heavy gust against horse and man, driving the sharp rain into their ears, and its cold damp breath into their very bones; and past them it would scour, far, far away, with a stunning roar, as if in ridicule of their weakness, and triumphant in the consciousness of its own strength and power.

The bay mare splashed away, through the mud and water, with drooping ears; now and then tossing her head as if to express her disgust at this very ungentlemanly behaviour of the elements, but keeping a good pace notwithstanding, until a gust of wind, more furious than any that had yet assailed them, caused her to stop suddenly and plant her four feet firmly against the ground to prevent her being blown over. It's a special mercy that she did this, for if she *had* been blown over, the vixenish mare was so light, and the gig was so light, and Tom Smart such a light weight into the bargain, that they must infallibly have all gone rolling over and over together, until they reached the confines of earth, or until the wind fell; and in either case the probability is, that neither the vixenish mare, nor the clay-coloured gig with the red wheels, nor Tom Smart, would ever have been fit for service again.

"Well, damn my straps and whiskers," says Tom Smart (Tom sometimes had an unpleasant knack of swearing), "Damn my straps and whiskers," says Tom, "if this ain't pleasant, blow me!"

You'll very likely ask me why, as Tom Smart had been pretty well blown already, he expressed this wish to be submitted to the same process again. I can't say—all I know is, that Tom Smart said so—or at least he always told my uncle he said so, and it's just the same thing.

"Blow me," says Tom Smart; and the mare neighed as if she were precisely of the same opinion.

"Cheer up, old girl," said Tom, patting the bay mare on the neck with the end of his whip. "It won't do pushing on. such a night as this; the first house we come to we'll put up at, so the faster you go the sooner it's over. Soho, old girl—gently—gently."

Whether the vixenish mare was sufficiently well acquainted with the tones of Tom's voice to comprehend his meaning, or whether she found it colder standing still than moving on, of course I can't say. But I can say that Tom had no sooner finished speaking, than she pricked up her ears, and started forward at a speed which made the clay-coloured gig rattle till you would have supposed every one of the red spokes was going to fly out on the turf of Marlborough Downs; and even Tom, whip as he was, couldn't stop or check her pace, until she drew up, of her own accord, before a roadside inn on the right-hand side of the way, about half a quarter of a mile from the end of the Downs.

Tom cast a hasty glance at the upper part of the house as he threw the reins to the hostler, and stuck the whip in the box. It was a strange old place, built of a kind of shingle, inlaid, as it were, with cross-beams, with gabled-topped windows projecting completely over the path-way, and a low door with a dark porch, and a couple of steep steps leading down into the house, instead of the modern fashion of half-a-dozen shallow ones leading up to it. It was a comfortable-looking place though, for there was a strong cheerful light in the bar window, which shed a bright ray across the road, and even lighted up the hedge on the other side ; and there was a red flickering light in the opposite window, one moment but faintly discernible, and the next gleaming strongly through the drawn curtains, which intimated that a rousing fire was blazing within. Marking these little evidences with the eye of an experienced traveller, Tom dismounted with as much agility as his half-frozen limbs would permit, and entered the house.

In less than five minutes' time, Tom was ensconced in the room opposite the bar—the very room where he had imagined the fire blazing—before a substantial matter-of-fact roaring fire, composed of something short of a bushel of coals, and wood enough to make half-a-dozen decent gooseberry bushes, piled half-way up the chimney, and roaring and crackling with a sound that of itself would have warmed the heart of any reasonable man. This was comfortable, but this was not all, for a smartly dressed girl, with a bright eye and a neat ankle, was laying a very clean white cloth on the table ; and as Tom sat with his slippered feet on the fender, and his back to the open door, he saw a charming prospect of the bar reflected in the glass over the chimney-piece, with delightful rows of green bottles and gold labels, together with jars of pickles and preserves, and cheeses and boiled hams, and rounds of beef arranged on shelves in the most tempting and delicious array. Well, this was comfortable too ; but even this was not all—for in the bar, seated at tea at the nicest possible little table, drawn close up before the brightest possible little fire, was a buxom widow of somewhere about eight and-forty or thereabouts, with a face as comfortable as the bar, who was evidently the landlady of the house, and the supreme ruler over all these agreeable possessions. There was only one drawback to the beauty of the whole picture, and that was a tall man—a very tall man—in a brown coat and bright basket buttons, and black whiskers and wavy black hair, who was seated at tea with the widow, and who it required no great penetration to discover was in a fair way of persuading her to be a widow no longer, but to confer upon him the privilege of sitting down in that bar, for and during the whole remainder of the term of his natural life.

Tom Smart was by no means of an irritable or envious disposition.

but somehow or other the tall man with the brown coat and the bright basket buttons did rouse what little gall he had in his composition, and did make him feel extremely indignant: the more especially as he could now and then observe, from his seat before the glass, certain little affectionate familiarities passing between the tall man and the widow, which sufficiently denoted that the tall man was as high in favour as he was in size. Tom was fond of hot punch —I may venture to say he was *very* fond of hot punch—and after he had seen the vixenish mare well fed and well littered down, and had eaten every bit of the nice little hot dinner which the widow tossed up for him with her own hands, he just ordered a tumbler of it, by way of experiment. Now, if there was one thing in the whole range of domestic art which the widow could manufacture better than another it was this identical article; and the first tumbler was adapted to Tom Smart's taste with such peculiar nicety, that he ordered a second with the least possible delay. Hot punch is a pleasant thing, gentlemen—an extremely pleasant thing under any circumstances—but in that snug old parlour, before the roaring fire, with the wind blowing outside till every timber in the old house creaked again, Tom Smart found it perfectly delightful. He ordered another tumbler, and then another—I am not quite certain whether he didn't order another after that—but the more he drank of the hot punch, the more he thought of the tall man.

"Confound his impudence!" said Tom to himself, "what business has he in that snug bar? Such an ugly villain too!" said Tom. "If the widow had any taste, she might surely pick up some better fellow than that." Here Tom's eye wandered from the glass on the chimney-piece to the glass on the table; and as he felt himself becoming gradually sentimental, he emptied the fourth tumbler of punch and ordered a fifth.

Tom Smart, gentlemen, had always been very much attached to the public line. It had long been his ambition to stand in a bar of his own in a green coat, knee-cords, and tops. He had a great notion of taking the chair at convivial dinners, and he had often thought how well he could preside in a room of his own in the talking way, and what a capital example he could set to his customers in the drinking department. All these things passed rapidly through Tom's mind as he sat drinking the hot punch by the roaring fire, and he felt very justly and properly indignant that the tall man should be in a fair way of keeping such an excellent house, while he, Tom Smart, was as far off from it as ever. So, after deliberating over the two last tumblers whether he hadn't a perfect right to pick a quarrel with the tall man for having contrived to get into the good graces of the buxom widow, Tom Smart at last arrived at the satisfactory conclusion that he was a very ill-used and persecuted individual, and had better go to bed.

Up a wide and ancient staircase the smart girl preceded Tom, shading the chamber candle with her hand, to protect it from the currents of air which in such a rambling old place might have found plenty of room to disport themselves in, without blowing the candle out, but which did blow it out nevertheless ; thus affording Tom's enemies an opportunity of asserting that it was he, and not the wind, who extinguished the candle, and that while he pretended to be blowing it alight again, he was in fact kissing the girl. Be this as it may, another light was obtained, and Tom was conducted through a maze of rooms, and a labyrinth of passages, to the apartment which had been prepared for his reception, where the girl bade him good-night, and left him alone.

It was a good large room with big closets, and a bed which might have served for a whole boarding-school, to say nothing of a couple of oaken presses that would have held the baggage of a small army ; but what struck Tom's fancy was a strange, grim-looking high-backed chair, carved in the most fantastic manner, with a flowered damask cushion, and the round knobs at the bottom of the legs carefully tied up in red cloth, as if it had got the gout in its toes. Of any other queer chair, Tom would only have thought it *was* a queer chair, and there would have been an end of the matter; but there was something about this particular chair, and yet he couldn't tell what it was, so odd and so unlike any other piece of furniture he had ever seen, that it seemed to fascinate him. He sat down before the fire, and stared at the old chair for half an hour ;—Deuce take the chair, it was such a strange old thing, he couldn't take his eyes off it.

"Well," said Tom, slowly undressing himself, and staring at the old chair all the while, which stood with a mysterious aspect by the bedside, "I never saw such a rum concern as that in my days. Very odd," said Tom, who had got rather sage with the hot punch, "Very odd." Tom shook his head with an air of profound wisdom, and looked at the chair again. He couldn't make anything of it though, so he got into bed, covered himself up warm, and fell asleep.

In about half an hour Tom woke up, with a start, from a confused dream of tall men and tumblers of punch ; and the first object that presented itself to his waking imagination was the queer chair.

"I won't look at it any more," said Tom to himself, and he squeezed his eyelids together, and tried to persuade himself he was going to sleep again. No use ; nothing but queer chairs danced before his eyes, kicking up their legs, jumping over each other's backs, and playing all kinds of antics.

"I may as well see one real chair as two or three complete sets of false ones," said Tom, bringing out his head from under the bedclothes. There it was, plainly descernible by the light of the fire looking as provoking as ever.

Tom gazed at the chair; and, suddenly as he looked at it, a most extraordinary change seemed to come over it. The carving of the back gradually assumed the lineaments and expression of an old shrivelled human face; the damask cushion became an antique, flapped waistcoat; the round knobs grew into a couple of feet, encased in red cloth slippers; and the old chair looked like a very ugly old man, of the previous century, with his arms akimbo. Tom sat up in bed, and rubbed his eyes to dispel the illusion. No. The chair was an ugly old gentleman; and what was more, he was winking at Tom Smart.

Tom was naturally a headlong careless sort of dog, and he had had five tumblers of hot punch into the bargain; so, although he was a little startled at first he began to grow rather indignant when he saw the old gentleman winking and leering at him with such an impudent air. At length he resolved that he wouldn't stand it; and as the old face still kept winking away as fast as ever, Tom said, in a very angry tone:

"What the devil are you winking at me for?"

"Because I like it, Tom Smart," said the chair; or the old gentleman, whichever you like to call him. He stopped winking though, when Tom spoke, and began grinning like a superannuated monkey.

"How do you know my name, old nut-cracker face!" inquired Tom Smart, rather staggered;—though he pretended to carry it off so well.

"Come, come, Tom," said the old gentleman, "that's not the way to address solid Spanish Mahogany. Dam'me, you couldn't treat me with less respect if I was veneered." When the old gentleman said this, he looked so fierce that Tom began to grow frightened.

"I didn't mean to treat you with any disrespect, sir," said Tom, in a much humbler tone than he had spoken in at first.

"Well, well," said the old fellow, "perhaps not—perhaps not. Tom——"

"Sir——"

"I know everything about you, Tom; everything. You're very poor, Tom."

"I certainly am," said Tom Smart. "But how came you to know that?"

"Never mind that," said the old gentleman; "you're much too fond of punch, Tom."

Tom Smart was just on the point of protesting that he hadn't tasted a drop since his last birthday, but when his eye encountered that of the old gentleman, he looked so knowing that Tom blushed, and was silent.

" Tom," said the old gentleman, " the widow's a fine woman—remarkably fine woman—eh, Tom ? " Here the old fellow screwed up his eyes, cocked up one of his wasted little legs, and looked altogether so unpleasantly amorous, that Tom was quite disgusted with the levity of his behaviour ;—at his time of life, too !

" I am her guardian, Tom," said the old gentleman.

" Are you ? " inquired Tom Smart.

" I knew her mother, Tom," said the old fellow ; " and her grandmother. She was very fond of me—made me this waistcoat, Tom."

" Did she ? " said Tom Smart.

" And these shoes," said the old fellow, lifting up one of the red-cloth mufflers ; " but don't mention it, Tom. I shouldn't like to have it known that she was so much attached to me. It might occasion some unpleasantness in the family." When the old rascal said this, he looked so extremely impertinent, that, as Tom Smart afterwards declared, he could have sat upon him without remorse.

" I have been a great favourite among the women in my time, Tom," said the profligate old debauchee ; " hundreds of fine women have sat in my lap for hours together. What do you think of that, you dog, eh ! " The old gentleman was proceeding to recount some other exploits of his youth, when he was seized with such a violent fit of creaking that he was unable to proceed.

" Just serves you right, old boy," thought Tom Smart ; but he didn't say anything.

" Ah ! " said the old fellow, " I am a good deal troubled with this now. I am getting old, Tom, and have lost nearly all my rails. I have had an operation performed, too—a small piece let into my back—and I found it a severe trial, Tom."

" I dare say you did, sir," said Tom Smart.

" However," said the old gentleman, " that's not the point. Tom ! I want you to marry the widow."

" Me, sir ! " said Tom.

" You," said the old gentleman.

" Bless your reverend locks," said Tom—(he had a few scattered horse-hairs left)—" bless your reverend locks, she wouldn't have me." And Tom sighed involuntarily, as he thought of the bar.

" Wouldn't she ? " said the old gentleman firmly.

" No, no," said Tom ; " there's somebody else in the wind. A tall man—a confoundedly tall man—with black whiskers."

" Tom," said the old gentleman, " she will never have him."

" Won't she ? " said Tom. " If you stood in the bar, old gentleman, you'd tell another story."

" Pooh, pooh," said the old gentleman. " I know all about that."

" About what ? " said Tom.

" The kissing behind the door, and all that sort of thing, Tom," said the old gentleman. And here he gave another impudent look, which made Tom very wroth, because, as you all know, gentlemen, to hear an old fellow, who ought to know better, talking about these things, is very unpleasant—nothing more so.

" I know all about that, Tom," said the old gentleman. " I have seen it done very often in my time, Tom, between more people than I should like to mention to you ; but it never came to anything after all."

" You must have seen some queer things," said Tom, with an inquisitive look.

" You may say that, Tom," replied the old fellow, with a very complicated wink. " I am the last of my family, Tom," said the old gentleman, with a melancholy sigh.

" Was it a large one ? " inquired Tom Smart.

" There were twelve of us, Tom," said the old gentleman ; " fine straight-backed, handsome fellows as you'd wish to see. None of your modern abortions—all with arms, and with a degree of polish, though I say it that should not, which would have done your heart good to behold."

" And what's become of the others, sir ? " asked Tom Smart.

The old gentleman applied his elbow to his eye as he replied, " Gone, Tom, gone. We had hard service, Tom, and they hadn't all my constitution. They got rheumatic about the legs and arms, and went into kitchens and other hospitals ; and one of 'em, with long service and hard usage, positively lost his senses :—he got so crazy that he was obliged to be burnt. Shocking thing that, Tom."

" Dreadful ! " said Tom Smart.

The old fellow paused for a few minutes, apparently struggling with his feelings of emotion, and then said :

" However, Tom, I am wandering from the point. This tall man, Tom, is a rascally adventurer. The moment he married the widow, he would sell off all the furniture, and run away. What would be the consequence ? She would be deserted and reduced to ruin, and I should catch my death of cold in some broker's shop."

" Yes, but——"

" Don't interrupt me," said the old gentleman. " Of you, Tom, I entertain a very different opinion ; for I well know that if you once settled yourself in a public-house you would never leave it as long as there was anything to drink within its walls."

" I am very much obliged to you for your good opinion, sir," said Tom Smart.

" Therefore," resumed the old gentleman, in a dictatorial tone, " you shall have her, and he shall not."

"What is to prevent it ?" said Tom Smart eagerly.

"This disclosure," replied the old gentleman ; "he is already married."

"How can I prove it ?" said Tom, starting half out of bed.

The old gentleman untucked his arm from his side, and having pointed to one of the oaken presses, immediately replaced it in its old position.

"He little thinks," said the old gentleman, "that in the right-hand pocket of a pair of trousers in that press he has left a letter entreating him to return to his disconsolate wife, with six—mark me, Tom—six babes, and all of them small ones."

As the old gentleman solemnly uttered these words his features grew less and less distinct and his figure more shadowy. A film came over Tom Smart's eyes. The old man seemed gradually blending into the chair, the damask waistcoat to resolve into a cushion, the red slippers to shrink into little red cloth bags. The light faded gently away, and Tom Smart fell back on his pillow and dropped asleep.

Morning aroused Tom from the lethargic slumber into which he had fallen on the disappearance of the old man. He sat up in bed, and for some minutes vainly endeavoured to recall the events of the preceding night. Suddenly they rushed upon him. He looked at the chair ; it was a fantastic and grim-looking piece of furniture, certainly, but it must have been a remarkably ingenious and lively imagination that could have discovered any resemblance between it and an old man.

"How are you, old boy ?" said Tom. He was bolder in the day-light—most men are.

The chair remained motionless, and spoke not a word.

"Miserable morning," said Tom. No. The chair would not be drawn into conversation.

"Which press did you point to ?—you can tell me that," said Tom. Devil a word, gentlemen, the chair would say.

"It's not much trouble to open it, anyhow," said Tom, getting out of bed very deliberately. He walked up to one of the presses. The key was in the lock ; he turned it, and opened the door. There *was* a pair of trousers there. He put his hand into the pocket, and drew forth the identical letter the old gentleman had described !

"Queer sort of thing, this," said Tom Smart, looking first at the chair and then at the press, and then at the letter, and then at the chair again. "Very queer," said Tom. But, as there was nothing in either to lessen the queerness, he thought he might as well dress himself, and settle the tall man's business at once—just to put him out of his misery.

Tom surveyed the rooms he passed through, on his way downstairs, with the scrutinising eye of a landlord; thinking it not impossible that before long they and their contents would be his property. The tall man was standing in the snug little bar, with his hands behind him, quite at home. He grinned vacantly at Tom. A casual observer might have supposed he did it only to show his white teeth; but Tom Smart thought that a consciousness of triumph was passing through the place where the tall man's mind would have been, if he had had any. Tom laughed in his face; and summoned the landlady.

"Good morning, ma'am," said Tom Smart, closing the door of the little parlour as the widow entered.

"Good morning, sir," said the widow. "What will you take for breakfast, sir?"

Tom was thinking how he should open the case, so he made no answer.

"There's a very nice ham," said the widow, "and a beautiful cold larded fowl. Shall I send 'em in, sir?"

These words roused Tom from his reflections. His admiration of the widow increased as she spoke. Thoughtful creature! Comfortable provider!

"Who is that gentleman in the bar, ma'am?" inquired Tom.

"His name is Jinkins, sir," said the widow, slightly blushing.

"He's a tall man," said Tom.

"He is a very fine man, sir," replied the widow, "and a very nice gentleman."

"Ah!" said Tom.

"Is there anything more you want, sir?" inquired the widow, rather puzzled by Tom's manner.

"Why, yes," said Tom. "My dear ma'am, will you have the kindness to sit down for one moment?"

The widow looked much amazed, but she sat down, and Tom sat down too, close beside her. I don't know how it happened, gentlemen—indeed my uncle used to tell me that Tom Smart said *he* didn't know how it happened either—but somehow or other the palm of Tom's hand fell upon the back of the widow's hand, and remained there while he spoke.

"My dear ma'am," said Tom Smart—he had always a great notion of committing the amiable—"My dear ma'am, you deserve a very excellent husband;—you do indeed."

"Lor, sir!" said the widow—as well she might: Tom's mode of commencing the conversation being rather unusual, not to say startling; the fact of his never having set eyes upon her before the previous night being taken into consideration. "Lor, sir!"

"I scorn to flatter, my dear ma'am," said Tom Smart. "You deserve a very admirable husband, and whoever he is, he'll be a very lucky man." As Tom said this his eye involuntarily wandered from the widow's face to the comforts around him.

The widow looked more puzzled than ever, and made an effort to rise. Tom gently pressed her hand, as if to detain her, and she kept her seat. Widows, gentlemen, are not usually timorous, as my uncle used to say.

"I am sure I am very much obliged to you, sir, for your good opinion," said the buxom landlady, half-laughing; "and if ever I marry again——"

"*If*," said Tom Smart, looking very shrewdly out of the right-hand corner of his left eye. "*If*——"

"Well," said the widow, laughing outright this time. "*When* I do, I hope I shall have as good a husband as you describe."

"Jinkins to wit," said Tom.

"Lor, sir!" exclaimed the widow.

"Oh, don't tell me," said Tom, "I know him."

"I am sure nobody who knows him knows anything bad of him," said the widow, bridling up at the mysterious air with which Tom had spoken.

"Hem!" said Tom Smart.

The widow began to think if was high time to cry, so she took out her handkerchief, and inquired whether Tom wished to insult her; whether he thought it like a gentleman to take away the character of another gentleman behind his back; why, if he had got anything to say, he didn't say it to the man, like a man, instead of terrifying a poor weak woman in that way; and so forth.

"I'll say it to him fast enough," said Tom, "only I want you to hear it first."

"What is it?" inquired the widow, looking intently in Tom's countenance.

"I'll astonish you," said Tom, putting his hand in his pocket.

"If it is that he wants money," said the widow, "I know that already, and you needn't trouble yourself."

"Pooh, nonsense, that's nothing," said Tom Smart. "*I* want money. 'Tan't that."

"Oh, dear, what can it be?" exclaimed the poor widow.

"Don't be frightened," said Tom Smart. He slowly drew forth the letter, and unfolded it. "You won't scream?" said Tom doubtfully.

"No, no," replied the widow; "let me see it."

"You won't go fainting away, or any of that nonsense?" said Tom.

"No, no," returned the widow hastily.

"And don't run out, and blow him up," said Tom, "because I'll do all that for you; you had better not exert yourself."

"Well, well," said the widow, "let me see it."

"I will," replied Tom Smart; and, with these words, he placed the letter in the widow's hand.

Gentlemen, I have heard my uncle say that Tom Smart said the widow's lamentations when she heard the disclosure would have pierced a heart of stone. Tom was certainly very tender-hearted, but they pierced his to the very core. The widow rocked herself to and fro, and wrung her hands.

"Oh, the deception and villainy of man!" said the widow.

"Frightful, my dear ma'am; but compose yourself," said Smart.

"Oh, I can't compose myself," shrieked the widow. "I shall never find anyone else I can love so much!"

"Oh yes you will, my dear soul," said Tom Smart, letting fall a shower of the largest sized tears, in pity for the widow's misfortunes. Tom Smart, in the energy of his compassion, had put his arm round the widow's waist; and the widow, in a passion of grief, had clasped Tom's hand. She looked up in Tom's face, and smiled through her tears. Tom looked down in hers, and smiled through his.

I never could find out, gentlemen, whether Tom did or did not kiss the widow at that particular moment. He used to tell my uncle he didn't, but I have my doubts about it. Between ourselves, gentlemen, I rather think he did.

At all events, Tom kicked the very tall man out at the front door half an hour after, and married the widow a month after. And he used to drive about the country, with the clay-coloured gig with red wheels, and the vixenish mare with the fast pace, till he gave up business many years afterwards, and went to France with his wife; and then the old house was pulled down.

CHARLES DICKENS

THE POOR RELATION'S STORY

He was very reluctant to take precedence of so many respected members of the family, by beginning the round of stories they were to relate as they sat in a goodly circle by the Christmas fire ; and he modestly suggested that it would be more correct if " John our esteemed host " (whose health he begged to drink) would have the kindness to begin. For as to himself, he said, he was so little used to lead the way that really—— But as they all cried out here, that he must begin, and agreed with one voice that he might, could, would, and should begin, he left off rubbing his hands, and took his legs out from under his arm-chair, and did begin.

I have no doubt (said the poor relation) that I shall surprise the assembled members of our family, and particularly John our esteemed host to whom we are so much indebted for the great hospitality with which he has this day entertained us, by the confession I am going to make. But, if you do me the honour to be surprised at anything that falls from a person so unimportant in the family as I am, I can only say that I shall be scrupulously accurate in all I relate.

I am not what I am supposed to be. I am quite another thing. Perhaps before I go further I had better glance at what I *am* supposed to be.

It is supposed, unless I mistake—the assembled members of our family will correct me if I do, which is very likely (here the poor relation looked mildly about him for contradiction)—that I am nobody's enemy but my own. That I never met with any particular success in anything. That I failed in business because I was unbusiness-like and credulous—in not being prepared for the interested designs of my partner. That I failed in love because I was ridiculously trustful—in thinking it impossible that Christiana could deceive me. That I failed in my expectations from my uncle Chill, on account of not being as sharp as he could have wished in worldly matters. That, through life, I have been rather put upon and disappointed in a general way. That I am at present a bachelor of between fifty-nine and sixty years of age, living on a limited income in the form of a quarterly allowance, to which I see that John our esteemed host wishes me to make no further allusion.

The supposition as to my present pursuits and habits is to the following effect.

I live in a lodging in the Clapham Road—a very clean back room, in a very respectable house—where I am expected not to be at home in the daytime, unless poorly; and which I usually leave in the morning at nine o'clock, on pretence of going to business. I take my breakfast—my roll and butter, and my half-pint of coffee—at the old-established coffee-shop near Westminster Bridge; and then I go into the City—I don't know why—and sit in Garraway's Coffee House, and on 'Change, and walk about, and look into a few offices and counting-houses where some of my relations or acquaintances are so good as to tolerate me, and where I stand by the fire if the weather happens to be cold. I get through the day in this way until five o'clock, and then I dine: at a cost, on the average, of one and threepence. Having still a little money to spend on my evening's entertainment, I look into the old-established coffee-shop as I go home, and take my cup of tea, and perhaps my bit of toast. So, as the large hand of the clock makes its way round to the morning hour again, I make my way round to the Clapham Road again, and go to bed when I get to my lodging—fire being expensive, and being objected to by the family on account of its giving trouble and making a dirt.

Sometimes one of my relations or acquaintances is so obliging as to ask me to dinner. These are holiday occasions, and then I generally walk in the Park. I am a solitary man, and seldom walk with anybody. Not that I am avoided because I am shabby; for I am not at all shabby, having always a very good suit of black on (or rather Oxford mixture, which has the appearance of black and wears much better); but I have got into a habit of speaking low, and being rather silent, and my spirits are not high, and I am sensible that I am not an attractive companion.

The only exception to this general rule is the child of my first cousin, Little Frank. I have a particular affection for that child, and he takes very kindly to me. He is a diffident boy by nature; and in a crowd he is soon run over, as I may say, and forgotten. He and I, however, get on exceedingly well. I have a fancy that the poor child will in time succeed to my peculiar position in the family. We talk but little; still, we understand each other. We walk about, hand in hand; and without much speaking he knows what I mean, and I know what he means. When he was very little indeed, I used to take him to the windows of the toy-shops, and show him the toys inside. It is surprising how soon he found out that I would have made him a great many presents if I had been in circumstances to do it.

Little Frank and I go and look at the outside of the Monument—he is very fond of the Monument—and at the Bridges, and at all the sights that are free. On two of my birthdays, we have dined on *à-la-mode* beef, and gone at half-price to the play, and been deeply interested. I was once walking with him in Lombard Street, which we often visit on account of my having mentioned to him that there are great riches there—he is very fond of Lombard Street—when a gentleman said to me as he passed by, "Sir, your little son has dropped his glove." I assure you, if you will excuse my remarking on so trivial a circumstance, this accidental mention of the child as mine quite touched my heart and brought the foolish tears into my eyes.

When Little Frank is sent to school in the country I shall be very much at a loss what to do with myself, but I have the intention of walking down there once a month and seeing him on a half-holiday. I am told he will then be at play upon the Heath; and if my visits should be objected to, as unsettling the child, I can see him from a distance without his seeing me, and walk back again. His mother comes of a highly genteel family, and rather disapproves, I am aware, of our being so much together. I know that I am not calculated to improve his retiring disposition; but I think he would miss me beyond the feeling of the moment if we were wholly separated.

When I die in the Clapham Road I shall not leave much more in this world than I shall take out of it; but I happen to have a miniature of a bright-faced boy, with a curling head, and an open shirt-frill waving down his bosom (my mother had it taken for me, but I can't believe that it was ever like), which will be worth nothing to sell, and which I shall beg may be given to Frank. I have written my dear boy a little letter with it, in which I have told him that I felt very sorry to part from him, though bound to confess that I knew no reason why I should remain here. I have given him some short advice, the best in my power, to take warning of the consequences of being nobody's enemy but his own; and I have endeavoured to comfort him for what I fear he will consider a bereavement, by pointing out to him that I was only a superfluous something to every one but him; and that having by some means failed to find a place in this great assembly, I am better out of it.

Such (said the poor relation, clearing his throat and beginning to speak a little louder) is the general impression about me. Now, it is a remarkable circumstance, which forms the aim and purpose of my story, that this is all wrong. This is not my life, and these are not my habits. I do not even live in the Clapham Road. Comparatively speaking, I am very seldom there. I reside, mostly, in a—I am almost ashamed to say the word, it sounds so full of pretension—in a Castle. I do not mean that it is an old baronial habitation, but still it is a building always known to every one by the name of a Castle. In it I preserve the particulars of my history; they run thus:

It was when I first took John Spatter (who had been my clerk) into partnership, and when I was still a young man of not more than five-and-twenty, residing in the house of my uncle Chill, from whom I had considerable expectations, that I ventured to propose to Christiana. I had loved Christiana a long time. She was very beautiful, and very winning in all respects. I rather mistrusted her widowed mother, who I feared was of a plotting and mercenary turn of mind; but I thought as well of her as I could, for Christiana's sake. I never had loved any one but Christiana, and she had been all the world, and oh far more than all the world, to me, from our childhood!

Christiana accepted me with her mother's consent, and I was rendered very happy indeed. My life at my uncle Chill's was of a spare dull kind, and my garret chamber was as dull, and bare, and cold as an upper prison room in some stern northern fortress. But, having Christiana's love, I wanted nothing upon earth. I would not have changed my lot with any human being.

Avarice was, unhappily, my uncle Chill's master-vice. Though he was rich, he pinched, and scraped, and clutched, and lived miserably. As Christiana had no fortune, I was for some time a little fearful of confessing our engagement to him; but at length I wrote him a letter, saying how it all truly was. I put it into his hand one night, on going to bed.

As I came downstairs next morning, shivering in the cold December air—colder in my uncle's unwarmed house than in the street, where the winter sun did sometimes shine, and which was at all events enlivened by cheerful faces and voices passing along—I carried a heavy heart towards the long, low breakfast-room in which my uncle sat. It was a large room with a small fire, and there was a great bay window in it which the rain had marked in the night as if with the tears of houseless people. It stared upon a raw yard, with a cracked stone pavement, and some rusted iron railings half uprooted, whence an ugly out-building that had once been a dissecting-room (in the time of the great surgeon who had mortgaged the house to my uncle) stared at it.

We rose so early always that at that time of the year we breakfasted by candle-light. When I went into the room my uncle was so contracted by the cold, and so huddled together in his chair behind the one dim candle, that I did not see him until I was close to the table.

As I held out my hand to him, he caught up his stick (being infirm, he always walked about the house with a stick), and made a blow at me, and said, " You fool ! "

" Uncle," I returned, " I didn't expect you to be so angry as this." Nor had I expected it, though he was a hard and angry old man.

" You didn't expect ! " said he ; " when did you ever expect ? When did you ever calculate, or look forward, you contemptible dog ? "

" These are hard words, uncle ! "

" Hard words ? Feathers, to pelt such an idiot as you with," said he. " Here ! Betsy Snap ! Look at him ! "

Betsy Snap was a withered, hard-favoured, yellow old woman—our only domestic—always employed, at this time of the morning, in rubbing my uncle's legs. As my uncle adjured her to look at me, he put his lean grip on the crown of her head, she kneeling beside him, and turned her face towards me. An involuntary thought connecting them both with the dissecting-room, as it must often have been in the surgeon's time, passed across my mind in the midst of my anxiety.

" Look at the snivelling milksop ! " said my uncle. " Look at the baby ! This is the gentleman who, people say, is nobody's enemy but his own. This is the gentleman who can't say no. This is the gentleman who was making such large profits in his business that he must needs take a partner, t'other day. This is the gentleman who is going to marry a wife without a penny, and who falls into the hands of Jezebels who are speculating on my death ! "

I knew, now, how great my uncle's rage was ; for nothing short of his being almost beside himself would have induced him to utter that concluding word, which he held in such repugnance that it was never spoken or hinted at before him on any account.

" On my death," he repeated, as if he were defying me by defying his own abhorrence of the word. " On my death—death—Death ! But I'll spoil the speculation. Eat your last under this roof, you feeble wretch, and may it choke you ! "

You may suppose that I had not much appetite for the breakfast to which I was bidden in these terms ; but I took my accustomed seat. I saw that I was repudiated henceforth by my uncle ; still I could bear that very well, possessing Christiana's heart.

He emptied his basin of bread and milk as usual, only that he took it on his knees with his chair turned away from the table where I sat. When he had done, he carefully snuffed out the candle ; and the cold, slate-coloured, miserable day looked in upon us.

" Now, Mr. Michael," said he, " before we part, I should like to have a word with these ladies in your presence."

" As you will, sir," I returned ; " but you deceive yourself, and wrong us cruelly, if you suppose that there is any feeling at stake in this contract but pure, disinterested, faithful love."

To this, he only replied, " You lie ! " and not one other word.

We went, through half-thawed snow and half-frozen rain, to the house where Christiana and her mother lived. My uncle knew them very well. They were sitting at their breakfast, and were surprised to see us at that hour.

" Your servant, ma'am," said my uncle to the mother. " You divine the purpose of my visit, I dare say, ma'am. I understand there is a world of pure, disinterested, faithful love cooped up here. I am happy to bring it all it wants, to make it complete. I bring you your son-in-law, ma'am—and you, your husband, miss. The gentleman is a perfect stranger to me, but I wish him joy of his wise bargain."

He snarled at me as he went out, and I never saw him again.

It is altogether a mistake (continued the poor relation) to suppose that my dear Christiana, over-persuaded and influenced by her mother, married a rich man, the dirt from whose carriage-wheels is often, in these changed times, thrown upon me as she rides by. No, no. She married me.

The way we came to be married rather sooner than we intended was this. I took a frugal lodging and was saving and planning for her sake, when, one day, she spoke to me with great earnestness, and said :

" My dear Michael, I have given you my heart. I have said that I loved you, and I have pledged myself to be your wife. I am as much yours through all changes of good and evil as if we had been married on the day when such words passed between us. I know you well, and know that if we should be separated and our union broken off, your whole life would be shadowed, and all that might, even now, be stronger in your character for the conflict with the world would then be weakened to the shadow of what it is ! "

" God help me, Christiana ! " said I. " You speak the truth."

" Michael ! " said she, putting her hand in mine, in all maidenly devotion, " let us keep apart no longer. It is but for me to say that I can live content upon such means as you have, and I well know you are happy. I say so from my heart. Strive no more alone ; let us strive together. My dear Michael, it is not right that I should keep secret from you what you do not suspect, but what distresses my whole life. My mother—without considering that what you have lost, you have lost for me, and on the assurance of my faith—sets her heart on riches, and urges another suit upon me, to my misery. I cannot bear this, for to bear it is to be untrue to you. I would rather share your struggles than look on. I want no better home than you can give me. I know that you will aspire and labour with a higher courage if I am wholly yours, and let it be so when you will!"

I was blest indeed, that day, and a new world opened to me. We were married in a very little while, and I took my wife to our happy home. That was the beginning of the residence I have spoken of; the Castle we have ever since inhabited together dates from that time. All our children have been born in it. Our first child—now married—was a little girl, whom we called Christiana. Her son is so like Little Frank that I hardly know which is which.

The current impression as to my partner's dealings with me is also quite erroneous. He did not begin to treat me coldly, as a poor simpleton, when my uncle and I so fatally quarrelled; nor did he afterwards gradually possess himself of our business and edge me out. On the contrary, he behaved to me with the utmost good faith and honour.

Matters between us took this turn:—On the day of my separation from my uncle, and even before the arrival at our counting-house of my trunks (which he sent after me, *not* carriage paid), I went down to our room of business, on our little wharf, overlooking the river; and there I told John Spatter what had happened. John did not say, in reply, that rich old relatives were palpable facts, and that love and sentiment were moonshine and fiction. He addressed me thus:

"Michael," said John, "we were at school together, and I generally had the knack of getting on better than you, and making a higher reputation."

"You had, John," I returned.

"Although," said John, "I borrowed your books and lost them; borrowed your pocket-money, and never repaid it; got you to buy my damaged knives at a higher price than I had given for them new; and to own to the windows that I had broken."

"All not worth mentioning, John Spatter," said I, "but certainly true."

"When you were first established in this infant business, which promises to thrive so well," pursued John, "I came to you, in my search for almost any employment, and you made me your clerk."

"Still not worth mentioning, my dear John Spatter," said I; "still, equally true."

"And finding that I had a good head for business, and that I was really useful *to* the business, you did not like to retain me in that capacity, and thought it an act of justice soon to make me your partner."

"Still less worth mentioning than any of those other little circumstances you have recalled, John Spatter," said I; "for I was, and am, sensible of your merits and my deficiencies."

"Now, my good friend," said John, drawing my arm through his, as he had had a habit of doing at school; while two vessels outside the windows of our counting-house—which were shaped like the stern windows of a ship—went lightly down the river with the tide, as John and I might then be sailing away in company, and in trust and confidence, on our voyage of life; "let there, under these friendly circumstances, be a right understanding between us. You are too easy, Michael. You are nobody's enemy but your own. If I were to give you that damaging character among our connection, with a shrug, and a shake of the head, and a sigh; and if I were further to abuse the trust you place in me——"

"But you never will abuse it at all, John," I observed.

"Never!" said he; "but I am putting a case—I say, and if I were further to abuse that trust by keeping this piece of our common affairs in the dark, and this other piece in the light, and again this other piece in the twilight, and so on, I should strengthen my strength, and weaken your weakness, day by day, until at last I found myself on the high road to fortune, and you left behind on some bare common, a hopeless number of miles out of the way."

"Exactly so," said I.

"To prevent this, Michael," said John Spatter, "or the remotest chance of this, there must be perfect openness between us. Nothing must be concealed, and we must have but one interest."

"My dear John Spatter," I assured him, "that is precisely what I mean."

"And when you are too easy," pursued John, his face glowing with friendship, "you must allow me to prevent that imperfection in your nature from being taken advantage of by any one; you must not expect me to humour it——"

"My dear John Spatter," I interrupted, "I *don't* expect you to humour it. I want to correct it."

"And I, too," said John.

"Exactly so!" cried I. "We both have the same end in view; and, honourably seeking it, and fully trusting one another, and having but one interest, ours will be a prosperous and happy partnership."

"I am sure of it!" returned John Spatter. And we shook hands most affectionately.

I took John home to my Castle, and we had a very happy day. Our partnership throve well. My friend and partner supplied what I wanted, as I had foreseen that he would; and by improving both the business and myself, amply acknowledged any little rise in life to which I had helped him.

I am not (said the poor relation, looking at the fire as he slowly rubbed his hands) very rich, for I never cared to be that ; but I have enough, and am above all moderate wants and anxieties. My Castle is not a splendid place, but it is very comfortable, and it has a warm and cheerful air, and is quite a picture of Home.

Our eldest girl, who is very like her mother, married John Spatter's eldest son. Our two families are closely united in other ties of attachment. It is very pleasant of an evening, when we are all assembled together—which frequently happens—and when John and I talk over old times, and the one interest there has always been between us.

I really do not know, in my Castle, what loneliness is. Some of our children or grandchildren are always about it, and the young voices of my descendants are delightful—oh, how delightful !—to me to hear. My dearest and most devoted wife, ever faithful, ever loving, ever helpful and sustaining and consoling, is the priceless blessing of my house ; from whom all its other blessings spring. We are rather a musical family, and when Christiana sees me, at any time, a little weary or depressed, she steals to the piano and sings a gentle air she used to sing when we were first betrothed. So weak a man am I that I cannot bear to hear it from any other source. They played it once at the Theatre when I was there with Little Frank ; and the child said, wondering, " Cousin Michael, whose hot tears are these that have fallen on my hand ? "

Such is my Castle, and such are the real particulars of my life therein preserved. I often take Little Frank home there. He is very welcome to my grandchildren, and they play together. At this time of the year—the Christmas and New Year time—I am seldom out of my Castle. For the associations of the season seem to hold me there, and the precepts of the season seem to teach me that it is well to be there.

" And the Castle is——" observed a grave, kind voice among the company.

" Yes. My Castle," said the poor relation, shaking his head as he still looked at the fire, " is in the Air. John our esteemed host suggests its situation accurately. My Castle is in the Air ! I have done. Will you be so good as to pass the story ! "

CHARLES DICKENS

THE STORY OF RICHARD DOUBLEDICK

In the year one thousand seven hundred and ninety-nine a relative of mine came limping down, on foot, to this town of Chatham. I call it this town, because if anybody present knows to a nicety where Rochester ends and Chatham begins, it is more than I do. He was a poor traveller, with not a farthing in his pocket. He sat by the fire in this very room, and he slept one night in a bed that will be occupied to-night by some one here.

My relative came down to Chatham to enlist in a cavalry regiment, if a cavalry regiment would have him; if not, to take King George's shilling from any corporal or sergeant who would put a bunch of ribbons in his hat. His object was to get shot; but he thought he might as well ride to death as be at the trouble of walking.

My relative's Christian name was Richard, but he was better known as Dick. He dropped his own surname on the road down, and took up that of Doubledick. He was passed as Richard Doubledick; age, twenty-two; height, five foot ten; native place, Exmouth, which he had never been near in his life. There was no cavalry in Chatham when he limped over the bridge here with half a shoe to his dusty feet, so he enlisted into a regiment of the line, and was glad to get drunk and forget all about it.

You are to know that this relative of mine had gone wrong, and run wild. His heart was in the right place, but it was sealed up. He had been betrothed to a good and beautiful girl, whom he had loved better than she—or perhaps even he—believed; but in an evil hour he had given her cause to say to him solemnly, "Richard, I will never marry another man. I will live single for your sake, but Mary Marshall's lips"—her name was Mary Marshall—"never address another word to you on earth. Go, Richard! Heaven forgive you!" This finished him. This brought him down to Chatham. This made him Private Richard Doubledick, with a determination to be shot.

There was not a more dissipated and reckless soldier in Chatham barracks, in the year one thousand seven hundred and ninety-nine, than Private Richard Doubledick. He associated with the dregs of every regiment ; he was as seldom sober as he could be, and was constantly under punishment. It became clear to the whole barracks that Private Richard Doubledick would very soon be flogged.

Now the Captain of Richard Doubledick's company was a young gentleman not above five years his senior, whose eyes had an expression in them which affected Private Richard Doubledick in a very remarkable way. They were bright, handsome, dark eyes—what are called laughing eyes generally, and, when serious, rather steady than severe—but they were the only eyes now left in his narrowed world that Private Richard Doubledick could not stand. Unabashed by evil report and punishment, defiant of everything else and everybody else, he had but to know that those eyes looked at him for a moment, and he felt ashamed. He could not so much as salute Captain Taunton in the street like any other officer. He was reproached and confused—troubled by the mere possibility of the Captain's looking at him. In his worst moments he would rather turn back, and go any distance out of his way, than encounter those two handsome, dark, bright eyes.

One day, when Private Richard Doubledick came out of the Black hole, where he had been passing the last eight-and-forty hours, and in which retreat he spent a good deal of his time, he was ordered to betake himself to Captain Taunton's quarters. In the stale and squalid state of a man just out of the Black hole he had less fancy than ever for being seen by the Captain ; but he was not so mad yet as to disobey orders, and consequently went up to the terrace overlooking the parade-ground, where the officers' quarters were, twisting and breaking in his hands, as he went along, a bit of the straw that had formed the decorative furniture of the Black hole.

" Come in ! " cried the Captain, when he knocked with his knuckles at the door. Private Richard Doubledick pulled off his cap, took a stride forward, and felt very conscious that he stood in the light of the dark, bright eyes. There was a silent pause. Private Richard Doubledick had put the straw in his mouth, and was gradually doubling it up into his windpipe and choking himself.

" Doubledick," said the Captain, " do you know where you are going to ? "

" To the devil, sir ? " faltered Doubledick.

" Yes," returned the Captain. " And very fast."

Private Richard Doubledick turned the straw of the Black hole in his mouth, and made a miserable salute of acquiescence.

" Doubledick," said the Captain, " since I entered His Majesty's service, a boy of seventeen, I have been pained to see many men of promise going that road ; but I have never been so pained to see a man determined to make the shameful journey as I have been, ever since you joined the regiment, to see you."

Private Richard Doubledick began to find a film stealing over the floor at which he looked; also to find the legs of the Captain's breakfast-table turning crooked, as if he saw them through water.

"I am only a common soldier, sir," said he. "It signifies very little what such a poor brute comes to."

"You are a man," returned the Captain, with grave indignation, "of education and superior advantages; and if you say that, meaning what you say, you have sunk lower than I had believed. How low that must be, I leave you to consider, knowing what I know of your disgrace, and seeing what I see."

"I hope to get shot soon, sir," said Private Richard Doubledick; "and then the regiment and the world together will be rid of me."

The legs of the table were becoming very crooked. Doubledick, looking up to steady his vision, met the eyes that had so strong an influence over him. He put his hand before his own eyes, and the breast of his disgrace-jacket swelled as if it would fly asunder.

"I would rather," said the young Captain, "see this in you, Doubledick, than I would see five thousand guineas counted out upon this table for a gift to my good mother. Have you a mother?"

"I am thankful to say she is dead, sir."

"If your praises," returned the Captain, "were sounded from mouth to mouth through the whole regiment, through the whole army, through the whole country, you would wish she had lived to say, with pride and joy, 'He is my son!'"

"Spare me, sir," said Doubledick; "she would never have heard any good of me. She would never have had any pride and joy in owning herself my mother. Love and compassion she might have had, and would have always had, I know; but not—Spare me, sir! I am a broken wretch, quite at your mercy!" And he turned his face to the wall, and stretched out his imploring hand.

"My friend——" began the Captain.

"God bless you, sir!" sobbed Private Richard Doubledick.

"You are at the crisis of your fate. Hold your course unchanged a little longer, and you know what must happen. *I* know even better than you can imagine, that, after that has happened, you are lost. No man who could shed those tears could bear those marks."

"I fully believe it, sir," in a low, shivering voice, said Private Richard Doubledick.

"But a man in any station can do his duty," said the young Captain, "and, in doing it, can earn his own respect, even if his case should be so very unfortunate and so very rare that he can earn no other man's. A common soldier, poor brute though you called him just now, has this advantage in the stormy times we live in, that he always does his duty before a host of sympathising witnesses. Do you doubt that he may so do it as to be extolled through a whole regiment, through a whole army, through a whole country? Turn while you may yet retrieve the past, and try."

"I will! I will ask for only one witness, sir," cried Richard, with a bursting heart.

"I understand you. I will be a watchful and a faithful one."

I have heard from Private Richard Doubledick's own lips that he dropped down upon his knee, kissed that officer's hand, arose and went out of the light of the dark, bright eyes, an altered man.

In that year, one thousand seven hundred and ninety-nine, the French were in Egypt, in Italy, in Germany, where not? Napoleon Bonaparte had likewise begun to stir against us in India, and most men could read the signs of the great troubles that were coming on. In the very next year, when we formed an alliance with Austria against him, Captain Taunton's regiment was on service in India. And there was not a finer non-commissioned officer in it—no, nor in the whole line—than Corporal Richard Doubledick.

In eighteen hundred and one the Indian army were on the coast of Egypt. Next year was the year of the proclamation of the short peace, and they were recalled. It had then become well known to thousands of men that wherever Captain Taunton, with the dark, bright eyes, led, there, close to him, ever at his side, firm as a rock, true as the sun, and brave as Mars, would be certain to be found, while life beat in their hearts, that famous soldier, Sergeant Richard Doubledick.

Eighteen hundred and five, besides being the great year of Trafalgar, was a year of hard fighting in India. That year saw such wonders done by a Sergeant-Major, who cut his way single-handed through a solid mass of men, recovered the colours of his regiment, which had been seized from the hand of a poor boy shot through the heart, and rescued his wounded Captain, who was down, and in a very jungle of horses' hoofs and sabres—saw such wonders done, I say, by this brave Sergeant-Major, that he was specially made the bearer of the colours he had won; and Ensign Richard Doubledick had risen from the ranks.

Sorely cut up in every battle, but always reinforced by the bravest of men—for the fame of following the old colours, shot through and through, which Ensign Richard Doubledick had saved, inspired all breasts—this regiment fought its way through the Peninsular War, up to the investment of Badajos in eighteen hundred and twelve. Again and again it had been cheered through the British ranks until the tears had sprung into men's eyes at the mere hearing of the mighty British voice, so exultant in their valour; and there was not a drummer-boy but knew the legend, that wherever the two friends, Major Taunton, with the dark, bright eyes, and Ensign Richard Doubledick, who was devoted to him, were seen to go, there the boldest spirits in the English army became wild to follow.

One day, at Badajos—not in the great storming, but in repelling a hot sally of the besieged upon our men at work in the trenches, who had given way—the two officers found themselves hurrying forward face to face against a party of French infantry, who made a stand. There was an officer at their head, encouraging his men—a courageous, handsome, gallant officer, of five-and-thirty, whom Doubledick saw hurriedly, almost momentarily, but saw well. He particularly noticed this officer waving his sword, and rallying his men with an eager and excited cry, when they fired in obedience to his gesture, and Major Taunton dropped. It was over in ten minutes more, and Doubledick returned to the spot where he had laid the best friend man ever had on a coat spread upon the wet clay. Major Taunton's uniform was opened at the breast, and on his shirt were three little spots of blood.

"Dear Doubledick," said he, "I am dying."

"For the love of Heaven, no!" exclaimed the other, kneeling down beside him, and passing his arm round his neck to raise his head. "Taunton! My preserver, my guardian angel, my witness! Dearest, truest, kindest of human beings! Taunton! For God's sake!"

The bright, dark eyes—so very, very dark now, in the pale face—smiled upon him; and the hand he had kissed thirteen years ago laid itself fondly on his breast.

"Write to my mother. You will see Home again. Tell her how we became friends. It will comfort her, as it comforts me."

He spoke no more, but faintly signed for a moment towards his hair as it fluttered in the wind. The Ensign understood him. He smiled again when he saw that, and, gently turning his face over on the supporting arm as if for rest, died, with his hand upon the breast in which he had revived a soul.

No dry eye looked on Ensign Richard Doubledick that melancholy day. He buried his friend on the field, and became a lone, bereaved man. Beyond his duty he appeared to have but two remaining cares in life—one, to preserve the little packet of hair he was to give to Taunton's mother; the other, to encounter that French officer who had rallied the men under whose fire Taunton fell. A new legend now began to circulate among our troops; and it was, that when he and the French officer came face to face once more, there would be weeping in France. The war went on—and through it went the exact picture of the French officer on the one side, and the bodily reality upon the other—until the battle of Toulouse was fought. In the returns sent home appeared these words: "Severely wounded, but not dangerously, Lieutenant Richard Doubledick."

At midsummer-time, in the year eighteen hundred and fourteen, Lieutenant Richard Doubledick, now a browned soldier, seven-and-thirty years of age, came home to England invalided. He brought the hair with him, near his heart. Many a French officer had he seen since that day; many a dreadful night, in searching with men and lanterns for his wounded, had he relieved French officers lying disabled; but the mental picture and the reality had never come together.

Though he was weak and suffered pain, he lost not an hour in getting down to Frome in Somersetshire, where Taunton's mother lived. In the sweet compassionate words that naturally present themselves to the mind to-night, "he was the only son of his mother, and she was a widow." It was a Sunday evening, and the lady sat at her quiet garden-window reading the Bible; reading to herself, in a trembling voice, that very passage in it, as I have heard him tell. He heard the words: "Young man, I say unto thee, arise!"

He had to pass the window; and the bright, dark eyes of his debased time seemed to look at him. Her heart told her who he was; she came to the door quickly, and fell upon his neck.

"He saved me from ruin, made me a human creature, won me from infamy and shame. O God for ever bless him! As He will, He will."

"He will!" the lady answered. "I know he is in Heaven!" Then she piteously cried, "But oh, my darling boy, my darling boy!"

Never from the hour when Private Richard Doubledick enlisted at Chatham had the Private, Corporal, Sergeant, Sergeant-Major, Ensign or Lieutenant breathed his right name, or the name of Mary Marshall, or a word of the story of his life, into any ear except his reclaimer's. That previous scene in his existence was closed. He had firmly resolved that his expiation should be to live unknown; to disturb no more the peace that had long grown over his old offences; to let it be revealed, when he was dead, that he had striven and suffered, and had never forgotten; and then, if they could forgive him and believe him—well, it would be time enough—time enough!

But that night, remembering the words he had cherished for two years, "Tell her how we became friends. It will comfort her, as it comforts me," he related everything. It gradually seemed to him as if in his maturity he had recovered a mother; it gradually seemed to her as if in her bereavement she had found a son. During his stay in England, the quiet garden into which he had slowly and painfully crept, a stranger, became the boundary of his home ; when he was able to rejoin his regiment in the spring, he left the garden, thinking this was indeed the first time he had ever turned his face towards the old colours with a woman's blessing !

He followed them—so ragged, so scarred and pierced now, that they would scarcely hold together—to Quatre Bras and Ligny. He stood beside them, in an awful stillness of many men, shadowy through the mist and drizzle of a wet June forenoon, on the field of Waterloo. And down to that hour the picture in his mind of the French officer had never been compared with the reality.

The famous regiment was in action early in the battle, and received its first check in many an eventful year, when he was seen to fall. But it swept on to avenge him, and left behind it no such creature in the world of consciousness as Lieutenant Richard Doubledick.

Through pits of mire, and pools of rain ; along deep ditches, once roads, that were pounded and ploughed to pieces by artillery, heavy waggons, tramp of men and horses, and the struggle of every wheeled thing that could carry wounded soldiers ; jolted among the dying and the dead, so disfigured by blood and mud as to be hardly recognisable for humanity ; undisturbed by the moaning of men and the shrieking of horses, which, newly taken from the peaceful pursuits of life, could not endure the sight of the stragglers lying by the wayside, never to resume their toilsome journey ; dead, as to any sentient life that was in it, and yet alive—the form that had been Lieutenant Richard Doubledick, with whose praises England rang, was conveyed to Brussels. There it was tenderly laid down in hospital ; and there it lay, week after week, through the long bright summer days, until the harvest, spared by war, had ripened and was gathered in.

Over and over again the sun rose and set upon the crowded city ; over and over again the moonlight nights were quiet on the plains of Waterloo ; and all that time was a blank to what had been Lieutenant Richard Doubledick. Rejoicing troops marched into Brussels, and marched out ; brothers and fathers, sisters, mothers and wives, came thronging thither, drew their lots of joy and agony, and departed ; so many times a day the bells rang : so many times the shadows of the great buildings changed ; so many lights sprang up at dusk ; so many feet passed here and there upon the pavements ; so many hours of sleep and cooler air of night succeeded : indifferent to all, a marble face lay on a bed, like the face of a recumbent statue on the tomb of Lieutenant Richard Doubledick.

Slowly labouring, at last, through a long heavy dream of confused time and place, presenting faint glimpses of army surgeons whom he knew, and of faces that had been familiar to his youth—dearest and kindest among them, Mary Marshall's, with a solicitude upon it more like reality than anything he could discern—Lieutenant Richard Doubledick came back to life. To the beautiful life of a calm autumn evening sunset, to the peaceful life of a fresh quiet room with a large window standing open; a balcony beyond, in which were moving leaves and sweet-smelling flowers; beyond, again, the clear sky, with the sun full in his sight, pouring its golden radiance on his bed. It was so tranquil and so lovely that he thought he had passed into another world. And he said in a faint voice, "Taunton, are you near me?"

A face bent over him. Not his, his mother's.

"I came to nurse you. We have nursed you many weeks. You were moved here long ago. Do you remember nothing?"

"Nothing."

The lady kissed his cheek, and held his hand, soothing him.

"Where is the regiment? What has happened? Let me call you mother. What has happened, mother?"

"A great victory, dear. The war is over, and the regiment was the bravest in the field."

His eyes kindled, his lips trembled, he sobbed, and the tears ran down his face. He was very weak, too weak to move his hand.

"Was it dark just now?" he asked presently.

"No."

"It was only dark to me. Something passed away, like a black shadow. But as it went, and the sun—oh the blessed sun, how beautiful it is!—touched my face, I thought I saw a light white cloud pass out at the door. Was there nothing that went out?"

She shook her head, and in a little while he fell asleep, she still holding his hand, and soothing him.

From that time he recovered. Slowly, for he had been desperately wounded in the head, and had been shot in the body, but making some little advance every day. When he had gained sufficient strength to converse as he lay in bed, he soon began to remark that Mrs. Taunton always brought him back to his own history. Then he recalled his preserver's dying words, and thought, "It comforts her."

One day he awoke out of a sleep, refreshed, and asked her to read to him. But the curtain of the bed, softening the light, which she always drew back when he awoke, that she might see him from her table at the bedside where she sat at work, was held undrawn; and a woman's voice spoke, which was not hers.

"Can you bear to see a stranger?" it said softly. "Will you like to see a stranger?"

"Stranger!" he repeated. The voice awoke old memories, before the days of Private Richard Doubledick.

" A stranger now, but not a stranger once," it said in tones that thrilled him. " Richard, dear Richard, lost through so many years, my name——"

He cried out her name, " Mary," and she held him in her arms, and his head lay on her bosom.

" I am not breaking a rash vow, Richard. These are not Mary Marshall's lips that speak. I have another name."

She was married.

" I have another name, Richard. Did you ever hear it ? "

" Never ! "

He looked into her face, so pensively beautiful, and wondered at the smile upon it through her tears.

" Think again, Richard. Are you sure you never heard my altered name ? "

" Never ! "

" Don't move your head to look at me, dear Richard. Let it lie here, while I tell my story. I loved a generous, noble man ; loved him with my whole heart ; loved him for years and years ; loved him faithfully, devotedly ; loved him with no hope of return ; loved him, knowing nothing of his highest qualities—not even knowing that he was alive. He was a brave soldier. He was honoured and beloved by thousands of thousands, when the mother of his dear friend found me, and showed me that in all his triumphs he had never forgotten me. He was wounded in a great battle. He was brought, dying, here, into Brussels. I came to watch and tend him, as I would have joyfully gone, with such a purpose, to the dreariest ends of the earth. When he knew no one else, he knew me. When he suffered most, he bore his sufferings barely murmuring, content to rest his head where yours rests now. When he lay at the point of death he married me, that he might call me Wife before he died. And the name, my dear love, that I took on that forgotten night——"

" I know it now ! " he sobbed. " The shadowy remembrance strengthens. It is come back. I thank Heaven that my mind is quite restored ! My Mary, kiss me ; lull this weary head to rest, or I shall die of gratitude. His parting words were fulfilled. I see Home again ! " Well ! They were happy. It was a long recovery but they were happy through it all. The snow had melted on the ground, and the birds were singing in the leafless thickets of the early spring, when those three were first able to ride out together, and when people flocked about the open carriage to cheer and congratulate Captain Richard Doubledick.

But even then it became necessary for the Captain, instead of returning to England, to complete his recovery in the climate of Southern France. They found a spot upon the Rhône, within a ride of the old town of Avignon, and within view of its broken bridge, which was all they could desire; they lived there, together, six months; then returned to England. Mrs. Taunton, growing old after three years—though not so old as that her bright, dark eyes were dimmed—and remembering that her strength had been benefited by the change, resolved to go back for a year to those parts. So she went with a faithful servant, who had often carried her son in his arms; and she was to be rejoined and escorted home, at the year's end, by Captain Richard Doubledick.

She wrote regularly to her children (as she called them now), and they to her. She went to the neighbourhood of Aix; and there, in their own château near the farmer's house she rented, she grew into intimacy with a family belonging to that part of France. The intimacy began in her often meeting among the vineyards a pretty child, a girl with a most compassionate heart, who was never tired of listening to the solitary English lady's stories of her poor son and the cruel wars. The family were as gentle as the child, and at length she came to know them so well that she accepted their invitation to pass the last month of her residence abroad under their roof. All this intelligence she wrote home, piecemeal as it came about, from time to time; and at last enclosed a polite note, from the head of the château, soliciting, on the occasion of his approaching mission to that neighbourhood, the honour of the company of cet homme si justement célèbre, Monsieur le Capitaine Richard Doubledick.

Captain Doubledick, now a hardy, handsome man in the full vigour of life, broader across the chest and shoulders than he had ever been before, dispatched a courteous reply, and followed it in person. Travelling through all that extent of country after three years of Peace, he blessed the better days on which the world had fallen. The corn was golden, not drenched in unnatural red; was bound in sheaves for food, not trodden under foot by men in mortal fight. The smoke rose up from peaceful hearths, not blazing ruins. The carts were laden with the fair fruits of the earth, not with wounds and death. To him who had so often seen the terrible reverse, these things were beautiful indeed; and they brought him in a softened spirit to the old château near Aix upon a deep blue evening.

It was a large château of the genuine old ghostly kind, with round towers and extinguishers, and a high leaden roof, and more windows than Aladdin's Palace. The lattice blinds were all thrown open after the heat of the day, and there were glimpses of rambling walls and corridors within. Then there were immense out-buildings fallen into partial decay, masses of dark trees, terrace-gardens, balustrades; tanks of water, too weak to play and too dirty to work; statues, weeds, and thickets of iron railing that seemed to have overgrown themselves like the shrubberies, and to have branched out in all manner of wild shapes. The entrance doors stood open, as doors often do in that country when the heat of the day is past; and the Captain saw no bell or knocker, and walked in.

He walked into a lofty stone hall refreshingly cool and gloomy after the glare of a Southern day's travel. Extending along the four sides of this hall was a gallery, leading to suites of rooms; and it was lighted from the top. Still no bell was to be seen.

"Faith," said the Captain, halting, ashamed of the clanking of his boots, "this is a ghostly beginning!"

He started back, and felt his face turn white. In the gallery, looking down at him, stood the French officer—the officer whose picture he had carried in his mind so long and so far. Compared with the original, at last—in every lineament how like it was!

He moved, and disappeared, and Captain Richard Doubledick heard his steps coming quickly down into the hall. He entered through an archway. There was a bright, sudden look upon his face, much such a look as it had worn in that fatal moment.

"Monsieur le Capitaine Richard Doubledick? Enchanted to receive him! A thousand apologies! The servants were all out in the air. There was a little fête among them in the garden. In effect, it was the fête day of my daughter, the little cherished and protected of Madame Taunton."

He was so gracious and so frank that Monsieur le Capitaine Richard Doubledick could not withhold his hand. "It is the hand of a brave Englishman," said the French officer, retaining it while he spoke. "I could respect a brave Englishman, even as my foe, how much more as my friend! I also am a soldier."

"He has not remembered me, as I have remembered him; he did not take such note of my face, that day, as I took of his," thought Captain Richard Doubledick. "How shall I tell him?"

The French officer conducted his guest into a garden and presented him to his wife, an engaging and beautiful woman, sitting with Mrs. Taunton in a whimsical old-fashioned pavilion. His daughter, her fair young face beaming with joy, came running to embrace him; and there was a boy-baby to tumble down among the orange trees on the broad steps, in making for his father's legs. A multitude of children visitors were dancing to sprightly music; and all the servants and peasants about the château were dancing too. It was a scene of innocent happiness that might have been invented for the climax of the scenes of peace which had soothed the Captain's journey.

He looked on, greatly troubled in his mind, until a resounding bell rang, and the French officer begged to show him his rooms. They went upstairs into the gallery from which the officer had looked down; and Monsieur le Capitaine Richard Doubledick was cordially welcomed to a grand outer chamber, and a smaller one within, all clocks and draperies, and hearths, and brazen dogs, and tiles, and cool devices, and elegance, and vastness.

"You were at Waterloo," said the French officer.

"I was," said Captain Richard Doubledick. "And at Badajos."

Left alone with the sound of his own stern voice in his ears, he sat down to consider, What shall I do, and how shall I tell him? At that time, unhappily, many deplorable duels had been fought between English and French officers, arising out of the recent war; and these duels, and how to avoid this officer's hospitality, were the uppermost thought in Captain Richard Doubledick's mind.

He was thinking, and letting the time run out in which he should have dressed for dinner, when Mrs. Taunton spoke to him outside the door, asking if he could give her the letter he had brought from Mary. "His mother, above all," the Captain thought. "How shall I tell *her*?"

"You will form a friendship with your host, I hope," said Mrs. Taunton, whom he hurriedly admitted, "that will last for life. He is so true-hearted and so generous, Richard, that you can hardly fail to esteem one another. If He had been spared," she kissed (not without tears) the locket in which she wore his hair, "he would have appreciated him with his own magnanimity, and would have been truly happy that the evil days were past which made such a man his enemy."

She left the room; and the Captain walked, first to one window, whence he could see the dancing in the garden, then to another window, whence he could see the smiling prospect and the peaceful vineyards.

"Spirit of my departed friend," said he, "is it through thee these better thoughts are rising in my mind? Is it thou who hast shown me, all the way I have been drawn to meet this man, the blessings of the altered time? Is it thou who hast sent thy stricken mother to me, to stay my angry hand? Is it from thee the whisper comes, that this man did his duty as thou didst,—and as I did, through thy guidance, which has wholly saved me here on earth,—and that he did no more?"

He sat down, with his head buried in his hands, and, when he rose up, made the second strong resolution of his life,—that neither to the French officer, nor to the mother of his departed friend, nor to any soul, while either of the two was living, would he breathe what only he knew. And when he touched that French officer's glass with his own, that day at dinner, he secretly forgave him in the name of the Divine Forgiver of injuries.

CHARLES DICKENS

BOOTS AT THE HOLLY-TREE

WHERE had he been in his time? he repeated, when I asked him the question. Lord, he had been everywhere! And what had he been? Bless you, he had been everything you could mention a'most!

Seen a good deal? Why, of course he had. I should say so, he could assure me, if I only knew about a twentieth part of what had come in *his* way. Why, it would be easier for him, he expected, to tell what he hadn't seen than what he had. Ah! A deal, it would.

What was the curiousest thing he had seen? Well! He didn't know. He couldn't momently name what was the curiousest thing he had seen,—unless it was a Unicorn,—and he see *him* once at a Fair. But supposing a young gentleman not eight year old was to run away with a fine young woman of seven, might I think *that* a queer start? Certain. Then that was a start as he himself had had his blessed eyes on, and he had cleaned the shoes they run away in—and they was so little that he couldn't get his hand into 'em.

Master Harry Walmers's father, you see, he lived at the Elmses, down away by Shooter's Hill there, six or seven miles from Lunnon. He was a gentleman of spirit, and good-looking, and held his head up when he walked, and had what you may call Fire about him. He wrote poetry, and he rode, and he ran, and he cricketed, and he danced, and he acted, and he done it all equally beautiful. He was uncommon proud of Master Harry as was his only child; but he didn't spoil him neither. He was a gentleman that had a will of his own and a eye of his own, and that would be minded. Consequently, though he made quite a companion of the fine bright boy, and was delighted to see him so fond of reading his fairy books, and was never tired of hearing him say my name is Norval, or hearing him sing his songs about Young May Moons is beaming love, and When he as adores thee has left but the name, and that; still he kept the command over the child, and the child *was* a child, and it's to be wished more of 'em was!

How did Boots happen to know all this? Why, through being under-gardener. Of course he couldn't be under-gardener, and be always about, in the summer-time, near the windows on the lawn, a mowing, and sweeping, and weeding, and pruning, and this and that, without getting acquainted with the ways of the family. Even supposing Master Harry hadn't come to him one morning early, and said, "Cobbs, how should you spell Norah, if you was asked?" and then began cutting it in print all over the fence.

He couldn't say he had taken particular notice of children before that; but really it was pretty to see them two mites a going about the place together, deep in love. And the courage of the boy! Bless your soul, he'd have throwed off his little hat, and tucked up his little sleeves, and gone in at a Lion, he would, if they had happened to meet one, and she had been frightened of him. One day he stops, along with her, where Boots was hoeing weeds in the gravel, and says, speaking up, "Cobbs," he says, "I like *you*." "Do you, sir? I'm proud to hear it." "Yes, I do, Cobbs. Why do I like you, do you think, Cobbs?" "Don't know, Master Harry, I am sure." "Because Norah likes you, Cobbs." "Indeed—sir? That's very gratifying." "Gratifying, Cobbs? It's better than millions of the brightest diamonds to be liked by Norah." "Certainly, sir." "You're going away, ain't you, Cobbs?" "Yes, sir." "Would you like another situation, Cobbs?" "Well, sir, I shouldn't object, if it was a good 'un." "Then, Cobbs," says he, "you shall be our Head Gardener when we are married." And he tucks her, in her little sky-blue mantle, under his arm, and walks away.

Boots could assure me that it was better than a picter, and equal to a play, to see them babies, with their long, bright, curling hair, their sparkling eyes, and their beautiful light tread, a rambling about the garden, deep in love. Boots was of opinion that the birds believed they was birds, and kept up with 'em, singing to please 'em. Sometimes they would creep under the Tulip-tree, and would sit there with their arms round one another's necks, and their soft cheeks touching, a reading about the Prince and the Dragon, and the good and bad enchanters, and the king's fair daughter. Sometimes he would hear them planning about having a house in a forest, keeping bees and a cow, and living entirely on milk and honey. Once he came upon them by the pond, and heard Master Harry say, "Adorable Norah, kiss me, and say you love me to distraction, or I'll jump in head-foremost." And Boots made no question he would have done it if she hadn't complied. On the whole, Boots said it had a tendency to make him feel as if he was in love himself—only he didn't exactly know who with.

"Cobbs," said Master Harry, one evening, when Cobbs was watering the flowers, "I am going on a visit, this present Midsummer, to my grandmamma's at York."

"Are you indeed, sir? I hope you'll have a pleasant time. I am going into Yorkshire, myself, when I leave here."

"Are you going to your grandmamma's, Cobbs?"

"No, sir. I haven't got such a thing."

"Not as a grandmamma, Cobbs?"

"No, sir."

The boy looked on at the watering of the flowers for a little while, and then said, "I shall be very glad indeed to go, Cobbs,—Norah's going."

"You'll be all right then, sir," says Cobbs, "with your beautiful sweetheart by your side."

"Cobbs," returned the boy, flushing, "I never let anybody joke about it, when I can prevent them."

"It wasn't a joke, sir," says Cobbs, with humility,—"wasn't so meant."

"I am glad of that, Cobbs, because I like you, you know, and you're going to live with us.—Cobbs!"

"Sir."

"What do you think my grandmamma gives me when I go down there?"

"I couldn't so much as make a guess, sir."

"A Bank of England five-pound note, Cobbs."

"Whew!" says Cobbs, "that's a spanking sum of money, Master Harry."

"A person could do a good deal with such a sum of money as that, —couldn't a person, Cobbs?"

"I believe you, sir!"

"Cobbs," said the boy, "I'll tell you a secret. At Norah's house, they have been joking her about me, and pretending to laugh at our being engaged,—pretending to make game of it, Cobbs!"

"Such, sir," says Cobbs, "is the depravity of human natur."

The boy, looking exactly like his father, stood for a few minutes with his glowing face towards the sunset, and then departed with, "Good-night, Cobbs. I'm going in."

If I was to ask Boots how it happened that he was a going to leave that place just at that present time, well, he couldn't rightly answer me. He did suppose he might have stayed there till now if he had been anyways inclined. But, you see, he was younger then, and he wanted change. That's what he wanted,—change. Mr. Walmers, he said to him when he gave him notice of his intentions to leave, "Cobbs," he says, "have you anythink to complain of? I make the inquiry because if I find that any of my people really has anythink to complain of, I wish to make it right if I can." "No, sir," says Cobbs; "thanking you, sir, I find myself as well sitiwated here as I could hope to be anywheres. The truth is, sir, that I'm a-going to seek my fortun'." "Oh, indeed, Cobbs!" he says; "I hope you may find it." And Boots could assure me—which he did, touching his hair with his boot-jack, as a salute in the way of his present calling—that he hadn't found it yet.

Well, sir! Boots left the Elmses when his time was up, and Master Harry, he went down to the old lady's at York, which old lady would have given that child the teeth out of her head (if she had had any), she was so wrapped up in him. What does that Infant do,—for Infant you may call him and be within the mark,—but cut away from that old lady's with his Norah, on a expedition to go to Gretna Green and be married!

Sir, Boots was at this identical Holly-Tree Inn (having left it several times since to better himself, but always come back through one thing or another), when, one summer afternoon, the coach drives up, and out of the coach gets them two children. The Guard says to our Governor, " I don't quite make out these little passengers, but the young gentleman's words was, that they was to be brought here." The young gentleman gets out; hands his lady out; gives the Guard something for himself; says to our Governor, " We're to stop here to-night, please. Sitting-room and two bedrooms will be required. Chops and cherry-pudding for two!" and tucks her, in her little sky-blue mantle, under his arm, and walks into the house much bolder than Brass.

Boots leaves me to judge what the amazement of that establishment was, when these two tiny creatures all alone by themselves was marched into the Angel,—much more so, when he, who had seen them without their seeing him, give the Governor his views of the expedition they was upon. " Cobbs," says the Governor, " if this is so, I must set off myself to York, and quiet their friends' minds. In which case you must keep your eye upon 'em, till I come back. But before I take these measures, Cobbs, I should wish you to find from themselves whether your opinion is correct." " Sir, to you," says Cobbs, " that shall be done directly."

So Boots goes upstairs to the Angel, and there he finds Master Harry on a e-normous sofa,—immense at any time, but looking like the Great Bed of Ware, compared with him,—a drying the eyes of Miss Norah with his pocket-hankecher. Their little legs was entirely off the ground, of course, and it really is not possible for Boots to express to me how small them children looked.

" It's Cobbs! It's Cobbs!" cried Master Harry, and comes running to him, and catching hold of his hand. Miss Norah comes running to him on t'other side and catching hold of his t'other hand, and they both jump for joy.

" I see you a getting out, sir," says Cobbs. " I thought it was you. I thought I couldn't be mistaken in your height and figure. What's the object of your journey, sir?—Matrimonial?"

"We are going to be married, Cobbs, at Gretna Green," returned the boy. "We have run away on purpose. Norah has been in rather low spirits, Cobbs; but she'll be happy, now we have found you to be our friend."

"Thank you, sir, and thank *you*, miss," says Cobbs, "for your good opinion. *Did* you bring any luggage with you, sir?"

If I will believe Boots when he gives me his word and honour upon it, the lady had got a parasol, a smelling-bottle, a round and a half of cold buttered toast, eight peppermint drops, and a hair-brush,—seemingly a doll's. The gentleman had got about half a dozen yards of string, a knife, three or four sheets of writing-paper folded up surprising small, a orange, and a Chaney mug with his name upon it.

"What may be the exact natur of your plans, sir?" says Cobbs.

"To go on," replied the boy,—which the courage of that boy was something wonderful!—"in the morning, and be married to-morrow."

"Just so, sir," says Cobbs. "Would it meet your views, sir, if I was to accompany you?"

When Cobbs said this, they both jumped for joy again, and cried out, "Oh, yes, yes, Cobbs! Yes!"

"Well, sir," says Cobbs. "If you will excuse my having the freedom to give an opinion, what I should recommend would be this. I'm acquainted with a pony, sir, which, put in a pheayton that I could borrow, would take you and Mrs. Harry Walmers, Junior (myself driving, if you approved), to the end of your journey in a very short space of time. I am not altogether sure, sir, that this pony will be at liberty to-morrow, but even if you had to wait over to-morrow for him, it might be worth your while. As to the small account here, sir, in case you was to find yourself running at all short, that don't signify; because I'm a part proprietor of this inn, and it could stand over."

Boots assures me that when they clapped their hands, and jumped for joy again, and called him "Good Cobbs!" and "Dear Cobbs!" and bent across him to kiss one another in the delight of their confiding hearts, he felt himself the meanest rascal for deceiving 'em that ever was born.

"Is there anything you want just at present, sir?" says Cobbs, mortally ashamed of himself.

"We should like some cakes after dinner," answered Master Harry, folding his arms, putting out one leg, and looking straight at him, "and two apples,—and jam. With dinner we should like to have toast-and-water. But Norah has always been accustomed to half a glass of currant wine at dessert. And so have I."

"It shall be ordered at the bar, sir," says Cobbs; and away he went.

Boots has the feeling as fresh upon him at this minute of speaking as he had then, that he would far rather have had it out in half-a-dozen rounds with the Governor than have combined with him; and that he wished with all his heart there was any impossible place where those two babies could make an impossible marriage, and live impossibly happy ever afterwards. However, as it couldn't be, he went into the Governor's plans, and the Governor set off for York in half an hour.

The way in which the women of that house—without exception—every one of 'em—married *and* single—took to that boy when they heard the story, Boots considers surprising. It was as much as he could do to keep 'em from dashing into the room and kissing him. They climbed up all sorts of places, at the risk of their lives, to look at him through a pane of glass. They was seven deep at the keyhole. They was out of their minds about him and his bold spirit.

In the evening, Boots went into the room to see how the runaway couple was getting on. The gentleman was on the window-seat, supporting the lady in his arms. She had tears upon her face, and was lying, very tired and half asleep, with her head upon his shoulder.

"Mrs. Harry Walmers, Junior, fatigued, sir?" says Cobbs.

"Yes, she is tired, Cobbs; but she is not used to be away from home, and she has been in low spirits again. Cobbs, do you think you could bring a biffin please?"

"I ask your pardon, sir," says Cobbs. "What was it you——?"

"I think a Norfolk biffin would rouse her, Cobbs. She is very fond of them."

Boots withdrew in search of the required restorative, and, when he brought it in, the gentleman handed it to the lady, and fed her with a spoon, and took a little himself; the lady being heavy with sleep, and rather cross. "What should you think, sir," says Cobbs, "of a chamber candlestick?" The gentleman approved; the chambermaid went first, up the great staircase; the lady, in her sky-blue mantle, followed, gallantly escorted by the gentleman; the gentleman embrace her at her door, and retired to his own apartment, where Boots softly locked him up.

Boots couldn't but feel with increased acuteness what a base deceiver he was, when they consulted him at breakfast (they had ordered sweet milk-and-water, and toast and currant jelly, over-night) about the pony. It really was as much as he could do, he don't mind confessing to me, to look them two young things in the face, and think what a wicked old father of lies he had grown up to be. Howsomever, he went on a lying like a Trojan about the pony. He told 'em that it did so unfort'nately happen that the pony was half clipped, you see, and that he couldn't be taken out in that state, for fear it should strike to his inside. But that he'd be finished clipping in the course of the day, and that to-morrow morning at eight o'clock the pheayton would be ready. Boots's view of the whole case, looking back on it in my room, is, that Mrs. Harry Walmers, Junior, was beginning to give in. She hadn't had her hair curled when she went to bed, and she didn't seem quite up to brushing it herself, and its getting in her eyes put her out. But nothing put out Master Harry. He sat behind his breakfast-cup, a tearing away at the jelly, as if he had been his own father.

After breakfast, Boots is inclined to consider that they drawed soldiers,—at least, he knows that many such was found in the fireplace, all on horseback. In the course of the morning, Master Harry rang the bell,—it was surprising how that there boy did carry on,—and said, in a sprightly way, "Cobbs, is there any good walks in this neighbourhood?"

"Yes, sir," says Cobbs. "There's Love-lane."

"Get out with you, Cobbs!"—that was that there boy's expression,—"you're joking."

"Begging your pardon, sir," says Cobbs, "there really is Love-lane. And a pleasant walk it is, and proud shall I be to show it to yourself and Mrs. Harry Walmers, Junior."

"Norah, dear," said Master Harry, "this is curious. We really ought to see Love-lane. Put on your bonnet, my sweetest darling, and we will go there with Cobbs."

Boots leaves me to judge what a Beast he felt himself to be, when that young pair told him, as they all three jogged along together, that they had made up their minds to give him two thousand guineas a year as head-gardener, on accounts of his being so true a friend to 'em. Boots could have wished at the moment that the earth would have opened and swallowed him up, he felt so mean, with their beaming eyes a looking at him, and believing him. Well, sir, he turned the conversation as well as he could, and he took 'em down Love-lane to the water-meadows, and there Master Harry would have drowned himself in half a moment more, a getting out a water-lily for her,—but nothing daunted that boy. Well, sir, they was tired out. All being so new and strange to 'em, they was tired as tired could be. And they laid down on a bank of daisies. like the children in the wood, leastways meadows, and fell asleep.

Boots don't know—perhaps I do,—but never mind, it don't signify either way—why it made a man fit to make a fool of himself to see them two pretty babies a lying there in the clear still sunny day, not dreaming half so hard when they was asleep as they done when they was awake. But, lord! when you come to think of yourself, you know, and what a game you have been up to ever since you was in your own cradle, and what a poor sort of a chap you are, and how it's always either Yesterday with you, or else To-morrow, and never To-day, that's where it is!

Well, sir, they woke up at last, and then one thing was getting pretty clear to Boots, namely, that Mrs. Harry Walmerses, Junior's temper was on the move. When Master Harry took her round the waist, she said he "teased her so"; and when he says, "Norah, my young May Moon, your Harry tease you?" she tells him, "Yes; and I want to go home!"

A biled fowl, and baked bread-and-butter pudding, brought Mrs. Walmers up a little; but Boots could have wished, he must privately own to me, to have seen her more sensible of the woice of love, and less abandoning of herself to currants. However, Master Harry, he kept up, and his noble heart was as fond as ever. Mrs. Walmers turned very sleepy about dusk, and began to cry. Therefore, Mrs. Walmers went off to bed as per yesterday; and Master Harry ditto repeated.

About eleven or twelve at night comes back the Governor in a chaise, along with Mr. Walmers and a elderly lady. Mr. Walmers looks amused and very serious, both at once, and says to our missis, "We are much indebted to you, ma'am, for your kind care of our little children, which we can never sufficiently acknowledge. Pray, ma'am, where is my boy?" Our missis says, "Cobbs has the dear child in charge, sir. Cobbs, show Forty!" Then he says to Cobbs, "Ah, Cobbs, I am glad to see *you*! I understood you was here!" And Cobbs says, "Yes, sir. Your most obedient, sir."

I may be surprised to hear Boots say it, perhaps; but Boots assures me that his heart beat like a hammer, going upstairs. "I beg your pardon, sir," says he, while unlocking the door; "I hope you are not angry with Master Harry. For Master Harry is a fine boy, sir, and will do you credit and honour." And Boots signifies to me, that, if the fine boy's father had contradicted him in the daring state of mind in which he then was, he thinks he should have "fetched him a crack," and taken the consequences.

But Mr. Walmers only says, "No, Cobbs. No, my good fellow. Thank you!" And, the door being opened, goes in.

Boots goes in too, holding the light, and he sees Mr. Walmers go up to the bedside, bend gently down, and kiss the little sleeping face. Then he stands looking at it for a moment, looking wonderfully like it (they do say he ran away with Mrs. Walmers); and then he gently shakes the little shoulder.

"Harry, my dear boy! Harry!"

Master Harry starts up and looks at him. Looks at Cobbs too. Such is the honour of that mite, that he looks at Cobbs, to see whether he has brought him into trouble.

" I am not angry, my child. I only want you to dress yourself and come home."

" Yes, pa."

Master Harry dresses himself quickly. His breast begins to swell when he has nearly finished, and it swells more and more as he stands, at last, a looking at his father: his father standing a looking at him, the quiet image of him.

" Please may I "—the spirit of that little creatur, and the way he kept his rising tears down !—" please, dear pa—may I—kiss Norah before I go ? "

" You may, my child."

So he takes Master Harry in his hand, and Boots leads the way with the candle, and they come to that other bedroom, where the elderly lady is seated by the bed, and poor little Mrs. Harry Walmers, Junior, is fast asleep. There the father lifts the child up to the pillow, and he lays his little face down for an instant by the little warm face of poor unconscious little Mrs. Harry Walmers, Junior, and gently draws it to him,—a sight so touching to the chambermaids who are peeping through the door, that one of them calls out, " It's a shame to part 'em ! " But this chambermaid was always, as Boots informs me, a soft-hearted one. Not that there was any harm in that girl. Far from it.

Finally, Boots says, that's all about it. Mr. Walmers drove away in the chaise, having hold of Master Harry's hand. The elderly lady and Mrs. Harry Walmers, Junior, that was never to be (she married a Captain long afterwards, and died in India), went off next day. In conclusion, Boots put it to me whether I hold with him in two opinions: firstly, that there are not many couples on their way to be married who are half as innocent of guile as those two children; secondly, that it would be a jolly good thing for a great many couples on their way to be married, if they could only be stopped in time, and brought back separately.

CHARLES DICKENS

DR. MANETTE'S MS.

I, Alexandre Manette, unfortunate physician, native of Beauvais, and afterwards resident in Paris, write this melancholy paper in my doleful cell in the Bastille, during the last month of the year 1767. I write it at stolen intervals, under every difficulty. I design to secrete it in the wall of the chimney, where I have slowly and laboriously made a place of concealment for it. Some pitying hand may find it there, when I and my sorrows are dust.

These words are formed by the rusty iron point with which I write with difficulty in scrapings of soot and charcoal from the chimney, mixed with blood, in the last month of the tenth year of my captivity. Hope has quite departed from my breast. I know from terrible warnings I have noted in myself that my reason will not long remain unimpaired, but I solemnly declare that I am at this time in the possession of my right mind—that my memory is exact and circumstantial—and that I write the truth as I shall answer for these my last recorded words, whether they be ever read by men or not, at the Eternal Judgment-seat.

One cloudy moonlight night, in the third week of December (I think the twenty-second of the month) in the year 1757, I was walking on a retired part of the quay by the Seine for the refreshment of the frosty air, at an hour's distance from my place of residence in the Street of the School of Medicine, when a carriage came along behind me, driven very fast. As I stood aside to let that carriage pass, apprehensive that it might otherwise run me down, a head was put out at the window, and a voice called to the driver to stop.

The carriage stopped as soon as the driver could rein in his horses, and the same voice called to me by my name. I answered. The carriage was then so far in advance of me that two gentlemen had time to open the door and alight before I came up with it. I observed that they were both wrapped in cloaks, and appeared to conceal themselves. As they stood side by side near the carriage door, I also observed that they both looked of about my own age, or rather younger, and that they were greatly alike, in stature, manner, voice, and (as far as I could see) face too.

" You are Doctor Manette ? " said one.

" I am."

" Doctor Manette, formerly of Beauvais," said the other ; " the young physician, originally an expert surgeon, who within the last year or two has made a rising reputation in Paris ? "

" Gentlemen," I returned, " I am that Doctor Manette of whom you speak so graciously."

" We have been to your residence," said the first, " and not being so fortunate as to find you there, and being informed that you were probably walking in this direction, we followed, in the hope of overtaking you. Will you please to enter the carriage ? "

The manner of both was imperious, and they both moved, as these words were spoken, so as to place me between themselves and the carriage door. They were armed. I was not.

" Gentlemen," said I, " pardon me ; but I usually inquire who does me the honour to seek my assistance, and what is the nature of the case to which I am summoned."

The reply to this was made by him who had spoken second. " Doctor, your clients are people of condition. As to the nature of the case, our confidence in your skill assures us that you will ascertain it for yourself better than we can describe it. Enough. Will you please to enter the carriage ? "

I could do nothing but comply, and I entered it in silence. They both entered after me—the last springing in, after putting up the steps. The carriage turned about, and drove on at its former speed.

I repeat this conversation exactly as it occurred. I have no doubt that it is, word for word, the same. I describe everything exactly as it took place, constraining my mind not to wander from the task. Where I make the broken marks that follow here, I leave off for the time, and put my paper in its hiding-place. * * * *

The carriage left the streets behind, passed the North Barrier, and emerged upon the country road. At two-thirds of a league from the Barrier—I did not estimate the distance at that time, but afterwards when I traversed it—it struck out of the main avenue, and presently stopped at a solitary house. We all three alighted, and walked, by a damp soft footpath in a garden where a neglected fountain had overflowed, to the door of the house. It was not opened immediately, in answer to the ringing of the bell, and one of my two conductors struck the man who opened it, with his heavy riding-glove, across the face.

There was nothing in this action to attract my particular attention, for I had seen common people struck more commonly than dogs. But the other of the two, being angry likewise, struck the man in like manner with his arm ; the look and bearing of the brothers were then so exactly alike, that I then first perceived them to be twin brothers.

From the time of our alighting at the outer gate (which we found locked, and which one of the brothers had opened to admit us, and had re-locked), I had heard cries proceeding from an upper chamber. I was conducted to this chamber straight, the cries growing louder as we ascended the stairs, and I found a patient in a high fever of the brain, lying on a bed.

The patient was a woman of great beauty, and young ; assuredly not much past twenty. Her hair was torn and ragged, and her arms were bound to her sides with sashes and handkerchiefs. I noticed that these bonds were all portions of a gentleman's dress. On one of them, which was a fringed scarf for a dress of ceremony, I saw the armorial bearings of a Noble, and the letter E.

I saw this, within the first minute of my contemplation of the patient ; for in her restless strivings she had turned over on her face on the edge of the bed, had drawn the end of the scarf into her mouth and was in danger of suffocation. My first act was to put out my hand to relieve her breathing ; and in moving the scarf aside, the embroidery in the corner caught my sight.

I turned her gently over, placed my hands upon her breast to calm her and keep her down, and looked into her face. Her eyes were dilated and wild, and she constantly uttered piercing shrieks, and repeated the words, " My husband, my father, and my brother ! " and then counted up to twelve, and said, " Hush ! " For an instant, and no more, she would pause to listen, and then the piercing shrieks would begin again, and she would repeat the cry, " My husband, my father, and my brother ! " and would count up to twelve, and say " Hush ! " There was no variation in the order, or the manner. There was no cessation, but the regular moment's pause, in the utterance of these sounds.

" How long," I asked, " has this lasted ? "

To distinguish the brothers, I will call them the elder and the younger ; by the elder, I mean him who exercised the most authority. It was the elder who replied, " Since about this hour last night."

" She has a husband, a father, and a brother ? "

" A brother."

" I do not address her brother ? "

He answered with great contempt, " No."

" She has some recent association with the number twelve ? "

The younger brother impatiently rejoined, " With twelve o'clock ? "

" See, gentlemen," said I, still keeping my hands upon her breast, " how useless I am, as you have brought me ! If I had known what

I was coming to see, I could have come provided. As it is, time must be lost. There are no medicines to be obtained in this lonely place."

The elder brother looked to the younger, who said haughtily, "There is a case of medicines here"; and brought it from a closet, and put it on the table. * * * *

I opened some of the bottles, smelt them, and put the stoppers to my lips. If I had wanted to use anything save narcotic medicines that were poisons in themselves, I would not have administered any of those.

"Do you doubt them?" asked the younger brother.

"You see, monsieur, I am going to use them," I replied, and said no more.

I made the patient swallow, with great difficulty, and after many efforts, the dose that I desired to give. As I intended to repeat it after a while, and as it was necessary to watch its influence, I then sat down by the side of the bed. There was a timid and suppressed woman in attendance (wife of the man downstairs), who had retreated into a corner. The house was damp and decayed, indifferently furnished—evidently, recently occupied and temporarily used. Some thick old hangings had been nailed up before the windows to deaden the sound of the shrieks. They continued to be uttered in their regular succession with the cry, "My husband, my father, and my brother!" the counting up to twelve, and "Hush!" The frenzy was so violent that I had not unfastened the bandages restraining the arms; but I had looked to them to see that they were not painful. The only spark of encouragement in the case was, that my hand upon the sufferer's breast had this much soothing influence, that for minutes at a time it tranquillised the figure. It had no effect upon the cries; no pendulum could be more regular.

For the reason that my hand had this effect (I assume), I had sat by the side of the bed for half an hour, with the two brothers looking on, before the elder said:

"There is another patient."

I was startled, and asked, "Is it a pressing case?"

"You had better see," he carelessly answered; and took up a light. * * * *

The other patient lay in a back room across a second staircase, which was a species of loft over a stable. There was a low plastered ceiling to a part of it; the rest was open to the ridge of the tiled roof, and there were beams across. Hay and straw were stored in that portion of the place, fagots for firing, and a heap of apples in sand. I had to pass through that part to get at the other. My memory is circumstantial and unshaken. I try it with these details and I see them all, in this my cell in the Bastille, near the close of the tenth year of my captivity, as I saw them all that night.

On some hay on the ground, with a cushion thrown under his head, lay a handsome peasant boy—a boy of not more than seventeen at the most. He lay on his back, with his teeth set, his right hand clenched on his breast, and his glaring eyes looking straight upward. I could not see where his wound was, as I kneeled on one knee over him ; but I could see that he was dying of a wound from a sharp point.

" I am a doctor, my poor fellow," said I. " Let me examine it."

" I do not want it examined," he answered ; " let it be."

It was under his hand, and I soothed him to let me move his hand away. The wound was a sword-thrust, received from twenty to twenty-four hours before, but no skill could have saved him if it had been looked to without delay. He was then dying fast. As I turned my eyes to the elder brother I saw him looking down at this handsome boy whose life was ebbing out, as if he were a wounded bird, or hare, or rabbit ; not at all as if he were a fellow-creature.

" How has this been done, monsieur ? " said I.

" A crazed young common dog ! A serf ! Forced my brother to draw upon him, and has fallen by my brother's sword—like a gentleman."

There was no touch of pity, sorrow, or kindred humanity in this answer. The speaker seemed to acknowledge that it was inconvenient to have that different order of creature dying there, and that it would have been better if he had died in the usual obscure routine of his vermin kind. He was quite incapable of any compassionate feeling about the boy, or about his fate.

The boy's eyes had slowly moved to him as he had spoken, and they now slowly moved to me.

" Doctor, they are very proud, these Nobles ; but we common dogs are proud too, sometimes. They plunder us, outrage us, beat us, kill us ; but we have a little pride left, sometimes. She—have you seen her, Doctor ? "

The shrieks and the cries were audible there, though subdued by the distance. He referred to them as if she were lying in our presence.

I said, " I have seen her."

" She is my sister, Doctor. They have had their shameful rights, these Nobles, in the modesty and virtue of our sisters, many years, but we have had good girls among us. I know it, and have heard my father say so. She was a good girl. She was betrothed to a good young man, too : a tenant of his. We were all tenants of his—that man's who stands there. The other is his brother the worst of a bad race."

It was with the greatest difficulty that the boy gathered bodily force to speak ; but his spirit spoke with a dreadful emphasis.

"We were so robbed by that man who stands there, as all we common dogs are by those superior Beings—taxed by him without mercy, obliged to work for him without pay, obliged to grind our corn at his mill, obliged to feed scores of his tame birds on our wretched crops, and forbidden for our lives to keep a single tame bird of our own, pillaged and plundered to that degree that when we chanced to have a bit of meat we ate it in fear, with the door barred, and the shutters closed, that his people should not see it and take it from us—I say, we were so robbed, and hunted, and were made so poor, that our father told us it was a dreadful thing to bring a child into the world, and that what we should most pray for was that our women might be barren and our miserable race die out!"

I had never before seen the sense of being oppressed, bursting forth like a fire. I had supposed that it must be latent in the people somewhere; but I had never seen it break out until I saw it in the dying boy.

"Nevertheless, Doctor, my sister married. He was ailing at that time, poor fellow, and she married her lover, that she might tend and comfort him in our cottage—our dog hut, as that man would call it. She had not been married many weeks, when that man's brother saw her and admired her, and asked that man to lend her to him—for what are husbands among us! He was willing enough, but my sister was good and virtuous, and hated his brother with a hatred as strong as mine. What did the two then, to persuade her husband to use his influence with her, to make her willing?"

The boy's eyes, which had been fixed on mine, slowly turned to the looker-on, and I saw in the two faces that all he said was true. The two opposing kinds of pride confronting one another, I can see, even in this Bastille; the gentleman's, all negligent indifference; the peasant's, all trodden-down sentiment and passionate revenge.

"You know, Doctor, that it is among the Rights of these Nobles to harness us common dogs to carts and drive us. They so harnessed him and drove him. You know that it is among their Rights to keep us in their grounds all night, quieting the frogs, in order that their noble sleep may not be disturbed. They kept him out in the unwholesome mists at night, and ordered him back into his harness in the day. But he was not persuaded. No! Taken out of harness one day at noon, to feed—if he could find food—he sobbed twelve times, once for every stroke of the bell, and died on her bosom."

Nothing human could have held life in the boy but his determination to tell all his wrong. He forced back the gathering shadows of death, as he forced his clenched right hand to remain clenched and to cover his wound.

"Then, with that man's permission and even with his aid, his brother took her away; in spite of what I know she must have told his brother—and what that is, will not be long unknown to you, Doctor, if it is now—his brother took her away—for his pleasure and diversion, for a little while. I saw her pass me on the road. When I took the tidings home, our father's heart burst; he never spoke one of the words that filled it. I took my young sister (for I have another to a place beyond the reach of this man, and where, at least, she will never be *his* vassal. Then I tracked the brother here, and last night) climbed in—a common dog, but sword in hand.—Where is the loft window? It was somewhere here?"

The room was darkening to his sight; the world was narrowing around him. I glanced about me, and saw that the hay and straw were trampled over the floor, as if there had been a struggle.

"She heard me, and ran in. I told her not to come near us till he was dead. He came in and first tossed me some pieces of money; then struck at me with a whip. But I, though a common dog, so struck at him as to make him draw. Let him break into as many pieces as he will the sword that he stained with my common blood; he drew to defend himself—thrust at me with all his skill for his life."

My glance had fallen, but a few moments before, on the fragments of a broken sword lying among the hay. That weapon was a gentleman's. In another place lay an old sword that seemed to have been a soldier's.

"Now, lift me up, Doctor; lift me up. Where is he?"

"He is not here," I said, supporting the boy, and thinking that he referred to the brother.

"He! Proud as these Nobles are, he is afraid to see me. Where is the man who was here? Turn my face to him."

I did so, raising the boy's head against my knee. But, invested for the moment with extraordinary power, he raised himself completely: obliging me to rise too, or I could not have still supported him.

"Marquis," said the boy, turned to him with his eyes opened wide, and his right hand raised, "in the days when all these things are to be answered for, I summon you and yours, to the last of your bad race, to answer for them. I mark this cross of blood upon you, as a sign that I do it. In the days when all these things are to be answered for, I summon your brother, the worst of the bad race to answer for them separately. I mark this cross of blood upon him, as a sign that I do it."

Twice he put his hand to the wound in his breast, and with his forefinger drew a cross in the air. He stood for an instant with the finger yet raised, and, as it dropped, he dropped with it, and I laid him down dead. * * * *

When I returned to the bedside of the young woman I found her raving in precisely the same order and continuity. I knew that this might last for many hours, and that it would probably end in the silence of the grave.

I repeated the medicines I had given her, and I sat at the side of the bed until the night was far advanced. She never abated the piercing quality of her shrieks, never stumbled in the distinctness or the order of her words. They were always "My husband, my father, and my brother! One, two, three, four, five, six, seven, eight, nine, ten, eleven, twelve. Hush!"

This lasted twenty-six hours from the time when I first saw her. I had come and gone twice, and was again sitting by her when she began to falter. I did what little could be done to assist that opportunity, and by-and-by she sank into a lethargy and lay like the dead.

It was as if the wind and rain had lulled at last after a long and fearful storm. I released her arms, and called the woman to assist me to compose her figure and the dress she had torn. It was then that I knew her condition to be that of one in whom the first expectations of being a mother had arisen; and it was then that I lost the little hope I had had of her.

"Is she dead?" asked the Marquis, whom I will still describe as the elder brother, coming booted into the room from his horse.

"Not dead," said I, "but like to die."

"What strength there is in these common bodies!" he said, looking down at her with some curiosity.

"There is prodigious strength," I answered him, "in sorrow and despair."

He first laughed at my words, and then frowned at them. He moved a chair with his foot near to mine, ordered the woman away, and said in a subdued voice:

"Doctor, finding my brother in this difficulty with these hinds, I recommended that your aid should be invited. Your reputation is high, and, as a young man with your fortune to make, you are probably mindful of your interest. The things that you see here are things to be seen and not spoken of."

I listened to the patient's breathing, and avoided answering.

"Do you honour me with your attention, Doctor?"

"Monsieur," said I, "in my profession the communications of patients are always received in confidence." I was guarded in my answer, for I was troubled in my mind with what I had heard and seen.

Her breathing was so difficult to trace, that I carefully tried the pulse and the heart. There was life and no more. Looking round as I resumed my seat, I found both the brothers intent upon me.* * * *

I write with so much difficulty, the cold is so severe, I am so fearful of being detected and consigned to an underground cell and total darkness, that I must abridge this narrative. There is no confusion or failure in my memory ; it can recall, and could detail, every word that was ever spoken between me and those brothers.

She lingered for a week. Towards the last, I could understand some few syllables that she said to me, by placing my ear close to her lips. She asked me where she was, and I told her ; who I was, and I told her. It was in vain that I asked her for her family name. She faintly shook her head upon the pillow, and kept her secret, as the boy had done.

I had no opportunity of asking her any question until I had told the brothers she was sinking fast and could not live another day. Until then, though no one was ever presented to her consciousness save the woman and myself, one or other of them had always jealously sat behind the curtain at the head of the bed when I was there. But when it came to that, they seemed careless what communication I might hold with her ; as if—the thought passed through my mind—I were dying too.

I always observed that their pride bitterly resented the younger brother's (as I call him) having crossed swords with a peasant, and that peasant a boy. The only consideration that appeared to affect the mind of either of them was the consideration that this was highly degrading to the family, and was ridiculous. As often as I caught the younger brother's eyes, their expression reminded me that he disliked me deeply for knowing what I knew from the boy. He was smoother and more polite to me than the elder ; but I saw this. I also saw that I was an incumbrance in the mind of the elder, too.

My patient died two hours before midnight—at a time, by my watch, answering almost to the minute when I had first seen her. I was alone with her when her forlorn young head drooped gently on one side, and all her earthly wrongs and sorrows ended.

The brothers were waiting in a room downstairs, impatient to ride away. I heard them, alone at the bedside, striking their boots with their riding-whips, and loitering up and down.

" At last she is dead ? " said the elder, when I went in.

" She is dead," said I.

" I congratulate you, my brother," were his words as he turned round.

He had before offered me money, which I had postponed taking. He now gave me a rouleau of gold. I took it from his hand, but laid it on the table. I had considered the question, and had resolved to accept nothing.

" Pray excuse me," said I. " Under the circumstances, no."

They exchanged looks, but bent their heads to me as I bent mine to them, and we parted without another word on either side. * * * *

I am weary, weary, weary—worn down by misery. I cannot read what I have written with this gaunt hand.

Early in the morning, the rouleau of gold was left at my door in a little box, with my name on the outside. From the first, I had anxiously considered what I ought to do. I decided, that day, to write privately to the Minister, stating the nature of the two cases to which I had been summoned, and the place to which I had gone: in effect, stating all the circumstances. I knew what Court influence was, and what the immunities of the Nobles were, and I expected that the matter would never be heard of; but I wished to relieve my own mind. I had kept the matter a profound secret, even from my wife; and this, too, I resolved to state in my letter. I had no apprehension whatever of my real danger; but I was conscious that there might be danger for others, if others were compromised by possessing the knowledge that I possessed.

I was much engaged that day, and could not complete my letter that night. I rose long before my usual time next morning to finish it. It was the last day of the year. The letter was lying before me just completed when I was told that a lady waited who wished to see me. * * * *

I am growing more and more unequal to the task I have set myself. It is so cold, so dark, my senses are so benumbed, and the gloom upon me is so dreadful.

The lady was young, engaging, and handsome, but not marked for long life. She was in great agitation. She presented herself to me as the wife of the Marquis St. Evrémonde. I connected the title by which the boy had addressed the elder brother with the initial letter embroidered on the scarf, and had no difficulty in arriving at the conclusion that I had seen that nobleman very lately.

My memory is still accurate, but I cannot write the words of our conversation. I suspect that I am watched more closely than I was, and I know not at what times I may be watched. She had in part suspected, and in part discovered, the main facts of the cruel story, of her husband's share in it, and my being resorted to. She did not know that the girl was dead. Her hope had been, she said in great distress, to show her, in secret, a woman's sympathy. Her hope had been to avert the wrath of Heaven from a House that had long been hateful to the suffering many.

She had reason for believing that there was a young sister living, and her greatest desire was to help that sister. I could tell her nothing but that there was such a sister; beyond that I knew nothing. Her inducement to come to me, relying on my confidence, had been the hope that I could tell her the name and place of abode. Whereas to this wretched hour I am ignorant of both. * * * *

These scraps of paper fail me. One was taken from me, with a warning, yesterday. I must finish my record to-day.

She was a good, compassionate lady, and not happy in her marriage. How could she be! The brother distrusted and disliked her, and his influence was all opposed to her; she stood in dread of him, and in dread of her husband too. When I handed her down to the door, there was a child, a pretty boy from two to three years old, in her carriage.

"For his sake, Doctor," she said, pointing to him in tears, "I would do all I can to make what poor amends I can. He will never prosper in his inheritance otherwise. I have a presentiment that if no other innocent atonement is made for this, it will one day be required of him. What I have left to call my own—it is little beyond the worth of a few jewels—I will make it the first charge of his life to bestow, with the compassion and lamenting of his dead mother, on this injured family, if the sister can be discovered."

She kissed the boy, and said, caressing him, "It is for thine own dear sake. Thou wilt be faithful, little Charles?" The child answered her bravely, "Yes!" I kissed her hand, and she took him in her arms, and went away caressing him. I never saw her more.

As she had mentioned her husband's name in the faith that I knew it, I added no mention of it to my letter. I sealed my letter, and, not trusting it out of my own hands, delivered it myself that day.

That night, the last night of the year, towards nine o'clock, a man in a black dress rang at my gate, demanded to see me, and softly followed my servant, Ernest Defarge, a youth, upstairs. When my servant came into the room where I sat with my wife—oh, my wife, beloved of my heart! My fair young English wife!—we saw the man, who was supposed to be at the gate, standing silent behind him.

An urgent case in the Rue St. Honoré, he said. It would not detain me, he had a coach in waiting.

It brought me here, it brought me to my grave. When I was clear of the house a black muffler was drawn tightly over my mouth from behind, and my arms were pinioned. The two brothers crossed the road from a dark corner, and identified me with a single gesture. The Marquis took from his pocket the letter I had written, showed it me, burnt it in the light of a lantern that was held, and extinguished the ashes with his foot. Not a word was spoken. I was brought here, I was brought to my living grave.

If it had pleased GOD to put it in the hard heart of either of the brothers, in all these frightful years, to grant me any tidings of my dearest wife—so much as to let me know by a word whether alive or dead—I might have thought that He had not quite abandoned them. But, now I believe that the mark of the red cross is fatal to them, and that they have no part in His mercies. And them and their descendants, to the last of their race, I, Alexandre Manette, unhappy prisoner, do this last night of the year 1767, in my unbearable agony, denounce to the times when all these things shall be answered for. I denounce them to Heaven and to earth.

CHARLES DICKENS

TO BE TAKEN WITH A GRAIN OF SALT

I HAVE always noticed a prevalent want of courage, even among persons of superior intelligence and culture, as to imparting their own psychological experiences when those have been of a strange sort. Almost all men are afraid that what they could relate in such wise would find no parallel or response in a listener's internal life, and might be suspected or laughed at. A truthful traveller, who should have seen some extraordinary creature in the likeness of a sea-serpent, would have no fear of mentioning it ; but the same traveller, having had some singular presentiment, impulse, vagary of thought, vision (so called), dream, or other remarkable mental impression, would hesitate considerably before he would own to it. To this reticence I attribute much of the obscurity in which such subjects are involved. We do not habitually communicate our experiences of these subjective things as we do our experiences of objective creation. The consequence is, that the general stock of experience in this regard appears exceptional, and really is so, in respect of being miserably imperfect.

In what I am going to relate, I have no intention of setting up, opposing, or supporting any theory whatever. I know the history of the Bookseller of Berlin, I have studied the case of the wife of a late Astronomer-Royal as related by Sir David Brewster, and I have followed the minutest details of a much more remarkable case of Spectral Illusion occurring within my private circle of friends. It may be necessary to state as to this last, that the sufferer (a lady) was in no degree, however distant, related to me. A mistaken assumption on that head might suggest an explanation of a part of my own case,—but only a part,—which would be wholly without foundation. It cannot be referred to my inheritance of any developed peculiarity, nor had I ever before any at all similar experience, nor have I ever had any at all similar experience since.

It does not signify how many years ago, or how few, a certain murder was committed in England, which attracted great attention. We hear more than enough of murderers as they rise in succession to their atrocious eminence, and I would bury the memory of this particular brute, if I could, as his body was buried, in Newgate Jail. I purposely abstain from giving any direct clue to the criminal's individuality. When the murder was first discovered, no suspicion fell—or I ought rather to say, for I cannot be too precise in my facts, it was nowhere publicly hinted that any suspicion fell—on the man who was afterwards brought to trial. As no reference was at that time made to him in the newspapers, it is obviously impossible that any description of him can at that time have been given in the newspapers. It is essential that this fact be remembered.

Unfolding at breakfast my morning paper, containing the account of that first discovery, I found it to be deeply interesting, and I read it with close attention. I read it twice, if not three times. The discovery had been made in a bedroom, and, when I laid down the paper, I was aware of a flash—rush—flow—I do not know what to call it,—no word I can find is satisfactorily descriptive,—in which I seemed to see that bedroom passing through my room, like a picture impossibly painted on a running river. Though almost instantaneous in its passing, it was perfectly clear; so clear that I distinctly, and with a sense of relief, observed the absence of the dead body from the bed.

It was in no romantic place that I had this curious sensation, but in chambers in Piccadilly, very near to the corner of St. James's Street. It was entirely new to me. I was in my easy-chair at the moment, and the sensation was accompanied with a peculiar shiver which started the chair from its position. (But it is to be noted that the chair ran easily on castors.) I went to one of the windows (there are two in the room, and the room is on the second floor) to refresh my eyes with the moving objects down in Piccadilly. It was a bright autumn morning, and the street was sparkling and cheerful. The wind was high. As I looked out, it brought down from the Park a quantity of fallen leaves, which a gust took, and whirled into a spiral pillar. As the pillar fell and the leaves dispersed, I saw two men on the opposite side of the way, going from west to east. They were one behind the other. The foremost man often looked back over his shoulder. The second man followed him, at a distance of some thirty paces, with his right hand menacingly raised. First, the singularity and steadiness of this threatening gesture in so public a thoroughfare attracted my attention; and next, the more remarkable circumstance that nobody heeded it. Both men threaded their way among the other passengers with a smoothness hardly consistent even with the action of walking on a pavement; and no single creature, that I could see, gave them place, touched them, or looked after them. In passing before my windows, they both stared up at me. I saw their two faces very distinctly, and I knew that I could recognise them anywhere. Not that I had consciously noticed anything very remarkable in either face, except that the man who went first had an unusually lowering appearance, and that the face of the man who followed him was of the colour of impure wax.

I am a bachelor, and my valet and his wife constitute my whole establishment. My occupation is in a certain Branch Bank, and I wish that my duties as head of a Department were as light as they are popularly supposed to be. They kept me in town that autumn, when I stood in need of change. I was not ill, but I was not well. My reader is to make the most that can be reasonably made of my feeling jaded, having a depressing sense upon me of a monotonous life, and being "slightly dyspeptic." I am assured by my renowned doctor that my real state of health at that time justified no stronger description, and I quote his own from his written answer to my request for it. As the circumstances of the murder, gradually unravelling, took stronger and stronger possession of the public mind, I kept them away from mine by knowing as little about them as was possible in the midst of the universal excitement. But I knew that a verdict of Wilful Murder had been found against the suspected murderer, and that he had been committed to Newgate for trial. I also knew that his trial had been postponed over one Sessions of the Central Criminal Court, on the ground of general prejudice and want of time for the preparation of the defence. I may further have known, but I believe I did not, when, or about when, the Sessions to which his trial stood postponed would come on.

My sitting-room, bedroom, and dressing-room are all on one floor. With the last there is no communication but through the bedroom. True, there is a door in it, once communicating with the staircase; but a part of the fitting of my bath has been—and had been then for some years—fixed across it. At the same period, and as a part of the same arrangement, the door had been nailed up and canvased over.

I was standing in my bedroom late one night, giving some directions to my servant before he went to bed. My face was towards the only available door of communication with the dressing-room, and it was closed. My servant's back was towards that door. While I was speaking to him, I saw it open, and a man look in, who very earnestly and mysteriously beckoned to me. That man was the man who had gone second of the two along Piccadilly, and whose face was the colour of impure wax. The figure, having beckoned, drew back, and closed the door. With no longer pause than was made by my crossing the bedroom, I opened the dressing-room door and looked in. I had a lighted candle already in my hand. I felt no inward expectation of seeing the figure in the dressing-room, and I did not see it there.

Conscious that my servant stood amazed, I turned round to him, and said: "Derrick, could you believe that in my cool senses I fancied I saw a——" As I there laid my hand upon his breast, with a sudden start he trembled violently, and said, "O Lord, yes, Sir! A dead man beckoning!"

Now I do not believe that this John Derrick, my trusty and attached servant for more than twenty years, had any impression whatever of having seen any such figure, until I touched him. The change in him was so startling, when I touched him, that I fully believe he derived his impression in some occult manner from me at that instant.

I bade John Derrick bring some brandy, and I gave him a dram, and was glad to take one myself. Of what had preceded that night's phenomenon I told him not a single word. Reflecting on it, I was absolutely certain that I had never seen that face before, except on the one occasion in Piccadilly. Comparing its expression when beckoning at the door with its expression when it had stared up at me as I stood at my window, I came to the conclusion that on the first occasion it had sought to fasten itself upon my memory, and that on the second occasion it had made sure of being immediately remembered.

I was not very comfortable that night, though I felt a certainty, difficult to explain, that the figure would not return. At daylight I fell into heavy sleep, from which I was awakened by John Derrick's coming to my bedside with a paper in his hand.

This paper, it appeared, had been the subject of an altercation at the door between its bearer and my servant. It was a summons to me to serve upon a Jury at the forthcoming Sessions of the Central Criminal Court at the Old Bailey. I had never before been summoned on such a Jury, as John Derrick well knew. He believed—I am not certain at this hour whether with reason or otherwise—that that class of Jurors were customarily chosen on a lower qualification than mine, and he had at first refused to accept the summons. The man who served it had taken the matter very coolly. He had said that my attendance or non-attendance was nothing to him; there the summons was; and I should deal with it at my own peril, and not at his.

For a day or two I was undecided whether to respond to this call, or take no notice of it. I was not conscious of the slightest mysterious bias, influence, or attraction, one way or other. Of that I am as strictly sure as of every other statement that I make here. Ultimately I decided, as a break in the monotony of my life, that I would go.

The appointed morning was a raw morning in the month of November. There was a dense brown fog in Piccadilly, and it became positively black and in the last degree oppressive east of Temple Bar. I found the passages and staircases of the Court House flaringly lighted with gas, and the Court itself similarly illuminated. I *think* that, until I was conducted by officers into the Old Court and saw its crowded state, I did not know that the Murderer was to be tried that day. I *think* that, until I was so helped into the Old Court with considerable difficulty, I did not know into which of the two Courts sitting my summons would take me. But this must not be received as a positive assertion, for I am not completely satisfied in my mind on either point. I took my seat in the place appropriated to Jurors in waiting, and I looked about the Court as well as I could through the cloud of fog and breath that was heavy in it. I noticed the black vapour hanging like a murky curtain outside the great windows, and I noticed the stifled sound of wheels on the straw or tan that was littered in the street; also, the hum of the people gathered there, which a shrill whistle, or a louder song or hail than the rest, occasionally pierced. Soon afterwards the Judges, two in number, entered, and took their seats. The buzz in the Court was awfully hushed. The direction was given to put the Murderer to the bar. He appeared there. And in that same instant I recognised in him the first of the two men who had gone down Piccadilly.

If my name had been called then, I doubt if I could have answered to it audibly. But it was called about sixth or eighth in the panel, and I was by that time able to say "Here!" Now, observe. As I stepped into the box, the prisoner, who had been looking on attentively, but with no sign of concern, became violently agitated, and beckoned to his attorney. The prisoner's wish to challenge me was so manifest, that it occasioned a pause, during which the attorney, with his hand upon the dock, whispered with his client, and shook his head. I afterwards had it from that gentleman, that the prisoner's first affrighted words to him were, "*At all hazards, challenge that man!*" But that, as he would give no reason for it, and admitted that he had not even known my name until he heard it called and I appeared, it was not done.

Both on the ground already explained, that I wish to avoid reviving the unwholesome memory of that Murderer, and also because a detailed account of his long trial is by no means indispensable to my narrative, I shall confine myself closely to such incidents in the ten days and nights during which we, the Jury, were kept together, as directly bear on my own curious personal experience. It is in that, and not in the Murderer, that I seek to interest my reader. It is to that, and not to a page of the Newgate Calendar, that I beg attention.

I was chosen Foreman of the Jury. On the second morning of the trial, after evidence had been taken for two hours (I heard the church clocks strike), happening to cast my eyes over my brother-jurymen, I found an inexplicable difficulty in counting them. I counted them several times, yet always with the same difficulty. In short, I made them one too many.

I touched the brother-juryman whose place was next me, and I whispered to him, "Oblige me by counting us." He looked surprised by the request, but turned his head and counted. "Why," says he, suddenly, "we are Thirt——but no, it's not possible. No. We are twelve." According to my counting that day, we were always right in detail, but in the gross we were always one too many. There was no appearance—no figure—to account for it; but I had now an inward foreshadowing of the figure that was surely coming.

The Jury were housed at the London Tavern. We all slept in one large room on separate tables, and we were constantly in the charge and under the eye of the officer sworn to hold us in safe-keeping. I see no reason for suppressing the real name of that officer. He was intelligent, highly polite, and obliging, and (I was glad to hear) much respected in the City. He had an agreeable presence, good eyes, enviable black whiskers, and a fine sonorous voice. His name was Mr. Harker.

When we turned into our twelve beds at night, Mr. Harker's bed was drawn across the door. On the night of the second day, not being disposed to lie down, and seeing Mr. Harker sitting on his bed, I went and sat beside him, and offered him a pinch of snuff. As Mr. Harker's hand touched mine in taking it from my box, a peculiar shiver crossed him, and he said, "Who is this?"

Following Mr. Harker's eyes, and looking along the room, I saw again the figure I expected,—the second of the two men who had gone down Piccadilly. I rose, and advanced a few steps; then stopped, and looked round at Mr. Harker. He was quite unconcerned, laughed, and said in a pleasant way, "I thought for a moment we had a thirteenth juryman, without a bed. But I see it is the moonlight."

Making no revelation to Mr. Harker, but inviting him to take a walk with me to the end of the room, I watched what the figure did. It stood for a few moments by the bedside of each of my eleven brother jurymen, close to the pillow. It always went to the right-hand side of the bed, and always passed out crossing the foot of the next bed. It seemed, from the action of the head, merely to look down pensively at each recumbent figure. It took no notice of me, or of my bed, which was that nearest to Mr. Harker's. It seemed to go out where the moonlight came in, through a high window, as by an aerial flight of stairs.

Next morning at breakfast, it appeared that everybody present had dreamed of the murdered man last night except myself and Mr. Harker.

I now felt as convinced that the second man who had gone down Piccadilly was the murdered man (so to speak), as if it had been borne into my comprehension by his immediate testimony. But even this took place, and in a manner for which I was not at all prepared.

On the fifth day of the trial, when the case for the prosecution was drawing to a close, a miniature of the murdered man, missing from his bedroom upon the discovery of the deed, and afterwards found in a hiding-place where the murderer had been seen digging, was put in evidence. Having been identified by the witness under examination, it was handed up to the Bench, and thence handed down to be inspected by the Jury. As an officer in a black gown was making his way with it across to me, the figure of the second man who had gone down Piccadilly impetuously started from the crowd, caught the miniature from the officer, and gave it to me with his own hands, at the same time saying, in a low and hollow tone,—before I saw the miniature, which was in a locket,—" *I was younger then, and my face was not then drained of blood.*" It also came between me and the brother juryman to whom I would have given the miniature, and between him and the brother juryman to whom he would have given it, and so passed it on through the whole of our number, and back into my possession. Not one of them, however, detected this.

At table, and generally when we were shut up together in Mr. Harker's custody, we had from the first naturally discussed the day's proceedings a good deal. On that fifth day, the case for the prosecution being closed, and we having that side of the question in a completed shape before us, our discussion was more animated and serious. Among our number was a vestryman,—the densest idiot I have ever seen at large,—who met the plainest evidence with the most preposterous objections, and who was sided with by two flabby parochial parasites ; all the three impanelled from a district so delivered over to fever that they ought to have been upon their own trial for five hundred murders. When these mischievous blockheads were at their loudest, which was towards midnight, while some of us were already preparing for bed, I again saw the murdered man. He stood grimly behind them, beckoning to me. On my going towards them, and striking into the conversation, he immediately retired. This was the beginning of a separate series of appearances, confined to that long room in which *we* were confined. Whenever a knot of my brother jurymen laid their heads together, I saw the head of the murdered man among theirs. Whenever their comparison of notes was going against him, he would solemnly and irresistibly beckon to me.

It will be borne in mind that down to the production of the miniature, on the fifth day of the trial, I had never seen the Appearance in Court. Three changes occurred now that we entered on the case for the defence. Two of them I will mention together, first. The figure was now in Court continually, and it never there addressed itself to me, but always to the person who was speaking at the time. For instance: the throat of the murdered man had been cut straight across. In the opening speech for the defence it was suggested that the deceased might have cut his own throat. At that very moment, the figure, with its throat in the dreadful condition referred to (this it had concealed before), stood at the speaker's elbow, motioning across and across its windpipe, now with the right hand, now with the left, vigorously suggesting to the speaker himself the impossibility of such a wound having been self-inflicted by either hand. For another instance: a witness to character, a woman, deposed to the prisoner's being the most amiable of mankind. The figure at that instant stood on the floor before her, looking her full in the face, and pointing out the prisoner's evil countenance with an extended arm and an outstretched finger.

The third change now to be added impressed me strongly as the most marked and striking of all. I do not theorise upon it; I accurately state it, and there leave it. Although the Appearance was not itself perceived by those whom it addressed, its coming close to such persons was invariably attended by some trepidation or disturbance on their part. It seemed to me as if it were prevented, by laws to which I was not amenable, from fully revealing itself to others, and yet as if it could invisibly, dumbly, and darkly overshadow their minds. When the leading counsel for the defence suggested that hypothesis of suicide, and the figure stood at the learned gentleman's elbow, frightfully sawing at its severed throat, it is undeniable that the counsel faltered in his speech, lost for a few seconds the thread of his ingenious discourse, wiped his forehead with his handkerchief, and turned extremely pale. When the witness to character was confronted by the Appearance, her eyes most certainly did follow the direction of its pointed finger, and rest in great hesitation and trouble upon the prisoner's face. Two additional illustrations will suffice. On the eighth day of the trial, after the pause which was every day made early in the afternoon for a few minutes' rest and refreshment, I came back into Court with the rest of the Jury some little time before the return of the Judges. Standing up in the box and looking about me, I thought the figure was not there, until, chancing to raise my eyes to the gallery, I saw it bending forward, and leaning ever a very decent woman, as if to assure itself whether the Judges had resumed their seats or not. Immediately afterwards that woman screamed, fainted and was carried out. So with the venerable, sagacious, and patient Judge who conducted the trial. When the case was over, and he settled himself and his papers to sum up, the murdered man, entering by the Judges' door, advanced to his Lordship's desk, and looked eagerly over his shoulder at the pages of his notes which he was turning. A change came over his Lordship's face; his hand stopped; the peculiar shiver, that I knew so well, passed over him; he faltered, "Excuse me, gentlemen, for a few moments. I am somewhat oppressed by the vitiated air"; and did not recover until he had drunk a glass of water.

Through all the monotony of six of those interminable ten days,—the same Judges and others on the bench, the same murderer in the dock, the same lawyers at the table, the same tones of question and answer rising to the roof of the Court, the same scratching of the Judge's pen, the same ushers going in and out, the same lights kindled at the same hour when there had been any natural light of day, the same foggy curtain outside the great windows when it was foggy, the same rain pattering and dripping when it was rainy, the same footmarks of turnkeys and prisoner day after day on the same sawdust, the same keys locking and unlocking the same heavy doors,—through all the wearisome monotony which made me feel as if I had been Foreman of the Jury for a vast period of time, and Piccadilly had flourished coevally with Babylon, the murdered man never lost one trace of his distinctness in my eyes, nor was he at any moment less distinct than anybody else. I must not omit, as a matter of fact, that I never once saw the Appearance which I call by the name of the murdered man look at the murderer. Again and again I wondered, "Why does he not?" But he never did.

Nor did he look at me, after the production of the miniature, until the last closing minutes of the trial arrived. We retired to consider at seven minutes before ten at night. The idiotic vestryman and his two parochial parasites gave us so much trouble that we twice returned into Court to beg to have certain extracts from the Judge's notes re-read. Nine of us had not the smallest doubt about those passages, neither, I believe, had any one in the Court; the dunder-headed triumvirate, however, having no idea but obstruction, disputed them for that very reason. At length we prevailed, and finally the Jury returned into Court at ten minutes past twelve.

The murdered man at that time stood directly opposite the Jury-box, on the other side of the Court. As I took my place, his eyes rested on me with great attention; he seemed satisfied, and slowly shook a great grey veil, which he carried on his arm for the first time, over his head and whole form. As I gave in our verdict, "Guilty," the veil collapsed, all was gone, and his place was empty.

The murderer, being asked by the Judge, according to usage whether he had anything to say before sentence of death should be passed upon him, indistinctly muttered something which was described in the leading newspapers of the following day as " a few rambling, incoherent, and half-audible words, in which he was understood to complain that he had not had a fair trial, because the Foreman of the Jury was prepossessed against him." The remarkable declaration that he really made was this : " *My Lord, I knew I was a doomed man, when the Foreman of the Jury came into the box. My Lord, I knew he would never let me off, because before I was taken, he somehow got to my bedside in the night, woke me, and put a rope round my neck.*"

CHARLES DICKENS

NO. 1 BRANCH LINE: THE SIGNALMAN

" HALLOA ! Below there ! "

When he heard a voice thus calling to him, he was standing at the door of his box, with a flag in his hand, furled round its short pole. One would have thought, considering the nature of the ground, that he could not have doubted from what quarter the voice came ; but instead of looking up to where I stood on the top of the steep cutting nearly over his head, he turned himself about, and looked down the Line. There was something remarkable in his manner of doing so, though I could not have said for my life what. But I know it was remarkable enough to attract my notice, even though his figure was foreshortened and shadowed, down in the deep trench, and mine was high above him, so steeped in the glow of an angry sunset that I had shaded my eyes with my hand before I saw him at all.

" Halloa ! Below ! "

From looking down the Line, he turned himself about again, and, raising his eyes, saw my figure high above him.

" Is there any path by which I can come down and speak to you ?"

He looked up at me without replying, and I looked down at him without pressing him too soon with a repetition of my idle question. Just then there came a vague vibration in the earth and air, quickly changing into a violent pulsation, and an oncoming rush that caused me to start back, as though it had force to draw me down. When such vapour as rose to my height from this rapid train had passed me, and was skimming away over the landscape, I looked down again, and saw him refurling the flag he had shown while the train went by.

I repeated my inquiry. After a pause, during which he seemed to regard me with fixed attention, he motioned with his rolled-up flag towards a point on my level, some two or three hundred yards distant. I called down to him, " All right ! " and made for that point. There, by dint of looking closely about me, I found a rough zigzag descending path notched out, which I followed.

The cutting was extremely deep, and unusually precipitate. It was made through a clammy stone, that became oozier and wetter as I went down. For these reasons, I found the way long enough to give me time to recall a singular air of reluctance or compulsion with which he had pointed out the path.

When I came down low enough upon the zigzag descent to see him again, I saw that he was standing between the rails on the way by which the train had lately passed, in an attitude as if he were waiting for me to appear. He had his left hand at his chin, and that left elbow rested on his right hand, crossed over his breast. His attitude was one of such expectation and watchfulness that I stopped a moment, wondering at it.

I resumed my downward way, and stepping out upon the level of the railroad, and drawing nearer to him, saw that he was a dark sallow man, with a dark beard and rather heavy eyebrows. His post was in as solitary and dismal a place as ever I saw. On either side, a dripping-wet wall of jagged stone, excluding all view but a strip of sky ; the perspective one way only a crooked prolongation of this great dungeon ; the shorter perspective in the other direction terminating in a gloomy red light, and the gloomier entrance to a black tunnel, in whose massive architecture there was a barbarous, depressing, and forbidding air. So little sunlight ever found its way to this spot, that it had an earthy, deadly smell ; and so much cold wind rushed through it, that it struck chill to me, as if I had left the natural world.

Before he stirred, I was near enough to him to have touched him. Not even then removing his eyes from mine, he stepped back one step, and lifted his hand.

This was a lonesome post to occupy (I said), and it had riveted my attention when I looked down from up yonder. A visitor was a rarity, I should suppose ; not an unwelcome rarity, I hoped ? In me, he merely saw a man who had been shut up within narrow limits all his life, and who, being at last set free, had a newly-awakened interest in these great works. To such purpose I spoke to him ; but I am far from sure of the terms I used ; for, besides that I am not happy in opening any conversation, there was something in the man that daunted me.

He directed a most curious look towards the red light near the tunnel's mouth, and looked all about it, as if something were missing from it, and then looked at me.

That light was part of his charge ? Was it not ?

He answered in a low voice, " Don't you know it is ? "

The monstrous thought came into my mind, as I perused the fixed eyes and the saturnine face, that this was a spirit, not a man. I have speculated since, whether there may have been infection in his mind.

In my turn I stepped back. But in making the action, I detected in his eyes some latent fear of me. This put the monstrous thought to flight.

" You look at me," I said, forcing a smile, " as if you had a dread of me."

" I was doubtful," he returned, " whether I had seen you before."

" Where ? "

He pointed to the red light he had looked at.

" There ? " I said.

Intently watchful of me, he replied (but without sound), " Yes."

" My good fellow, what should I do there ? However, be that as it may, I never was there, you may swear."

" I think I may," he rejoined. " Yes ; I am sure I may."

His manner cleared, like my own. He replied to my remarks with readiness, and in well-chosen words. Had he much to do there ? Yes ; that was to say, he had enough responsibility to bear ; but exactness and watchfulness were what was required of him, and of actual work—manual labour—he had next to none. To change that signal, to trim those lights, and to turn this iron handle now and then, was all he had to under that head. Regarding those many long and lonely hours of which I seemed to make so much, he could only say that the routine of his life had shaped itself into that form, and he had grown used to it. He had taught himself a language down here,—if only to know it by sight, and to have formed his own crude ideas of its pronunciation, could be called learning it. He had also worked at fractions and decimals, and tried a little algebra ; but he was, and had been as a boy, a poor hand at figures. Was it necessary for him when on duty always to remain in that channel of damp air, and could he never rise into the sunshine from between those high stone walls ? Why, that depended upon times and circumstances. Under some conditions there would be less upon the Line than under others, and the same held good as to certain hours of the day and night. In bright weather, he did choose occasions for getting a little above those lower shadows ; but, being at all times liable to be called by his electric bell, and at such times listening for it with redoubled anxiety, the relief was less than I would suppose.

He took me into his box, where there was a fire, a desk for an official book in which he had to make certain entries, a telegraphic instrument with its dial, face, and needles, and the little bell of which he had spoken. On my trusting that he would excuse the remark that he had been well educated, and (I hoped I might say without offence) perhaps educated above that station, he observed that instances of slight incongruity in such wise would rarely be found wanting among large bodies of men ; that he had heard it was so in workhouses, in the police force, even in that last desperate resource, the army; and that he knew it was so, more or less, in any great railway staff. He had been, when young (if I could believe it, sitting in that hut,—he scarcely could), a student of natural philosophy, and had attended lectures; but he had run wild, misused his opportunities, gone down, and never risen again. He had no complaint to offer about that. He had made his bed, and he lay upon it. It was far too late to make another.

All that I have here condensed he said in a quiet manner, with his grave dark regards divided between me and the fire. He threw in the word "Sir" from time to time, and especially when he referred to his youth,—as though to request me to understand that he claimed to be nothing but what I found him. He was several times interrupted by the little bell, and had to read off messages and send replies. Once he had to stand without the door, and display a flag as a train passed, and make some verbal communication to the driver. In the discharge of his duties, I observed him to be remarkably exact and vigilant, breaking off his discourse at a syllable, and remaining silent until what he had to do was done.

In a word, I should have set this man down as one of the safest of men to be employed in that capacity, but for the circumstance that while he was speaking to me he twice broke off with a fallen colour, turned his face towards the little bell when it did NOT ring, opened the door of the hut (which was kept shut to exclude the unhealthy damp), and looked out towards the red light near the mouth of the tunnel. On both of those occasions he came back to the fire with the inexplicable air upon him which I had remarked, without being able to define, when we were so far asunder.

Said I, when I rose to leave him, "You almost make me think that I have met with a contented man."

(I am afraid I must acknowledge that I said it to lead him on.)

"I believe I used to be so," he rejoined, in the low voice in which he had first spoken; "but I am troubled, sir, I am troubled."

He would have recalled the words if he could. He had said them, however, and I took them up quickly.

"With what? What is your trouble?"

"It is very difficult to impart, sir. It is very, very difficult to speak of. If ever you make me another visit, I will try to tell you."

"But I expressly intend to make you another visit. Say, when shall it be?"

"I go off early in the morning, and I shall be on again at ten to-morrow night, sir."

"I will come at eleven."

He thanked me, and went out at the door with me. "I'll show my white light, sir," he said, in his peculiar low voice, "till you have found the way up. When you have found it, don't call out! And when you are at the top, don't call out!"

His manner seemed to make the place strike colder to me, but I said no more than "Very well."

"And when you come down to-morrow night, don't call out! Let me ask you a parting question. What made you cry, 'Halloa! Below there!' to-night?"

"Heaven knows," said I, "I cried something to that effect——"

"Not to that effect, sir. Those were the very words. I know them well."

"Admit those were the very words. I said them, no doubt, because I saw you below."

"For no other reason?"

"What other reason could I possibly have?"

"You have no feeling that they were conveyed to you in any supernatural way?"

"No."

He wished me good-night, and held up his light. I walked by the side of the down Line of rails (with a very disagreeable sensation of a train coming behind me) until I found the path. It was easier to mount than to descend, and I got back to my inn without any adventure.

Punctual to my appointment, I placed my foot on the first notch of the zigzag next night as the distant clocks were striking eleven. He was waiting for me at the bottom, with his white light on. "I have not called out," I said, when we came close together; "may I speak now?" "By all means, sir." "Good-night, then, and here's my hand." "Good-night, sir, and here's mine." With that we walked side by side to his box, entered it, closed the door, and sat down by the fire.

"I have made up my mind, sir," he began bending forward as soon as we were seated, and speaking in a tone but a little above a whisper, "that you shall not have to ask me twice what troubles me. I took you for some one else yesterday evening. That troubles me."

"That mistake?"

"No. That some one else."

"Who is it?"

"I don't know."

"Like me?"

"I don't know. I never saw the face. The left arm is across the face, and the right arm is waved—violently waved. This way."

I followed his action with my eyes, and it was the action of an arm gesticulating, with the utmost passion and vehemence, "For God's sake, clear the way!"

" One moonlight night," said the man, " I was sitting here, when I heard a voice cry, ' Halloa ! Below there ! ' I started up, looked from that door, and saw this some one else standing by the red light near the tunnel, waving as I just now showed you. The voice seemed hoarse with shouting, and it cried, ' Look out ! Look out ! ' And then again, ' Halloa ! Below there ! Look out ! ' I caught up my lamp, turned it on red, and ran towards the figure, calling, ' What's wrong ? What has happened ? Where ? ' It stood just outside the blackness of the tunnel. I advanced so close upon it that I wondered at its keeping the sleeve across its eyes. I ran right up at it, and had my hand stretched out to pull the sleeve away, when it was gone."

" Into the tunnel ? " said I.

" No. I ran on into the tunnel, five hundred yards. I stopped, and held my lamp above my head, and saw the figures of the measured distance, and saw the wet stains stealing down the walls and trickling through the arch. I ran out again faster than I had run in (for I had a mortal abhorrence of the place upon me), and I looked all round the red light with my own red light, and I went up the iron ladder to the gallery atop of it, and I came down again, and ran back here. I telegraphed both ways. ' An alarm has been given. Is anything wrong ? ' The answer came back, both ways, ' All well.' "

Resisting the slow touch of a frozen finger tracing out my spine, I showed him how that this figure must be a deception of his sense of sight ; and how that figures, originating in disease of the delicate nerves that minister to the functions of the eye, were known to have often troubled patients, some of whom had become conscious of the nature of their affliction, and had even proved it by experiments upon themselves. " As to an imaginary cry," said I, " do but listen for a moment to the wind in this unnatural valley while we speak so low, and to the wild harp it makes of the telegraph wires."

That was all very well, he returned, after we had sat listening for a while, and he ought to know something of the wind and the wires,—he who so often passed long winter nights there, alone and watching. But he would beg to remark that he had not finished.

I asked his pardon, and he slowly added these words, touching my arm :

" Within six hours after the Appearance, the memorable accident on this Line happened, and within ten hours the dead and wounded were brought along through the tunnel over the spot where the figure had stood."

A disagreeable shudder crept over me, but I did my best against it. It was not to be denied, I rejoined, that this was a remarkable coincidence, calculated deeply to impress his mind. But it was unquestionable that remarkable coincidences did continually occur, and they must be taken into account in dealing with such a subject. Though to be sure I must admit, I added (for I thought I saw that he was going to bring the objecton to bear upon me), men of common sense did not allow much for coincidences in making the ordinary calculations of life.

He again begged to remark that he had not finished.

I again begged his pardon for being betrayed into interruptions.

" This," he said, again laying his hand upon my arm, and glancing over his shoulder with hollow eyes, " was just a year ago. Six or seven months passed, and I had recovered from the surprise and shock, when one morning, as the day was breaking, I, standing at the door, looked towards the red light, and saw the spectre again." He stopped, with a fixed look at me.

" Did it cry out ? "

" No. It was silent."

" Did it wave its arm ? "

" No. It leaned against the shaft of the light with both hands before the face. Like this."

Once more I followed his action with my eyes. It was an action of mourning. I have seen such an attitude on stone figures on tombs.

" Did you go up to it ? "

" I came in and sat down, partly to collect my thoughts, partly because it had turned me faint. When I went to the door again, daylight was above me, and the ghost was gone."

" But nothing followed ? Nothing came of this ? "

He touched me on the arm with his forefinger twice or thrice, giving a ghastly nod each time :

" That very day, as a train came out of the tunnel, I noticed, at a carriage window on my side, what looked like a confusion of hands and heads, and something waved. I saw it just in time to signal the driver, Stop ! He shut off, and put his brake on, but the train drifted past here a hundred and fifty yards or more. I ran after it, and, as I went along, heard terrible screams and cries. A beautiful young lady had died instantaneously in one of the compartments, and was brought in here, and laid down on this floor between us."

Involuntarily I pushed my chair back, as I looked from the boards at which he pointed to himself.

" True, sir. True. Precisely as it happened, so I tell it you."

I could think of nothing to say, to any purpose, and my mouth was very dry. The wind and the wires took up the story with a long lamenting wail.

He resumed, " Now, sir, mark this, and judge how my mind is troubled. The spectre came back a week ago. Ever since, it has been there, now and again, by fits and starts."

" At the light ? "

" At the Danger-light."

" What does it seem to do ? "

He repeated, if possible with increased passion and vehemence, that former gesticulation of " For God's sake, clear the way ! "

Then he went on. " I have no peace or rest for it. It calls to me, for many minutes together, in an agonised manner, ' Below there ! Look out ! Look out ! ' It stands waving to me. It rings my little bell——"

I caught at that. " Did it ring your bell yesterday evening when I was here, and you went to the door ? "

" Twice."

" Why, see," said I, " how your imagination misleads you. My eyes were on the bell, and my ears were open to the bell, and if I am a living man, it did NOT ring at those times. No, nor at any other time, except when it was rung in the natural course of physical things by the station communicating with you."

He shook his head. " I have never made a mistake as to that yet, sir. I have never confused the spectre's ring with the man's. The ghost's ring is a strange vibration in the bell that it derives from nothing else, and I have not asserted that the bell stirs to the eye. I don't wonder that you failed to hear it. But *I* heard it."

" And did the spectre seem to be there when you looked out ? "

" It WAS there."

" Both times ? "

He repeated firmly : " Both times."

" Will you come to the door with me, and look for it now ? "

He bit his under lip as though he were somewhat unwilling, but arose. I opened the door, and stood on the step, while he stood in the doorway. There was the Danger-light. There was the dismal mouth of the tunnel. There were the high, wet stone walls of the cutting. There were the stars above them.

" Do you see it ? " I asked him, taking particular note of his face. His eyes were prominent and strained, but not very much more so, perhaps, than my own had been when I had directed them earnestly towards the same spot.

" No," he answered. " It is not there."

" Agreed," said I.

We went in again, shut the door, and resumed our seats. I was thinking how best to improve this advantage, if it might be called one, when he took up the conversation in such a matter-of-course way, so assuming that there could be no serious question of fact between us, that I felt myself placed in the weakest of positions.

" By this time you will fully understand, sir," he said, " that what troubles me so dreadfully is the question, What does the spectre mean ? "

I was not sure, I told him, that I did fully understand.

" What is its warning against ? " he said, ruminating, with his eyes on the fire, and only by times turning them on me. " What is the danger ? Where is the danger ? There is danger overhanging somewhere on the Line. Some dreadful calamity will happen. It is not to be doubted this third time, after what has gone before. But surely this is a cruel haunting of *me*. What can I do ? "

He pulled out his handkerchief, and wiped the drops from his heated forehead.

" If I telegraph Danger on either side of me, or on both, I can give no reason for it," he went on, wiping the palms of his hands. " I should get into trouble and do no good. They would think I was mad. This is the way it would work,—Message : ' Danger ! Take care ! ' Answer : ' What Danger ? Where ? ' Message : ' Don't know. But for God's sake, take care !' They would displace me. What else could they do ? "

His pain of mind was most pitiable to see. It was the mental torture of a conscientious man, oppressed beyond endurance by an unintelligible responsibility involving life.

" When it first stood under the Danger-light," he went on, putting his dark hair back from his head, and drawing his hands outward across and across his temples in an extremity of feverish distress, " why not tell me where that accident was to happen,—if it must happen ? Why not tell me how it could be averted,—if it could have been averted ? When on its second coming it hid its face, why not tell me, instead, ' She is going to die. Let them keep her at home ' ? If it came, on those two occasions, only to show me that its warnings were true, and so to prepare me for the third, why not warn me plainly now ? And I, Lord help me ! A mere poor signalman on this solitary station ! Why not go to somebody with credit to be believed, and power to act ? "

When I saw him in this state, I saw that for the poor man's sake, as well as for the public safety, what I had to do for the time was to compose his mind. Therefore, setting aside all question of reality or unreality between us, I represented to him that whoever thoroughly discharged his duty must do well, and that at least it was his comfort that he understood his duty, though he did not understand these confounding Appearances. In this effort I succeeded far better than in the attempt to reason him out of his conviction. He became calm ; the occupations incidental to his post as the night advanced began to make larger demands on his attention : and I left him at two in the morning. I had offered to stay through the night, but he would not hear of it.

That I more than once looked back at the red light as I ascended the pathway, that I did not like the red light, and that I should have slept but poorly if my bed had been under it, I see no reason to conceal. Nor did I like the two sequences of the accident and the dead girl. I see no reason to conceal that either.

But what ran most in my thoughts was the consideration how ought I to act, having become the recipient of this disclosure ? I had proved the man to be intelligent, vigilant, painstaking, and exact ; but how long might he remain so, in his state of mind ? Though in a subordinate position, still he held a most important trust, and would I (for instance) like to stake my own life on the chances of his continuing to execute it with precision ?

Unable to overcome a feeling that there would be something treacherous in my communicating what he had told me to his superiors in the Company, without first being plain with himself and proposing a middle course to him, I ultimately resolved to offer to accompany him (otherwise keeping his secret for the present) to the wisest medical practitioner we could hear of in those parts, and to take his opinion. A change in his time of duty would come round next night, he had apprised me, and he would be off an hour or two after sunrise, and on again soon after sunset. I had appointed to return accordingly.

Next evening was a lovely evening, and I walked out early to enjoy it. The sun was not yet quite down when I traversed the field-path near the top of the deep cutting. I would extend my walk for an hour, I said to myself, half an hour on and half an hour back, and it would then be time to go to my signalman's box.

Before pursuing my stroll, I stepped to the brink, and mechanically looked down, from the point from which I had first seen him. I cannot describe the thrill that seized upon me, when, close at the mouth of the tunnel, I saw the appearance of a man, with his left sleeve across his eyes, passionately waving his right arm.

The nameless horror that oppressed me passed in a moment, for in a moment I saw that this appearance of a man was a man indeed, and that there was a little group of other men standing at a short distance, to whom he seemed to be rehearsing the gesture he made. The Danger-light was not yet lighted. Against its shaft a little low hut entirely new to me, had been made of some wooden supports and tarpaulin. It looked no bigger than a bed.

With an irresistible sense that something was wrong—with a flashing self-reproachful fear that fatal mischief had come of my leaving the man there, and causing no one to be sent to overlook or correct what he did,—I descended the notched path with all the speed I could make.

" What is the matter ? " I asked the men.

" Signalman killed this morning, sir."

" Not the man belonging to that box ? "

" Yes, sir."

" Not the man I know ? "

" You will recognise him, sir, if you knew him," said the man who spoke for the others, solemnly uncovering his own head, and raising an end of the tarpaulin, " for his face is quite composed."

" Oh, how did this happen, how did this happen ? " I asked, turning from one to another as the hut closed in again.

" He was cut down by an engine, sir. No man in England knew his work better. But somehow he was not clear of the outer rail. It was just at broad day. He had struck the light, and had the lamp in his hand. As the engine came out of the tunnel, his back was towards her, and she cut him down. That man drove her, and was showing how it happened. Show the gentleman, Tom."

The man who wore a rough dark dress, stepped back to his former place at the mouth of the tunnel.

" Coming round the curve in the tunnel, sir," he said, " I saw him at the end, like as if I saw him down a perspective-glass. There was no time to check speed, and I knew him to be very careful. As he didn't seem to take heed of the whistle, I shut it off when we were running down upon him, and called to him as loud as I could call."

" What did you say ? "

" I said, ' Below there ! Look out ! Look out ! For God's sake, clear the way ! "

I started.

" Ah ! it was a dreadful time, sir. I never left off calling to him. I put this arm before my eyes not to see, and I waved this arm to the last ; but it was no use."

Without prolonging the narrative to dwell on any one of its curious circumstances more than on any other, I may, in closing it, point out the coincidence that the warning of the engine-driver included, not only the words which the unfortunate signalman had repeated to me as haunting him, but also the words which I myself—not he—had attached, and that only in my own mind, to the gesticulation he had imitated.